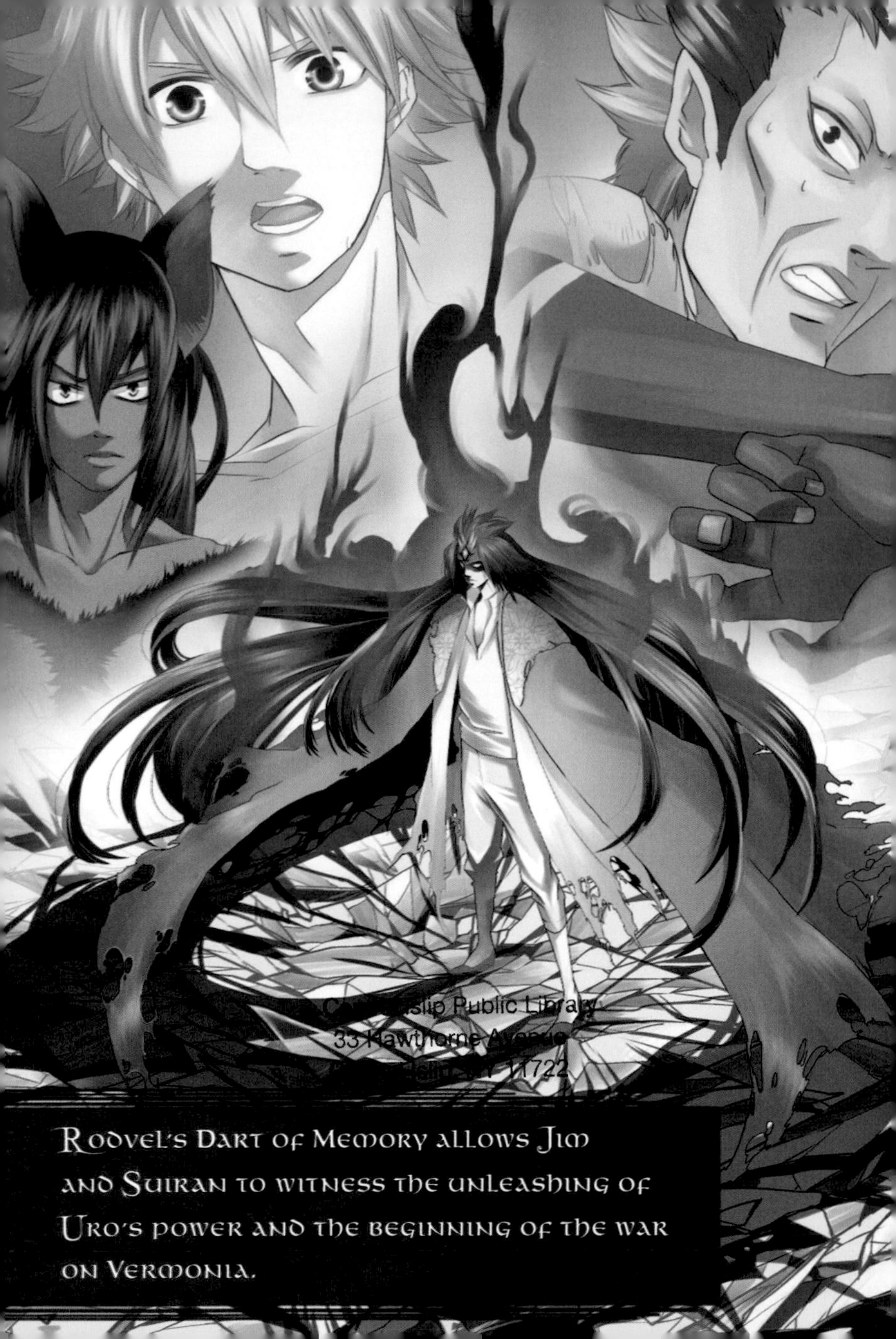

Rodvel's Dart of Memory allows Jim and Suiran to witness the unleashing of Uro's power and the beginning of the war on Vermonia.

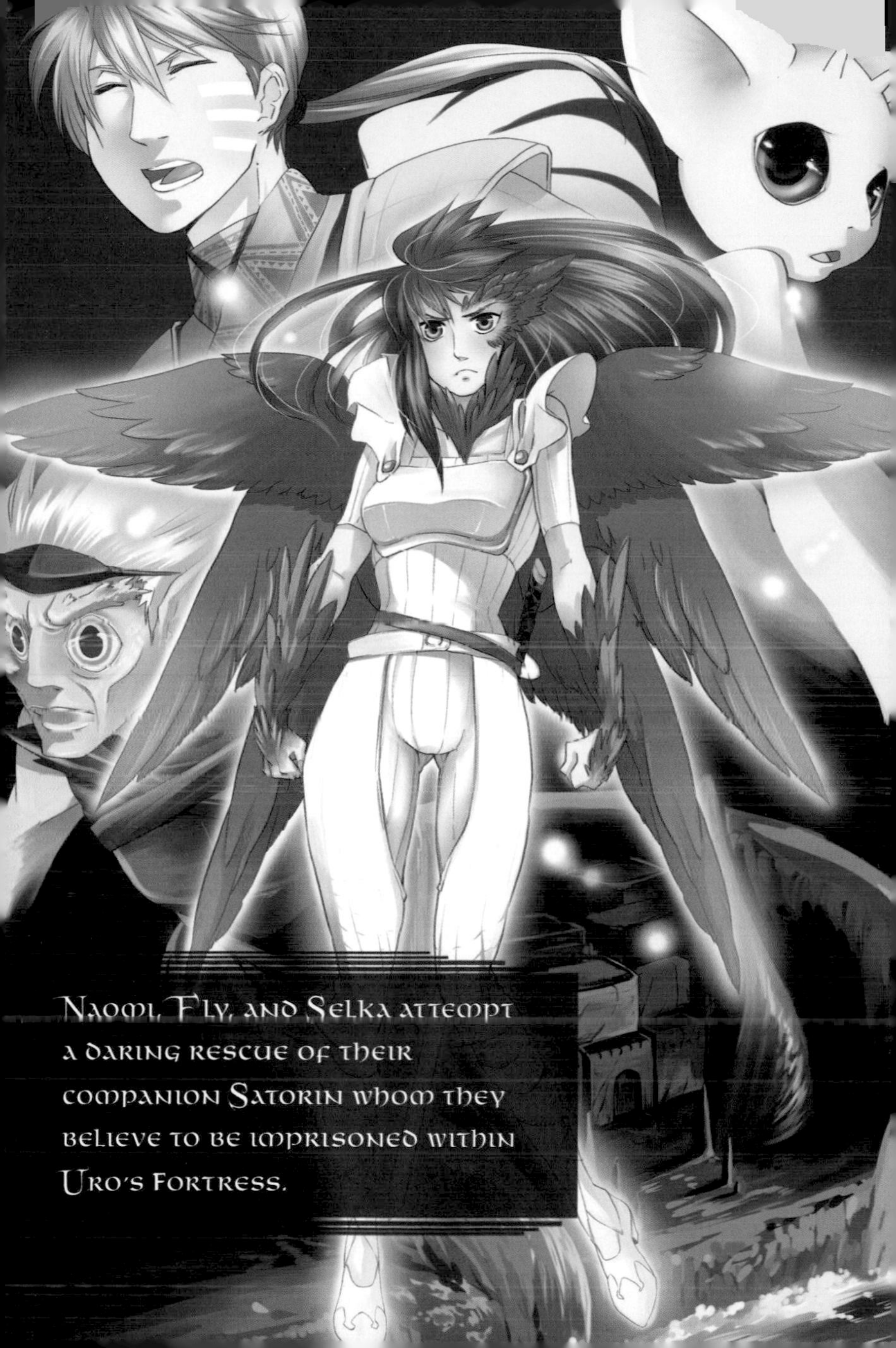
Naomi, Fly, and Selka attempt a daring rescue of their companion Satorin whom they believe to be imprisoned within Uro's Fortress.

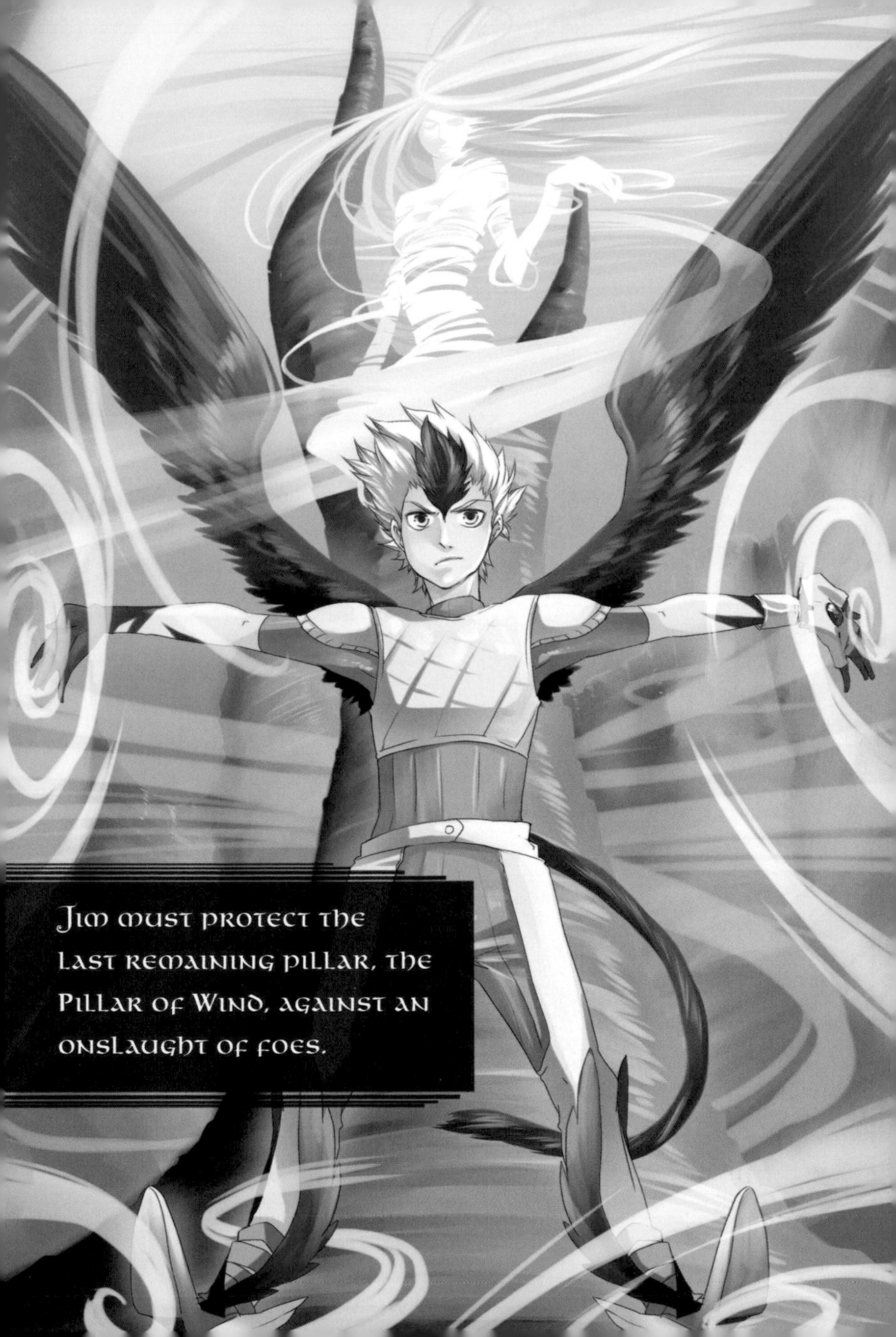
Jim must protect the last remaining pillar, the Pillar of Wind, against an onslaught of foes.

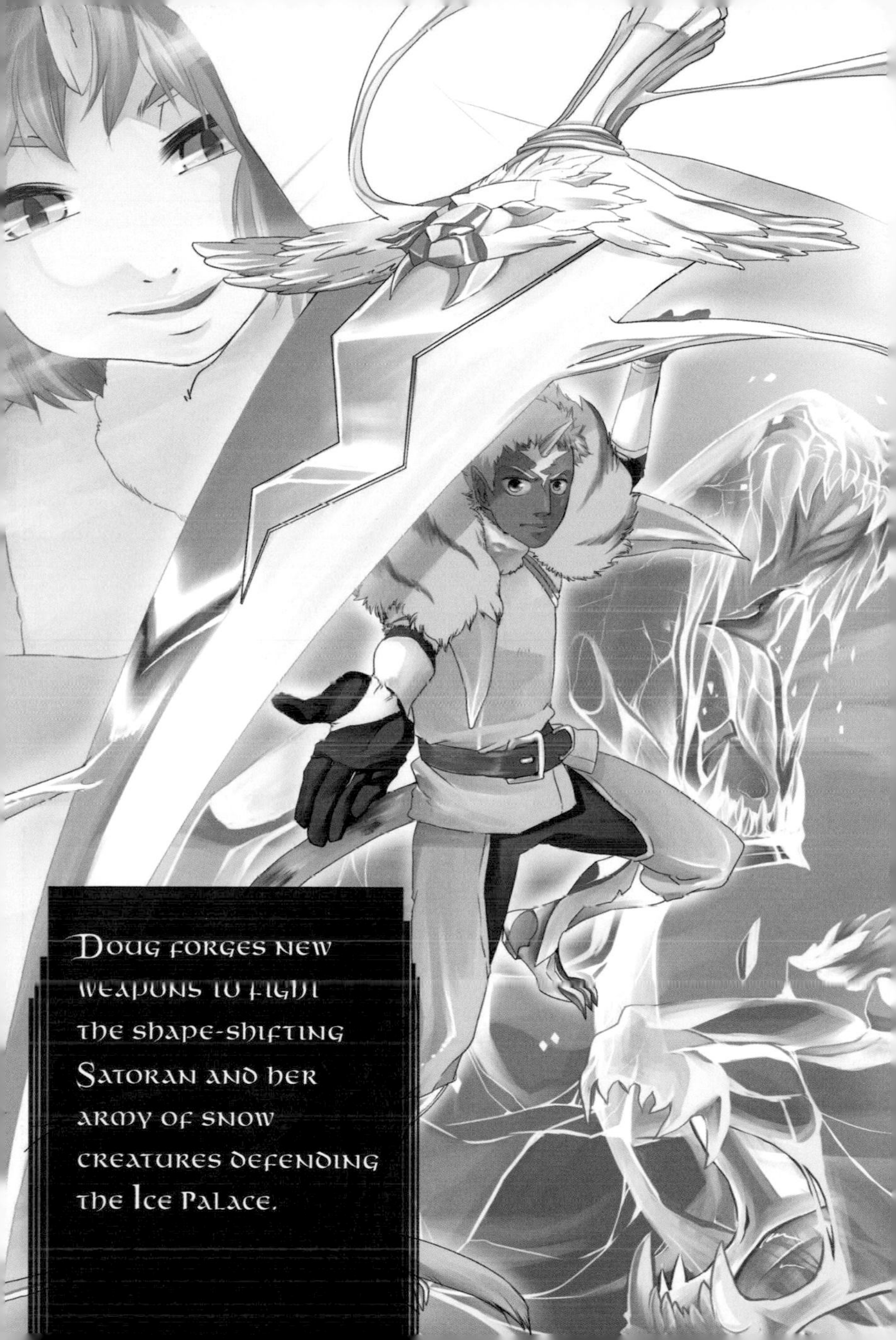
Doug forges new weapons to fight the shape-shifting Satoran and her army of snow creatures defending the Ice Palace.

VERMONIA

Battle for the Turtle Realm

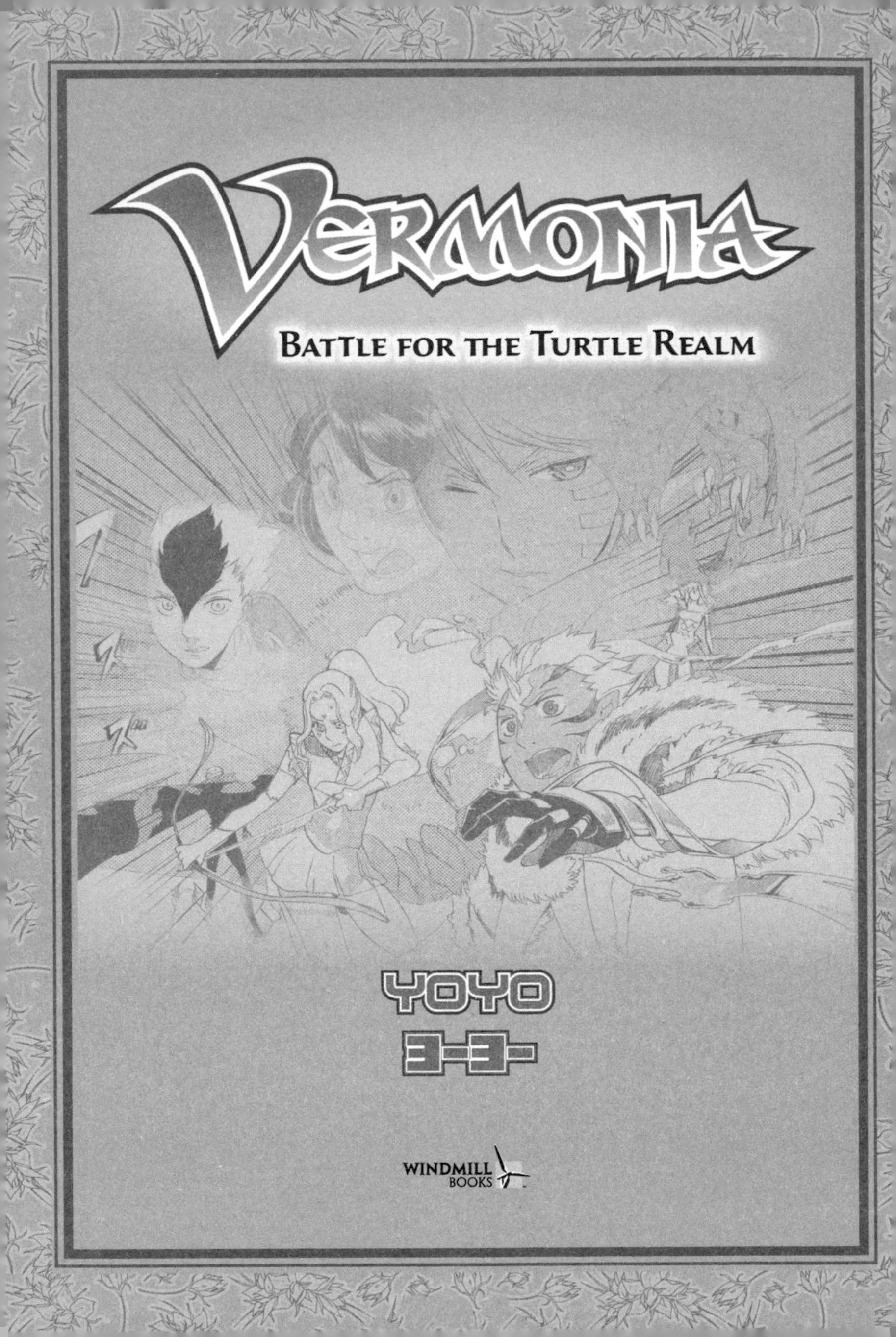

YOYO

ヨーヨー

WINDMILL BOOKS

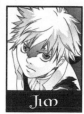

Jim

Bass Player
Blue Star Warrior

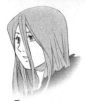

Sassella

Cursed Village Girl

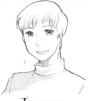

Lamto

Freed Prisoner of Uro

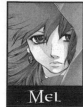

Mel

Lead Vocalist
Blue Star Warrior

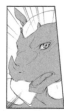

Miranda

Warrior of the Umli

The teenaged warriors Doug, Naomi, Jim, and Mel have gone through many trials since their abrupt departure from their homeland on Blue Star. Each of them has unlocked the power of their animal guardian to fight the monsters controlled by General Uro, destroyer of Vermonia. They've come through these battles stronger and even more determined to help the inhabitants of the Turtle Realm in their struggle against Uro and his conquering forces.

In volume 6, with the Turtle Realm teetering on the last pillar of magic, with Mel and the squelp guide, Satorin, still held prisoner by Uro's Captain Acidulous and the evil Deras, Doug, Jim, and Naomi are forced to split into three separate rescue expeditions.

Doug leads his team to the Ice Palace where his new admirer, Yuui, proves her worth with her magic lights to guide them through the snow. Jim and his beloved Princess Rainbow rush on the airship Vleste to the Pillar of Wind to make a last stand against Uro's army. Naomi and the Potonawi brave Fly infiltrate Uro's castle, searching for Satorin.

The countdown to defeat is upon the young friends. The superiority of Uro's forces hastens the outcome. What can turn the tide? Will Naomi's mysterious arrival in Blue Star make a difference?

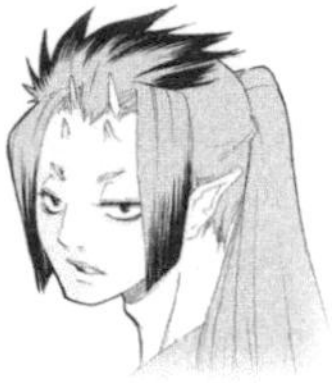

General Uro

Master of Dark Yami Magic

Yuui

Rescued Potonawi Girl

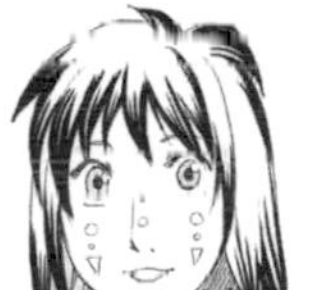

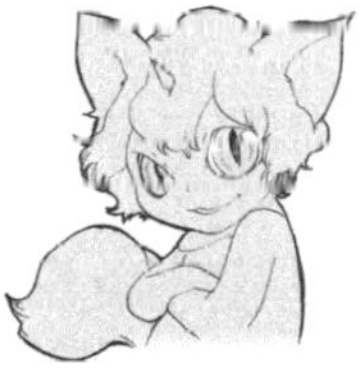

Satoran

Shape-shifting Monster

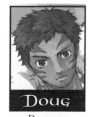

Doug

Drummer
Blue Star Warrior

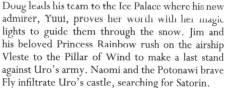

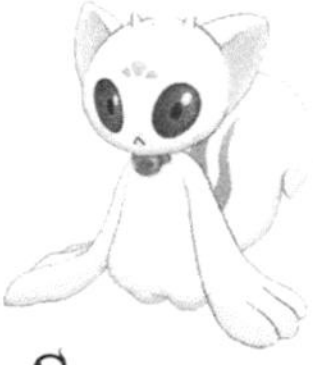

Satorin

Magical Squelp

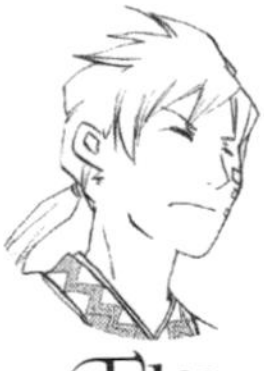

Fly

Potonawi Warrior

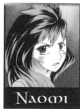

Naomi

Lead Guitarist
Blue Star Warrior

FOR MORE INFORMATION GO TO VERMONIA.COM

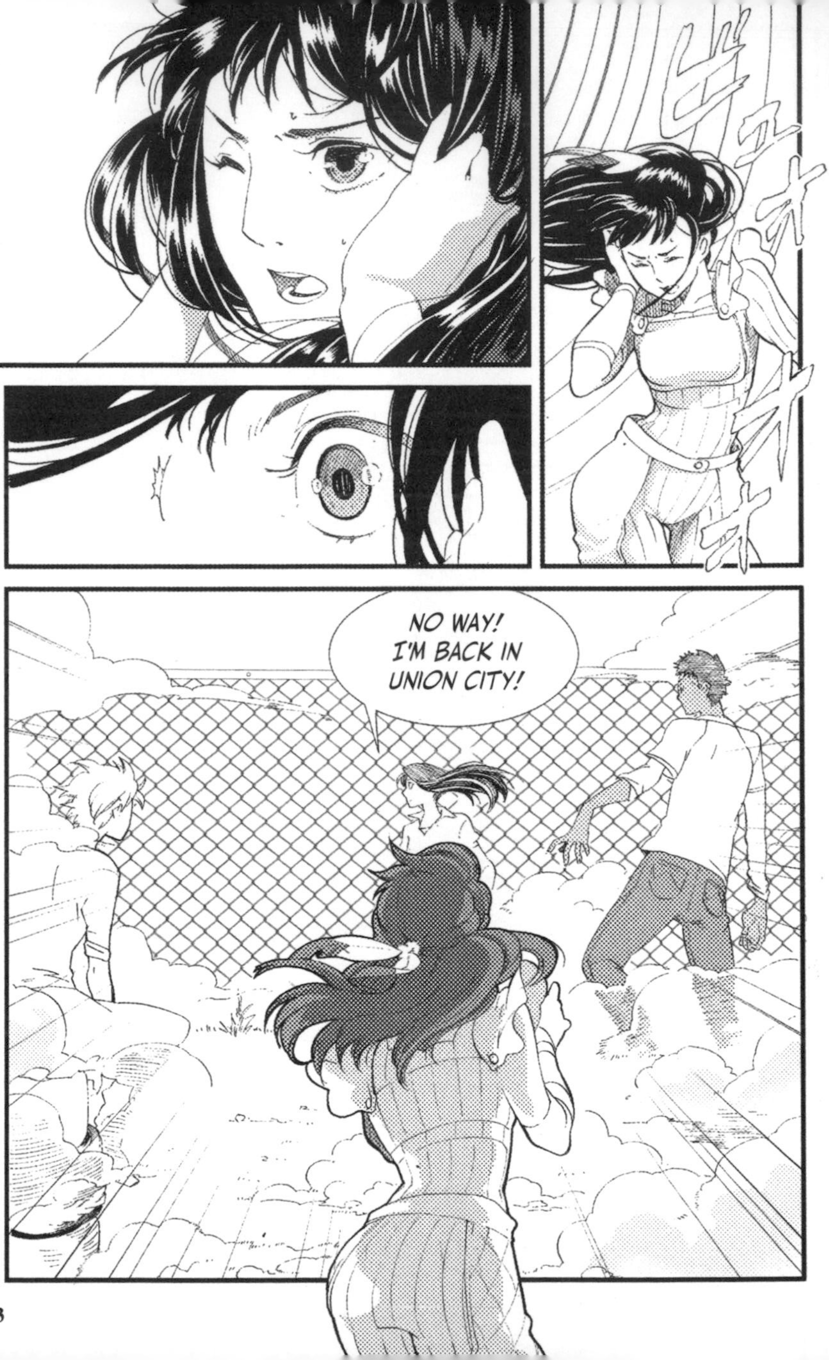
NO WAY! I'M BACK IN UNION CITY!

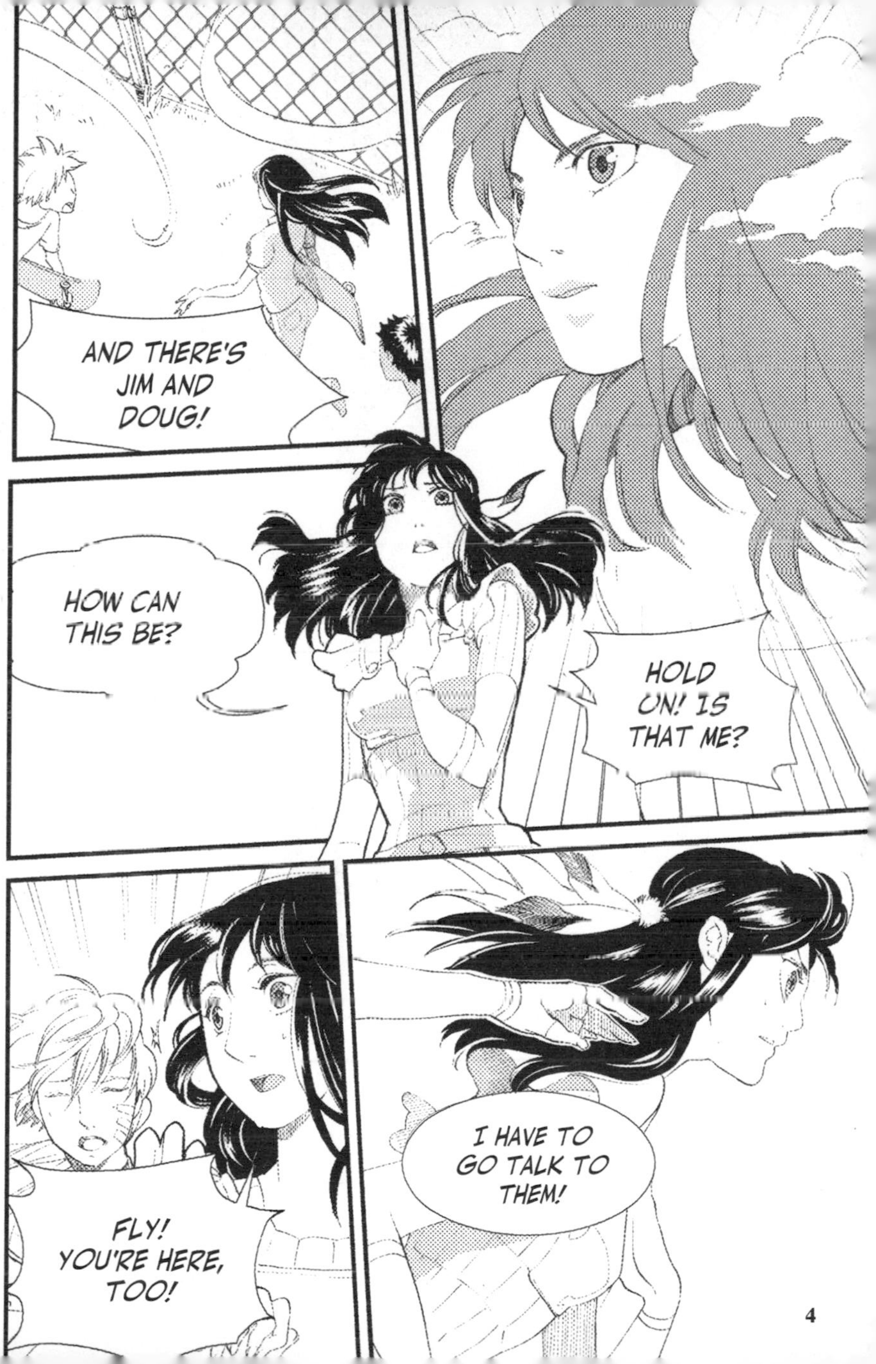
AND THERE'S JIM AND DOUG!
HOLD ON! IS THAT ME?
HOW CAN THIS BE?
I HAVE TO GO TALK TO THEM!
FLY! YOU'RE HERE, TOO!

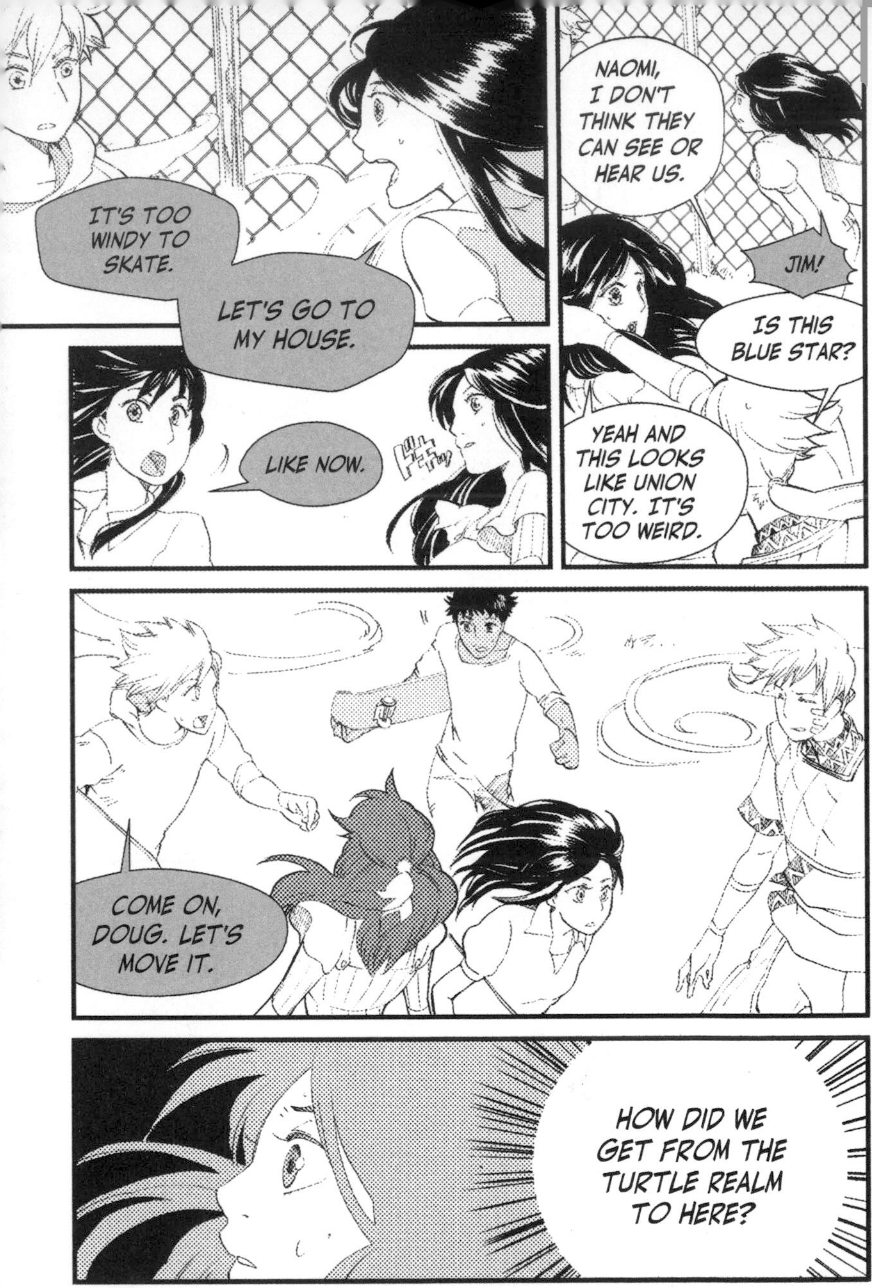
NAOMI, I DON'T THINK THEY CAN SEE OR HEAR US.
JIM!
IS THIS BLUE STAR?
YEAH AND THIS LOOKS LIKE UNION CITY. IT'S TOO WEIRD.
IT'S TOO WINDY TO SKATE.
LET'S GO TO MY HOUSE.
LIKE NOW.
COME ON, DOUG. LET'S MOVE IT.
HOW DID WE GET FROM THE TURTLE REALM TO HERE?

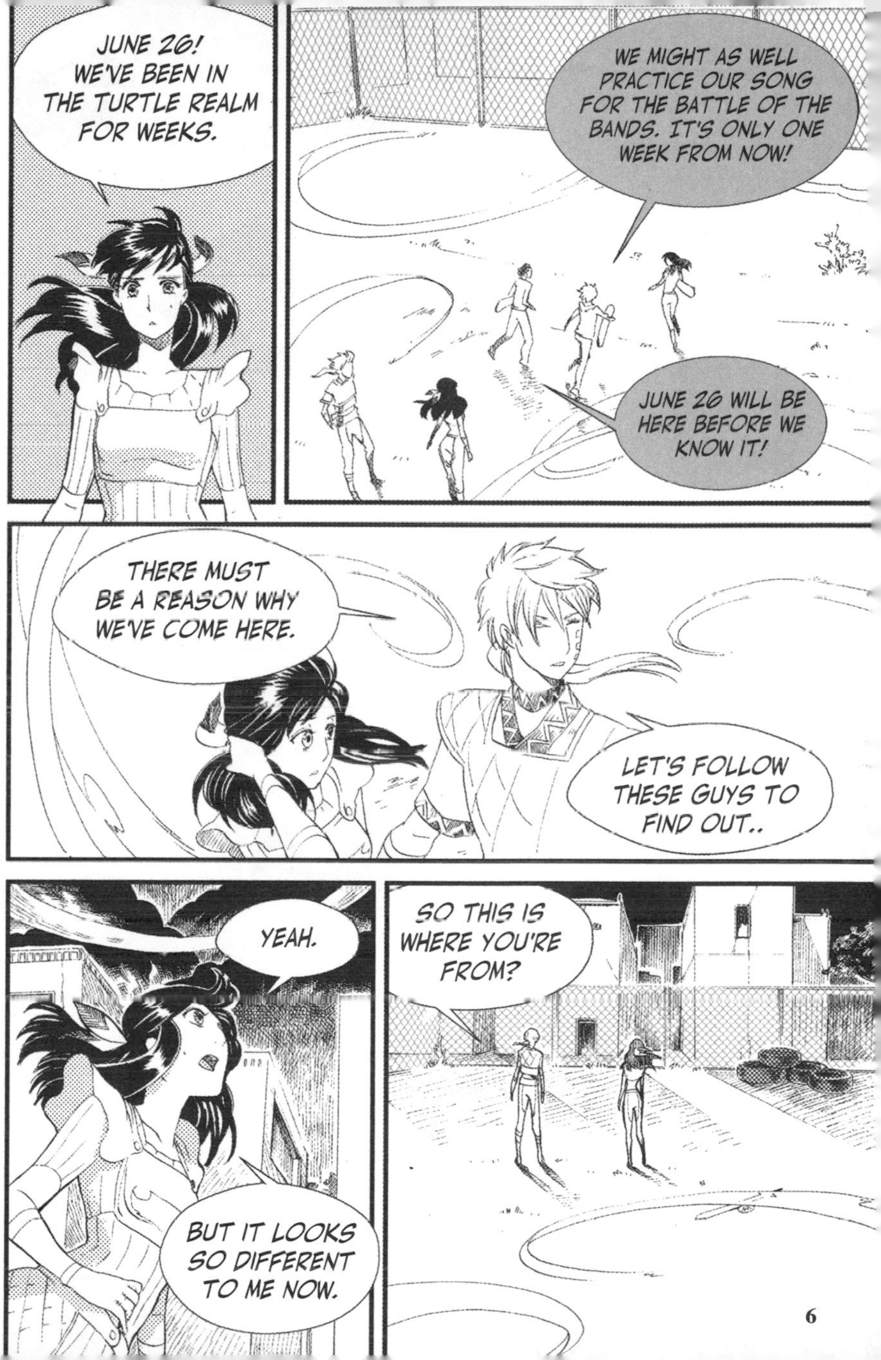
WE MIGHT AS WELL PRACTICE OUR SONG FOR THE BATTLE OF THE BANDS. IT'S ONLY ONE WEEK FROM NOW!
JUNE 26 WILL BE HERE BEFORE WE KNOW IT!
JUNE 26! WE'VE BEEN IN THE TURTLE REALM FOR WEEKS.
THERE MUST BE A REASON WHY WE'VE COME HERE.
LET'S FOLLOW THESE GUYS TO FIND OUT..
SO THIS IS WHERE YOU'RE FROM?
YEAH.
BUT IT LOOKS SO DIFFERENT TO ME NOW.

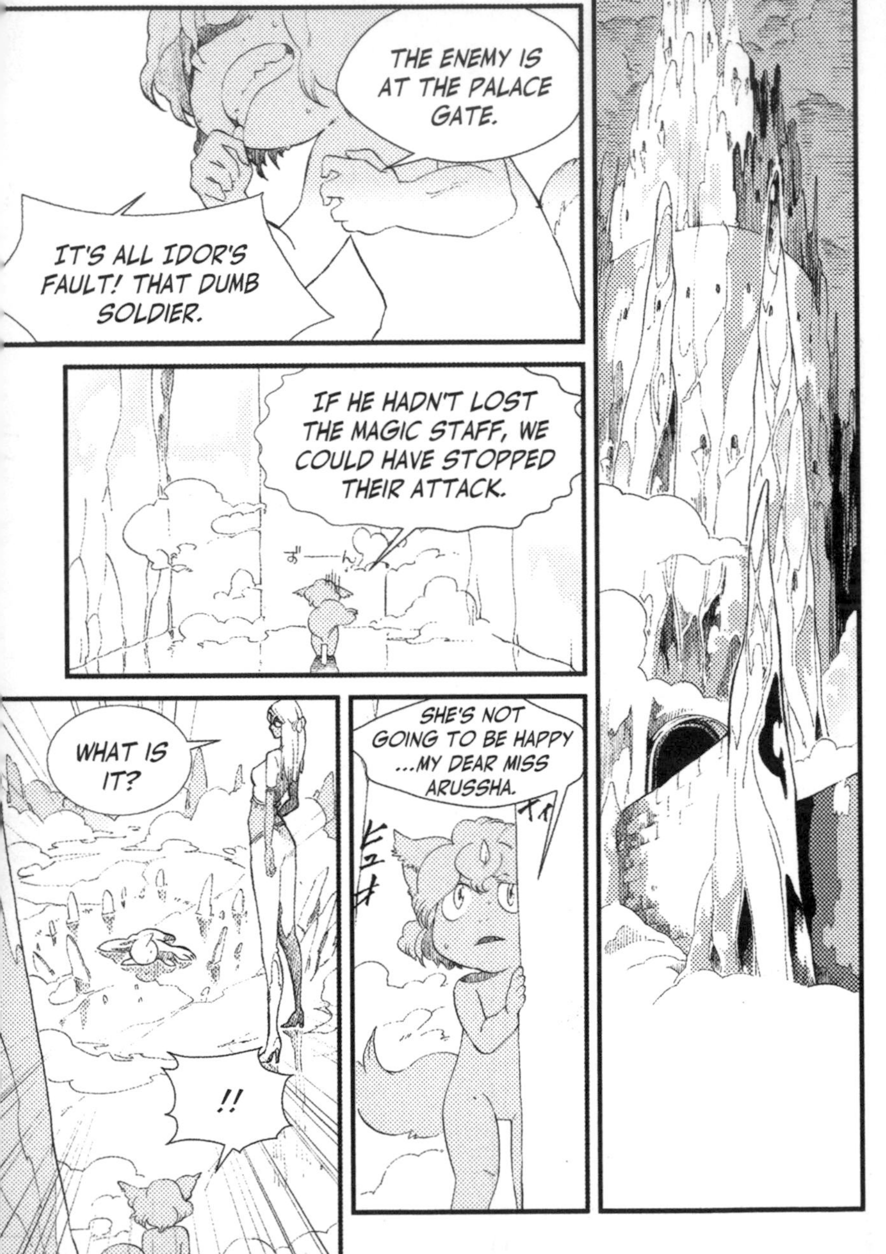
THE ENEMY IS AT THE PALACE GATE.
IT'S ALL IDOR'S FAULT! THAT DUMB SOLDIER.
IF HE HADN'T LOST THE MAGIC STAFF, WE COULD HAVE STOPPED THEIR ATTACK.
SHE'S NOT GOING TO BE HAPPY ...MY DEAR MISS ARUSSHA.
WHAT IS IT?
!!

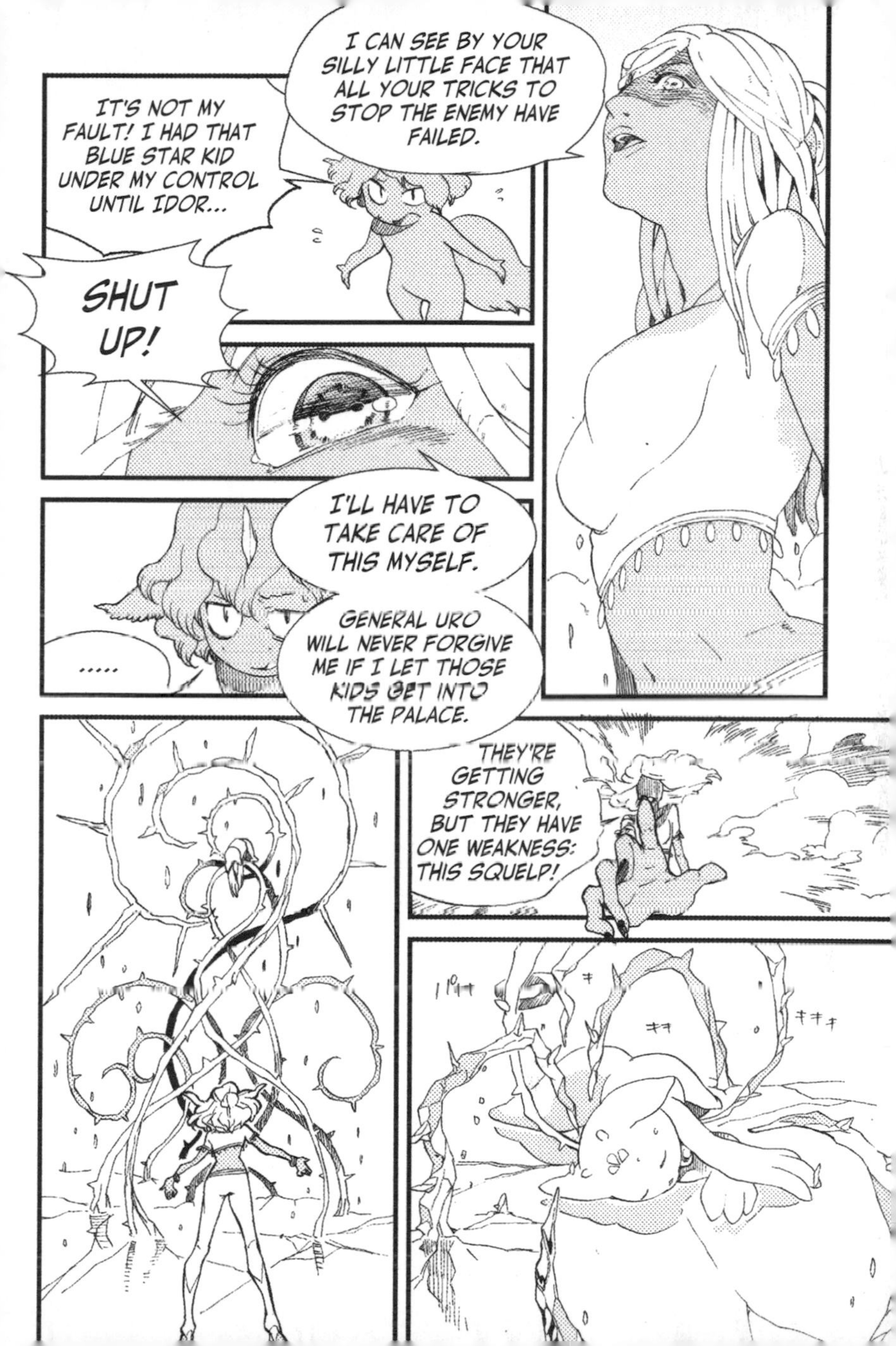
I CAN SEE BY YOUR SILLY LITTLE FACE THAT ALL YOUR TRICKS TO STOP THE ENEMY HAVE FAILED.
IT'S NOT MY FAULT! I HAD THAT BLUE STAR KID UNDER MY CONTROL UNTIL IDOR...
SHUT UP!
I'LL HAVE TO TAKE CARE OF THIS MYSELF.
.....
GENERAL URO WILL NEVER FORGIVE ME IF I LET THOSE KIDS GET INTO THE PALACE.
THEY'RE GETTING STRONGER, BUT THEY HAVE ONE WEAKNESS: THIS SQUELP!

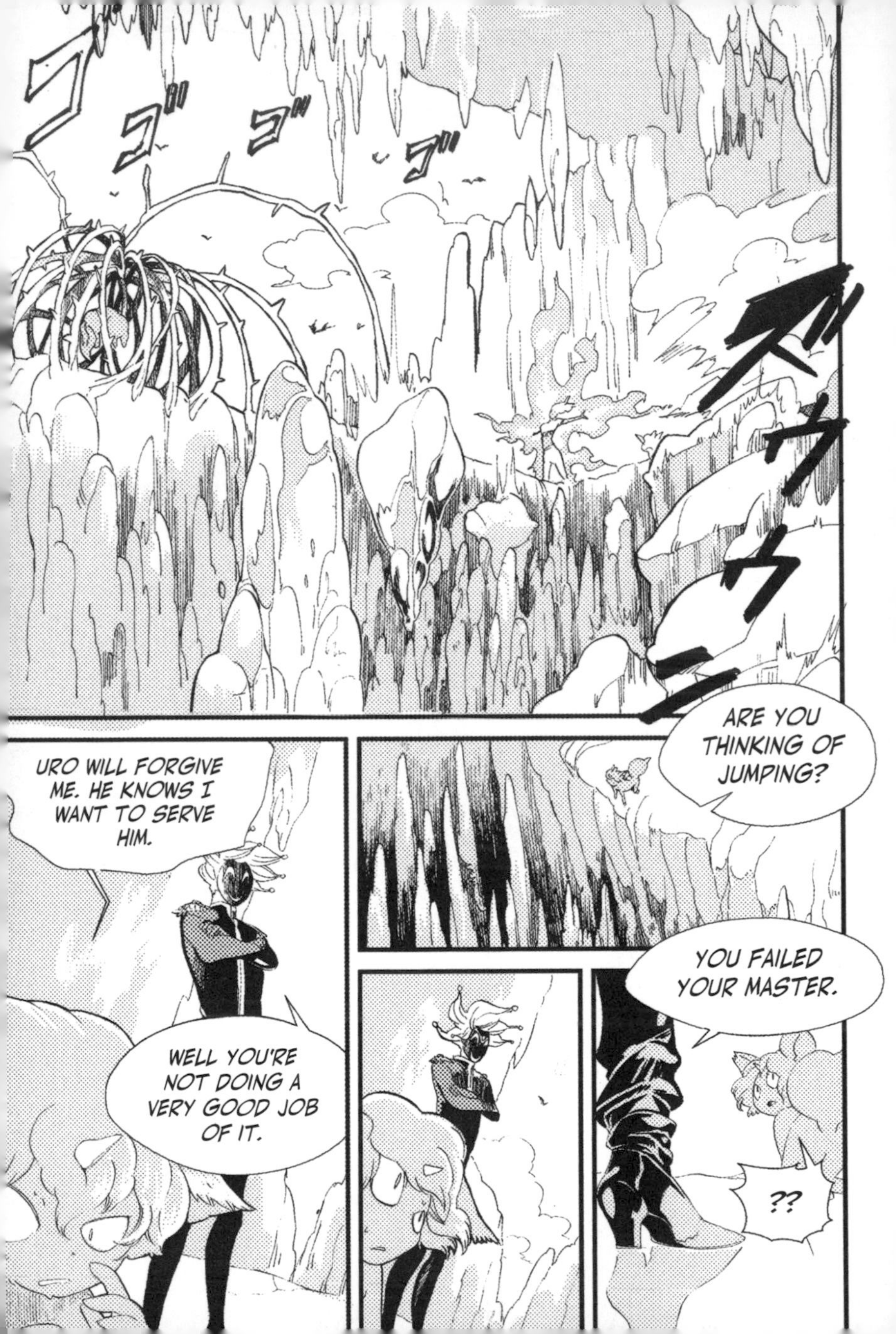
ゴゴゴゴ
ズウウン
ARE YOU THINKING OF JUMPING?
YOU FAILED YOUR MASTER.
??
URO WILL FORGIVE ME. HE KNOWS I WANT TO SERVE HIM.
WELL YOU'RE NOT DOING A VERY GOOD JOB OF IT.

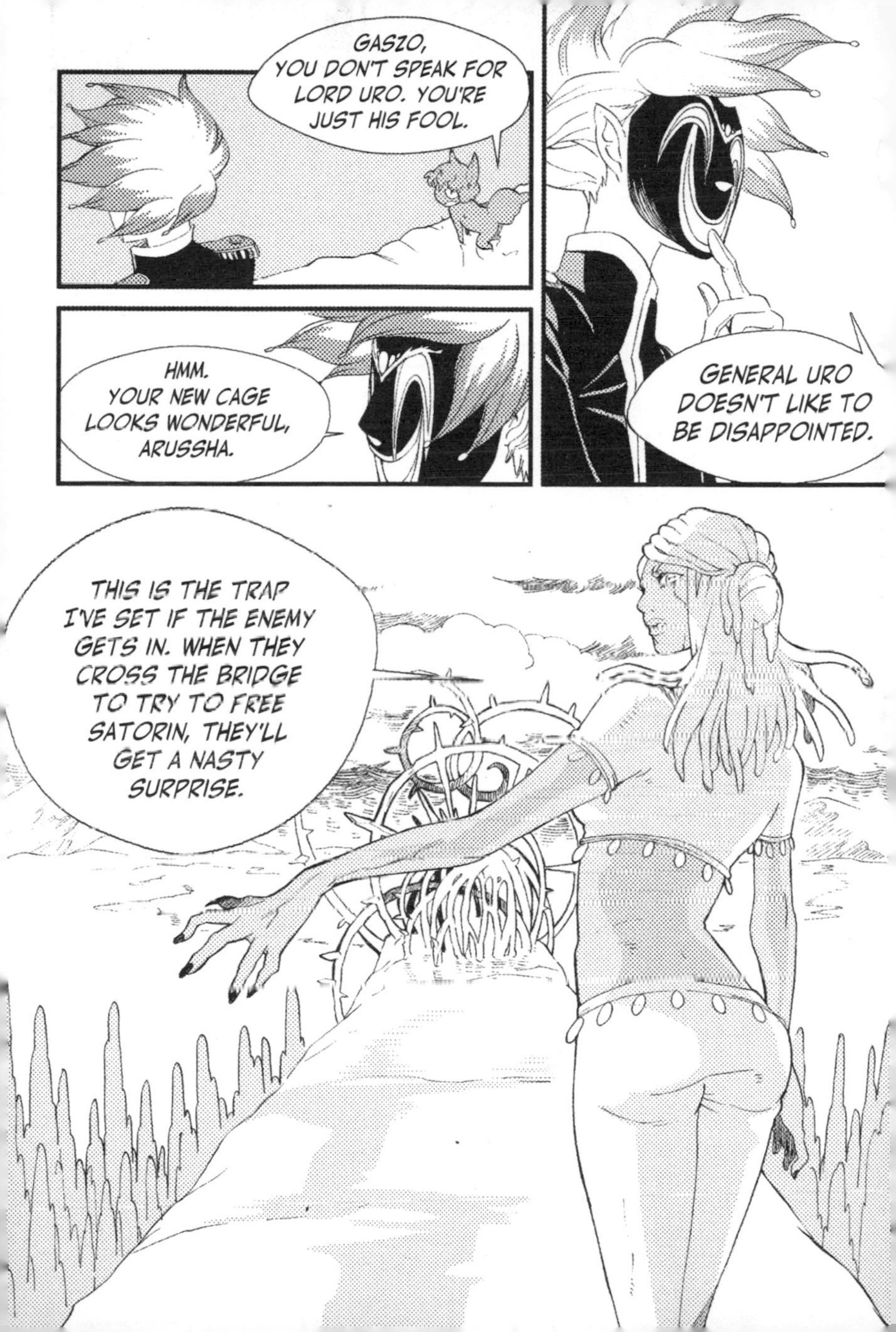
GENERAL URO DOESN'T LIKE TO BE DISAPPOINTED.
GASZO, YOU DON'T SPEAK FOR LORD URO. YOU'RE JUST HIS FOOL.
HMM. YOUR NEW CAGE LOOKS WONDERFUL, ARUSSHA.
THIS IS THE TRAP I'VE SET IF THE ENEMY GETS IN. WHEN THEY CROSS THE BRIDGE TO TRY TO FREE SATORIN, THEY'LL GET A NASTY SURPRISE.

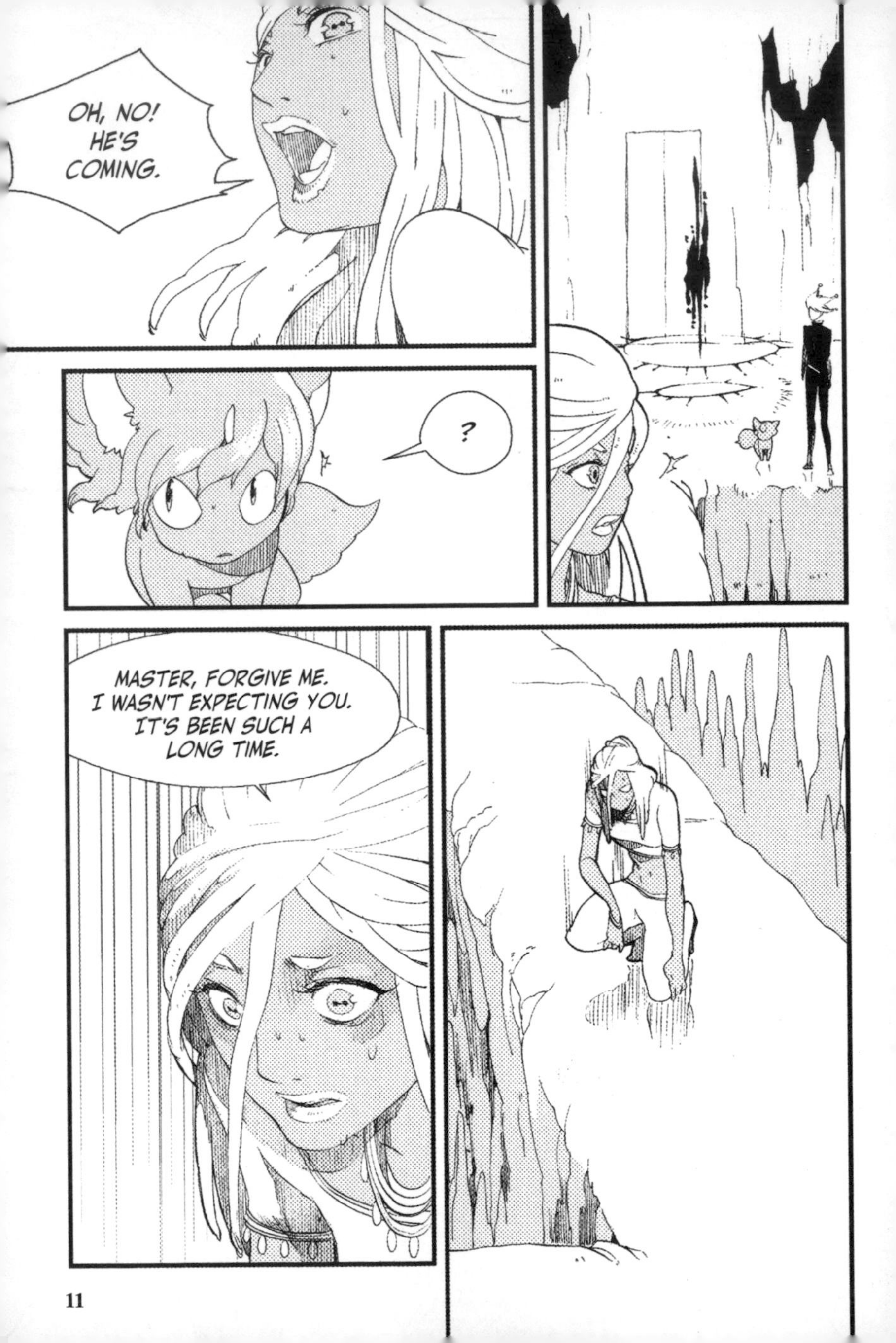
OH, NO! HE'S COMING.
?
MASTER, FORGIVE ME. I WASN'T EXPECTING YOU. IT'S BEEN SUCH A LONG TIME.

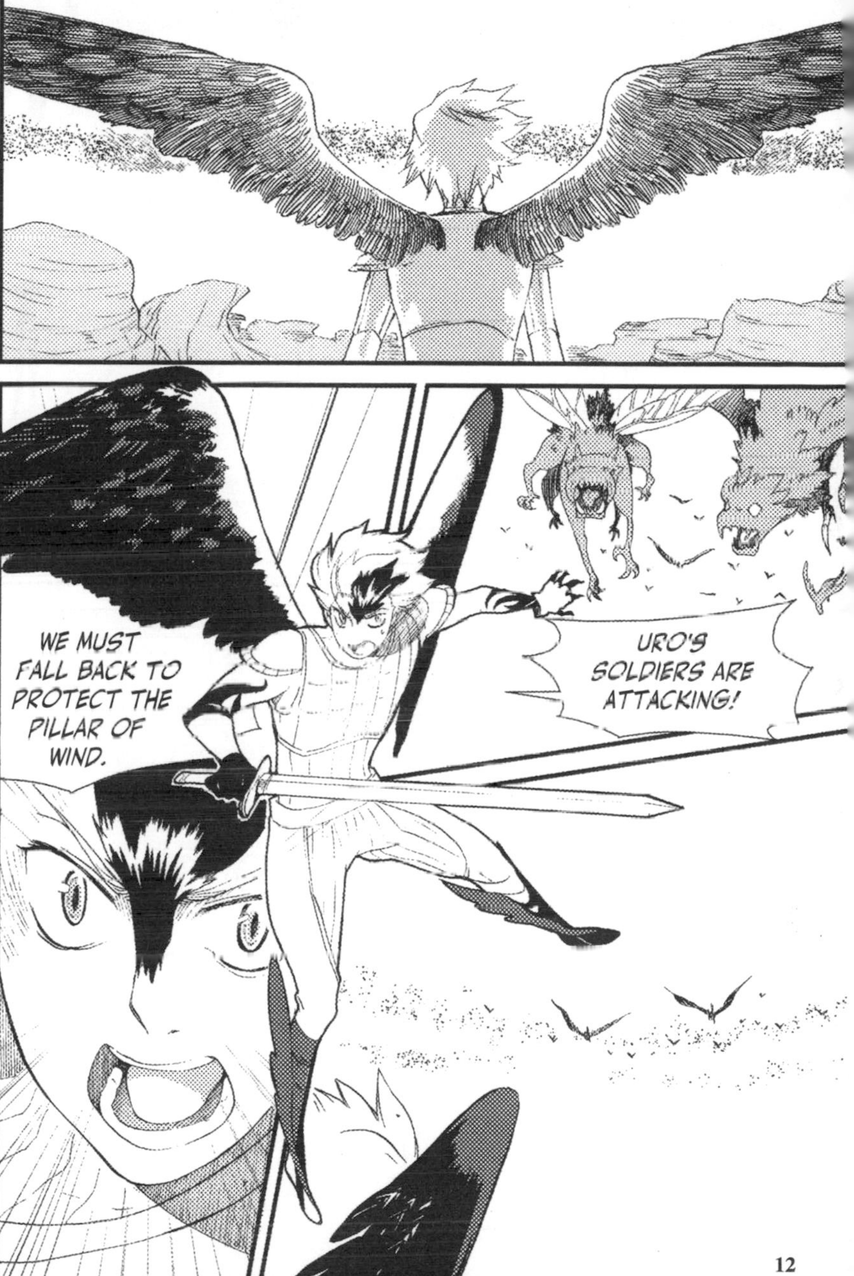
URO'S SOLDIERS ARE ATTACKING!
WE MUST FALL BACK TO PROTECT THE PILLAR OF WIND.

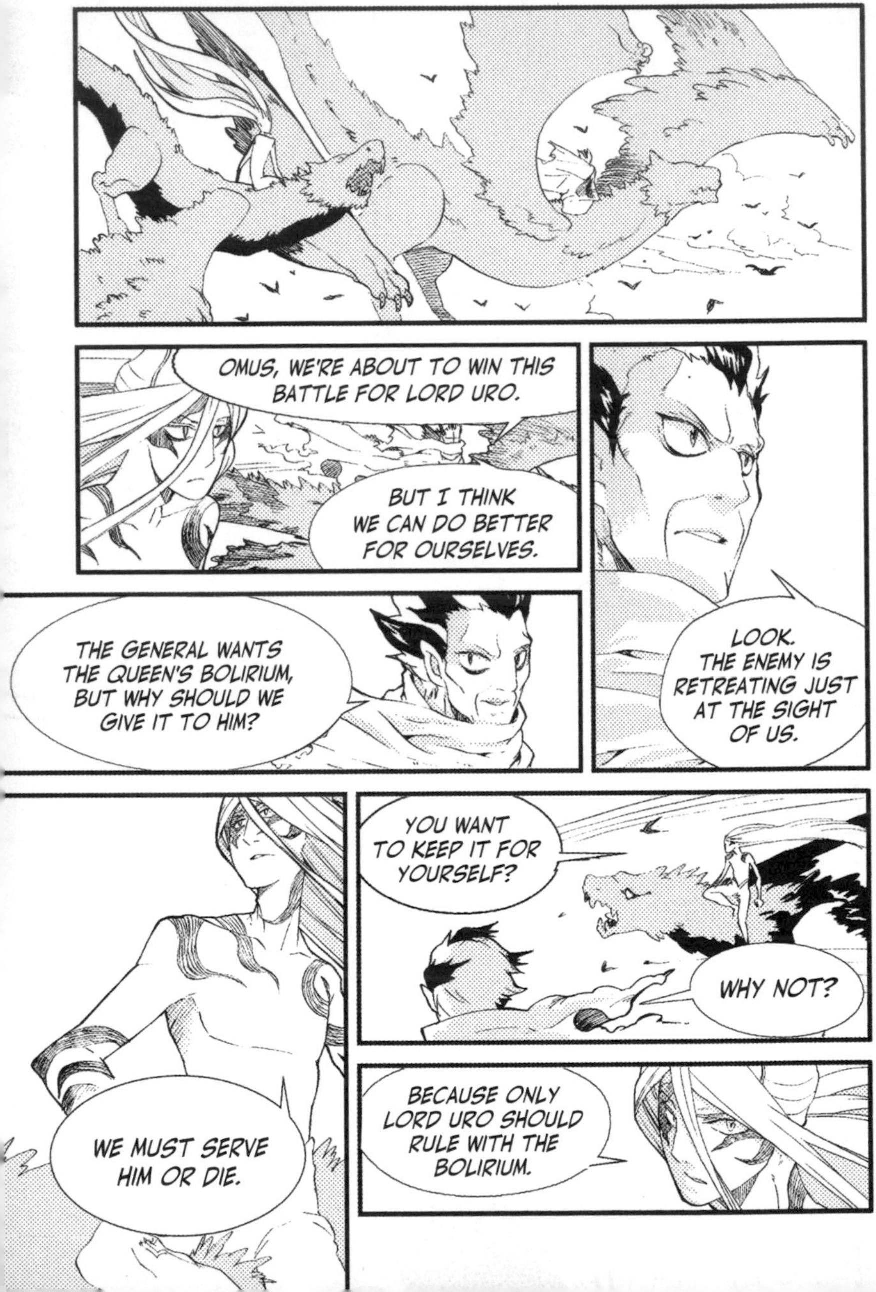
LOOK. THE ENEMY IS RETREATING JUST AT THE SIGHT OF US.
OMUS, WE'RE ABOUT TO WIN THIS BATTLE FOR LORD URO.
BUT I THINK WE CAN DO BETTER FOR OURSELVES.
THE GENERAL WANTS THE QUEEN'S BOLIRIUM, BUT WHY SHOULD WE GIVE IT TO HIM?
YOU WANT TO KEEP IT FOR YOURSELF?
WHY NOT?
BECAUSE ONLY LORD URO SHOULD RULE WITH THE BOLIRIUM.
WE MUST SERVE HIM OR DIE.

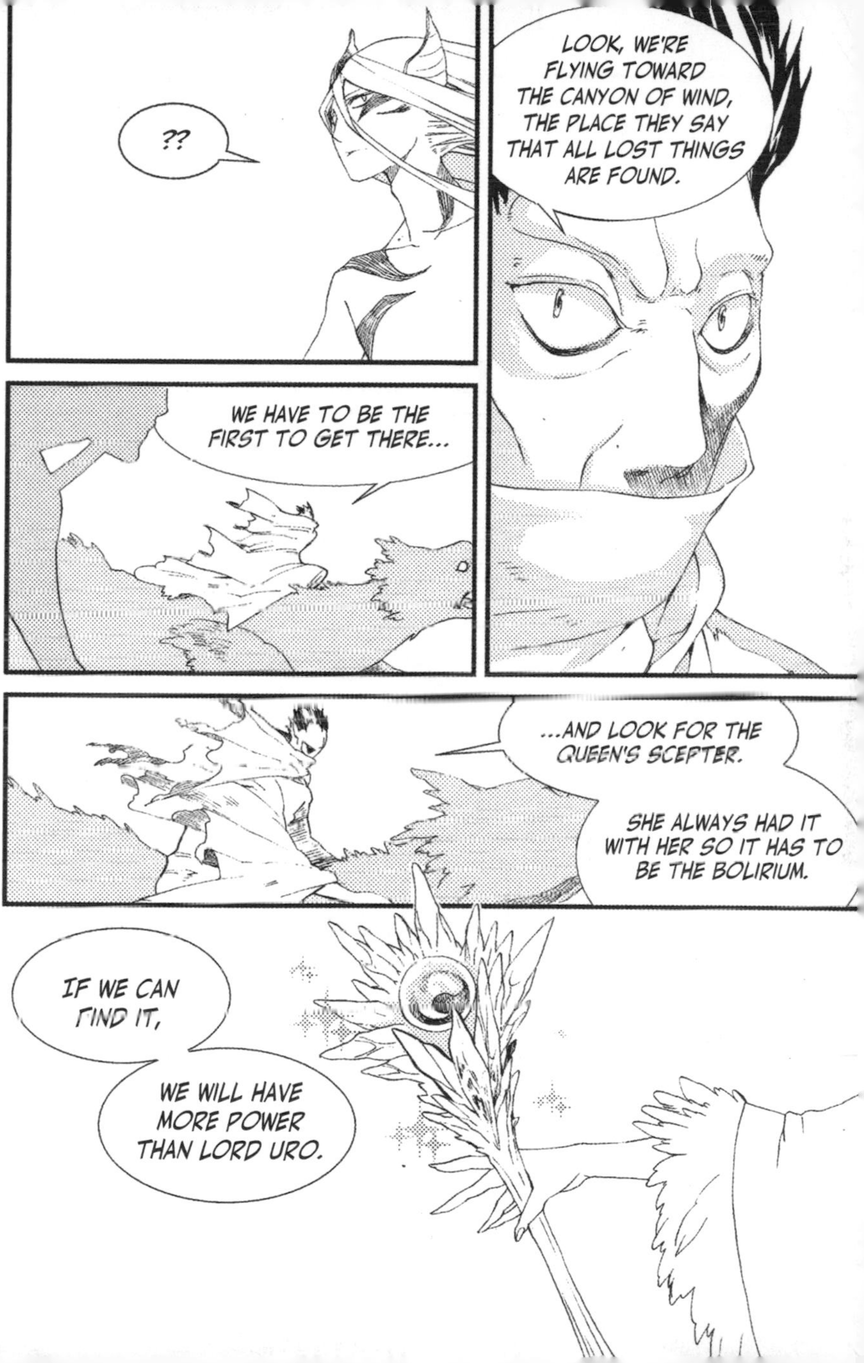
LOOK, WE'RE FLYING TOWARD THE CANYON OF WIND, THE PLACE THEY SAY THAT ALL LOST THINGS ARE FOUND.
??
WE HAVE TO BE THE FIRST TO GET THERE...
...AND LOOK FOR THE QUEEN'S SCEPTER.
SHE ALWAYS HAD IT WITH HER SO IT HAS TO BE THE BOLIRIUM.
IF WE CAN FIND IT,
WE WILL HAVE MORE POWER THAN LORD URO.

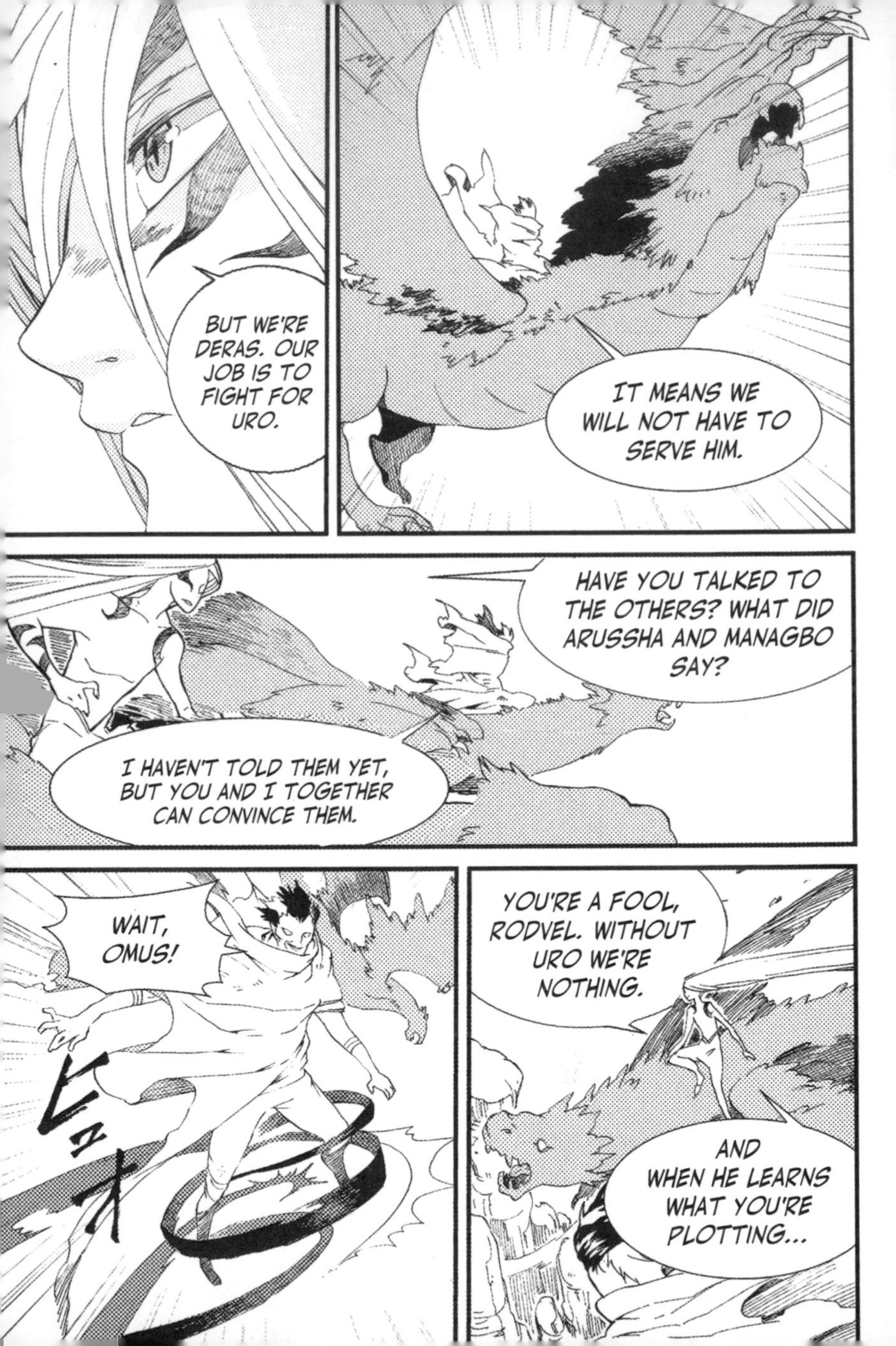
IT MEANS WE WILL NOT HAVE TO SERVE HIM.
BUT WE'RE DERAS. OUR JOB IS TO FIGHT FOR URO.
HAVE YOU TALKED TO THE OTHERS? WHAT DID ARUSSHA AND MANAGBO SAY?
I HAVEN'T TOLD THEM YET, BUT YOU AND I TOGETHER CAN CONVINCE THEM.
YOU'RE A FOOL, RODVEL. WITHOUT URO WE'RE NOTHING.
AND WHEN HE LEARNS WHAT YOU'RE PLOTTING...
WAIT, OMUS!
ヒュオ

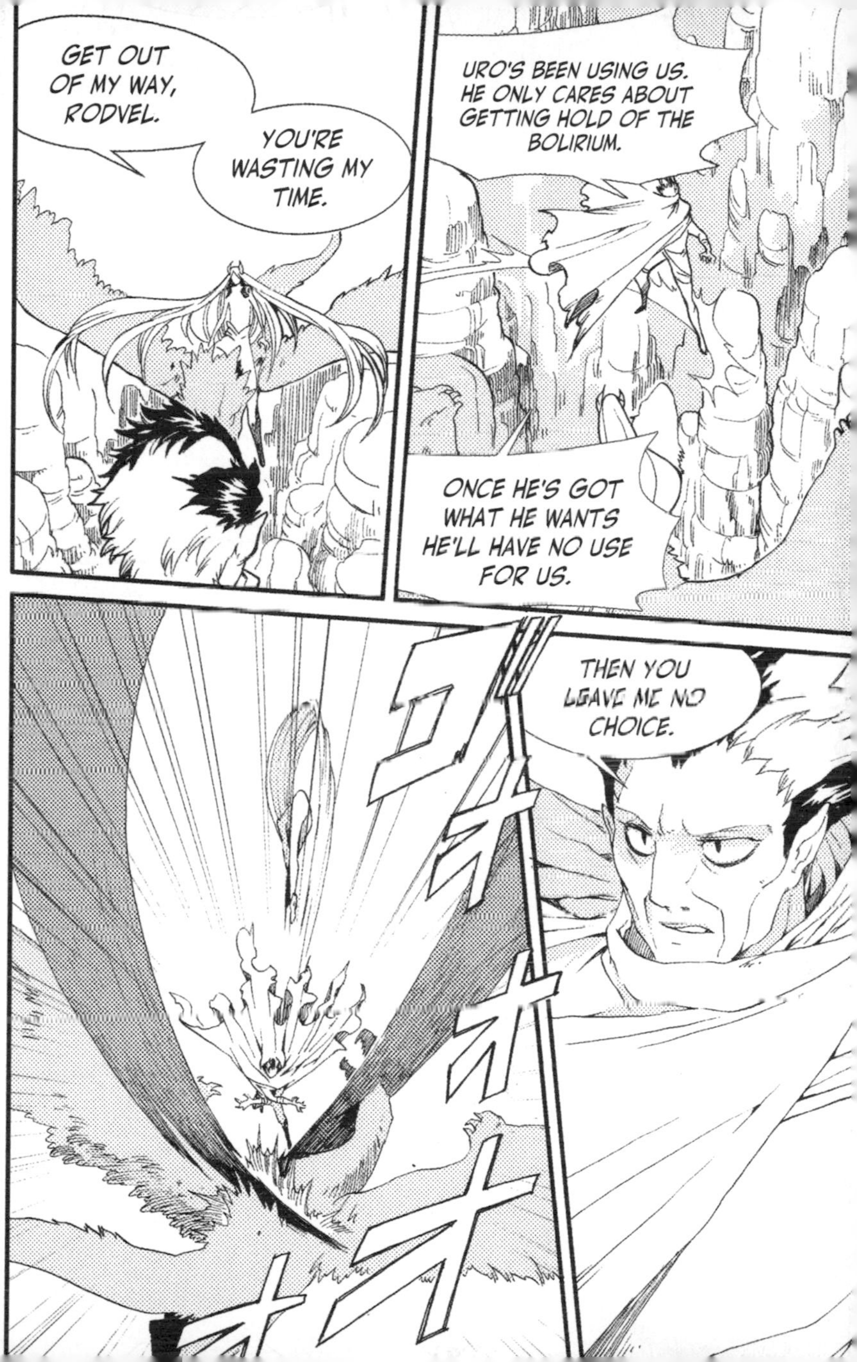
URO'S BEEN USING US. HE ONLY CARES ABOUT GETTING HOLD OF THE BOLIRIUM.
ONCE HE'S GOT WHAT HE WANTS HE'LL HAVE NO USE FOR US.
GET OUT OF MY WAY, RODVEL.
YOU'RE WASTING MY TIME.
THEN YOU LEAVE ME NO CHOICE.

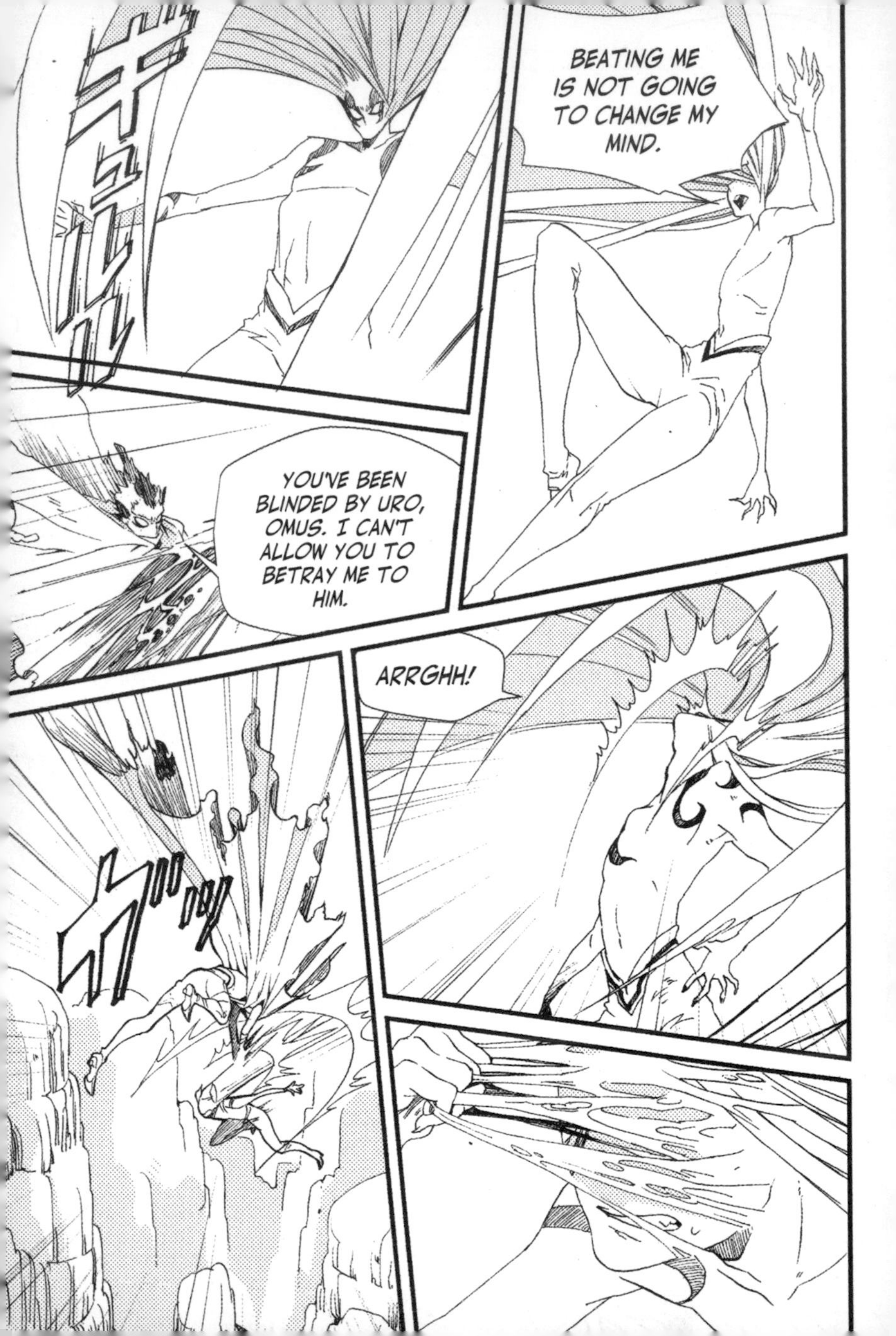
BEATING ME IS NOT GOING TO CHANGE MY MIND.
YOU'VE BEEN BLINDED BY URO, OMUS. I CAN'T ALLOW YOU TO BETRAY ME TO HIM.
ARRGHH!

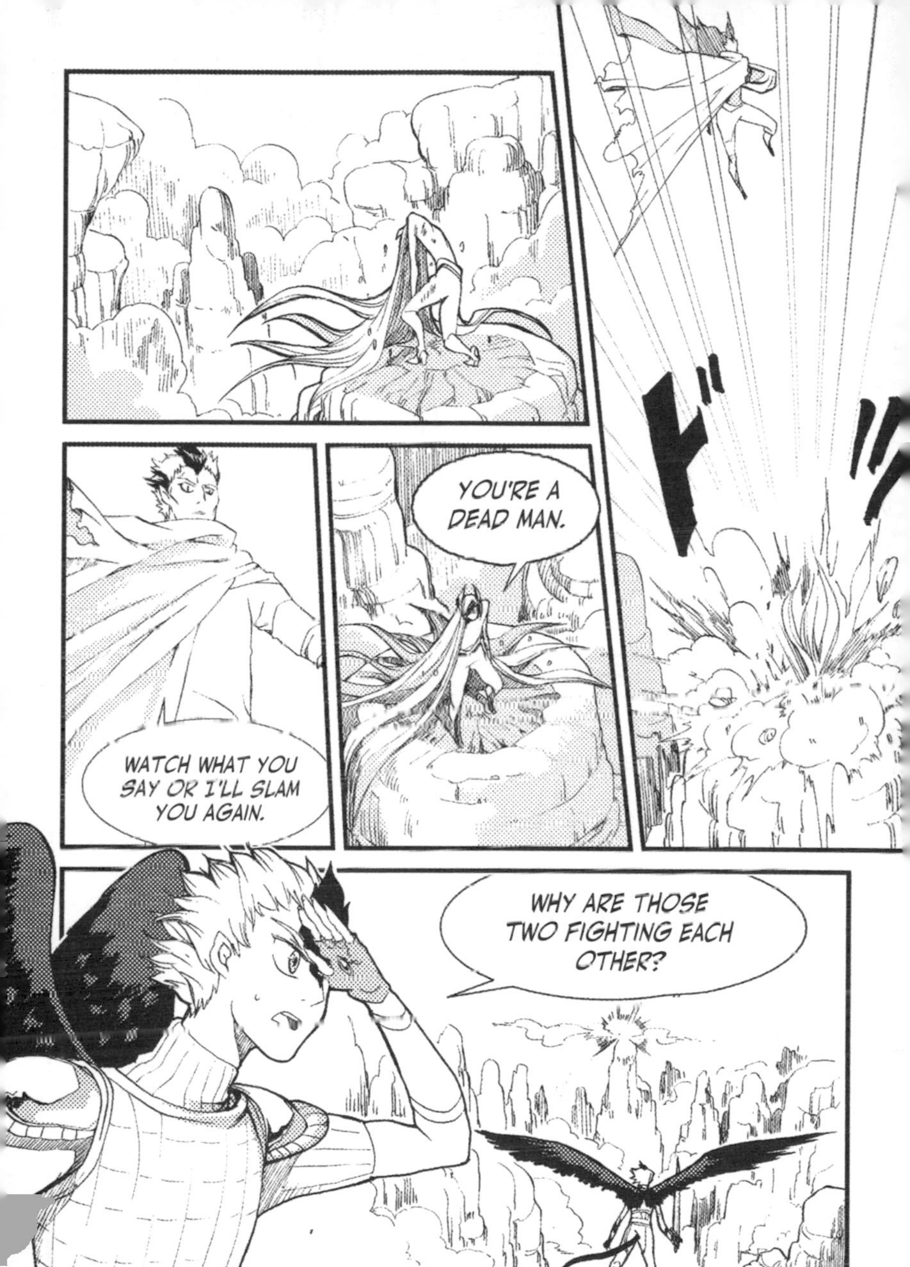
YOU'RE A DEAD MAN.
WATCH WHAT YOU SAY OR I'LL SLAM YOU AGAIN.
WHY ARE THOSE TWO FIGHTING EACH OTHER?

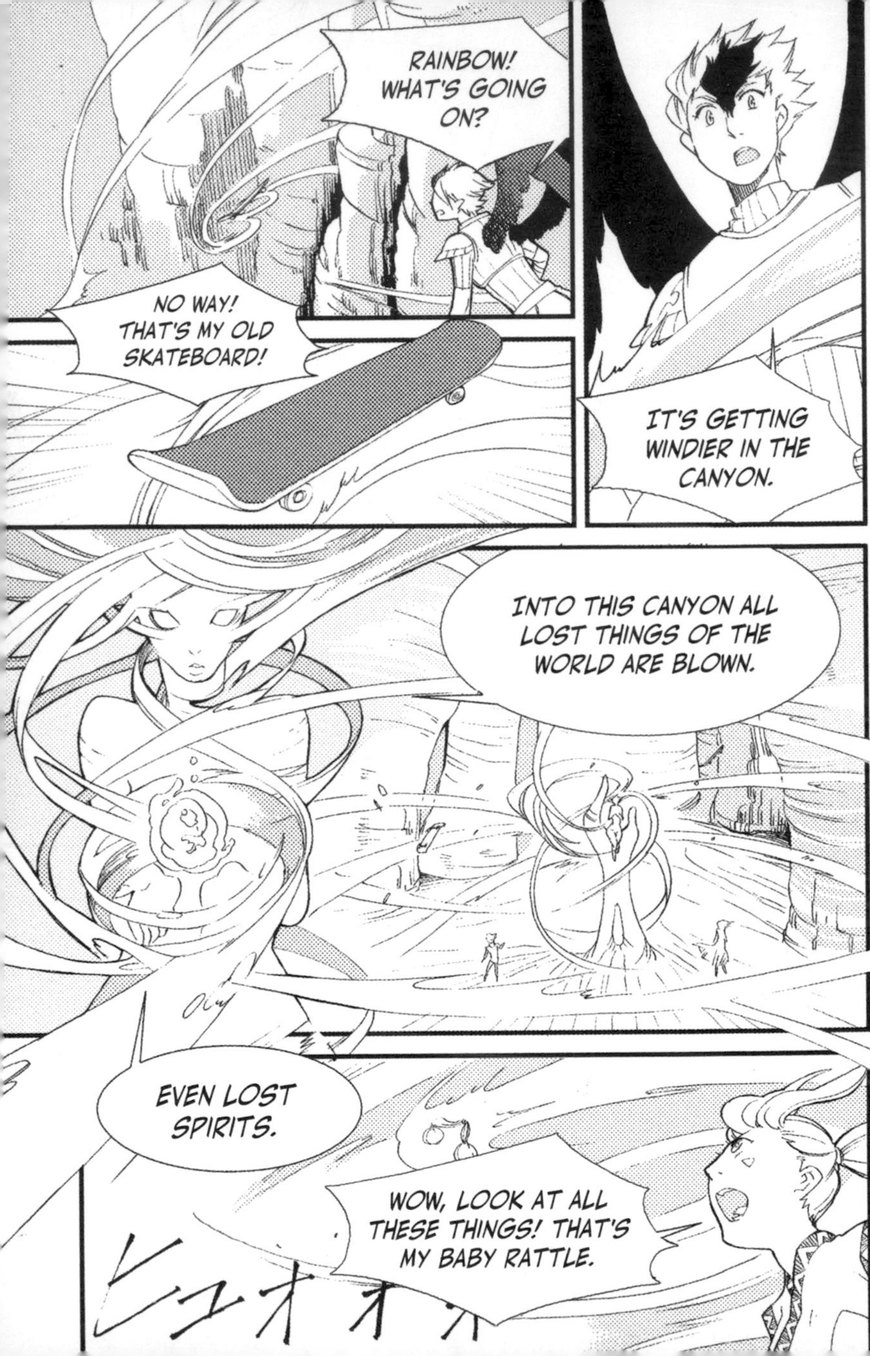
IT'S GETTING WINDIER IN THE CANYON.
RAINBOW! WHAT'S GOING ON?
NO WAY! THAT'S MY OLD SKATEBOARD!
INTO THIS CANYON ALL LOST THINGS OF THE WORLD ARE BLOWN.
EVEN LOST SPIRITS.
WOW, LOOK AT ALL THESE THINGS! THAT'S MY BABY RATTLE.
ヒュオオオ

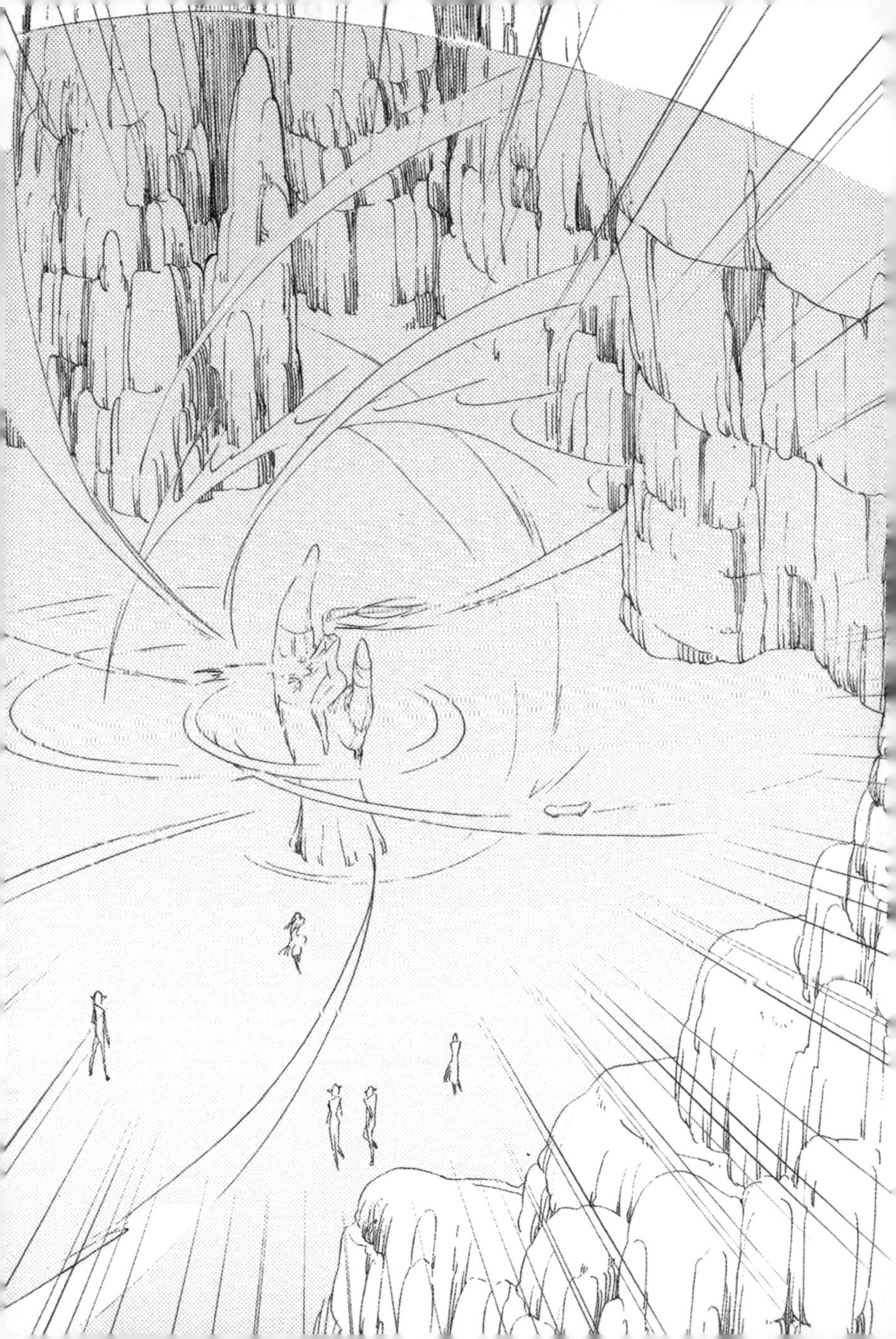

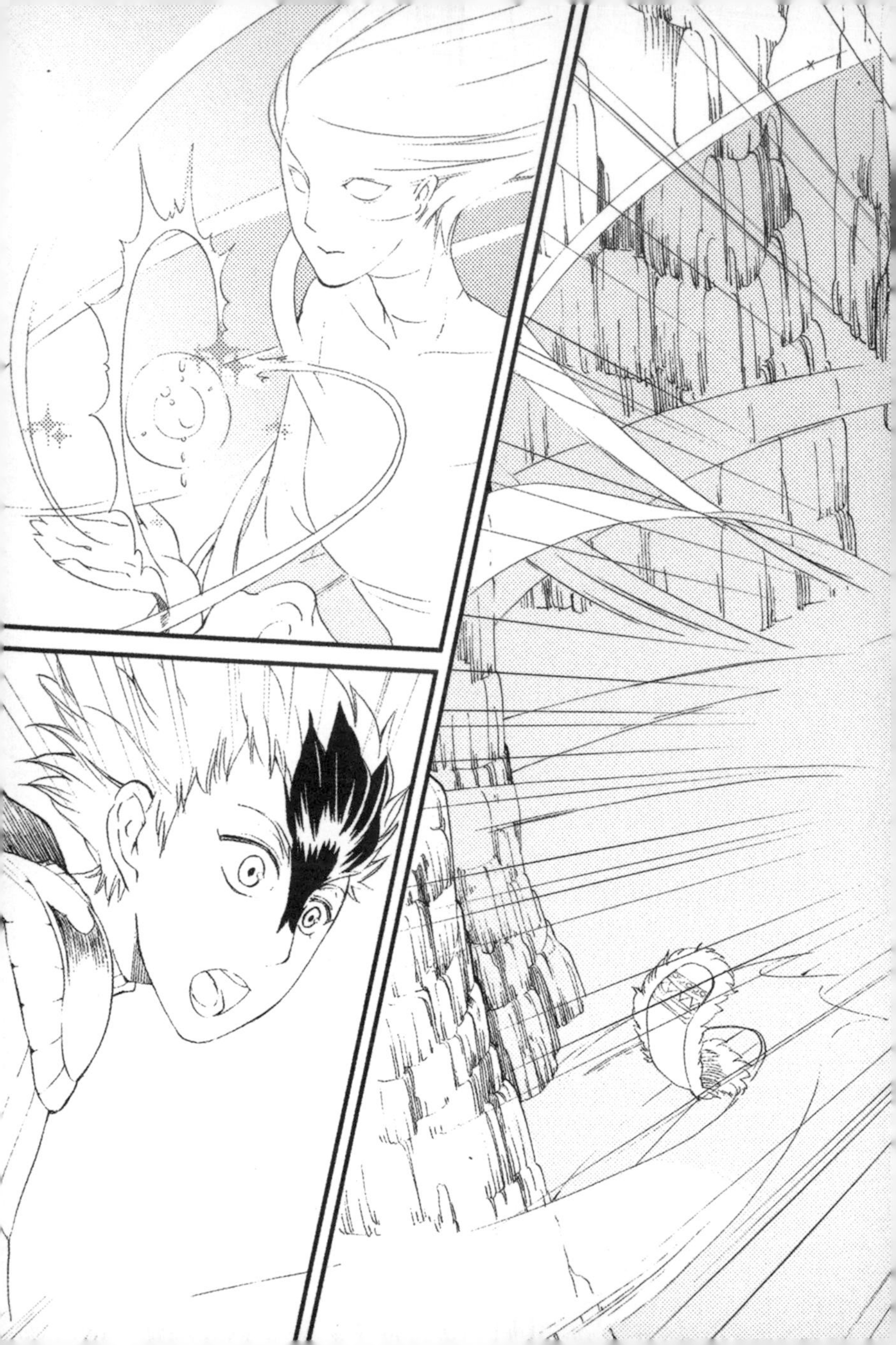

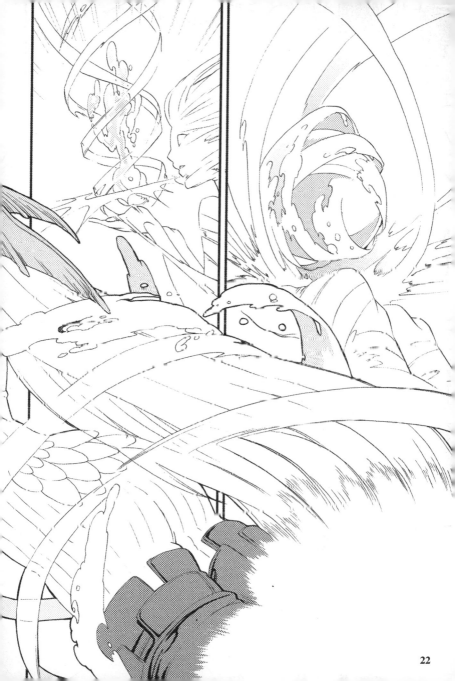

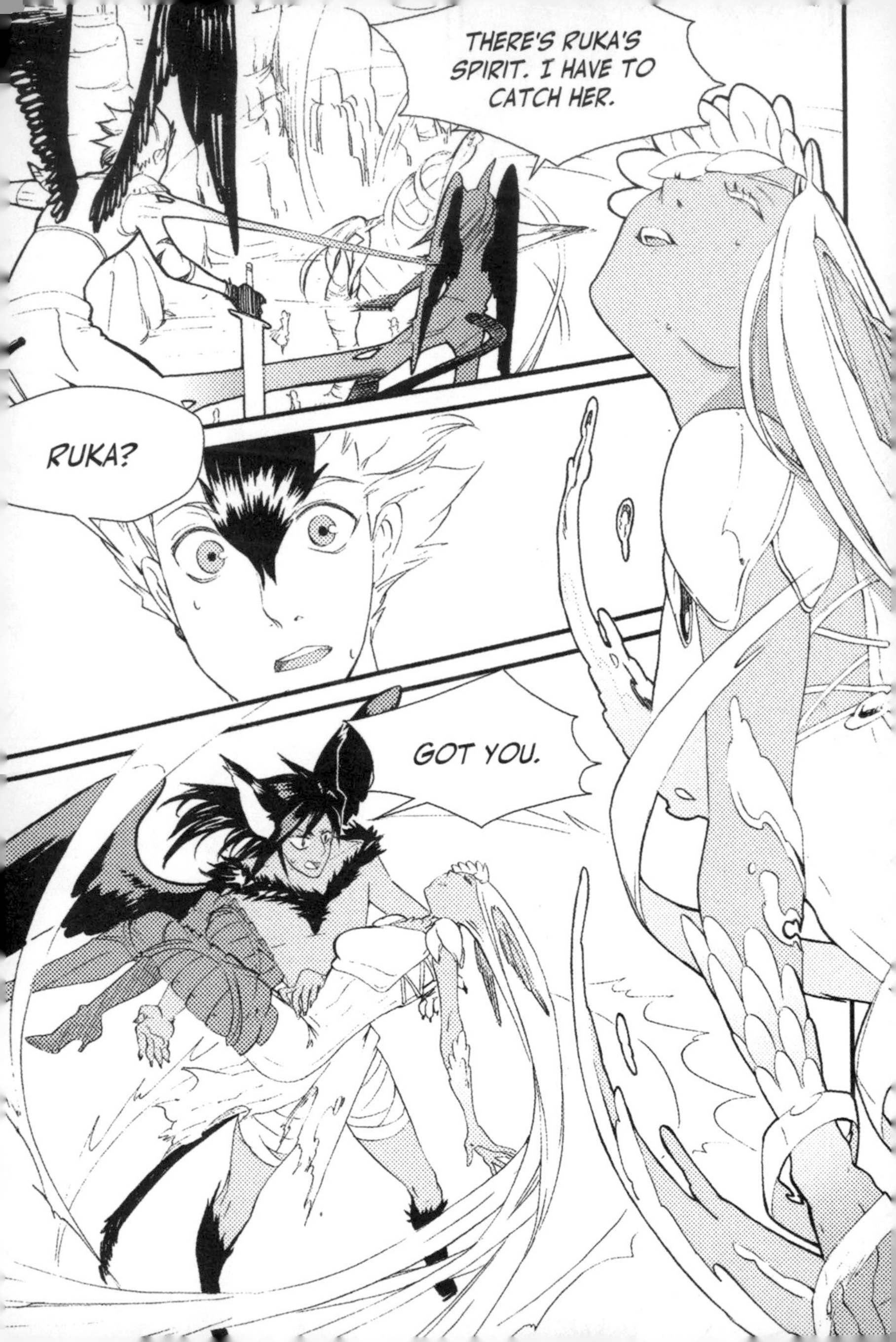
THERE'S RUKA'S SPIRIT. I HAVE TO CATCH HER.
RUKA?
GOT YOU.

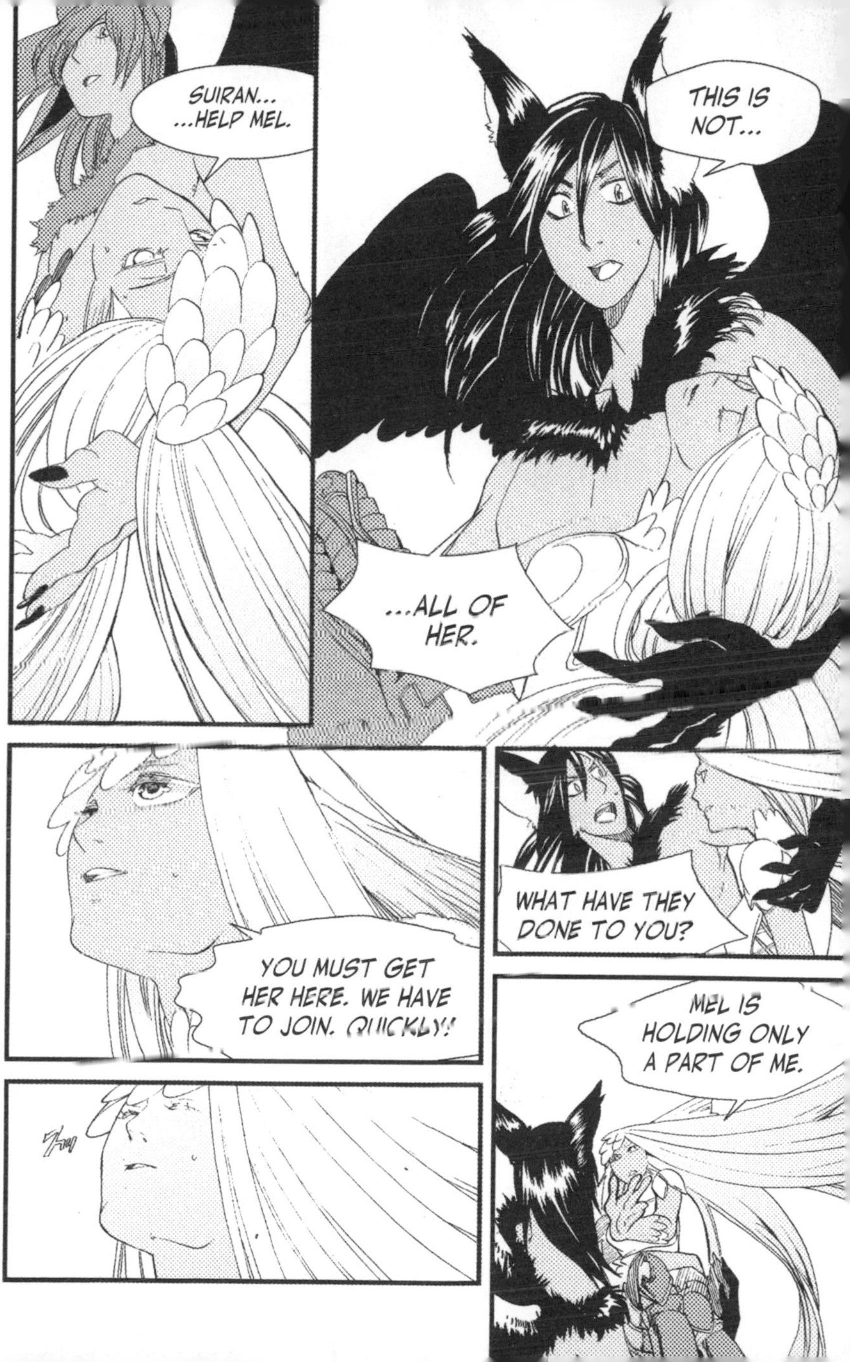
THIS IS NOT...
...ALL OF HER.
SUIRAN... ...HELP MEL.
WHAT HAVE THEY DONE TO YOU?
YOU MUST GET HER HERE. WE HAVE TO JOIN. QUICKLY!
MEL IS HOLDING ONLY A PART OF ME.

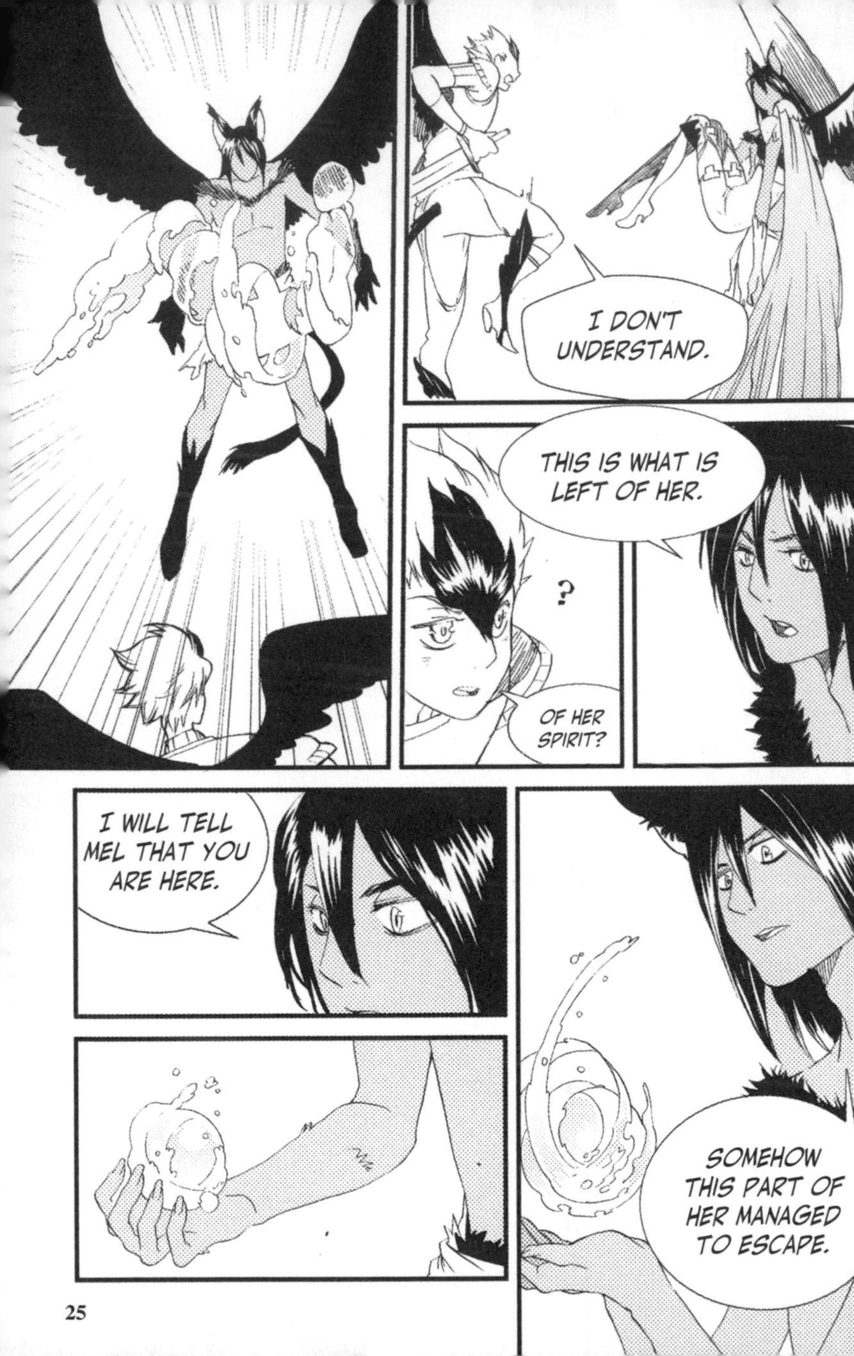
I DON'T UNDERSTAND.
THIS IS WHAT IS LEFT OF HER.
?
OF HER SPIRIT?
SOMEHOW THIS PART OF HER MANAGED TO ESCAPE.
I WILL TELL MEL THAT YOU ARE HERE.

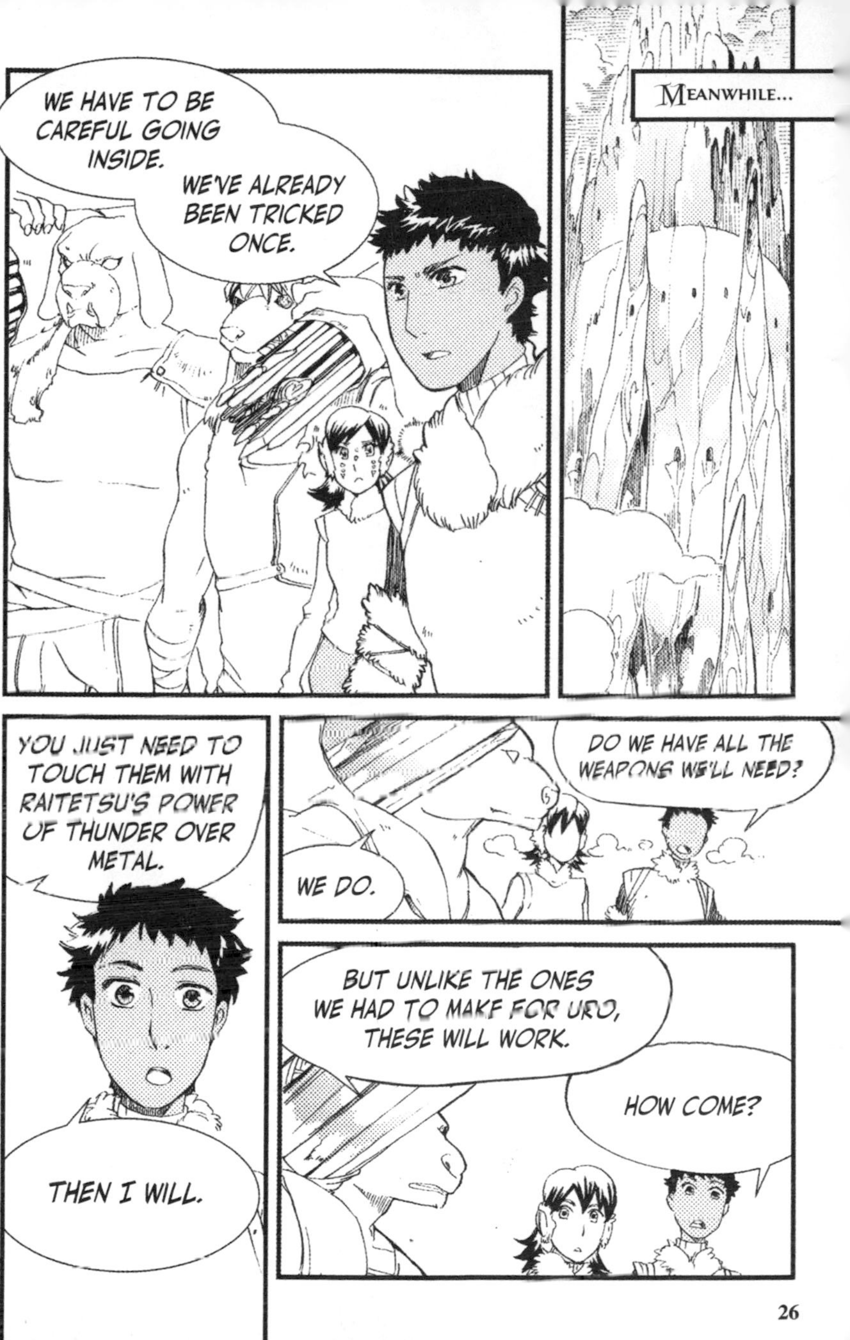
MEANWHILE...
WE HAVE TO BE CAREFUL GOING INSIDE.
WE'VE ALREADY BEEN TRICKED ONCE.
DO WE HAVE ALL THE WEAPONS WE'LL NEED?
WE DO.
BUT UNLIKE THE ONES WE HAD TO MAKE FOR URO, THESE WILL WORK.
HOW COME?
YOU JUST NEED TO TOUCH THEM WITH RAITETSU'S POWER OF THUNDER OVER METAL.
THEN I WILL.

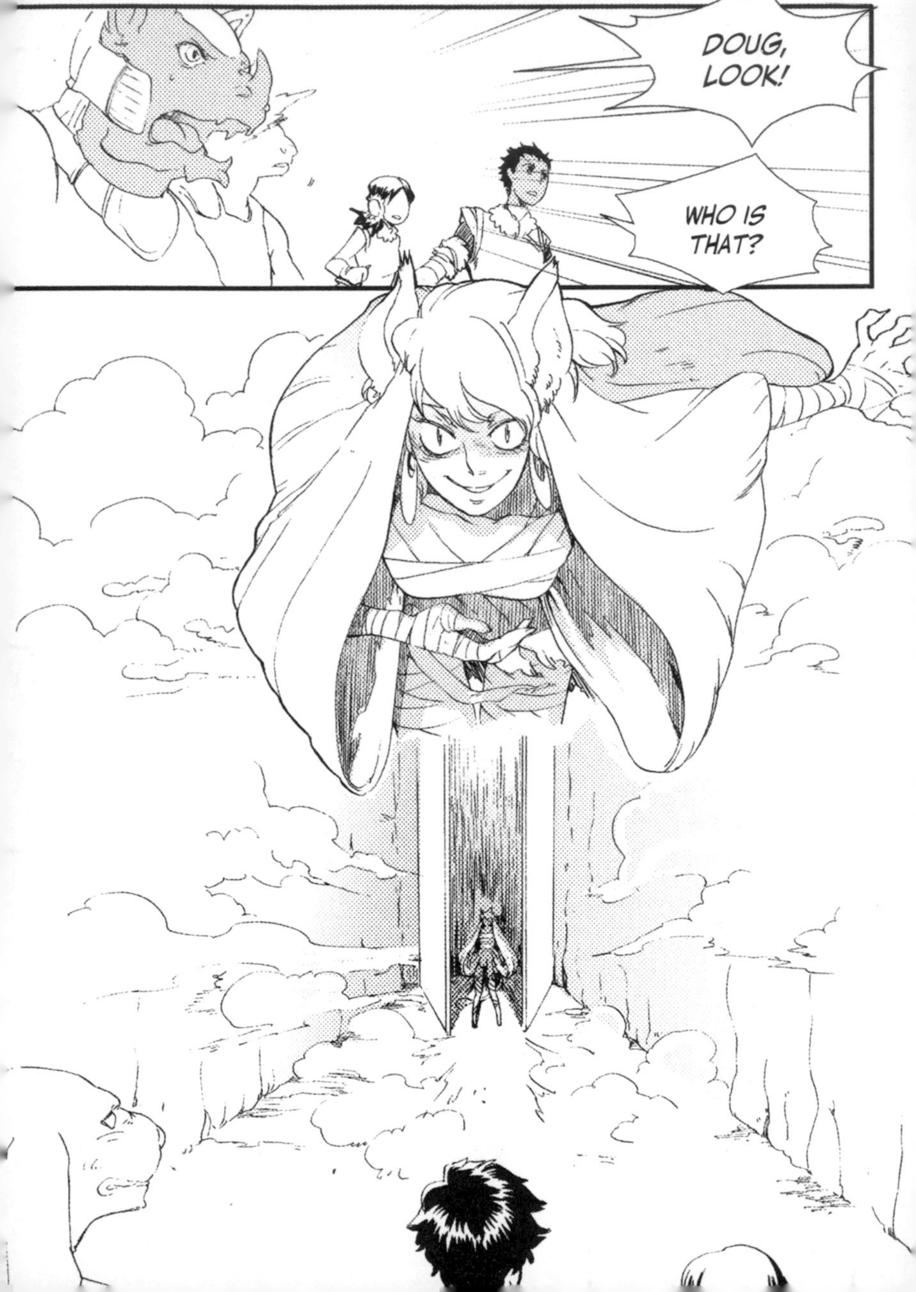
DOUG, LOOK!
WHO IS THAT?

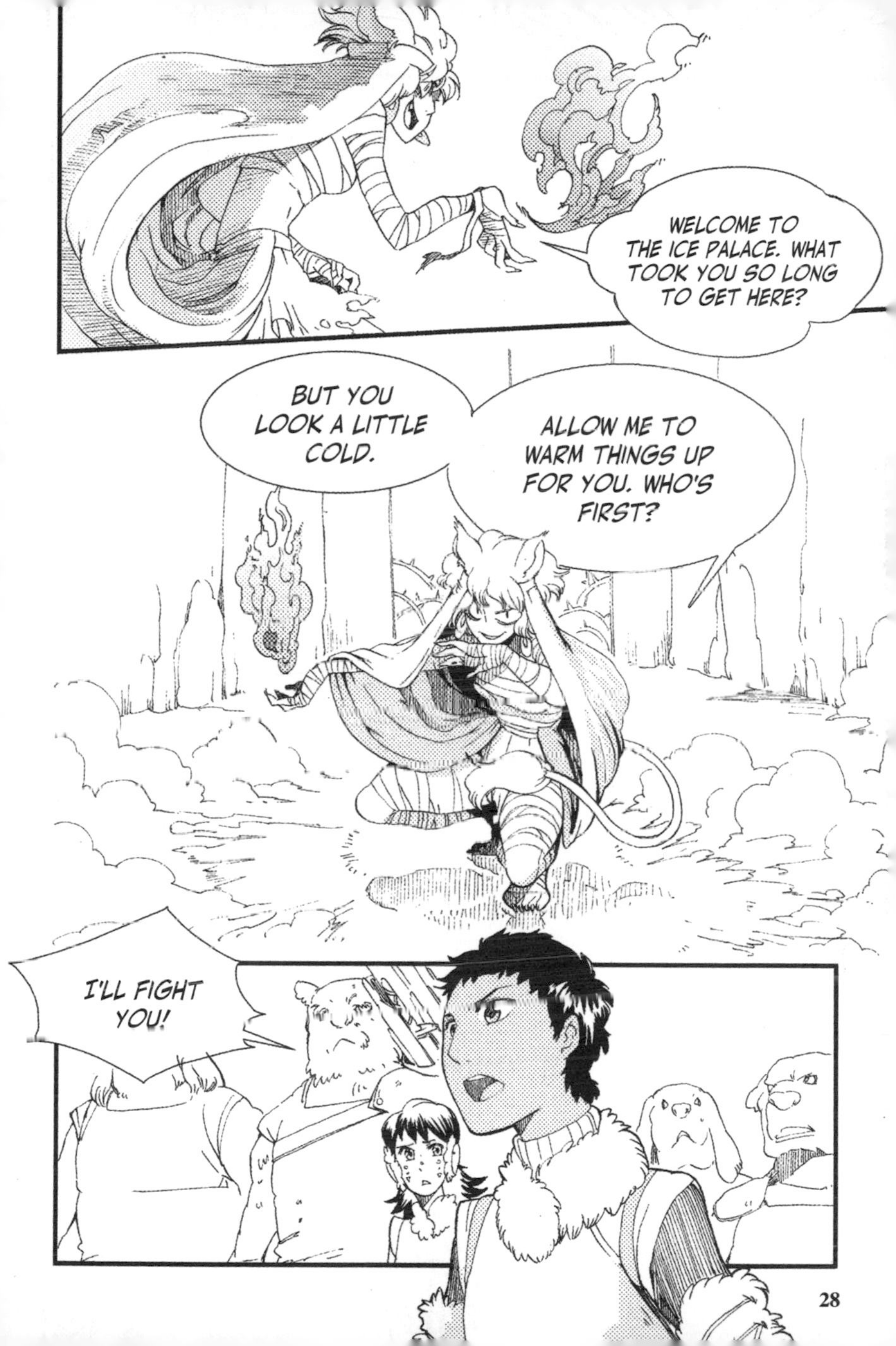
WELCOME TO THE ICE PALACE. WHAT TOOK YOU SO LONG TO GET HERE?
BUT YOU LOOK A LITTLE COLD.
ALLOW ME TO WARM THINGS UP FOR YOU. WHO'S FIRST?
I'LL FIGHT YOU!

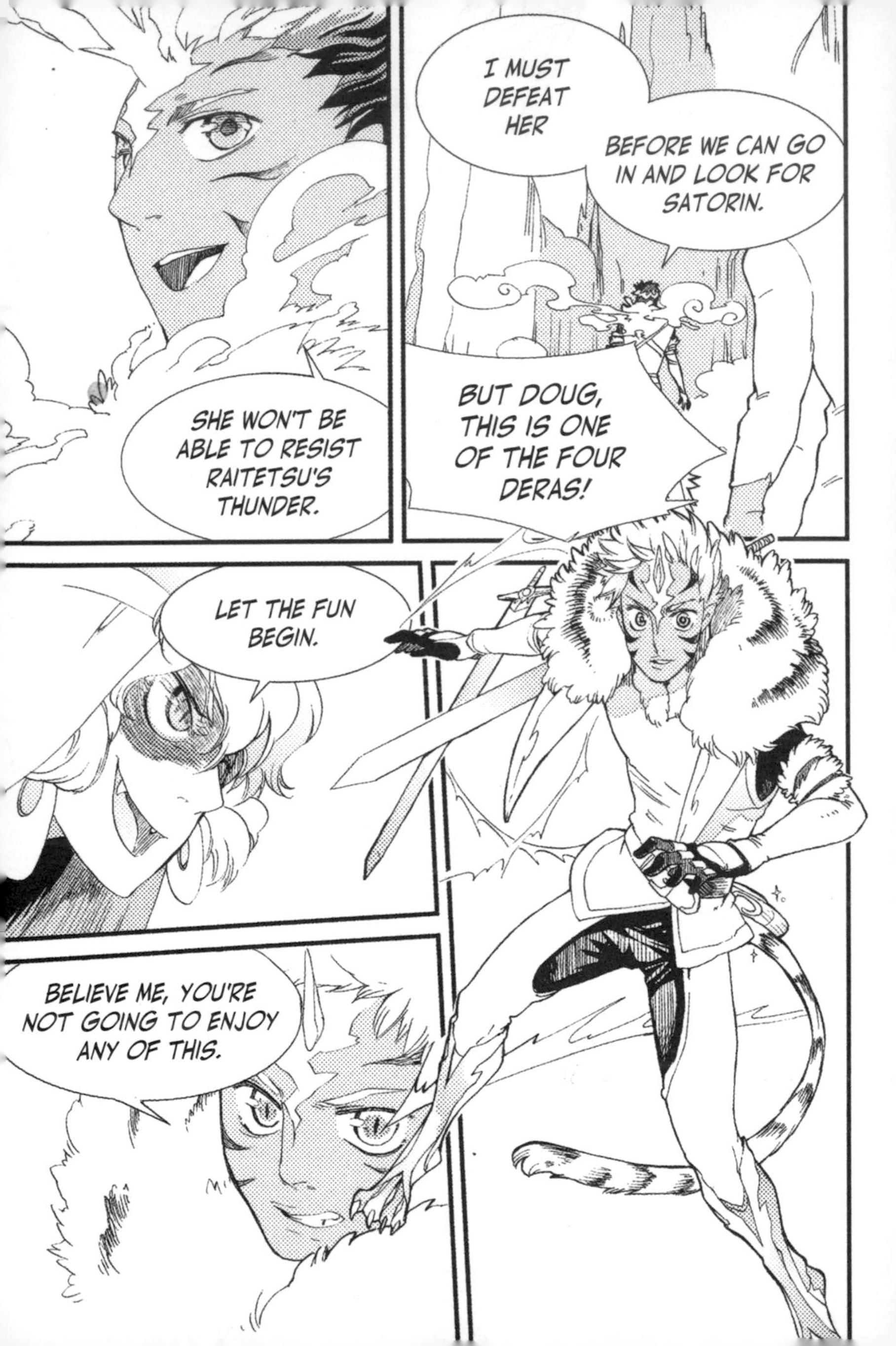
I MUST DEFEAT HER
BEFORE WE CAN GO IN AND LOOK FOR SATORIN.
BUT DOUG, THIS IS ONE OF THE FOUR DERAS!
SHE WON'T BE ABLE TO RESIST RAITETSU'S THUNDER.
LET THE FUN BEGIN.
BELIEVE ME, YOU'RE NOT GOING TO ENJOY ANY OF THIS.

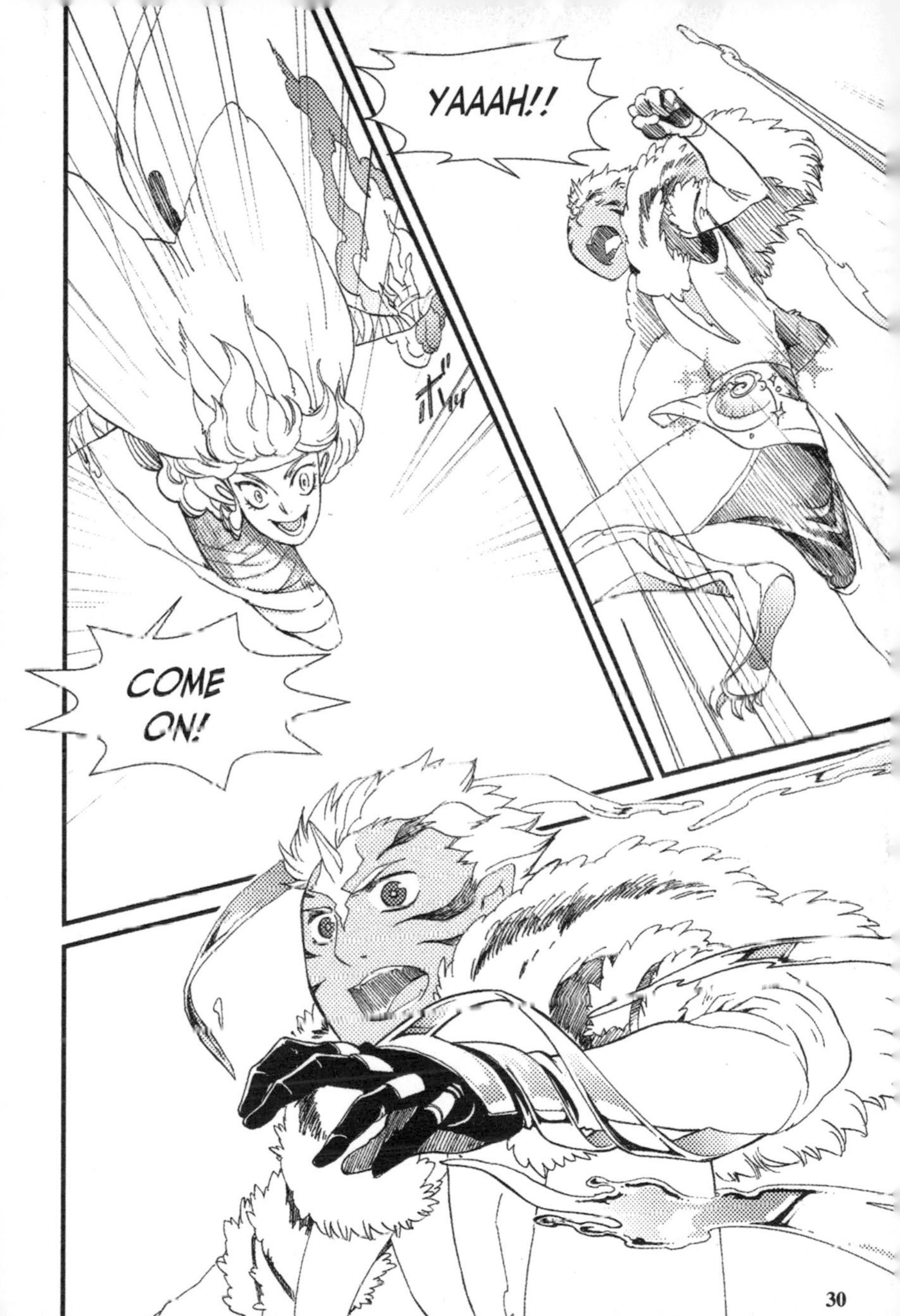
YAAAH!!
COME ON!

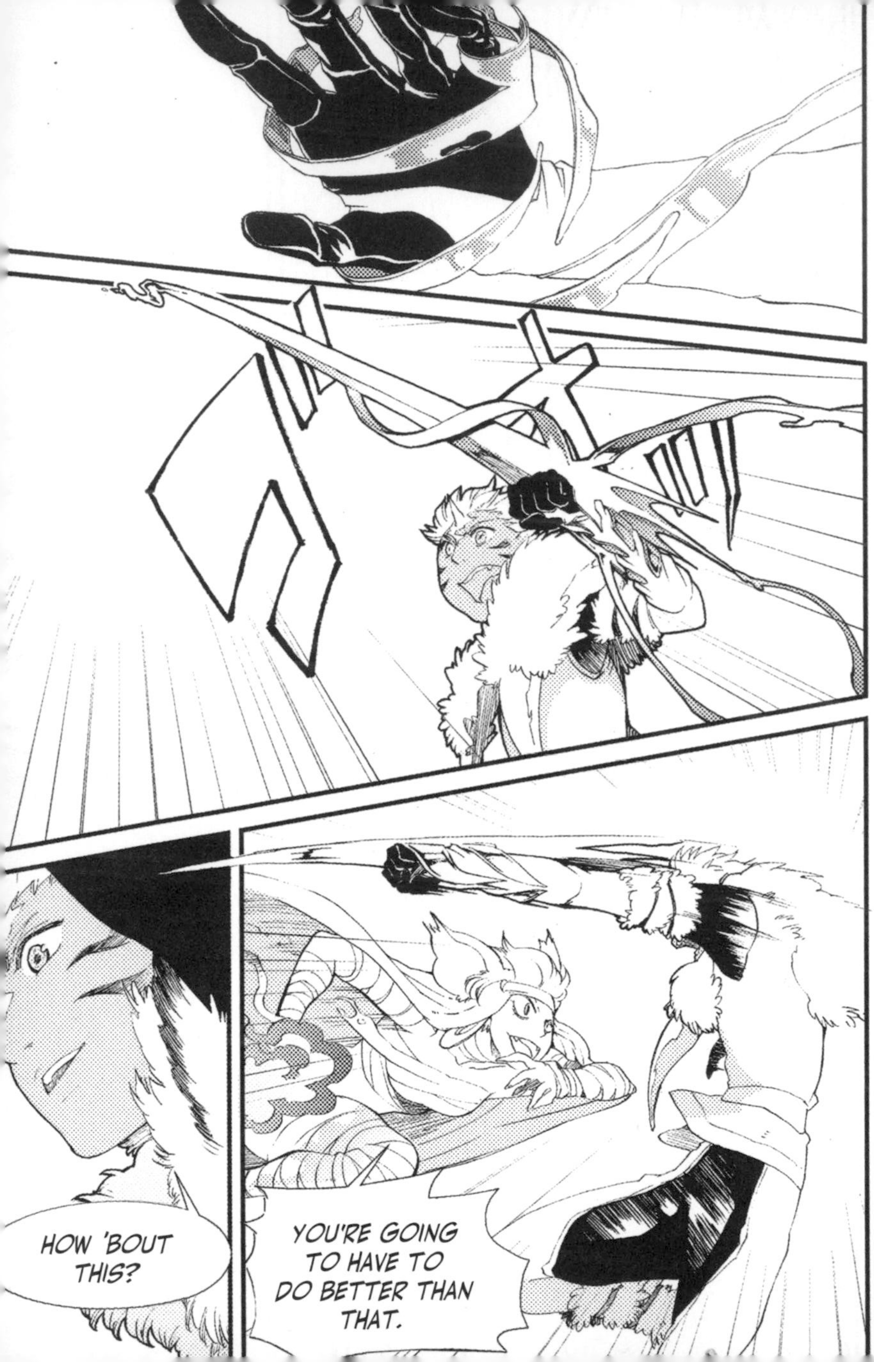
YOU'RE GOING TO HAVE TO DO BETTER THAN THAT.
HOW 'BOUT THIS?

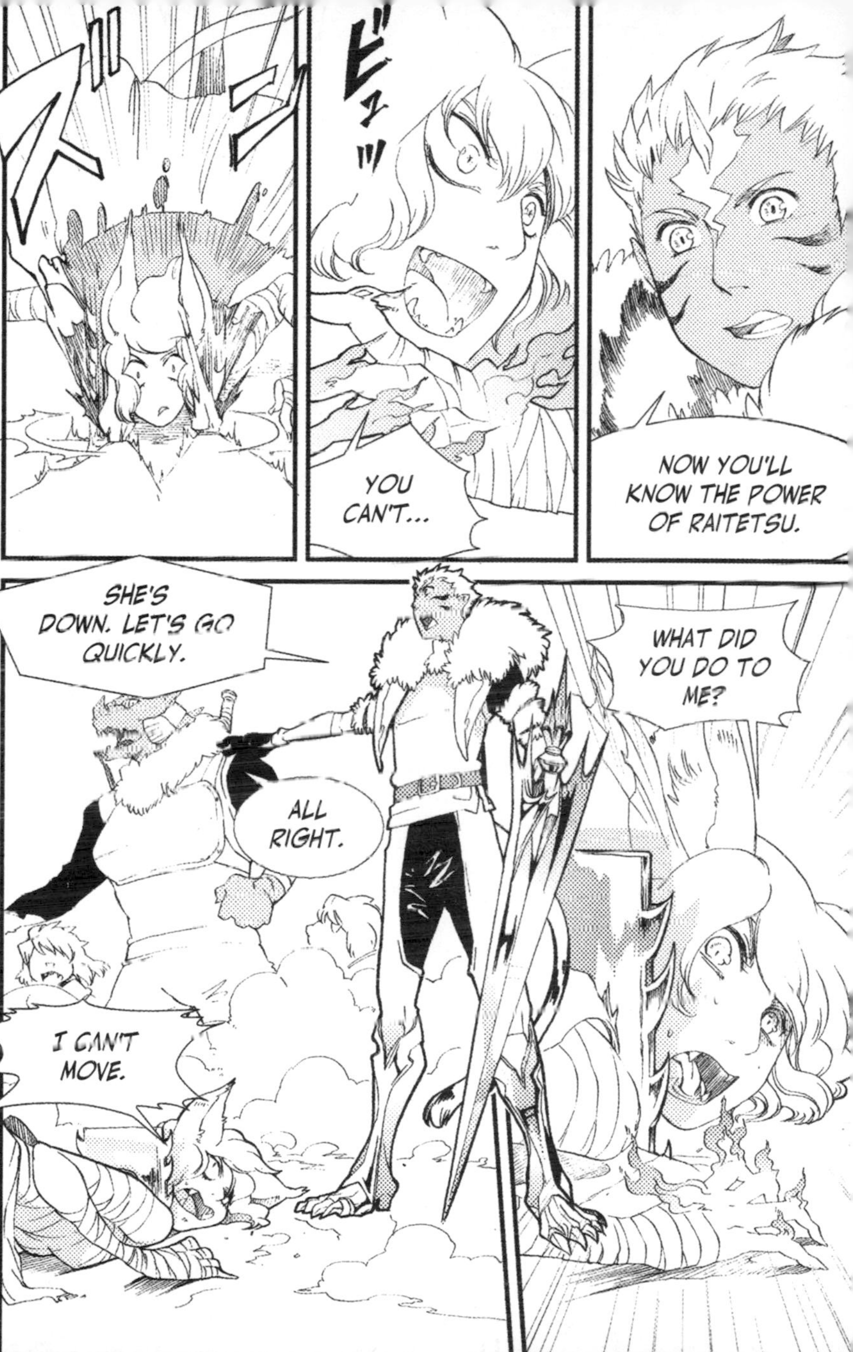
NOW YOU'LL KNOW THE POWER OF RAITETSU.
YOU CAN'T...
WHAT DID YOU DO TO ME?
SHE'S DOWN. LET'S GO QUICKLY.
ALL RIGHT.
I CAN'T MOVE.

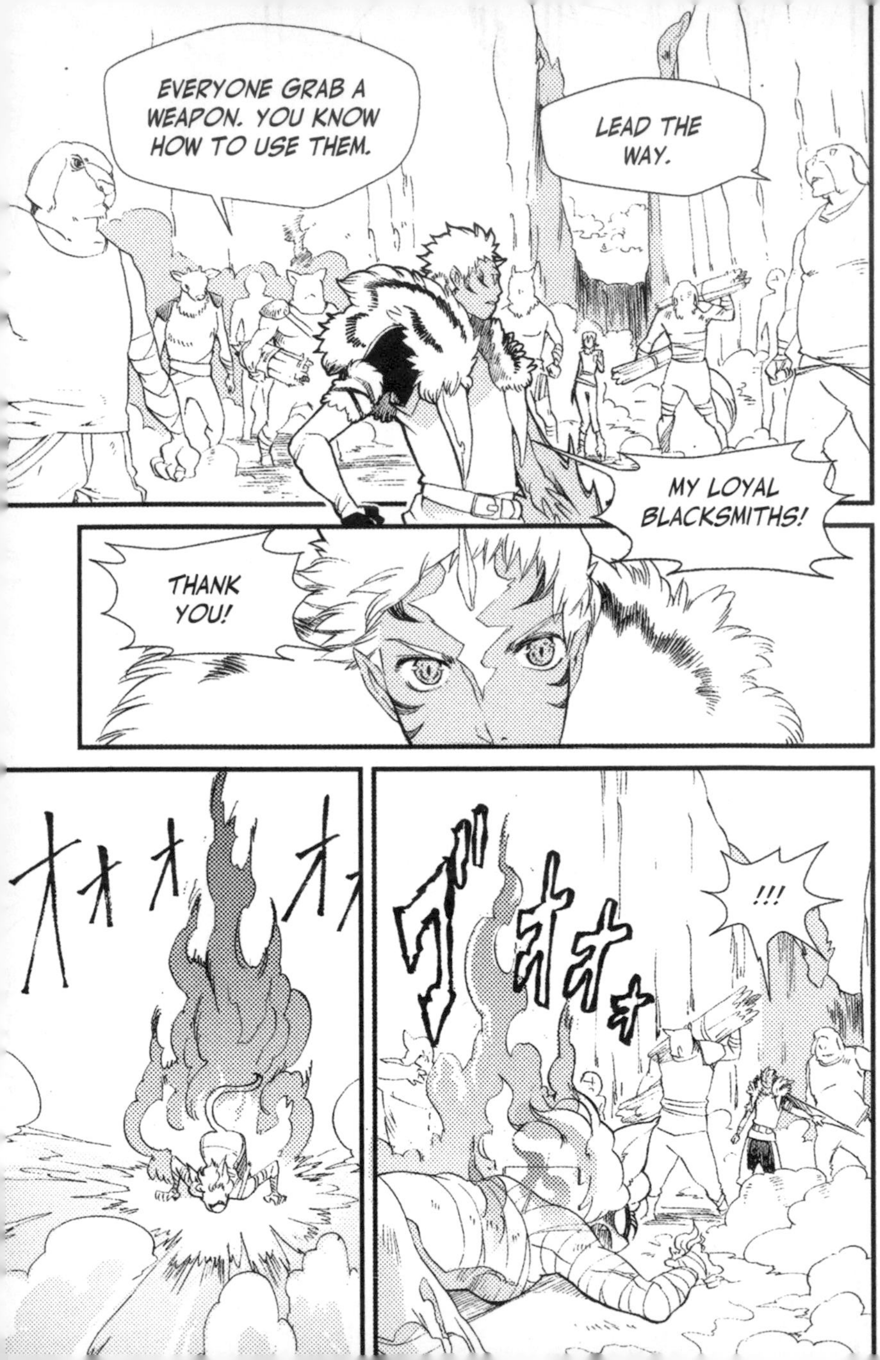
EVERYONE GRAB A WEAPON. YOU KNOW HOW TO USE THEM.
LEAD THE WAY.
MY LOYAL BLACKSMITHS!
THANK YOU!
!!!

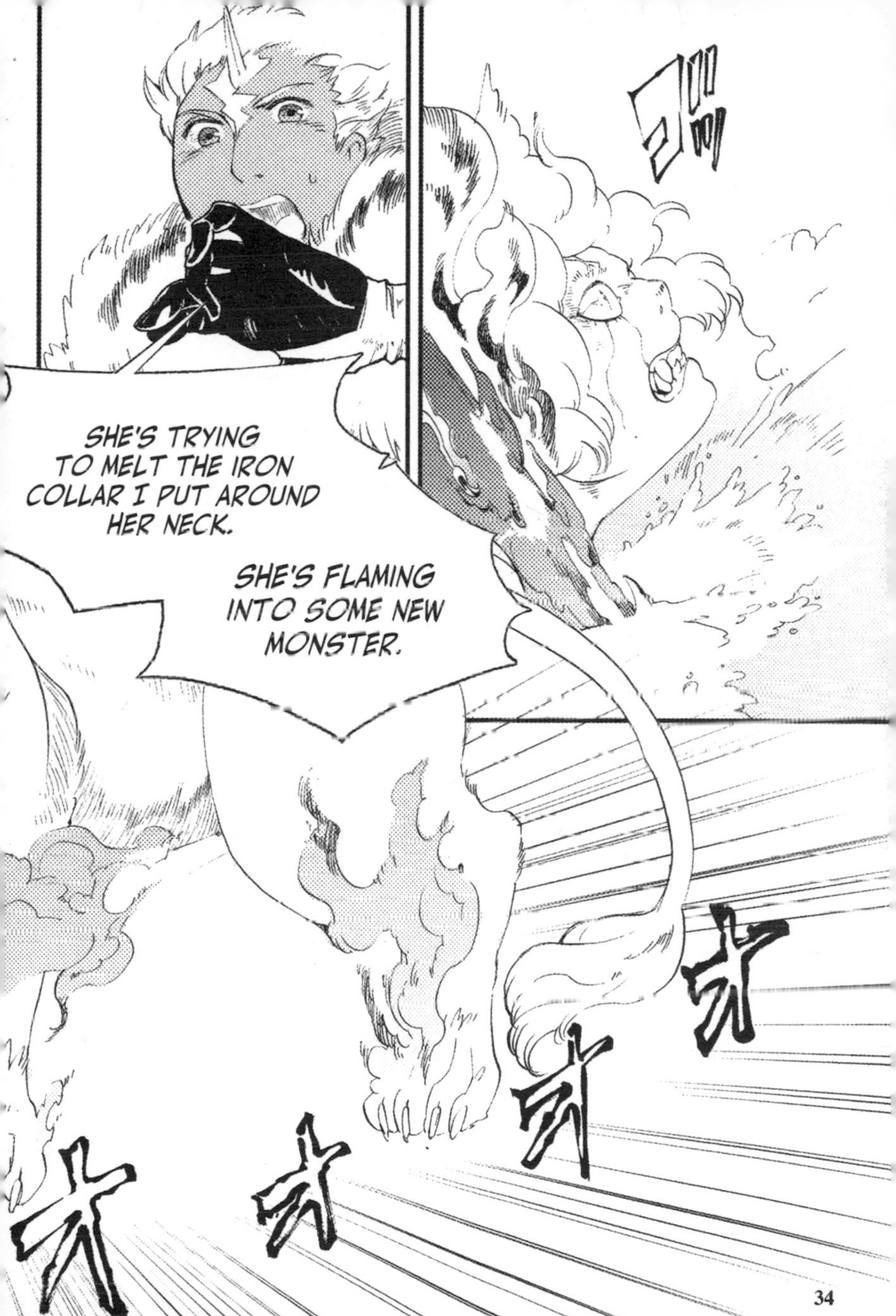
SHE'S TRYING TO MELT THE IRON COLLAR I PUT AROUND HER NECK.
SHE'S FLAMING INTO SOME NEW MONSTER.

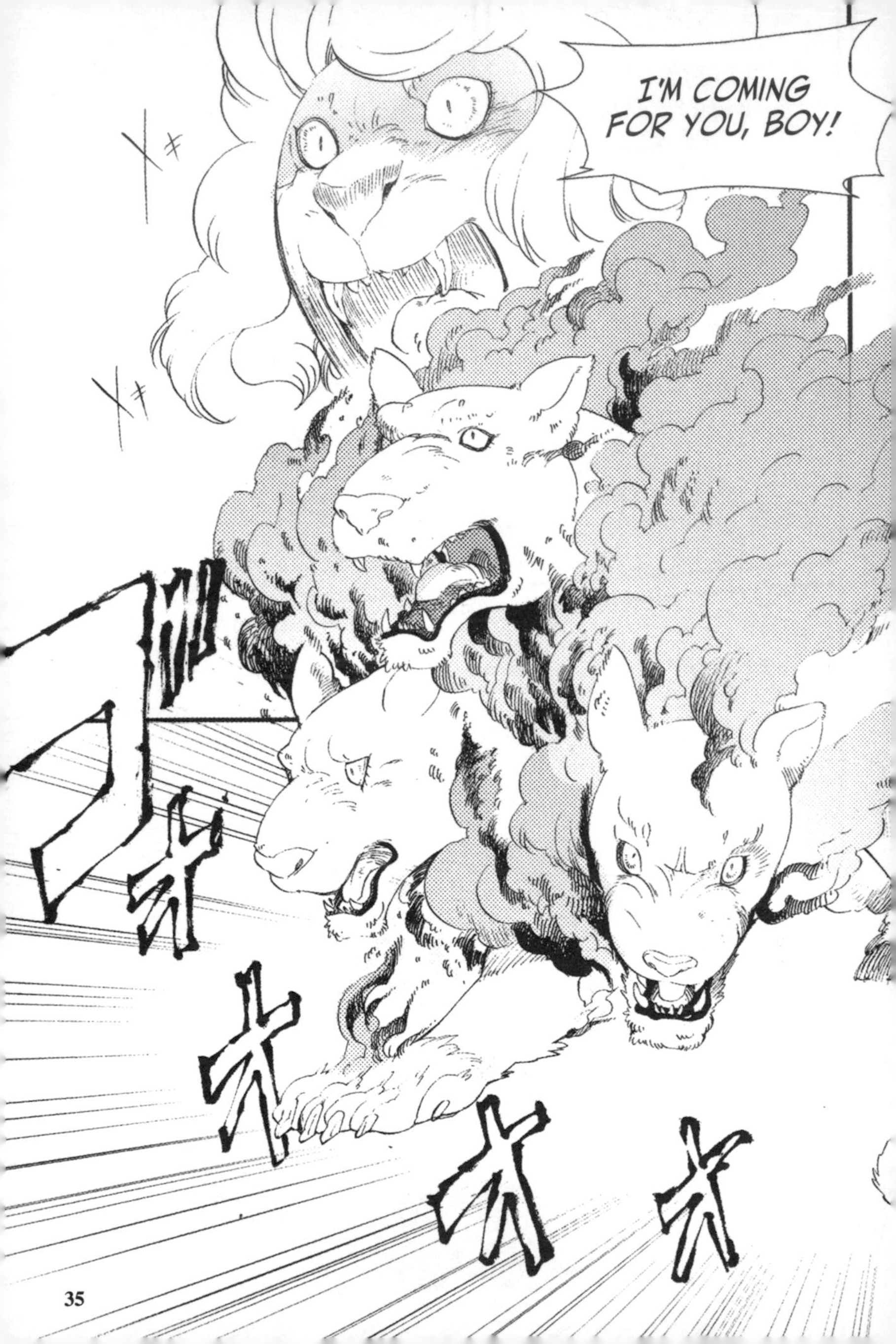
I'M COMING FOR YOU, BOY!

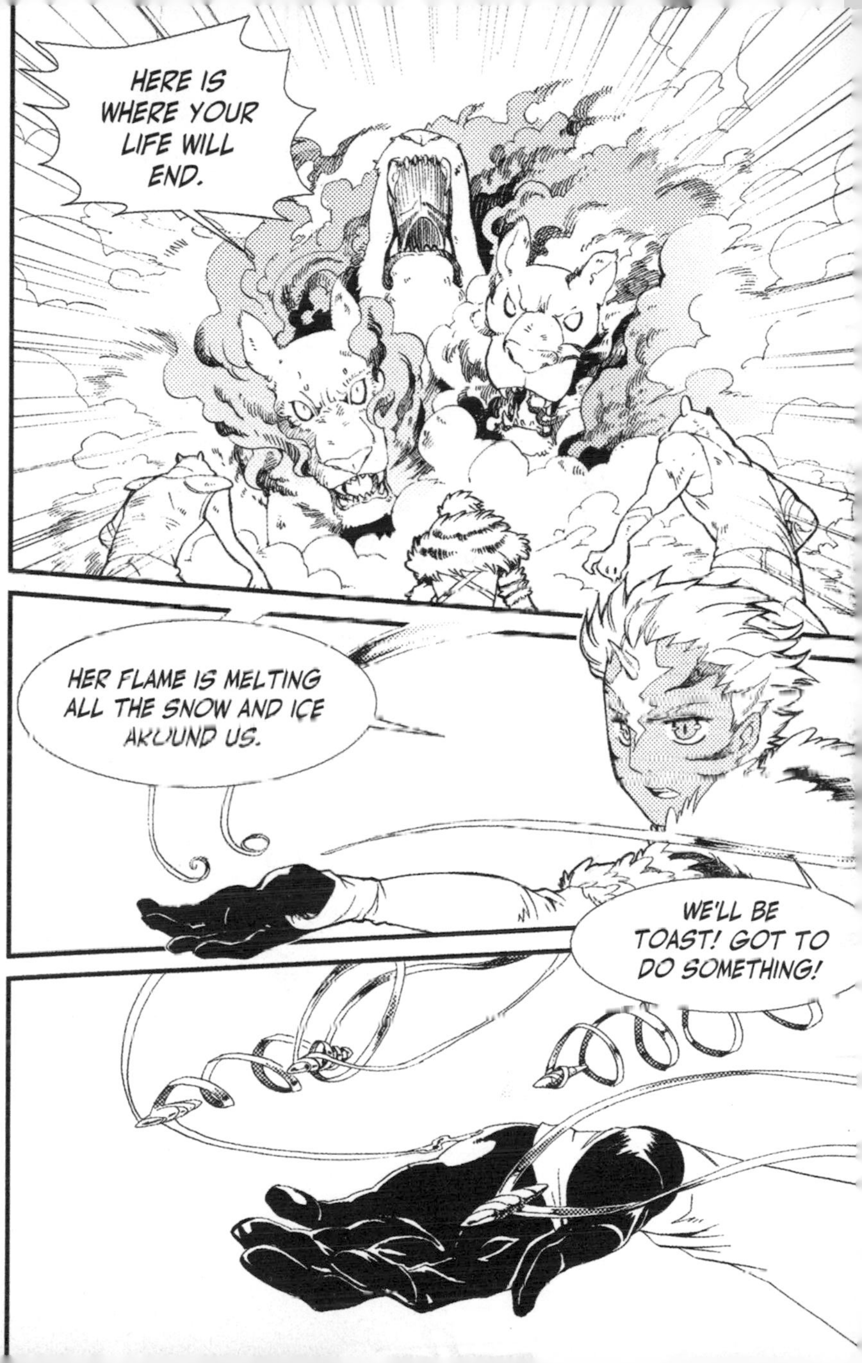
HERE IS WHERE YOUR LIFE WILL END.
HER FLAME IS MELTING ALL THE SNOW AND ICE AROUND US.
WE'LL BE TOAST! GOT TO DO SOMETHING!

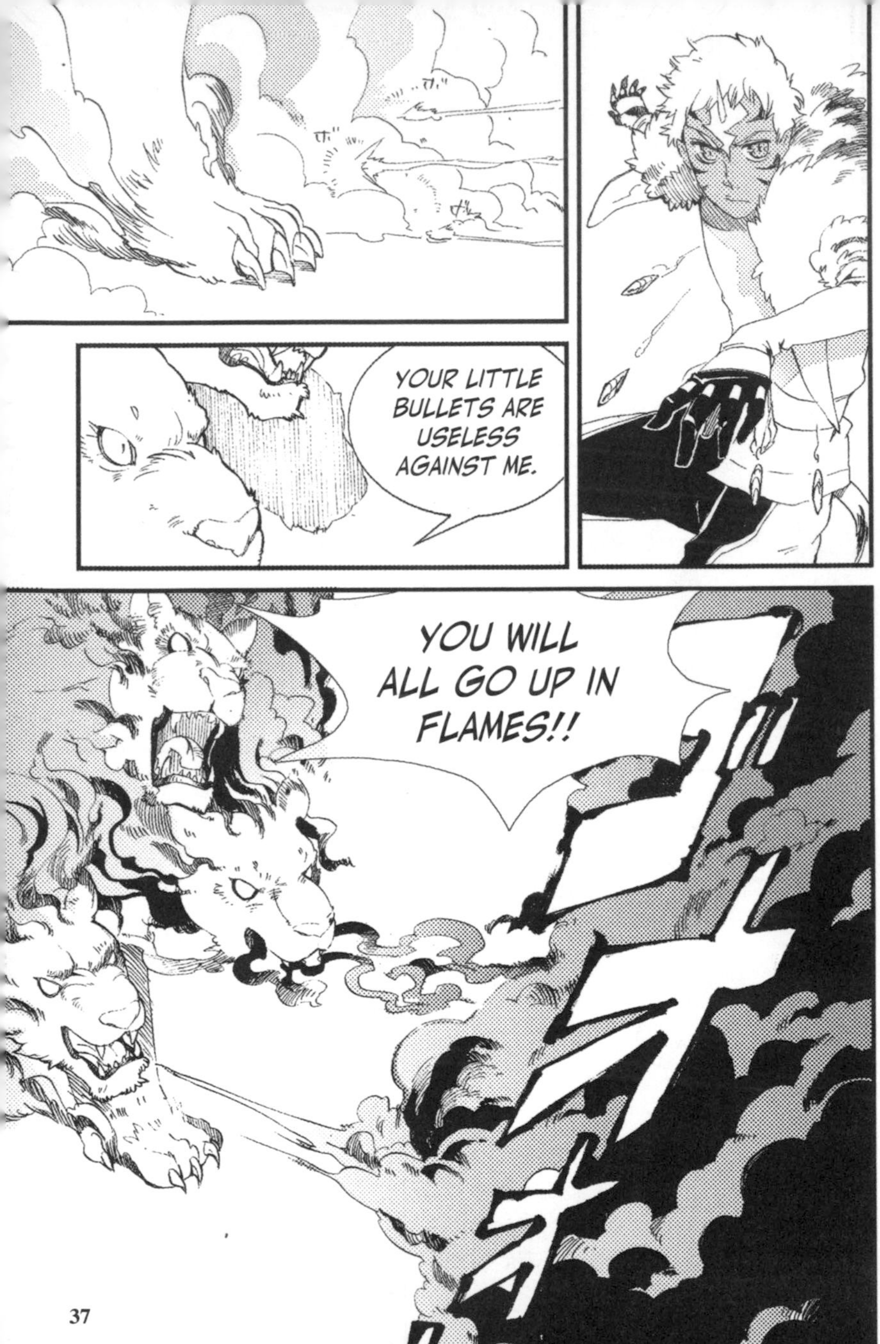
YOUR LITTLE BULLETS ARE USELESS AGAINST ME.
YOU WILL ALL GO UP IN FLAMES!!

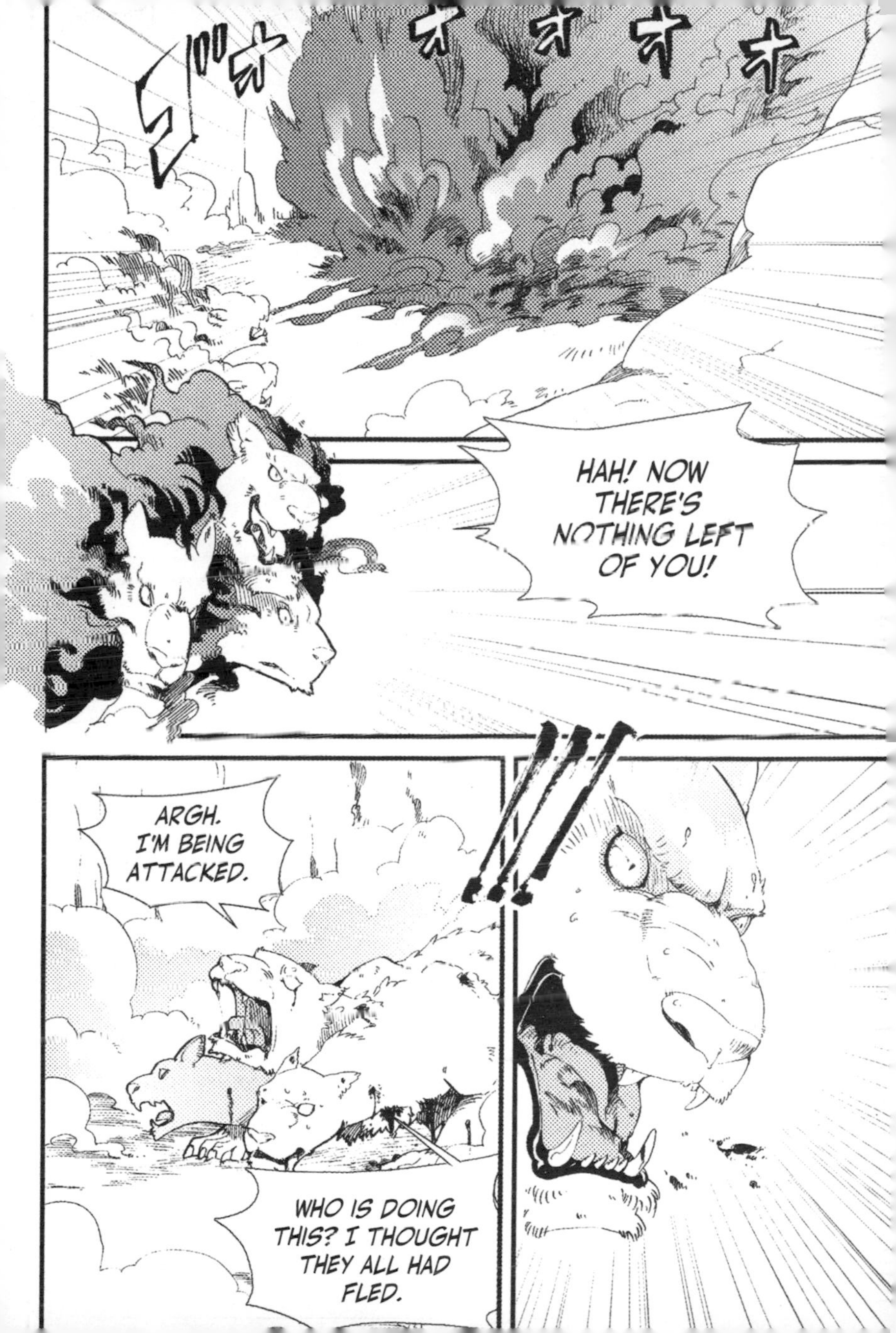
HAH! NOW THERE'S NOTHING LEFT OF YOU!
ARGH. I'M BEING ATTACKED.
WHO IS DOING THIS? I THOUGHT THEY ALL HAD FLED.

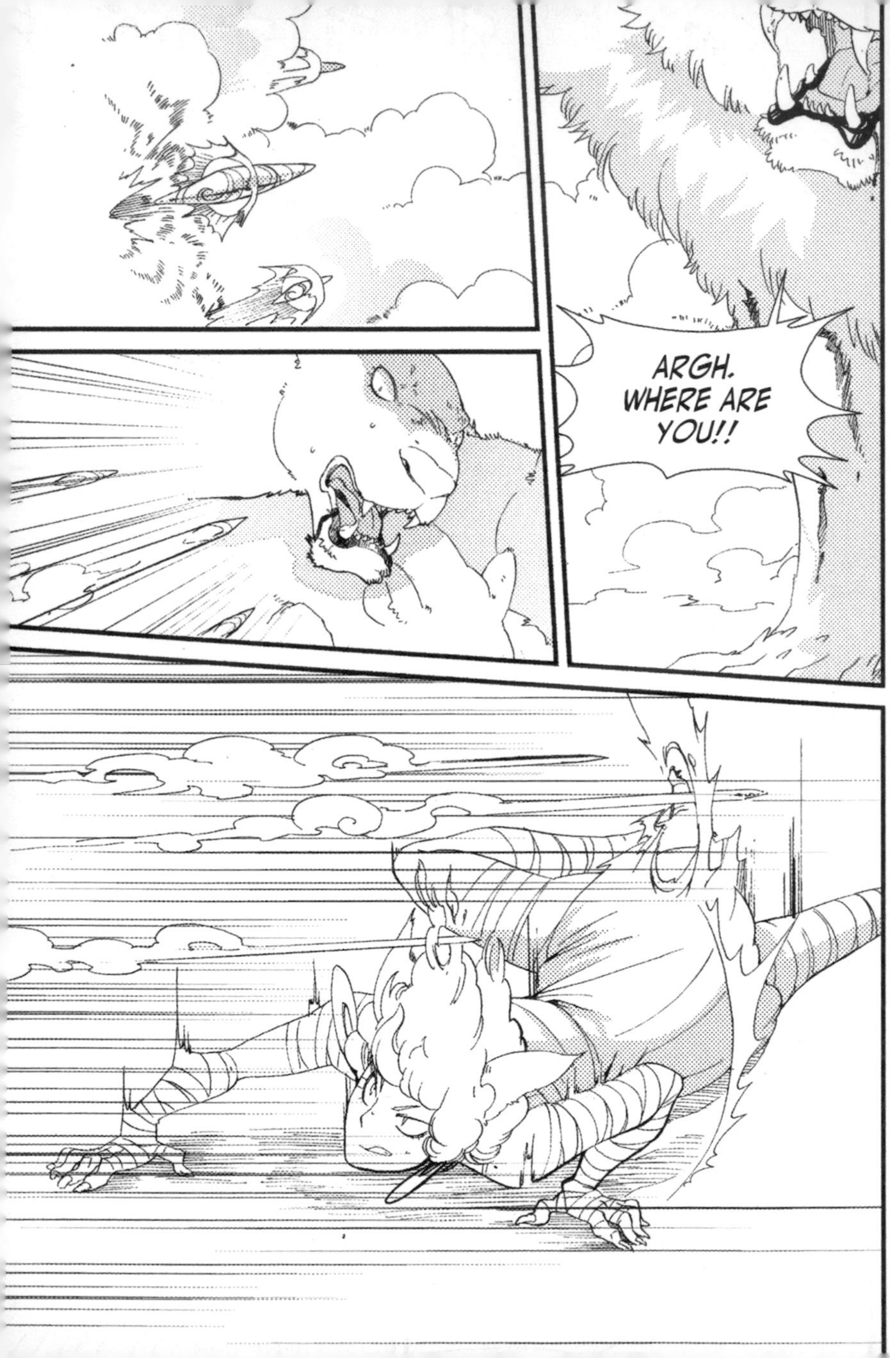
ARGH. WHERE ARE YOU!!

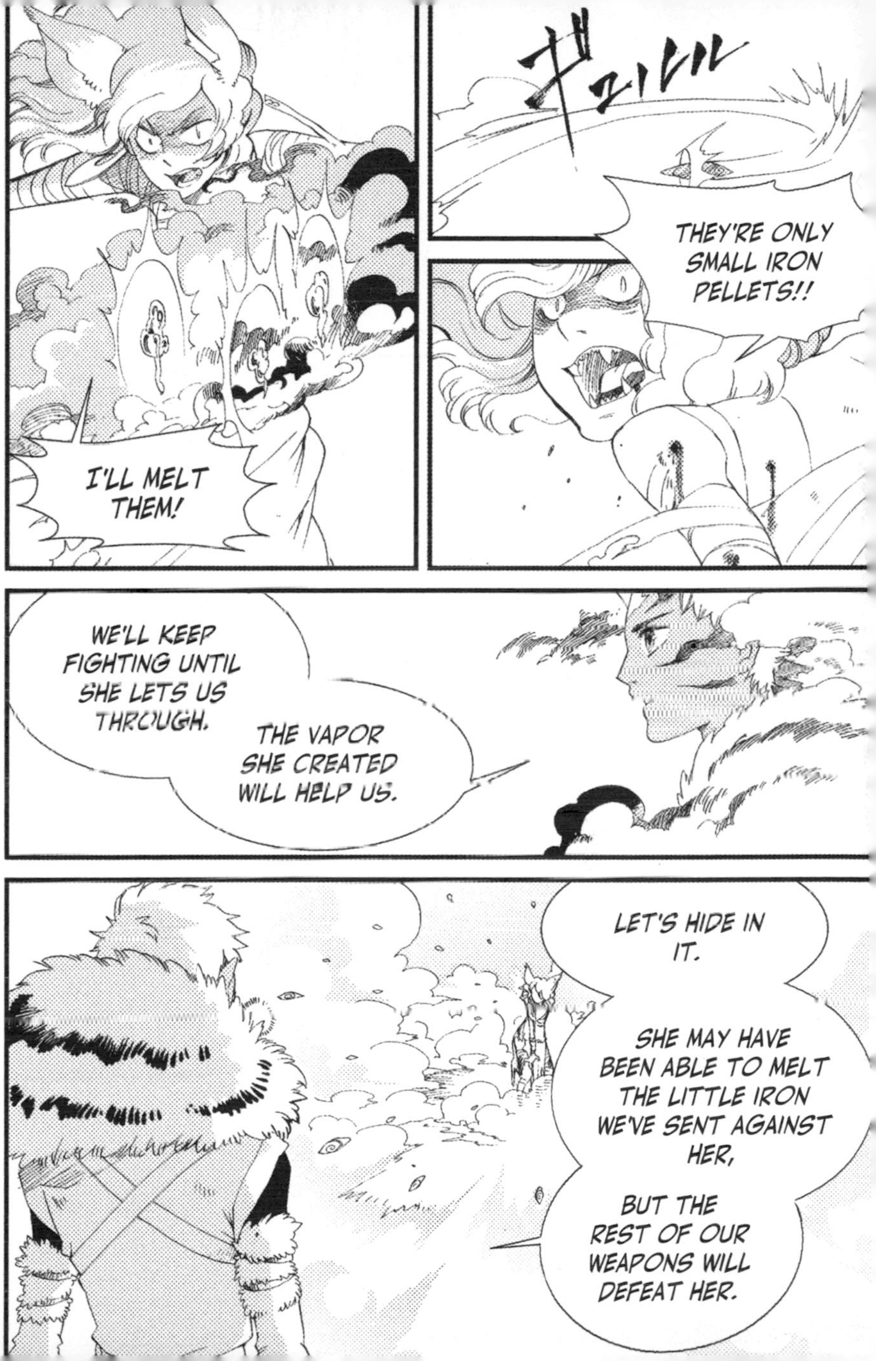
THEY'RE ONLY SMALL IRON PELLETS!!
I'LL MELT THEM!
WE'LL KEEP FIGHTING UNTIL SHE LETS US THROUGH.
THE VAPOR SHE CREATED WILL HELP US.
LET'S HIDE IN IT.
SHE MAY HAVE BEEN ABLE TO MELT THE LITTLE IRON WE'VE SENT AGAINST HER,
BUT THE REST OF OUR WEAPONS WILL DEFEAT HER.

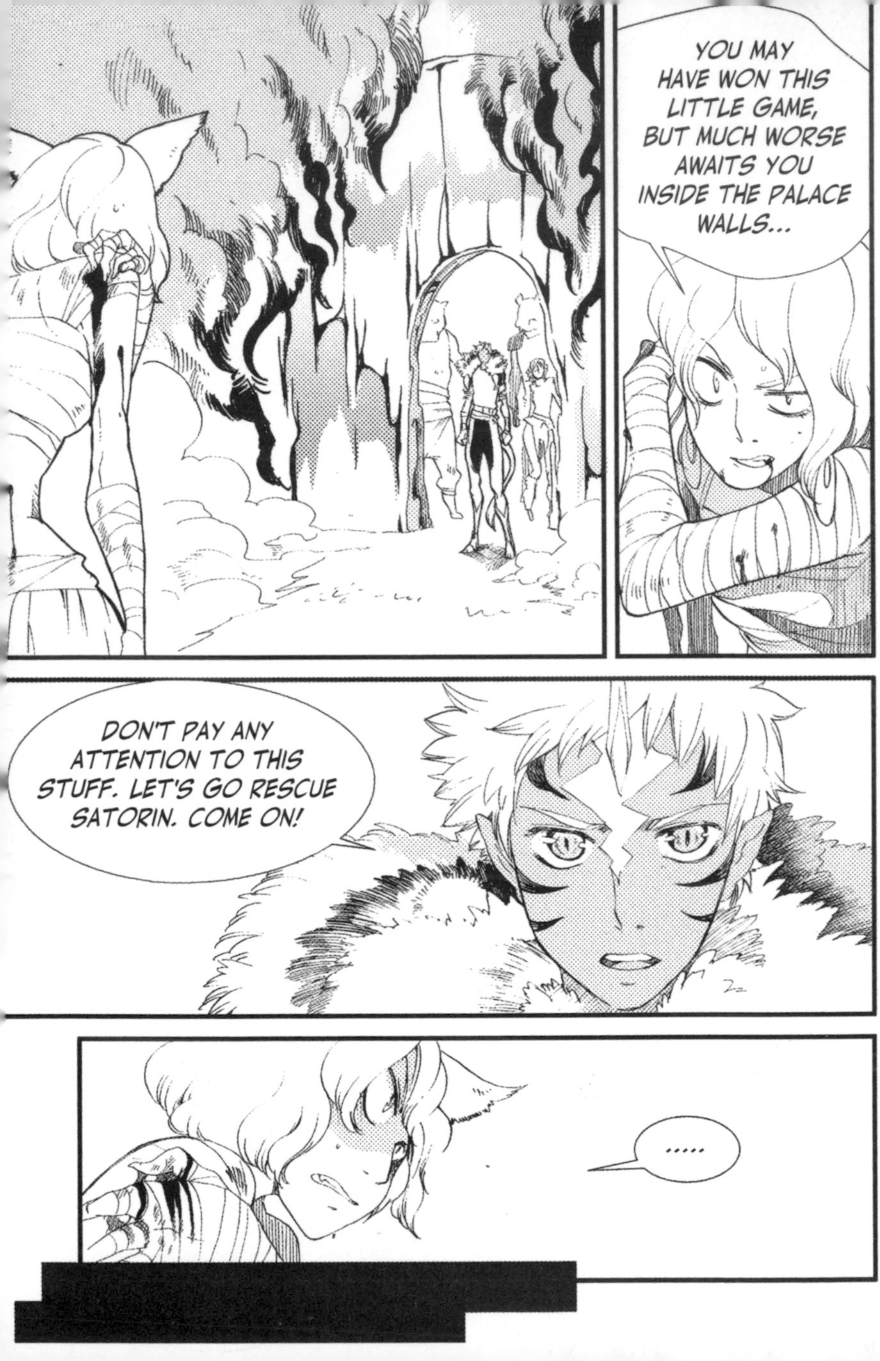
YOU MAY HAVE WON THIS LITTLE GAME, BUT MUCH WORSE AWAITS YOU INSIDE THE PALACE WALLS...
DON'T PAY ANY ATTENTION TO THIS STUFF. LET'S GO RESCUE SATORIN. COME ON!
......

[redacted]

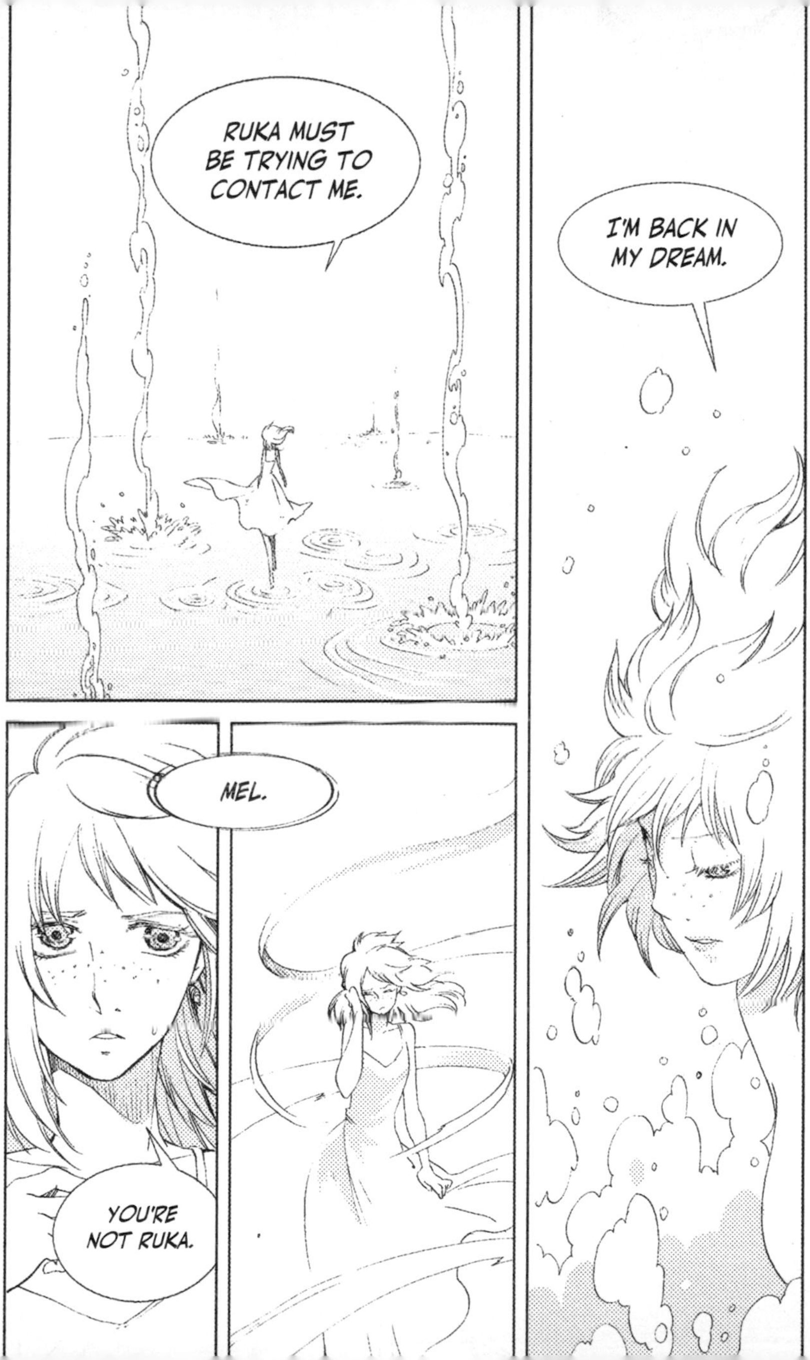
I'M BACK IN MY DREAM.
RUKA MUST BE TRYING TO CONTACT ME.
MEL.
YOU'RE NOT RUKA.

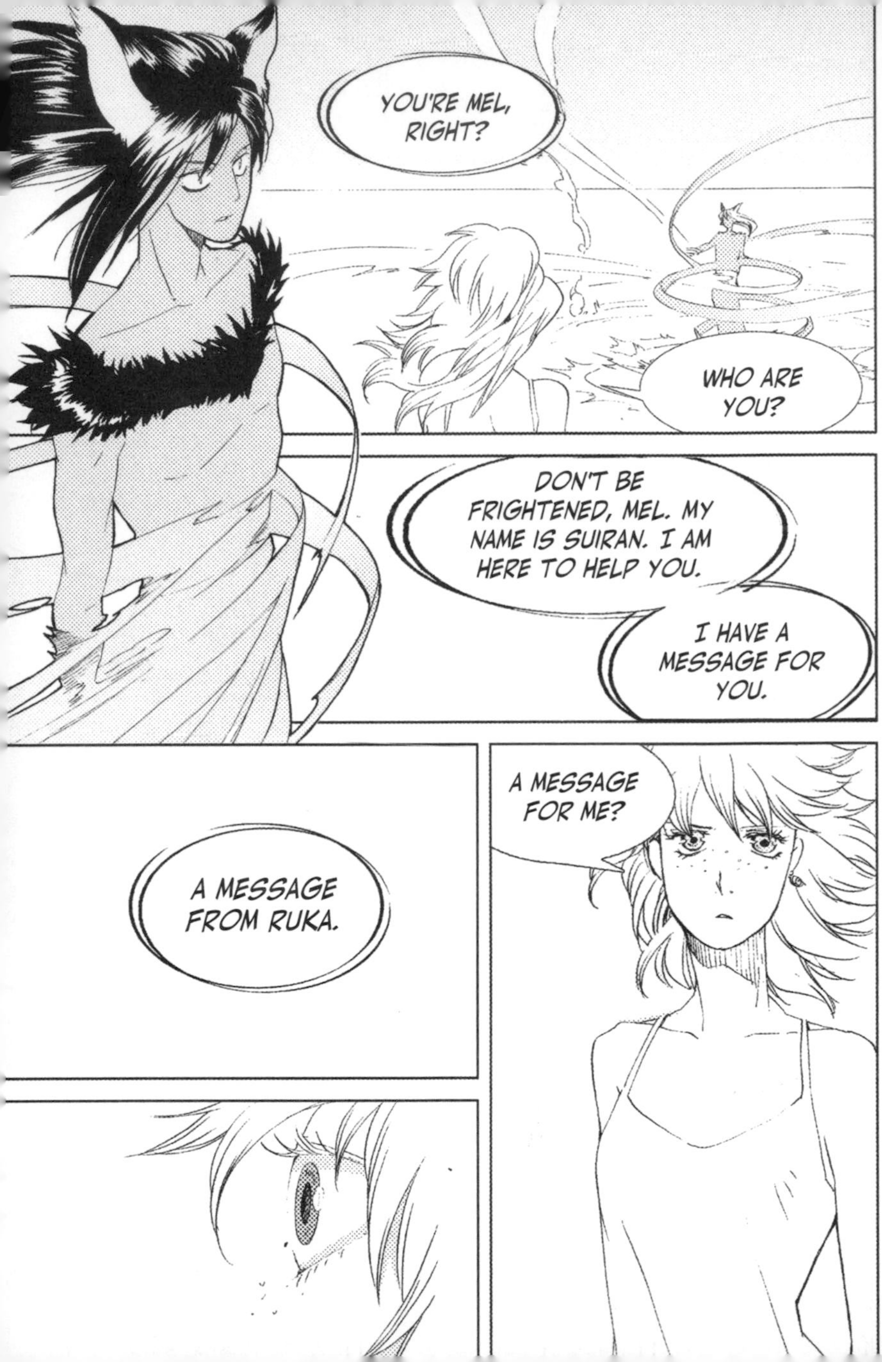
WHO ARE YOU?
YOU'RE MEL, RIGHT?
DON'T BE FRIGHTENED, MEL. MY NAME IS SUIRAN. I AM HERE TO HELP YOU.
I HAVE A MESSAGE FOR YOU.
A MESSAGE FOR ME?
A MESSAGE FROM RUKA.

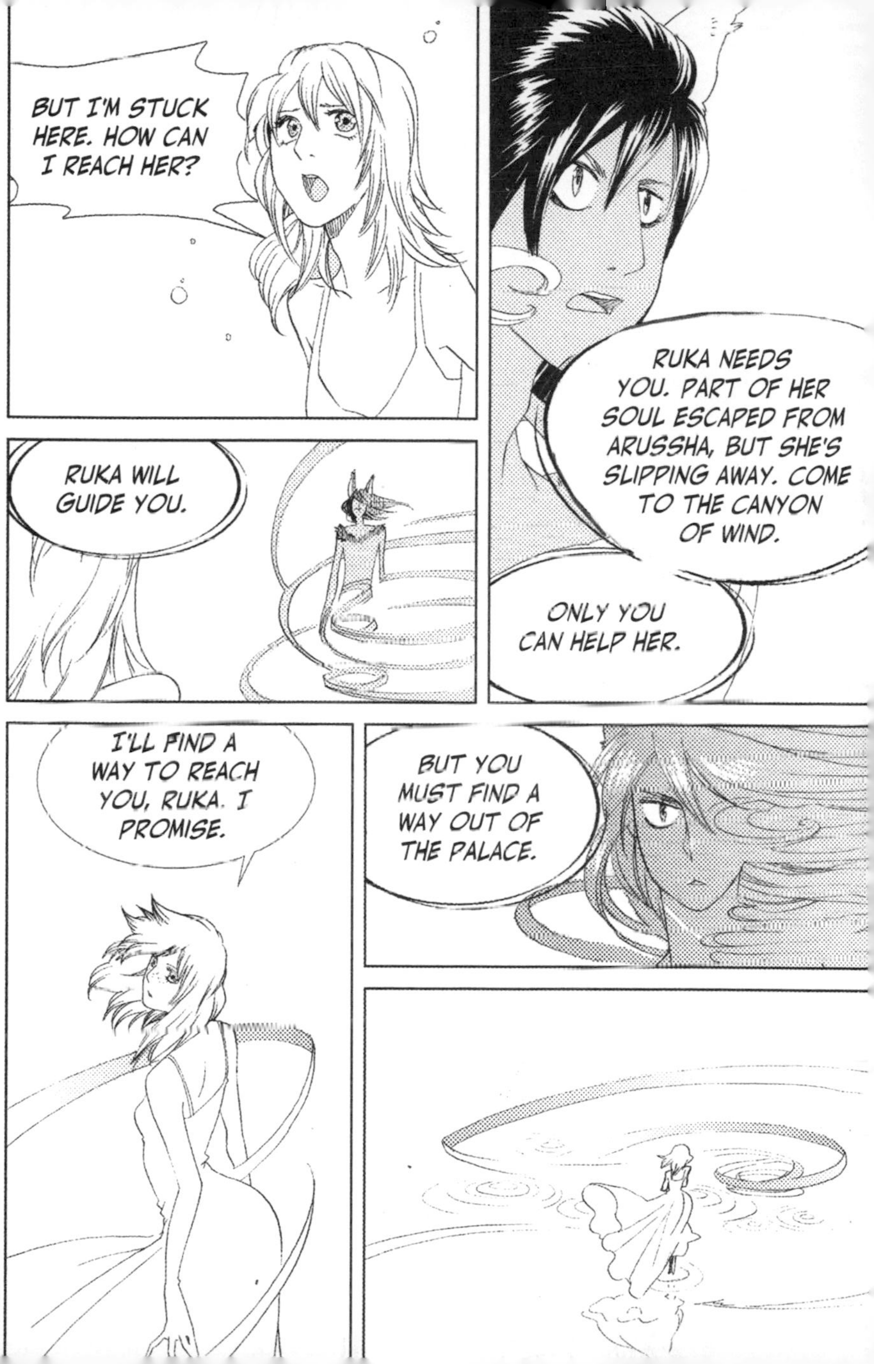
RUKA NEEDS YOU. PART OF HER SOUL ESCAPED FROM ARUSSHA, BUT SHE'S SLIPPING AWAY. COME TO THE CANYON OF WIND.
ONLY YOU CAN HELP HER.
BUT I'M STUCK HERE. HOW CAN I REACH HER?
RUKA WILL GUIDE YOU.
BUT YOU MUST FIND A WAY OUT OF THE PALACE.
I'LL FIND A WAY TO REACH YOU, RUKA. I PROMISE.

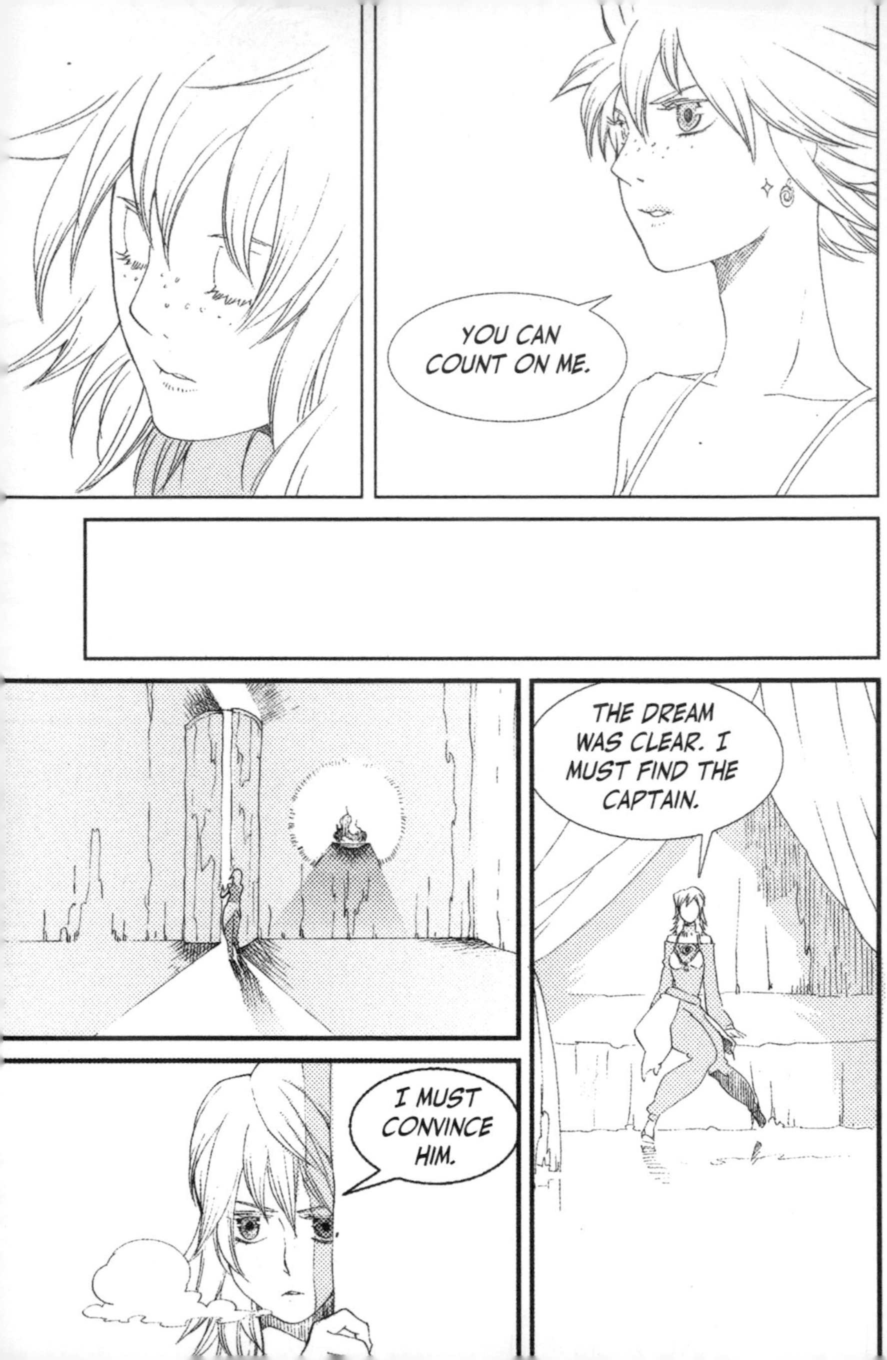
YOU CAN COUNT ON ME.
THE DREAM WAS CLEAR. I MUST FIND THE CAPTAIN.
I MUST CONVINCE HIM.

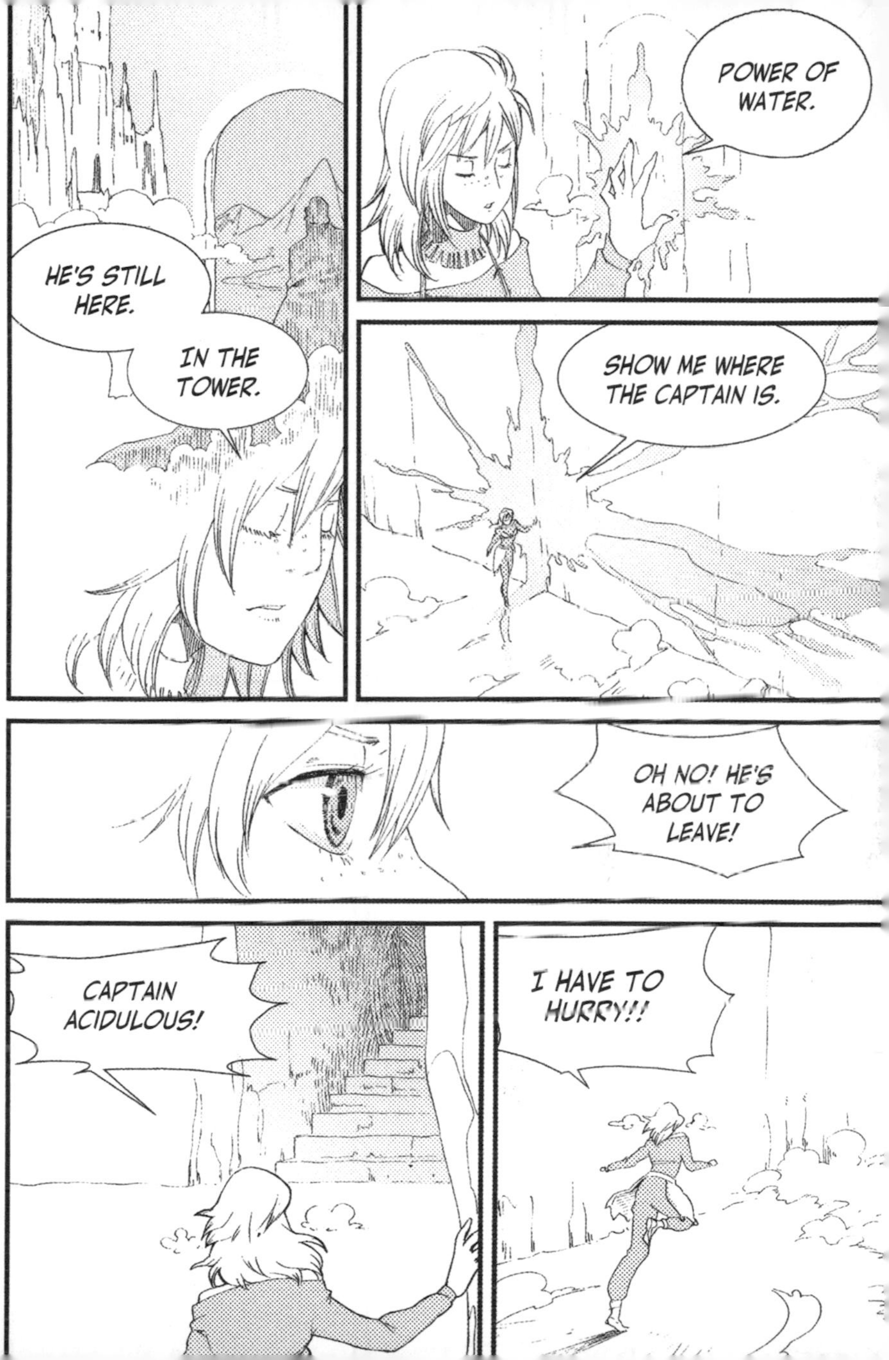
POWER OF WATER.
SHOW ME WHERE THE CAPTAIN IS.
HE'S STILL HERE.
IN THE TOWER.
OH NO! HE'S ABOUT TO LEAVE!
I HAVE TO HURRY!!
CAPTAIN ACIDULOUS!

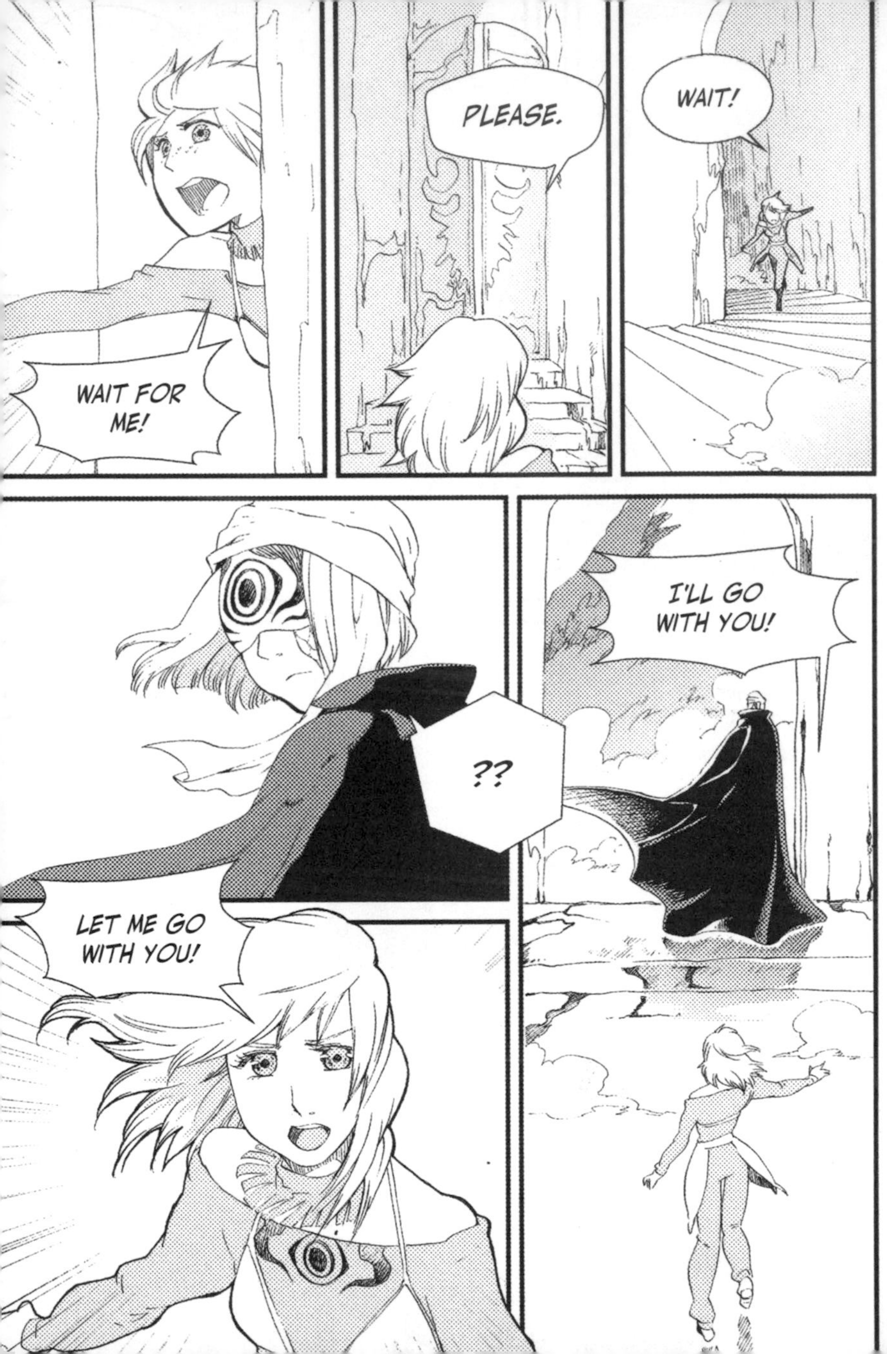
WAIT!
PLEASE.
WAIT FOR ME!
I'LL GO WITH YOU!
??
LET ME GO WITH YOU!

I HATE TO STAY IN THIS COLD PLACE.

IT'S BETTER IF I COME WITH YOU.

!

.....

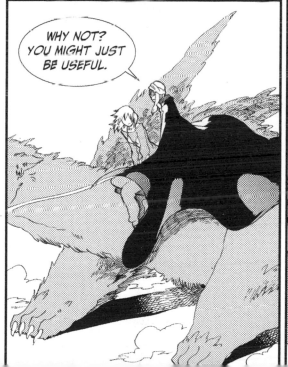

WHY NOT? YOU MIGHT JUST BE USEFUL.

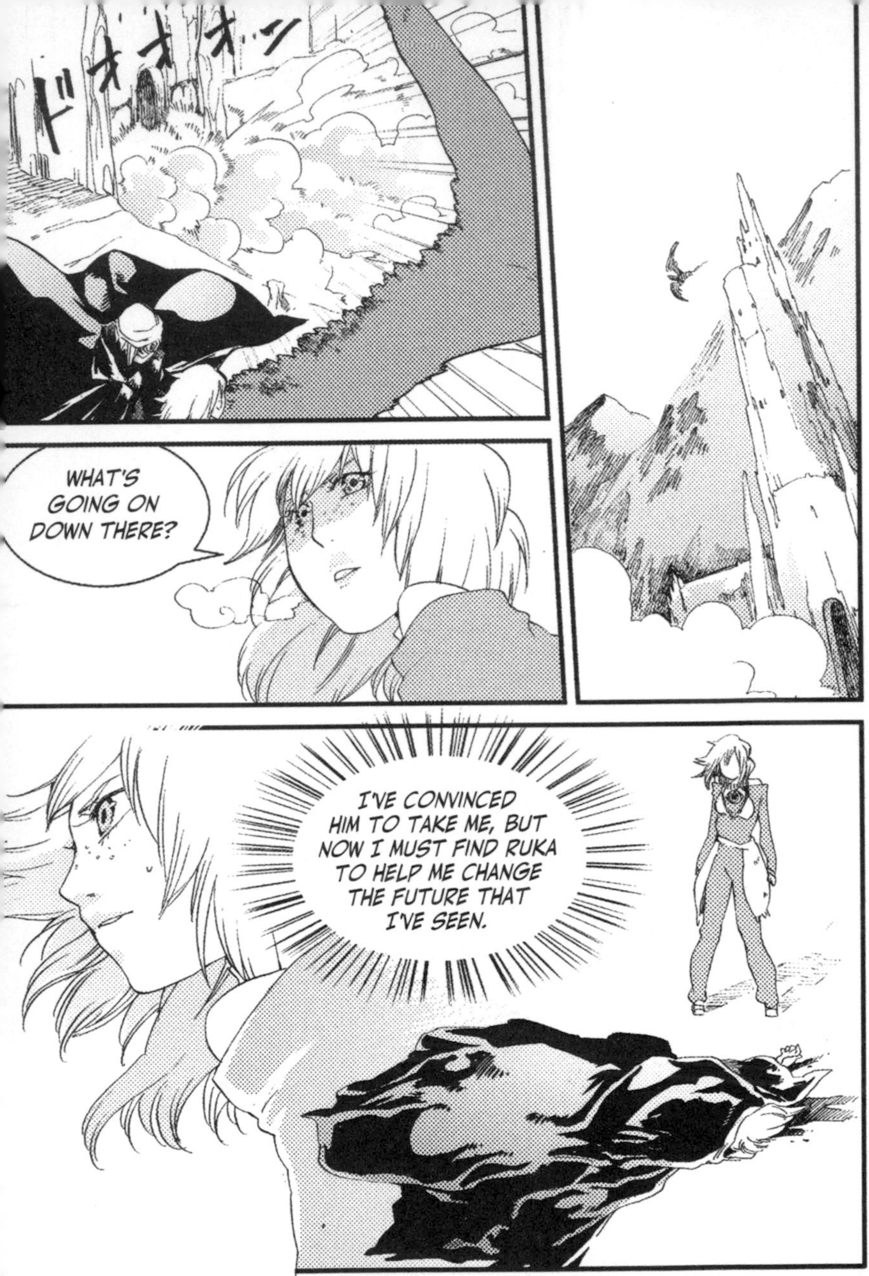
ドオオオ‥ン
WHAT'S GOING ON DOWN THERE?
I'VE CONVINCED HIM TO TAKE ME, BUT NOW I MUST FIND RUKA TO HELP ME CHANGE THE FUTURE THAT I'VE SEEN.

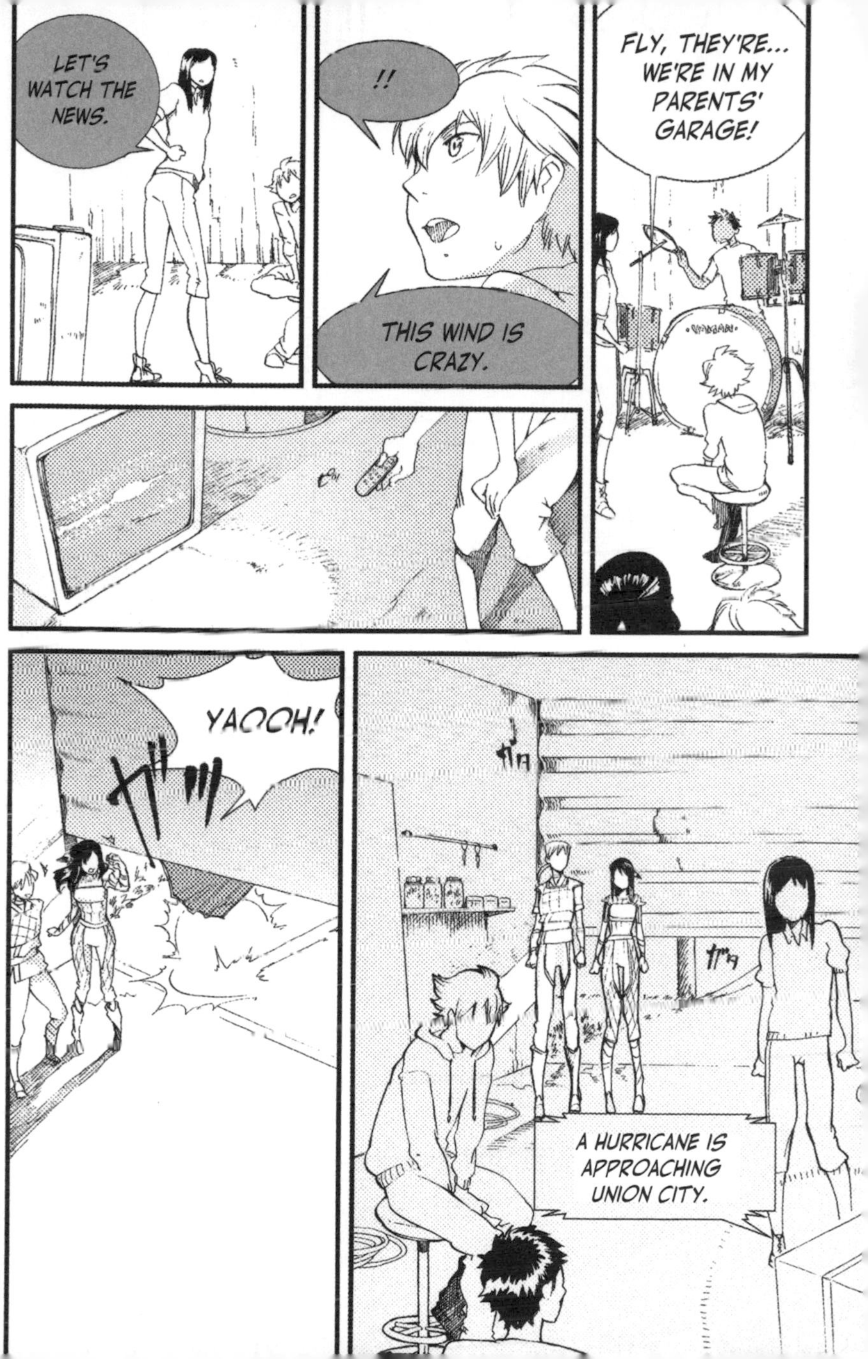
LET'S WATCH THE NEWS.
!!
THIS WIND IS CRAZY.
FLY, THEY'RE... WE'RE IN MY PARENTS' GARAGE!
YAOOH!
A HURRICANE IS APPROACHING UNION CITY.

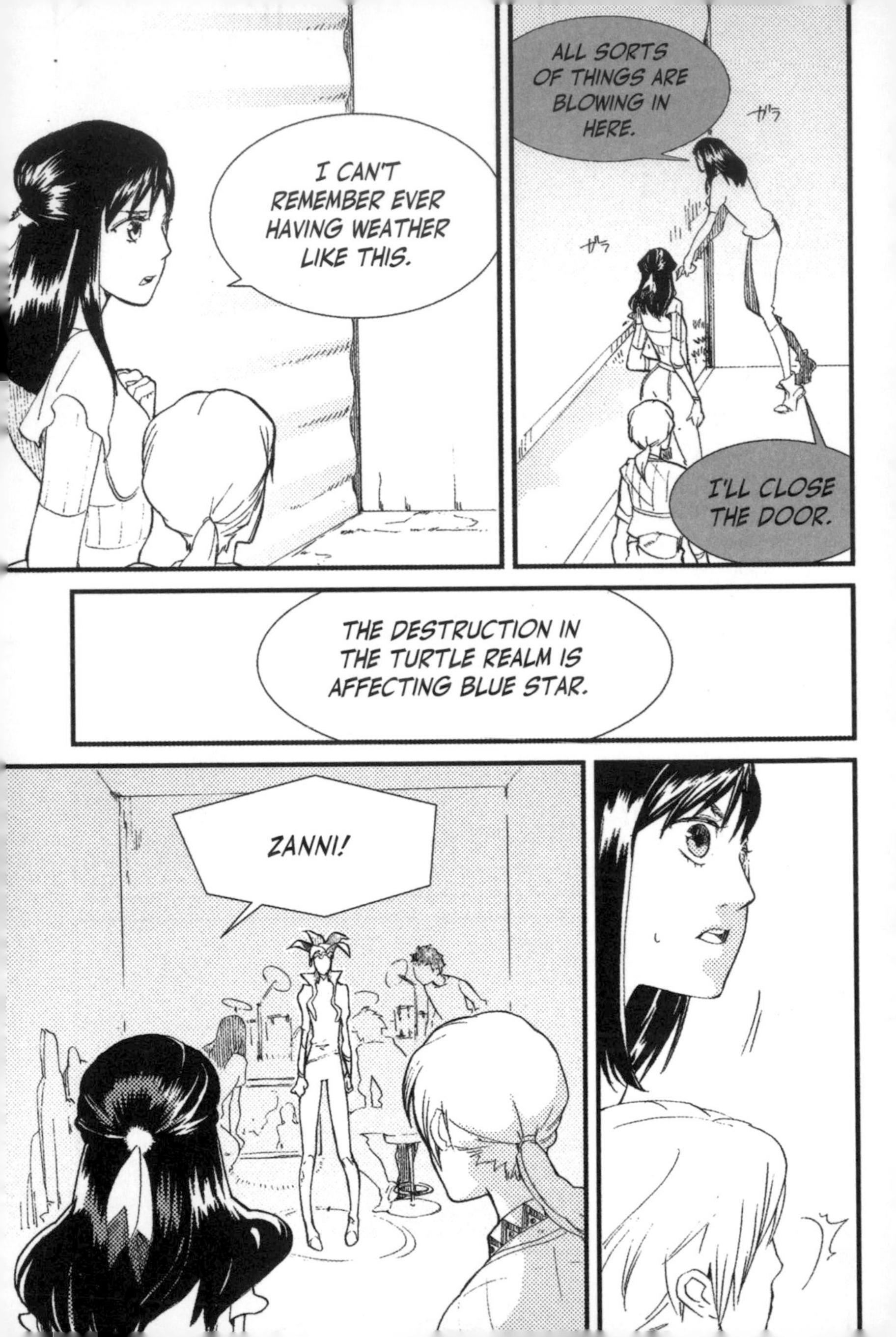
ALL SORTS OF THINGS ARE BLOWING IN HERE.
I'LL CLOSE THE DOOR.
I CAN'T REMEMBER EVER HAVING WEATHER LIKE THIS.
THE DESTRUCTION IN THE TURTLE REALM IS AFFECTING BLUE STAR.
ZANNI!

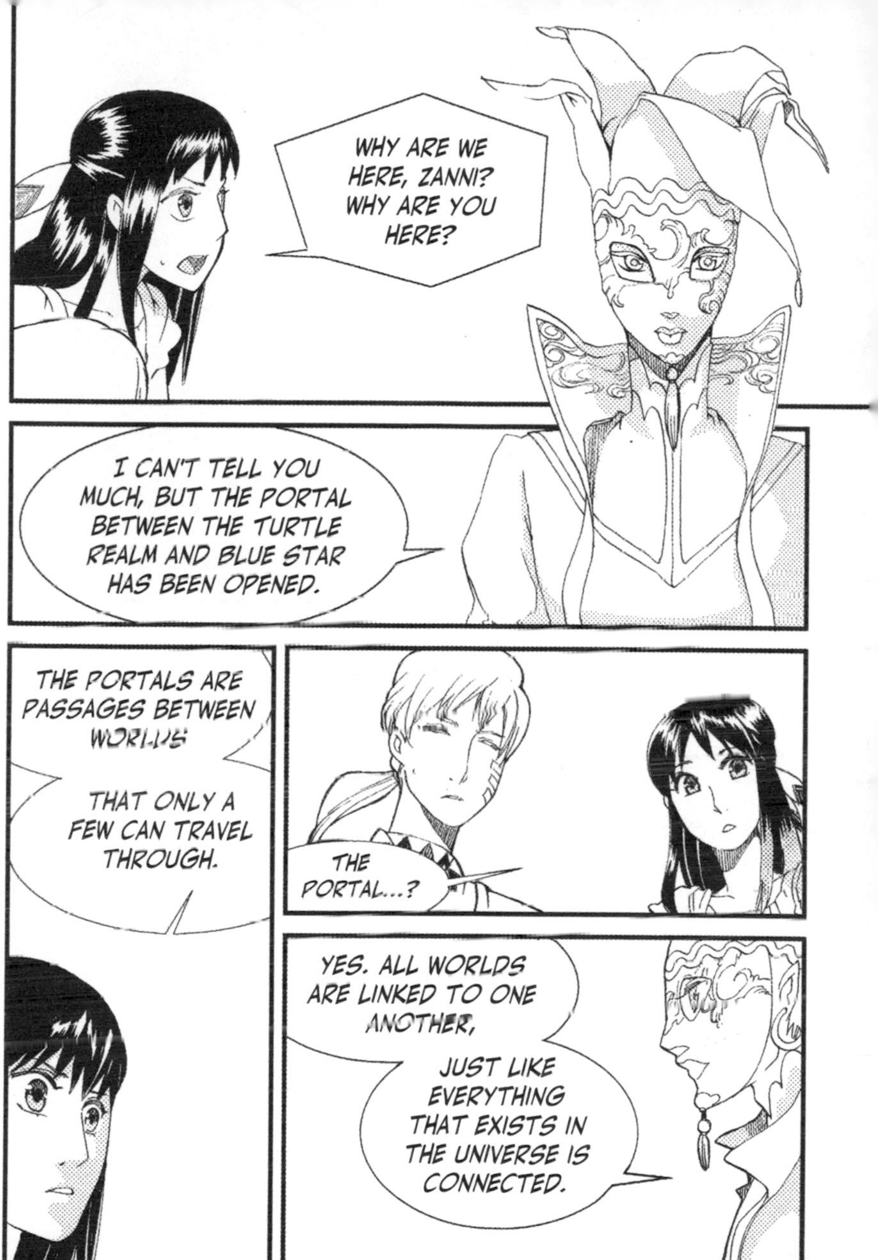
WHY ARE WE HERE, ZANNI? WHY ARE YOU HERE?
I CAN'T TELL YOU MUCH, BUT THE PORTAL BETWEEN THE TURTLE REALM AND BLUE STAR HAS BEEN OPENED.
THE PORTAL...?
YES. ALL WORLDS ARE LINKED TO ONE ANOTHER,
JUST LIKE EVERYTHING THAT EXISTS IN THE UNIVERSE IS CONNECTED.
THE PORTALS ARE PASSAGES BETWEEN WORLDS
THAT ONLY A FEW CAN TRAVEL THROUGH.

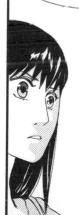

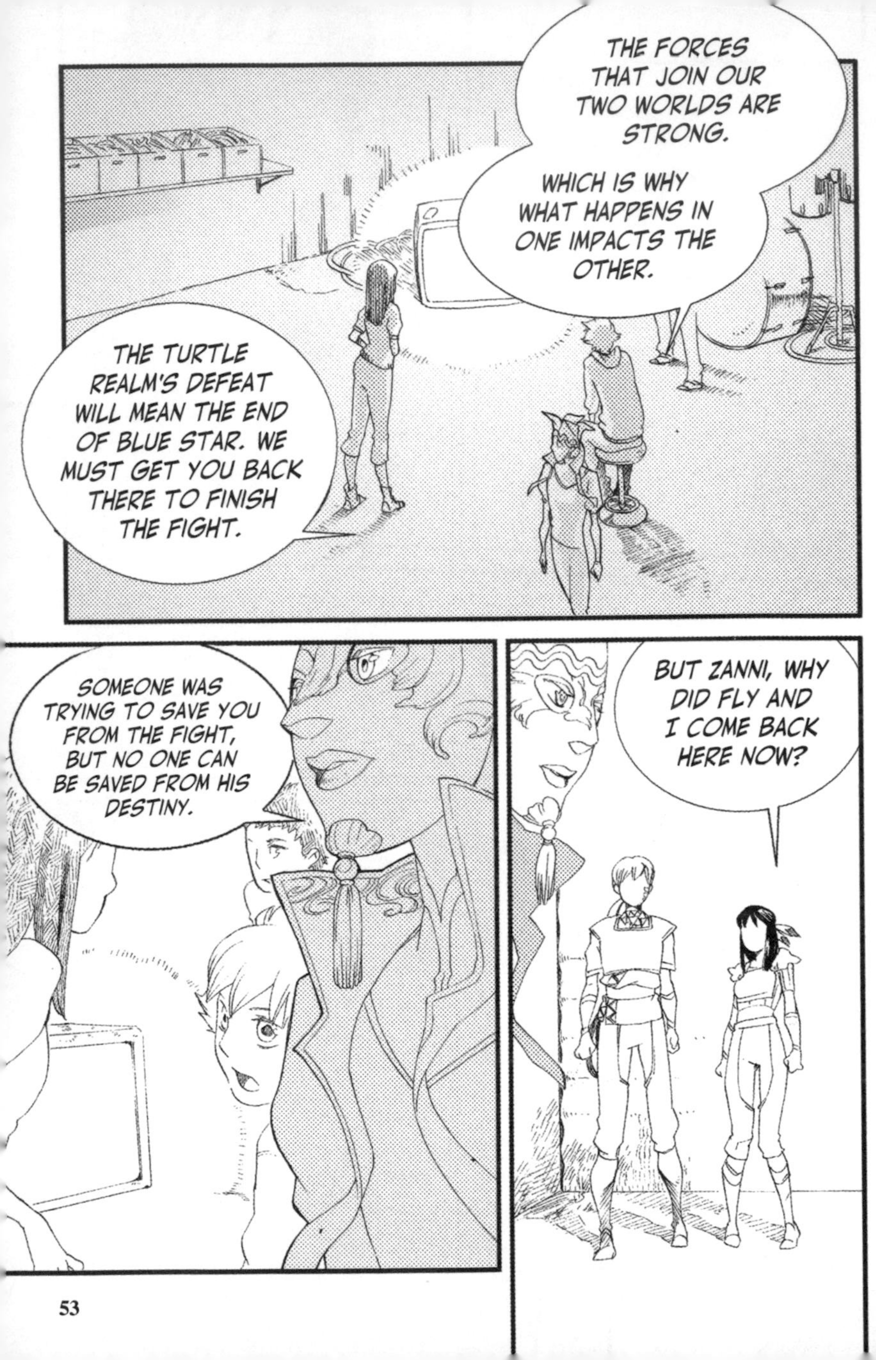
THE FORCES THAT JOIN OUR TWO WORLDS ARE STRONG.
WHICH IS WHY WHAT HAPPENS IN ONE IMPACTS THE OTHER.
THE TURTLE REALM'S DEFEAT WILL MEAN THE END OF BLUE STAR. WE MUST GET YOU BACK THERE TO FINISH THE FIGHT.
BUT ZANNI, WHY DID FLY AND I COME BACK HERE NOW?
SOMEONE WAS TRYING TO SAVE YOU FROM THE FIGHT, BUT NO ONE CAN BE SAVED FROM HIS DESTINY.

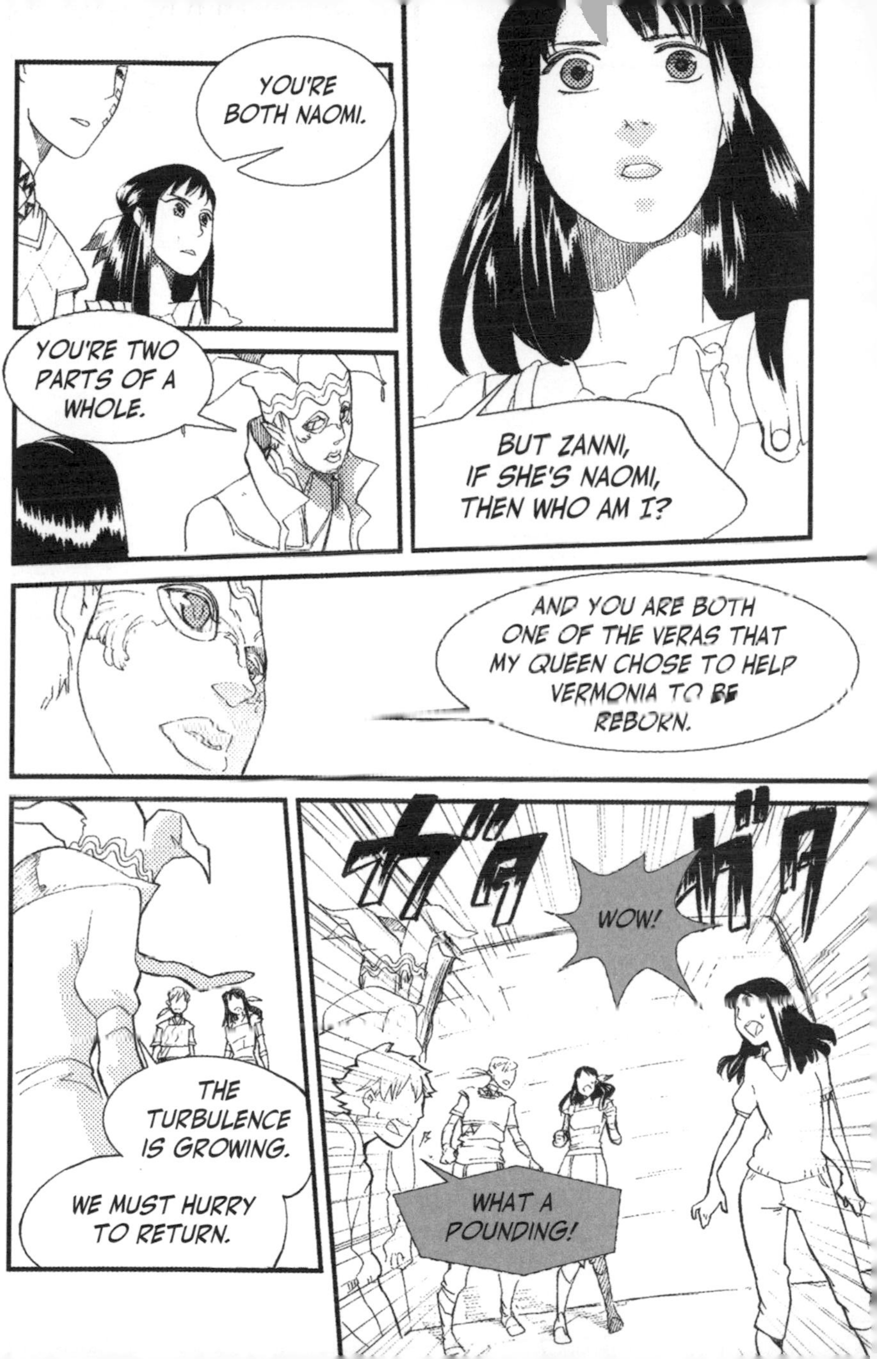
YOU'RE BOTH NAOMI.
YOU'RE TWO PARTS OF A WHOLE.
BUT ZANNI, IF SHE'S NAOMI, THEN WHO AM I?
AND YOU ARE BOTH ONE OF THE VERAS THAT MY QUEEN CHOSE TO HELP VERMONIA TO BE REBORN.
THE TURBULENCE IS GROWING.
WE MUST HURRY TO RETURN.
WOW!
WHAT A POUNDING!

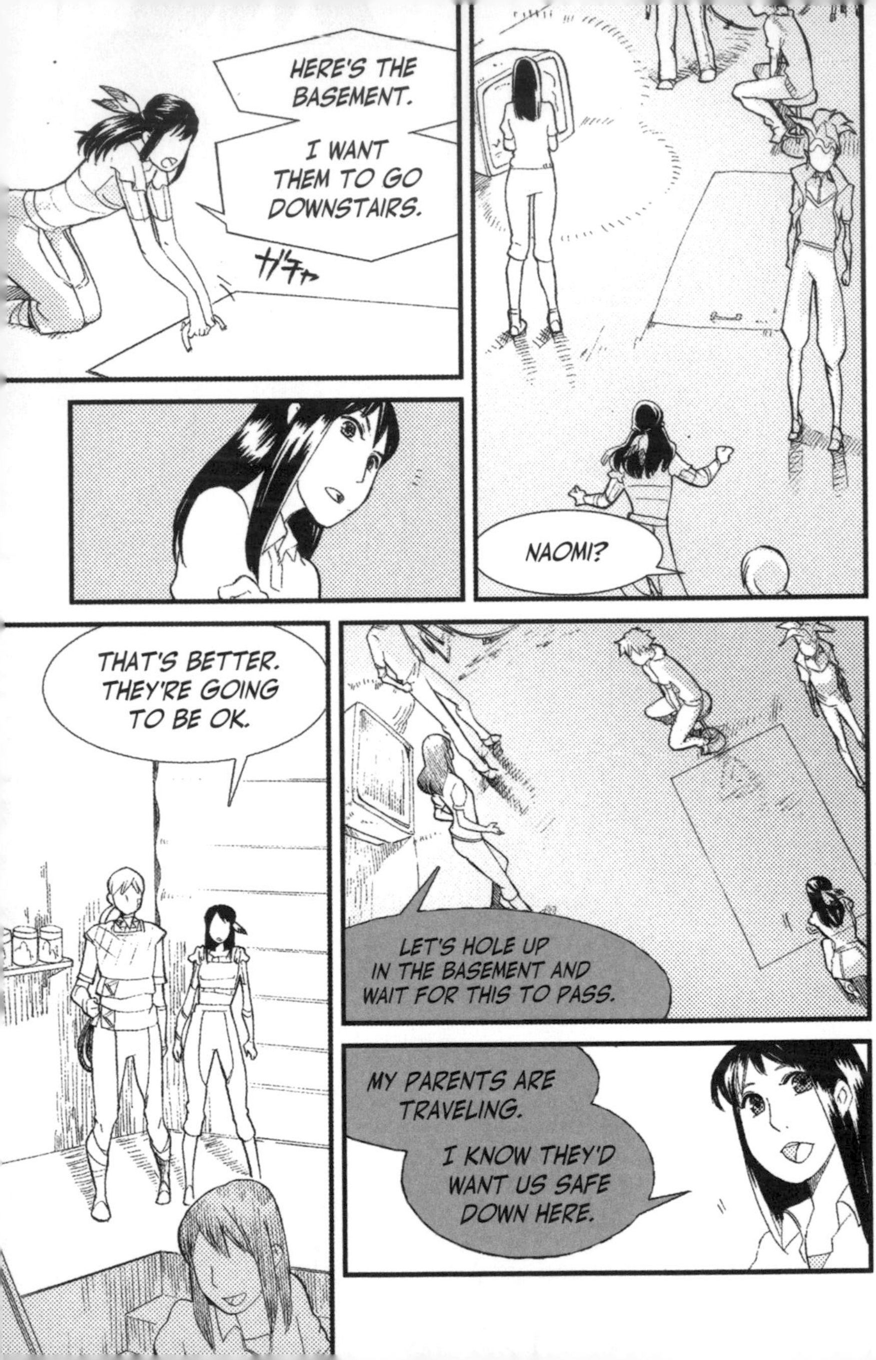
NAOMI?
HERE'S THE BASEMENT.
I WANT THEM TO GO DOWNSTAIRS.
ガチャ
LET'S HOLE UP IN THE BASEMENT AND WAIT FOR THIS TO PASS.
MY PARENTS ARE TRAVELING.
I KNOW THEY'D WANT US SAFE DOWN HERE.
THAT'S BETTER. THEY'RE GOING TO BE OK.

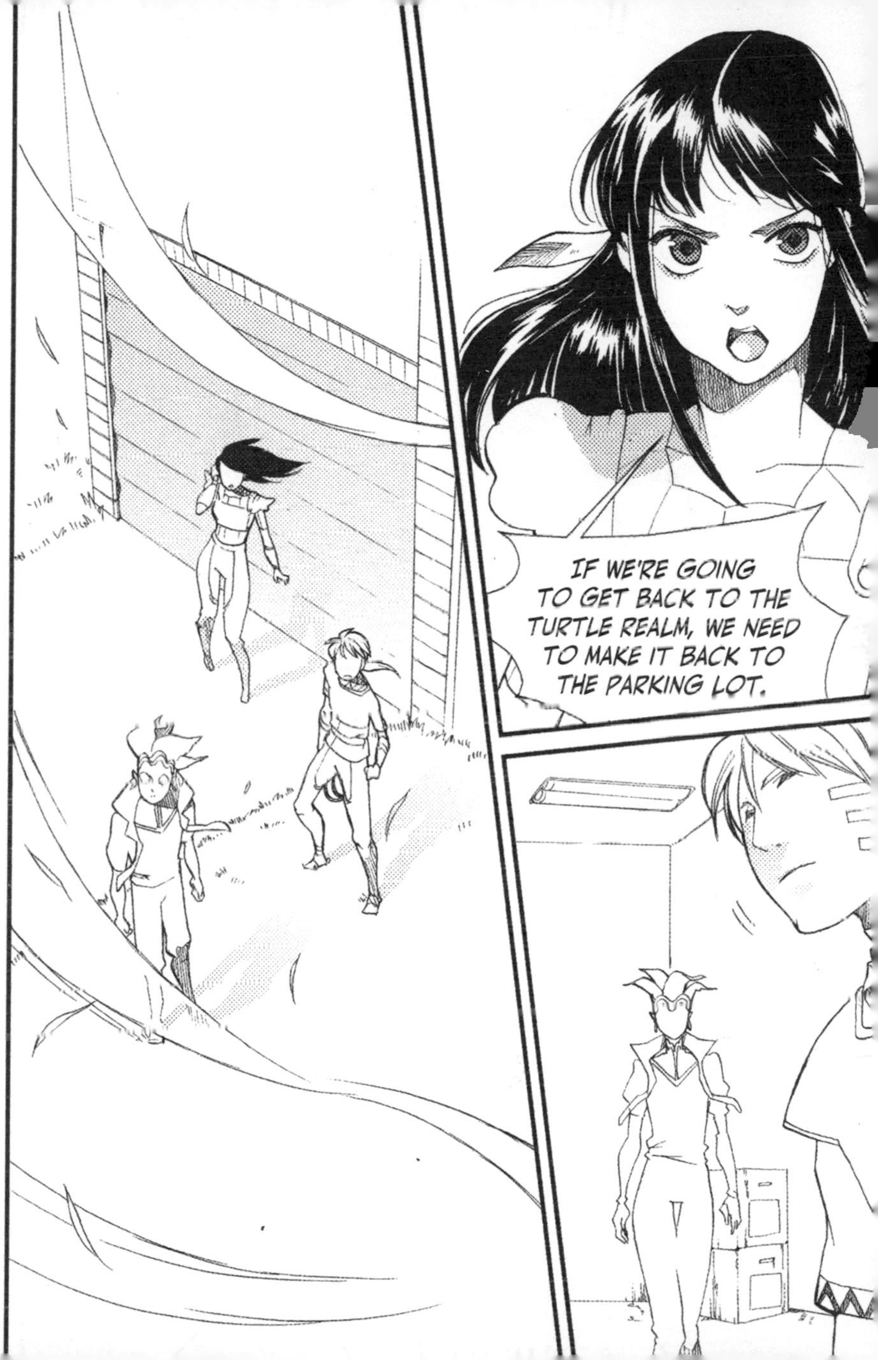
IF WE'RE GOING TO GET BACK TO THE TURTLE REALM, WE NEED TO MAKE IT BACK TO THE PARKING LOT.

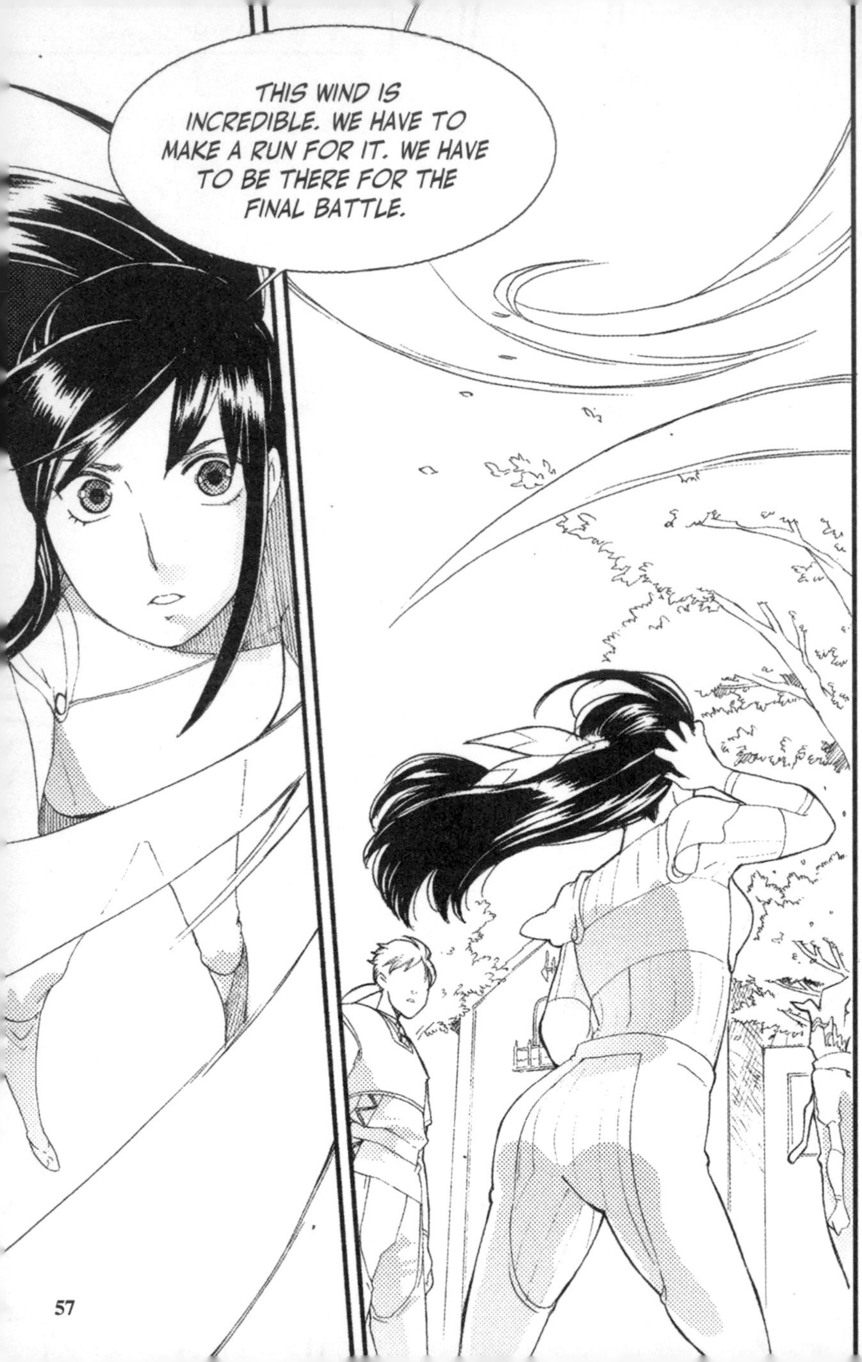
THIS WIND IS INCREDIBLE. WE HAVE TO MAKE A RUN FOR IT. WE HAVE TO BE THERE FOR THE FINAL BATTLE.

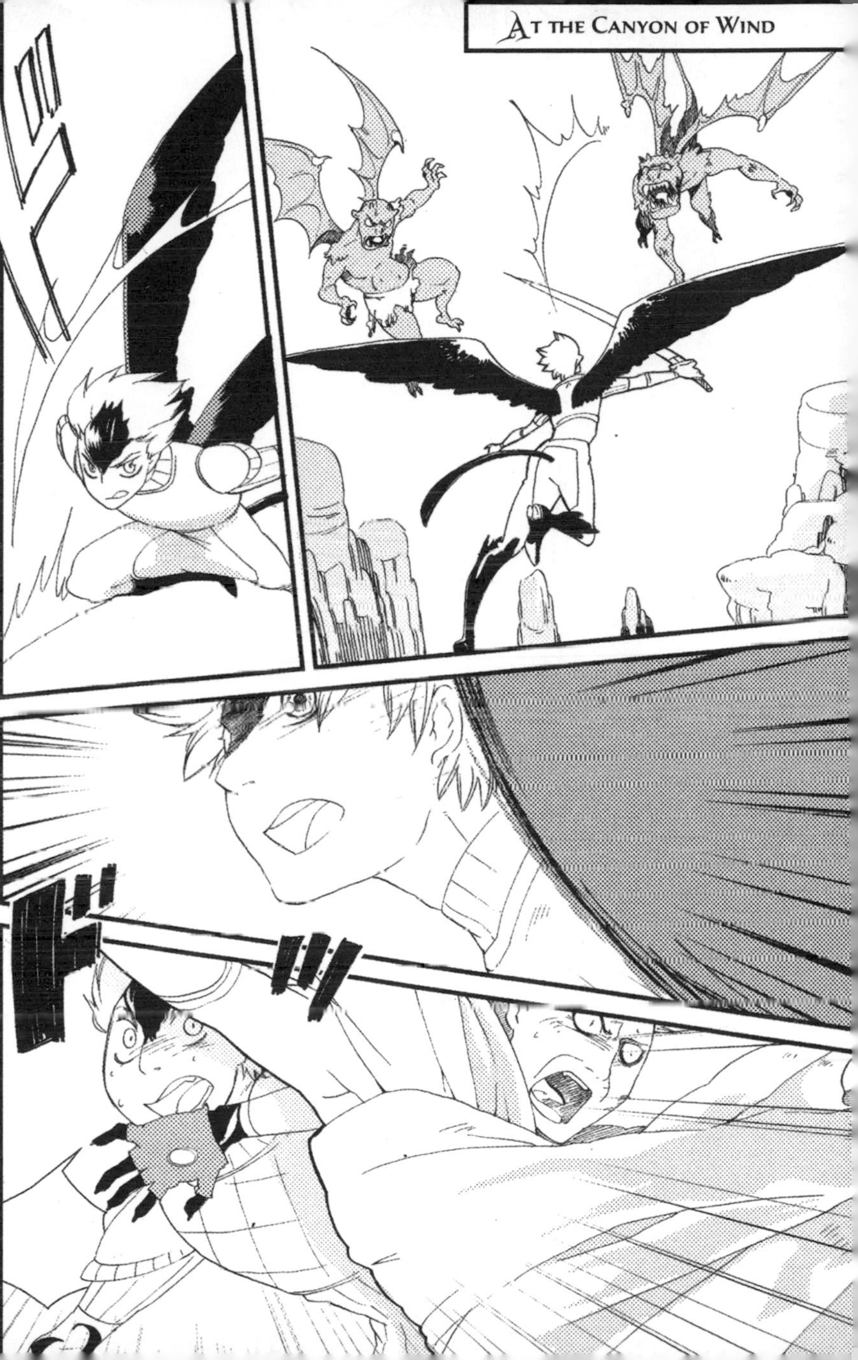

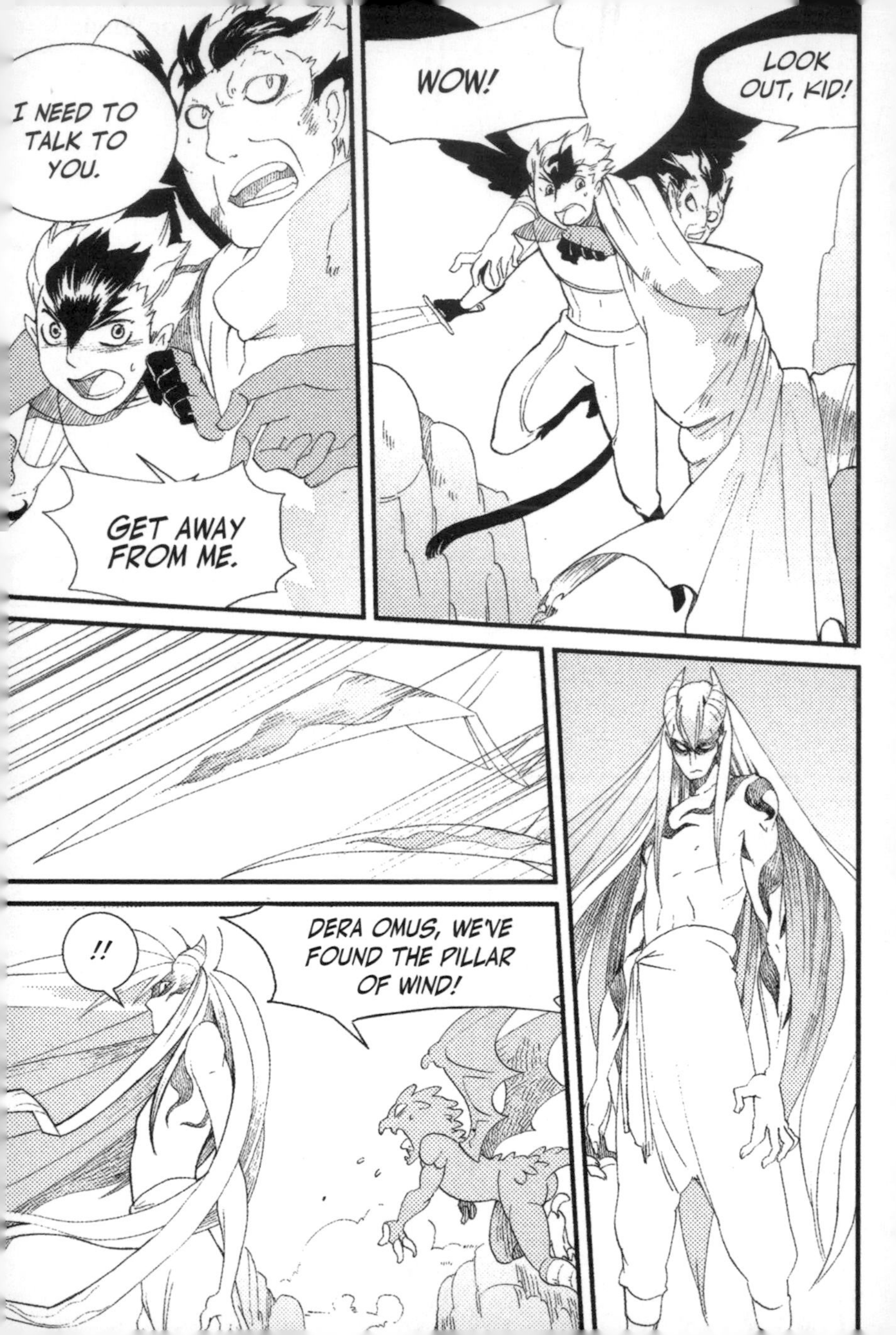
I NEED TO TALK TO YOU.
GET AWAY FROM ME.
WOW!
LOOK OUT, KID!
!!
DERA OMUS, WE'VE FOUND THE PILLAR OF WIND!

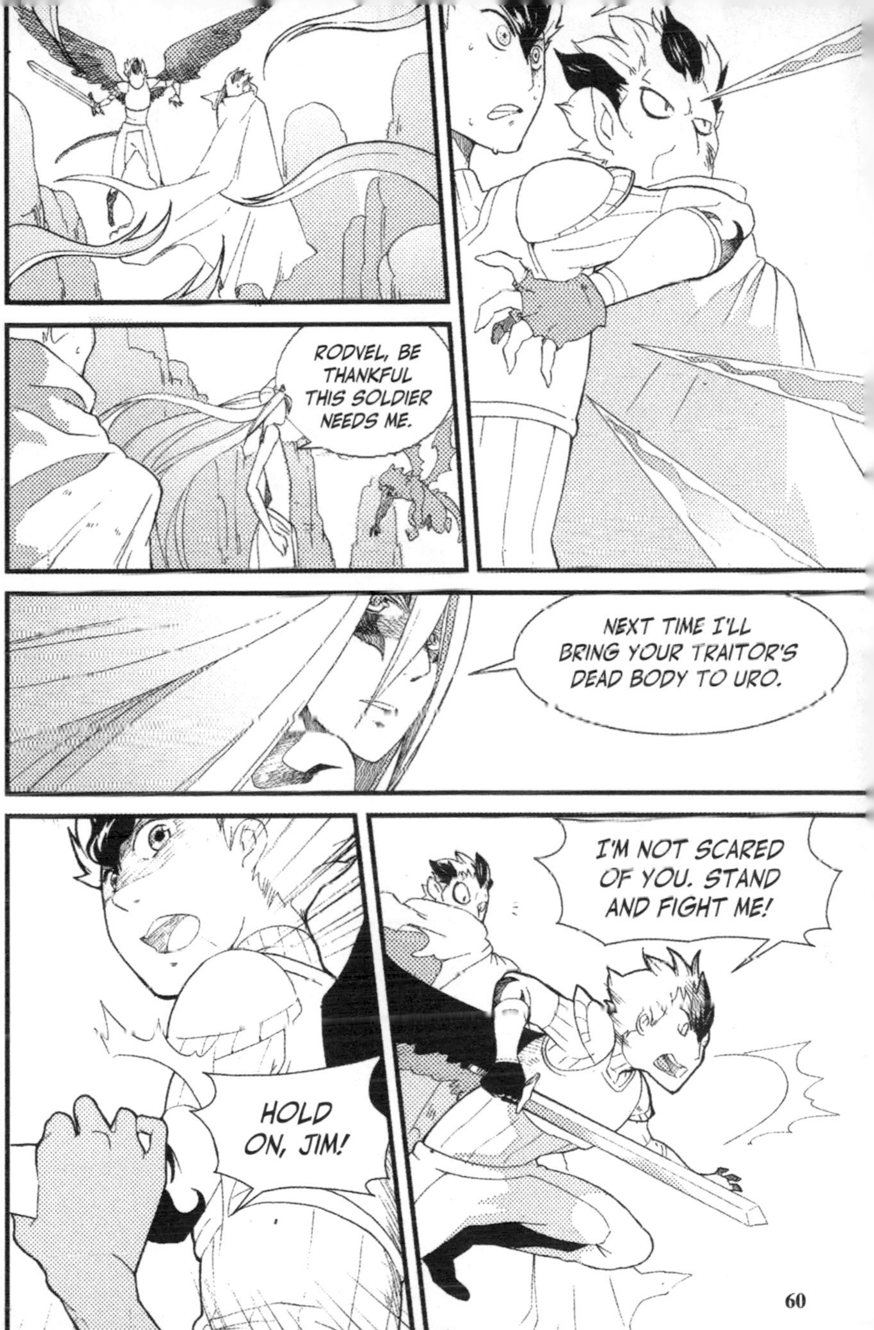
RODVEL, BE THANKFUL THIS SOLDIER NEEDS ME.
NEXT TIME I'LL BRING YOUR TRAITOR'S DEAD BODY TO URO.
I'M NOT SCARED OF YOU. STAND AND FIGHT ME!
HOLD ON, JIM!

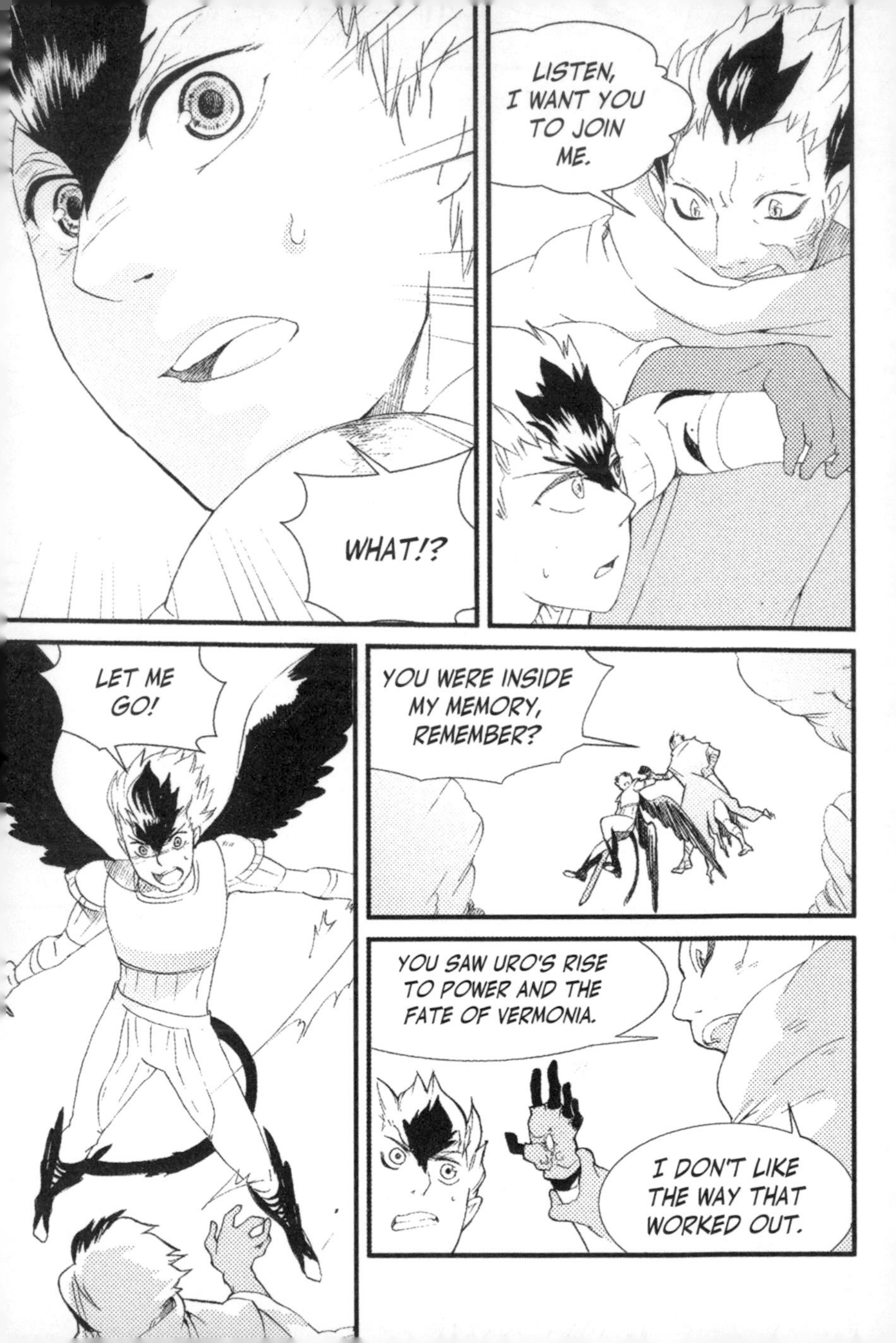
LISTEN, I WANT YOU TO JOIN ME.
WHAT!?
YOU WERE INSIDE MY MEMORY, REMEMBER?
YOU SAW URO'S RISE TO POWER AND THE FATE OF VERMONIA.
I DON'T LIKE THE WAY THAT WORKED OUT.
LET ME GO!

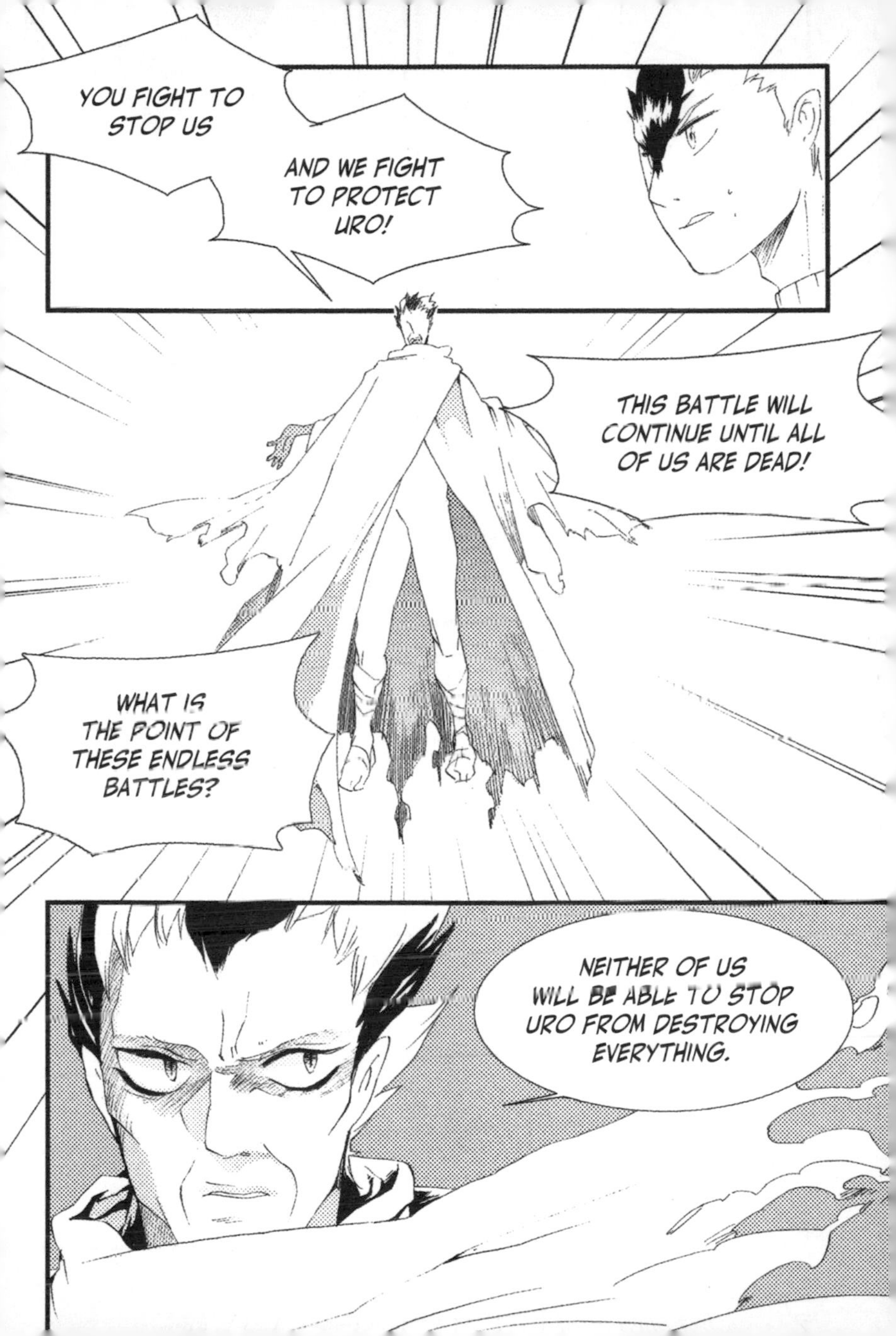
YOU FIGHT TO STOP US
AND WE FIGHT TO PROTECT URO!
THIS BATTLE WILL CONTINUE UNTIL ALL OF US ARE DEAD!
WHAT IS THE POINT OF THESE ENDLESS BATTLES?
NEITHER OF US WILL BE ABLE TO STOP URO FROM DESTROYING EVERYTHING.

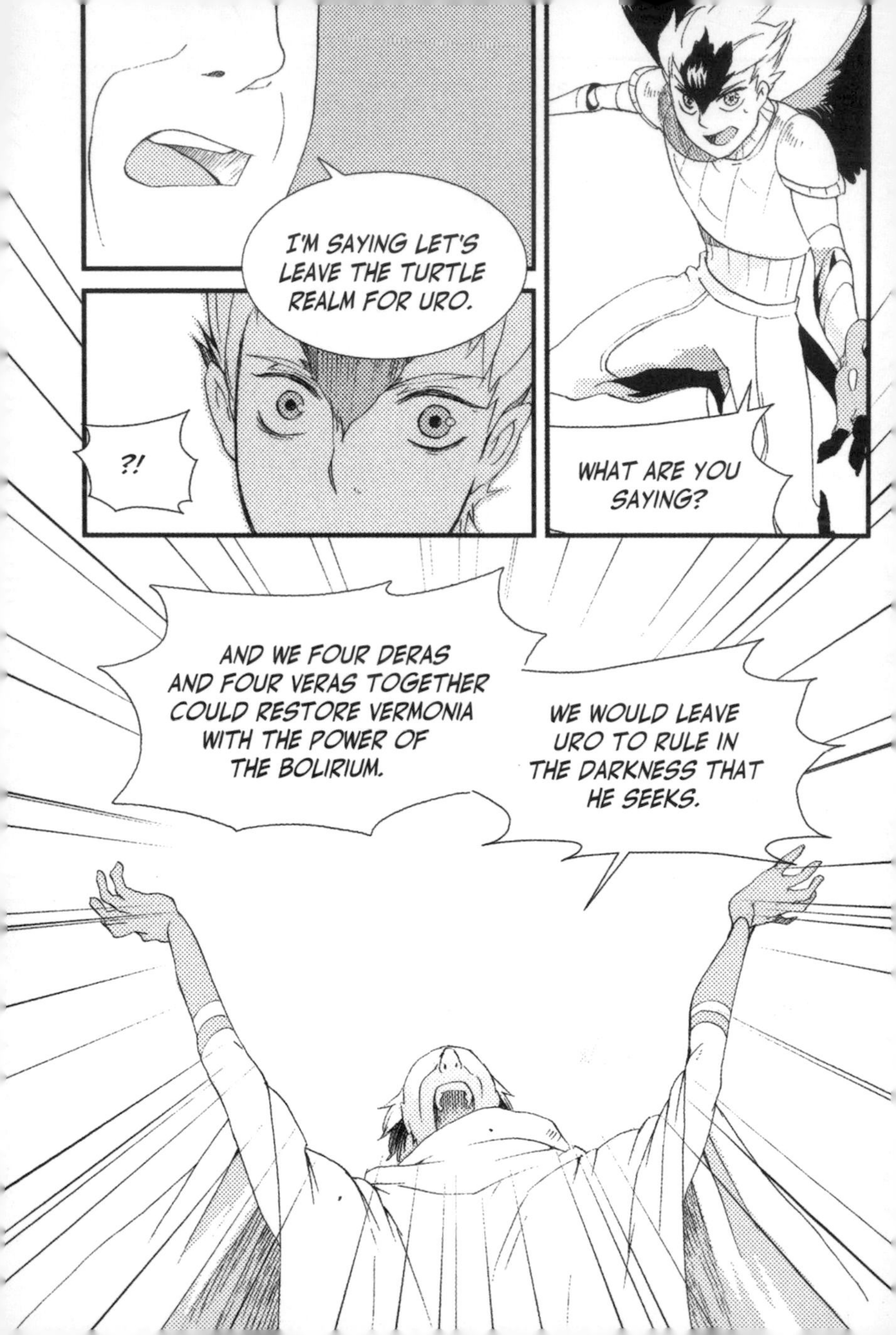
WHAT ARE YOU SAYING?
I'M SAYING LET'S LEAVE THE TURTLE REALM FOR URO.
?!
WE WOULD LEAVE URO TO RULE IN THE DARKNESS THAT HE SEEKS.
AND WE FOUR DERAS AND FOUR VERAS TOGETHER COULD RESTORE VERMONIA WITH THE POWER OF THE BOLIRIUM.

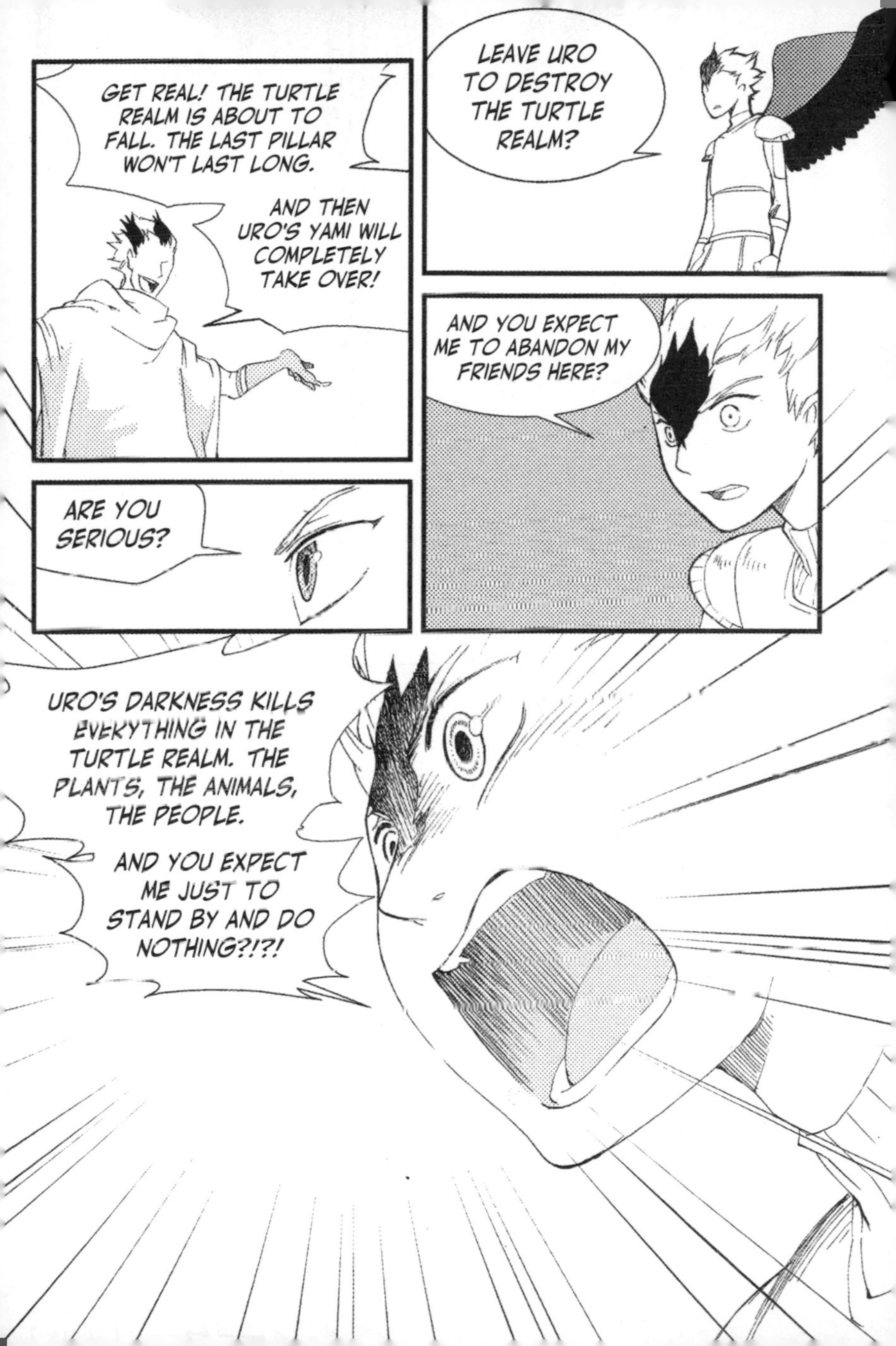
LEAVE URO TO DESTROY THE TURTLE REALM?
GET REAL! THE TURTLE REALM IS ABOUT TO FALL. THE LAST PILLAR WON'T LAST LONG.
AND THEN URO'S YAMI WILL COMPLETELY TAKE OVER!
AND YOU EXPECT ME TO ABANDON MY FRIENDS HERE?
ARE YOU SERIOUS?
URO'S DARKNESS KILLS EVERYTHING IN THE TURTLE REALM. THE PLANTS, THE ANIMALS, THE PEOPLE.
AND YOU EXPECT ME JUST TO STAND BY AND DO NOTHING?!?!

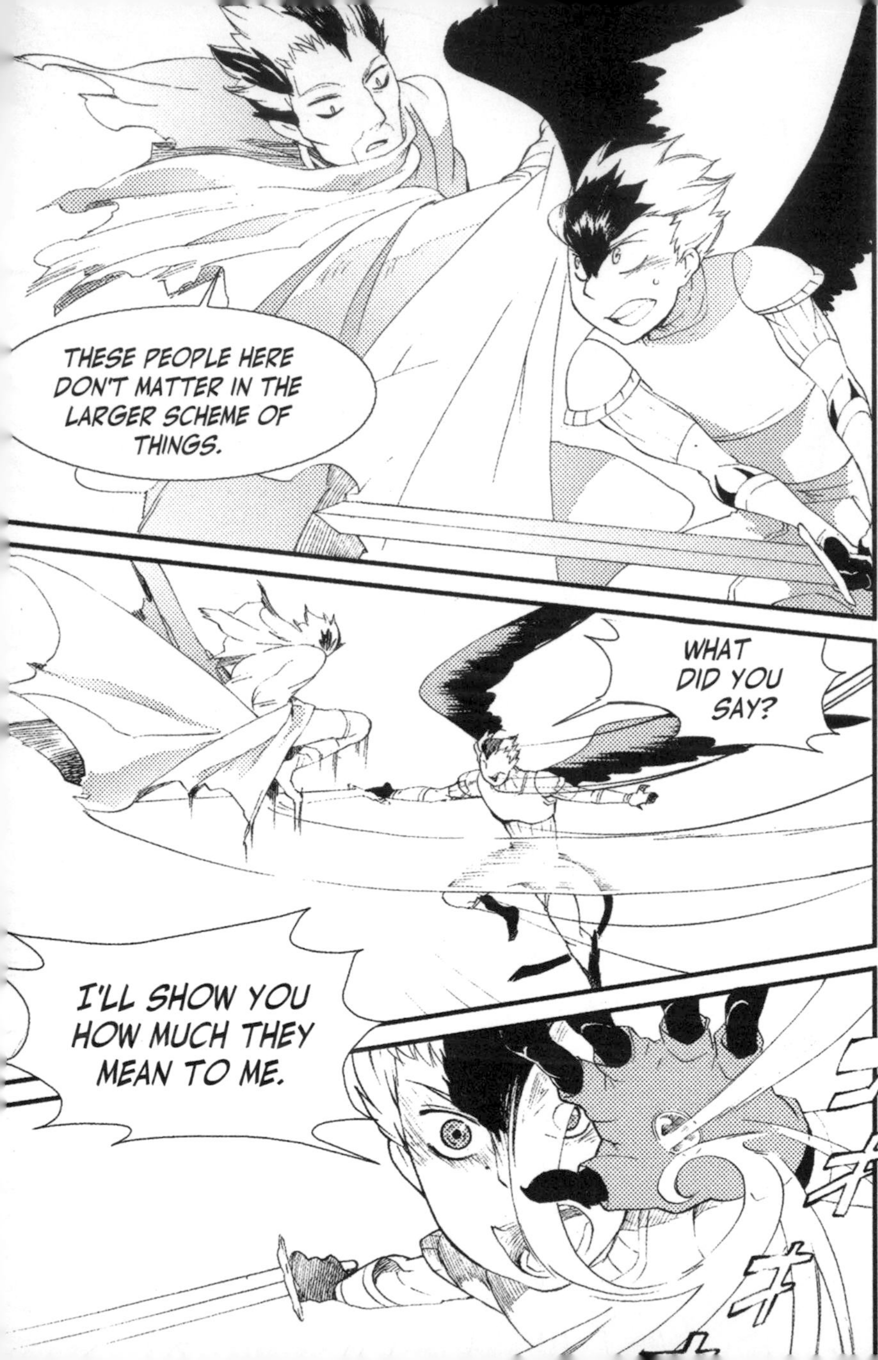
THESE PEOPLE HERE DON'T MATTER IN THE LARGER SCHEME OF THINGS.
WHAT DID YOU SAY?
I'LL SHOW YOU HOW MUCH THEY MEAN TO ME.

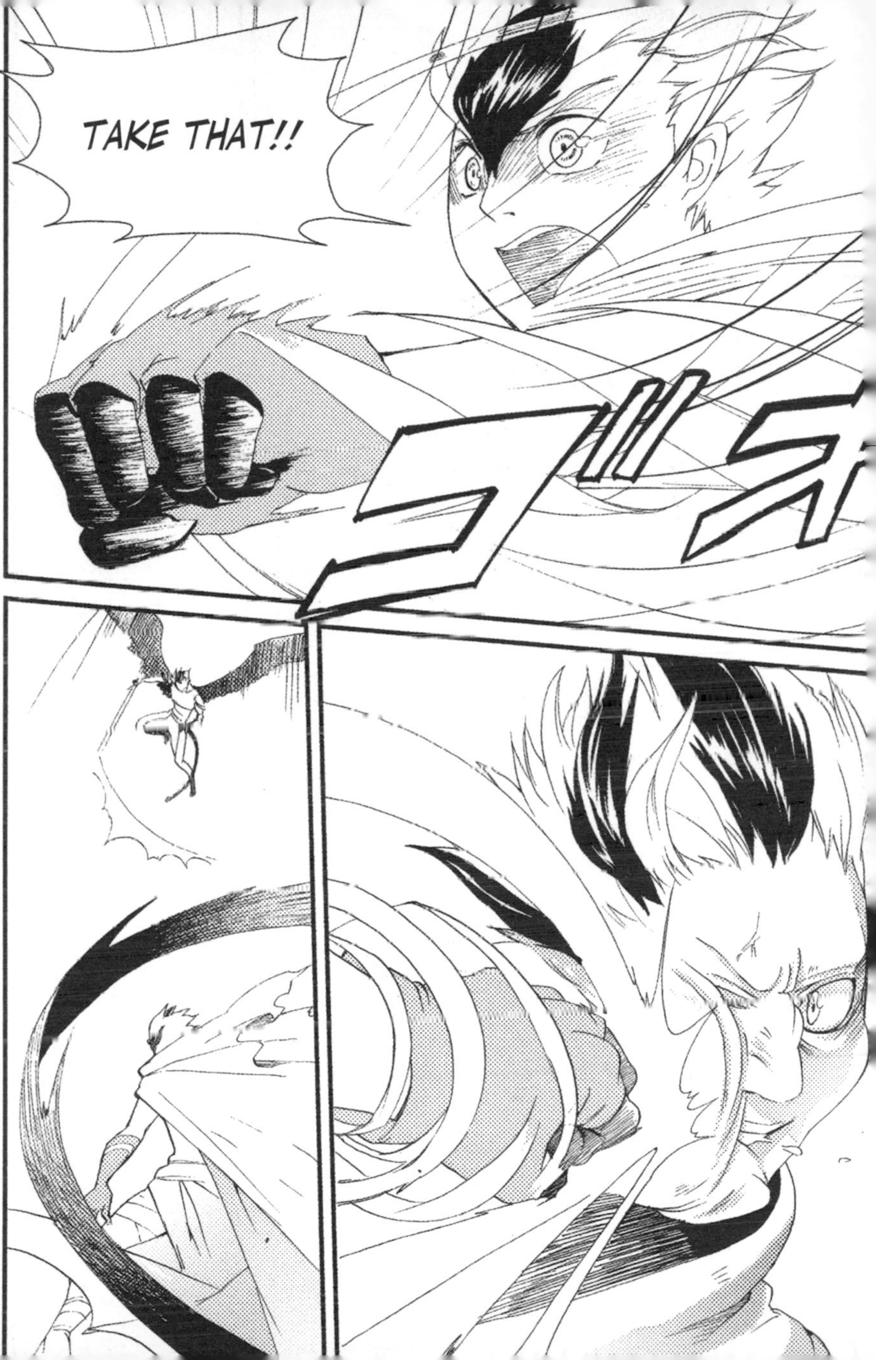
TAKE THAT!!

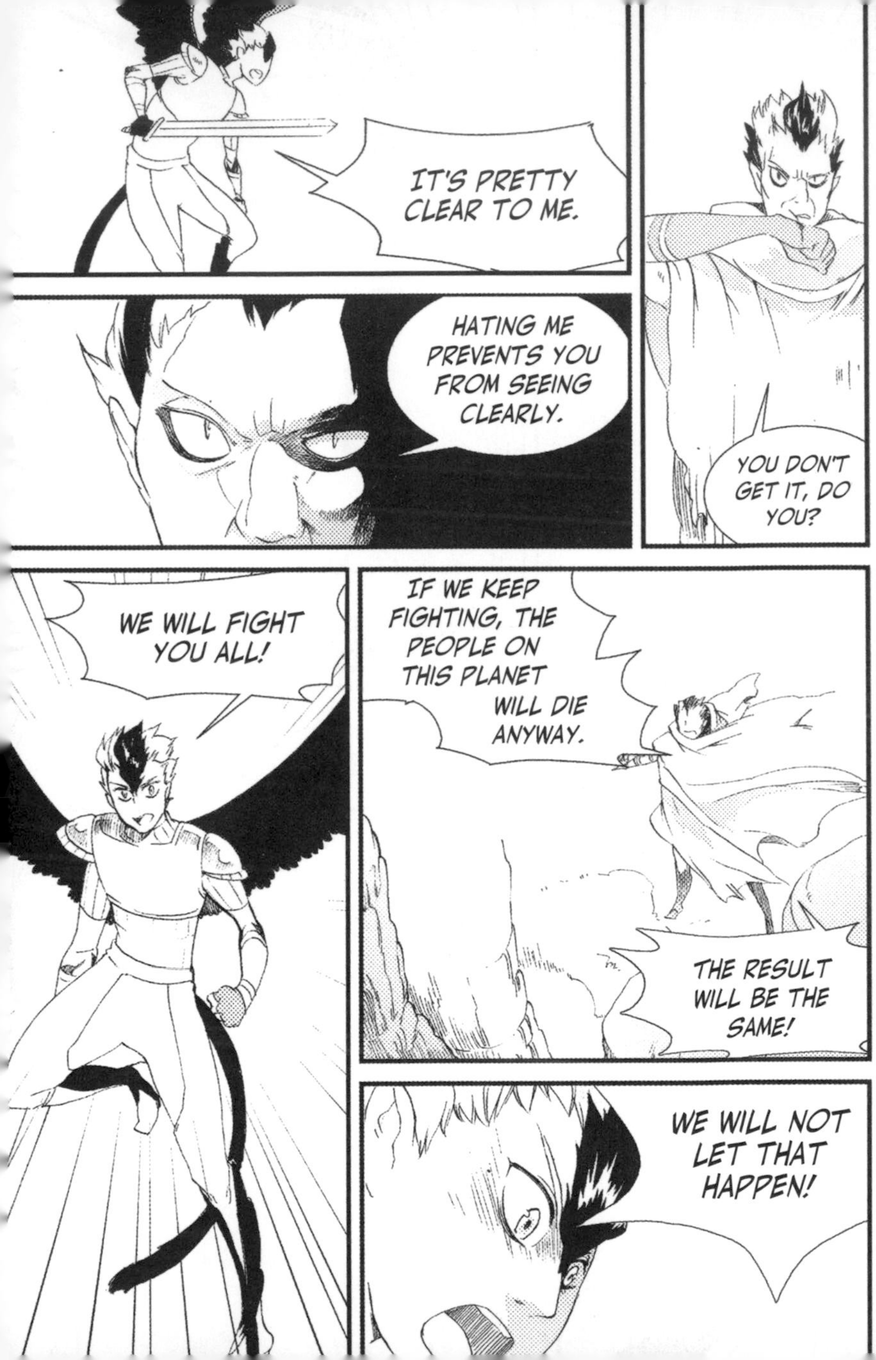
YOU DON'T GET IT, DO YOU?
IT'S PRETTY CLEAR TO ME.
HATING ME PREVENTS YOU FROM SEEING CLEARLY.
IF WE KEEP FIGHTING, THE PEOPLE ON THIS PLANET WILL DIE ANYWAY.
THE RESULT WILL BE THE SAME!
WE WILL NOT LET THAT HAPPEN!
WE WILL FIGHT YOU ALL!

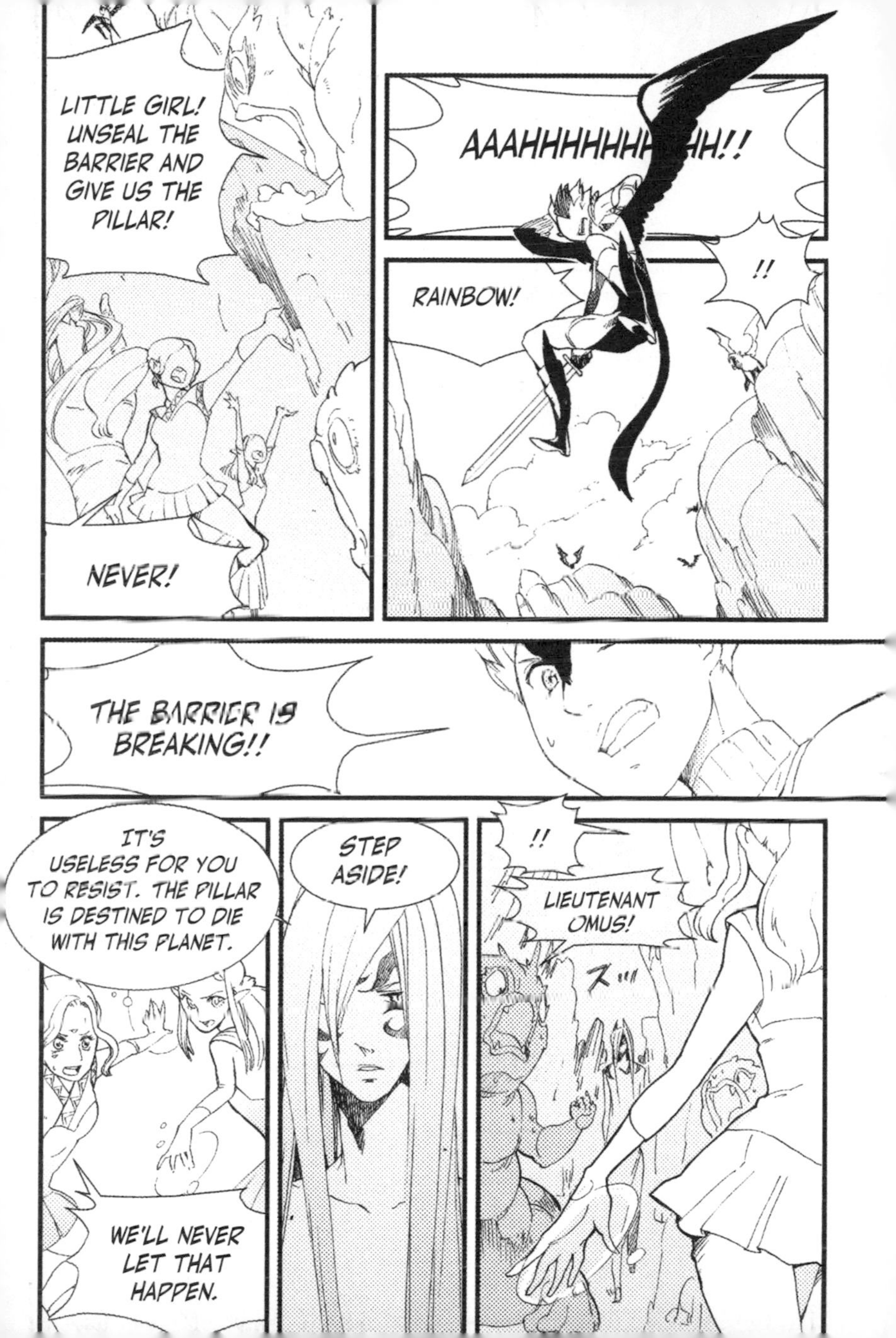
LITTLE GIRL! UNSEAL THE BARRIER AND GIVE US THE PILLAR!
NEVER!
AAAHHHHHHHHHH!!
RAINBOW!
!!
THE BARRIER IS BREAKING!!
IT'S USELESS FOR YOU TO RESIST. THE PILLAR IS DESTINED TO DIE WITH THIS PLANET.
WE'LL NEVER LET THAT HAPPEN.
STEP ASIDE!
!!
LIEUTENANT OMUS!

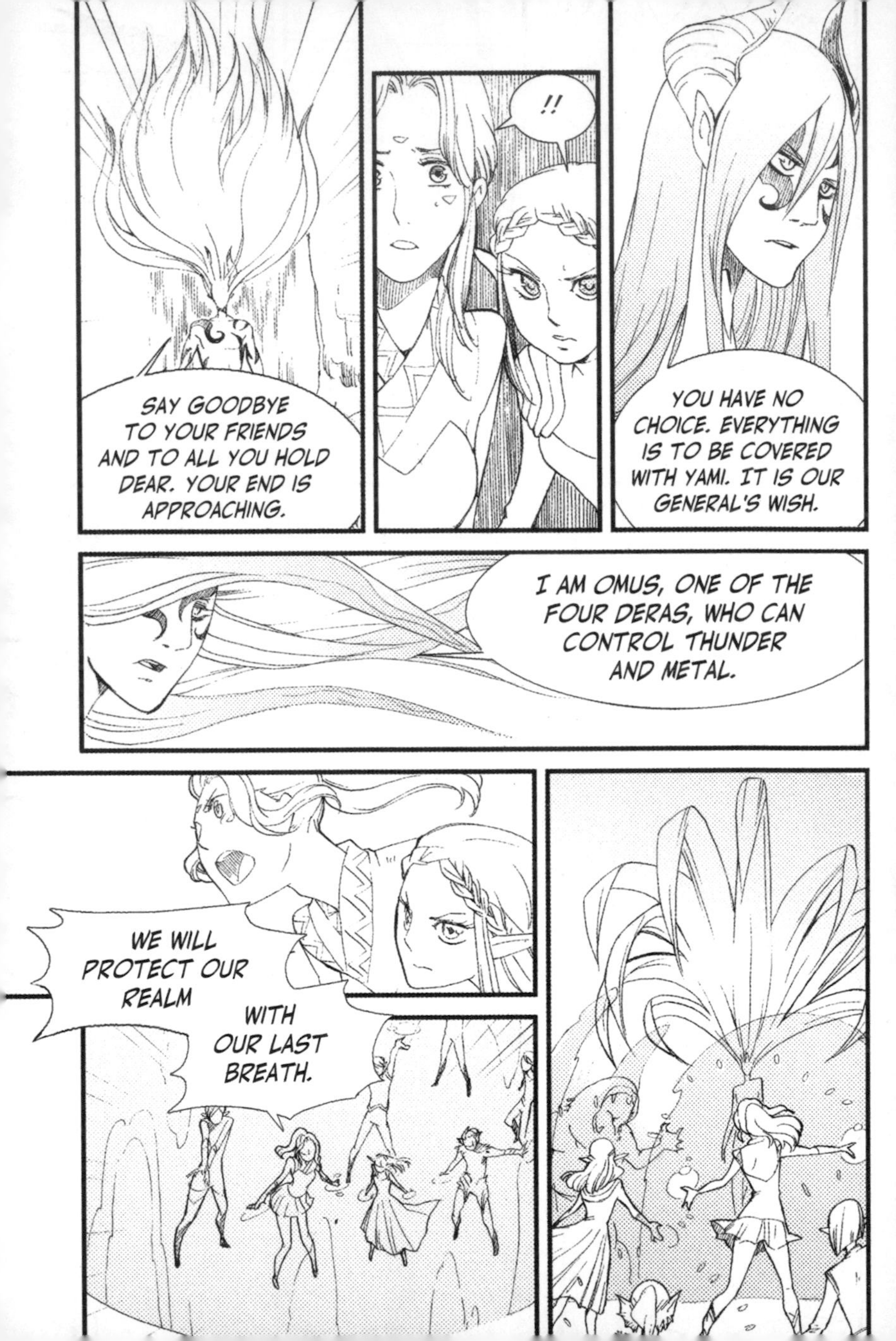
SAY GOODBYE TO YOUR FRIENDS AND TO ALL YOU HOLD DEAR. YOUR END IS APPROACHING.
!!
YOU HAVE NO CHOICE. EVERYTHING IS TO BE COVERED WITH YAMI. IT IS OUR GENERAL'S WISH.
I AM OMUS, ONE OF THE FOUR DERAS, WHO CAN CONTROL THUNDER AND METAL.
WE WILL PROTECT OUR REALM
WITH OUR LAST BREATH.

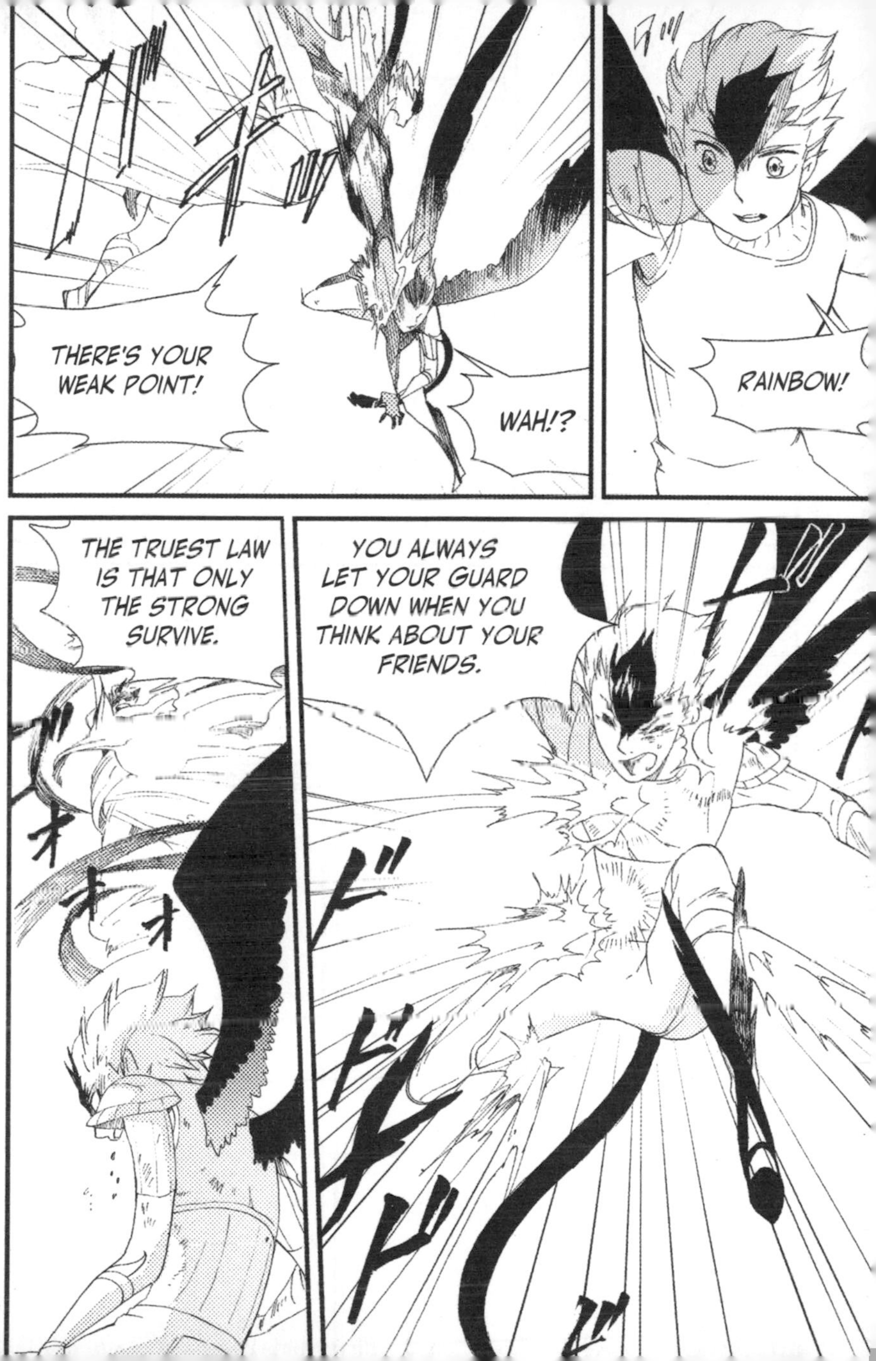
RAINBOW!
THERE'S YOUR WEAK POINT!
WAH!?
YOU ALWAYS LET YOUR GUARD DOWN WHEN YOU THINK ABOUT YOUR FRIENDS.
THE TRUEST LAW IS THAT ONLY THE STRONG SURVIVE.

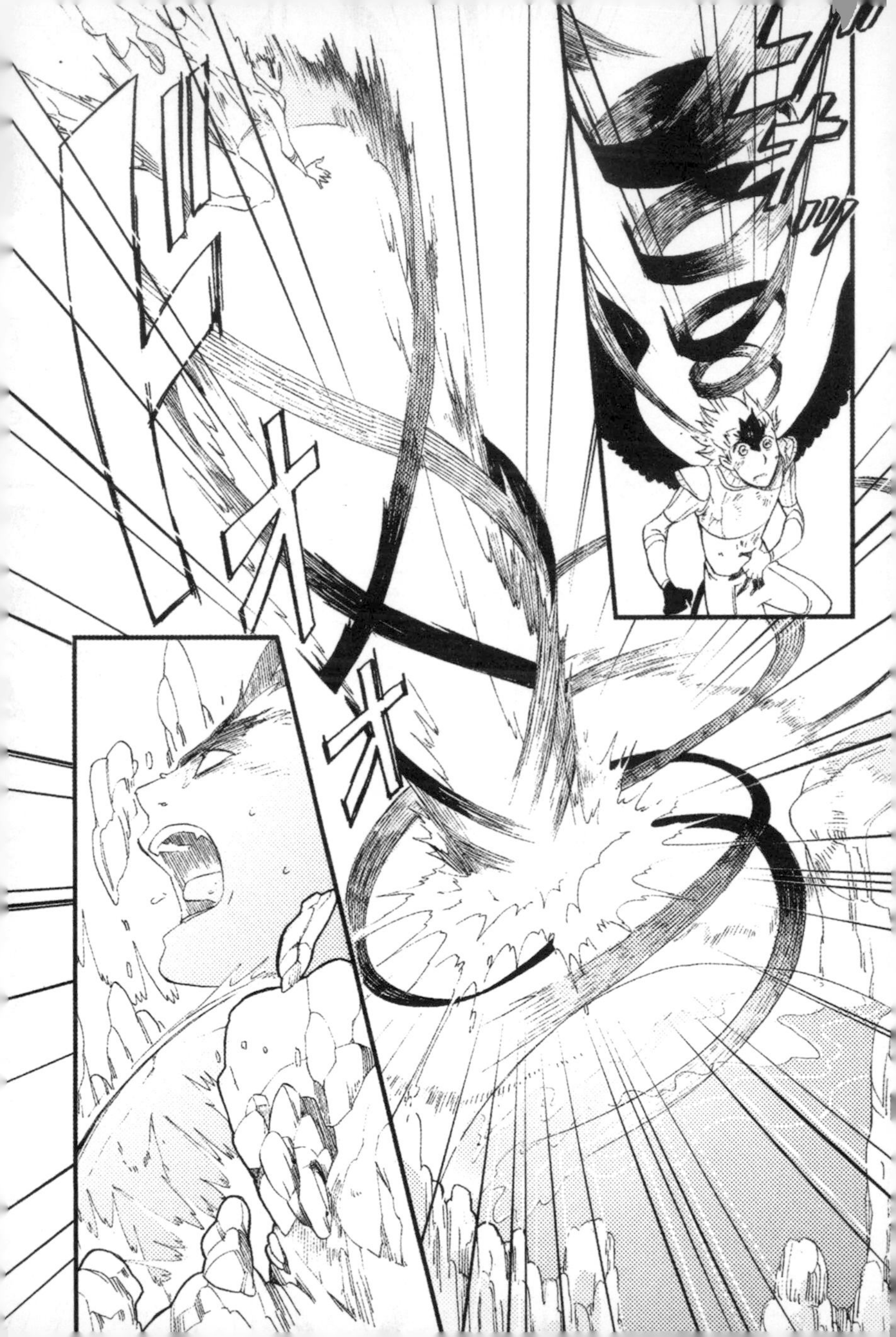
ゴオオ

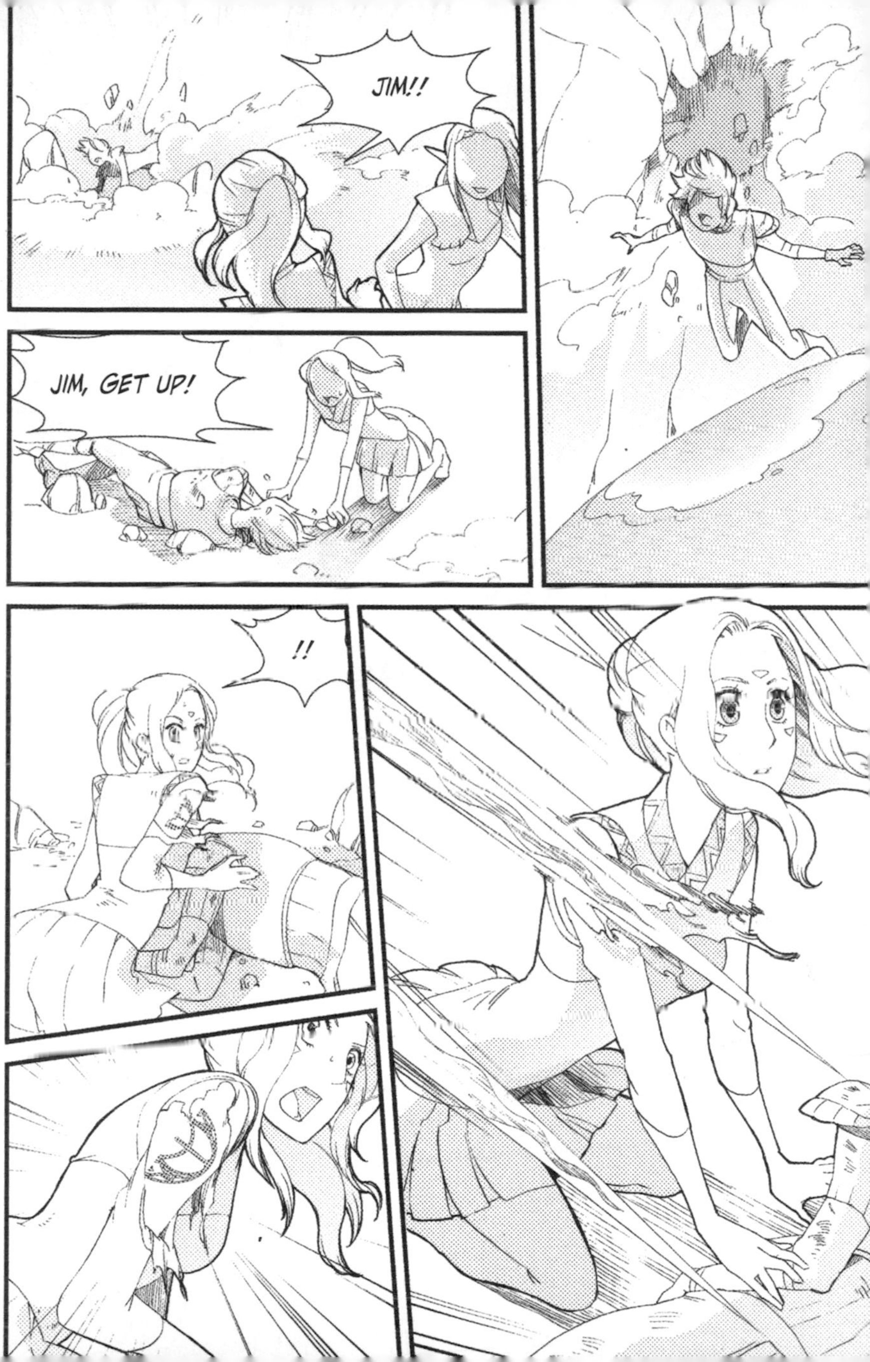
JIM!!
JIM, GET UP!
!!

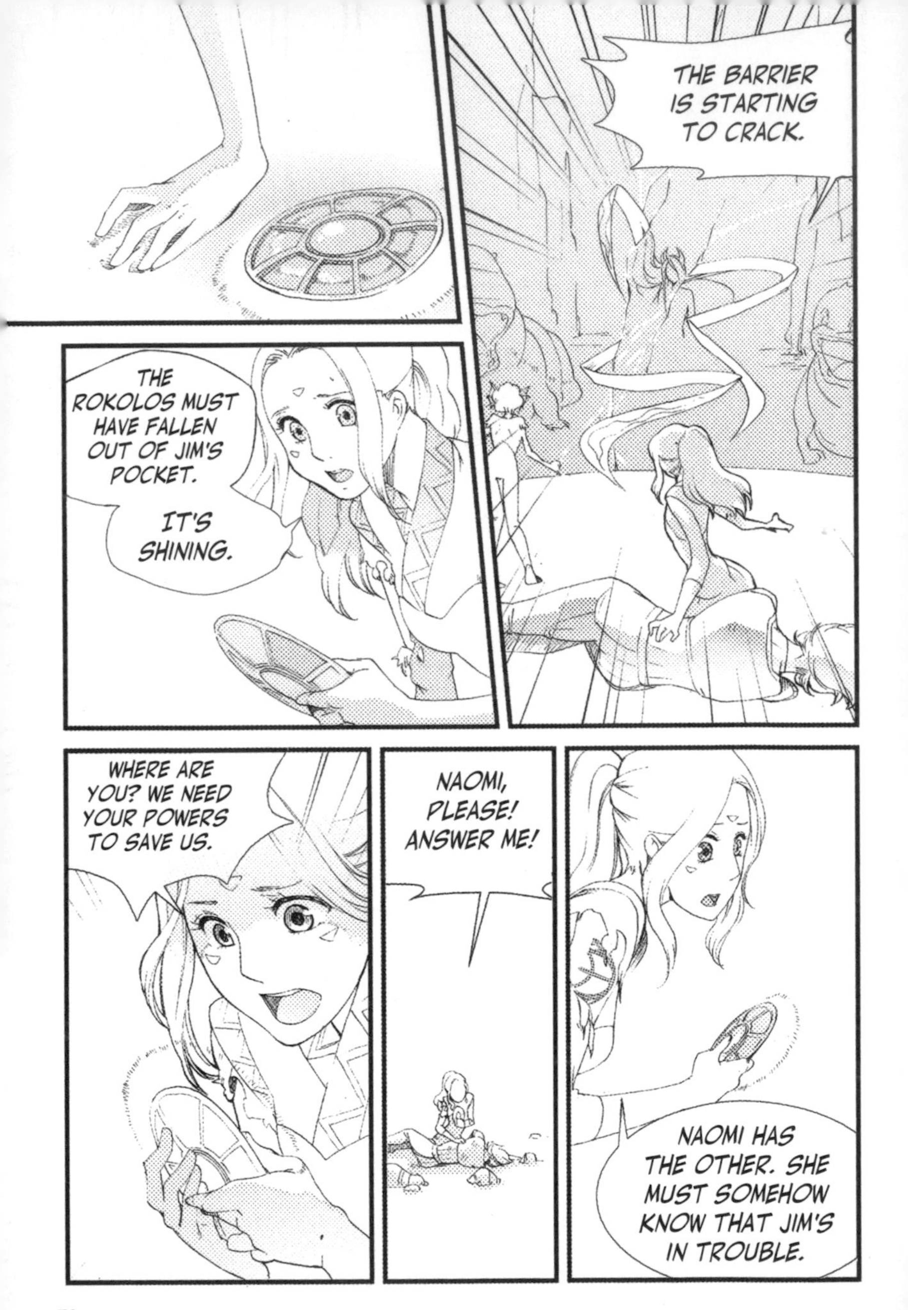
THE BARRIER IS STARTING TO CRACK.
THE ROKOLOS MUST HAVE FALLEN OUT OF JIM'S POCKET.
IT'S SHINING.
NAOMI HAS THE OTHER. SHE MUST SOMEHOW KNOW THAT JIM'S IN TROUBLE.
NAOMI, PLEASE! ANSWER ME!
WHERE ARE YOU? WE NEED YOUR POWERS TO SAVE US.

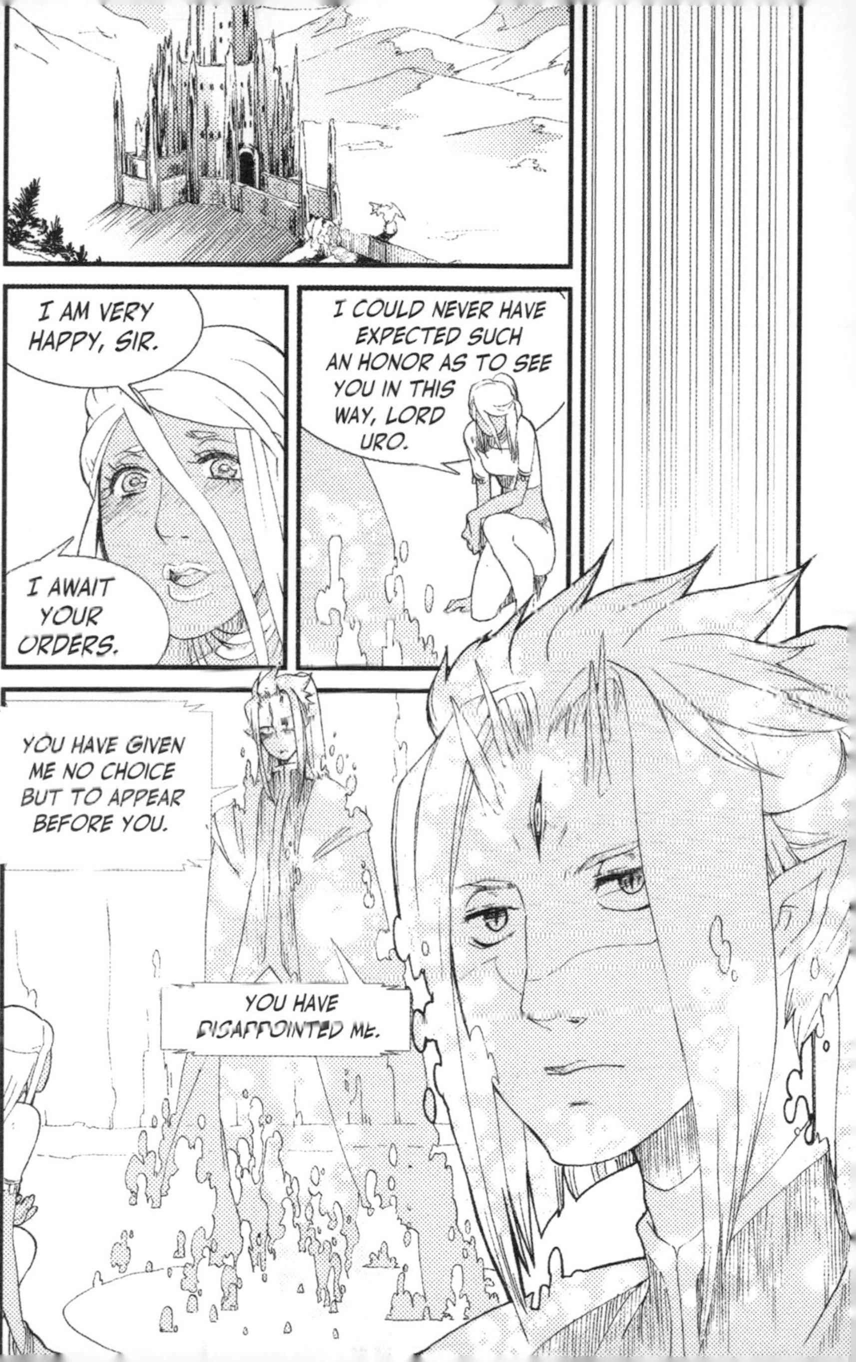
I COULD NEVER HAVE EXPECTED SUCH AN HONOR AS TO SEE YOU IN THIS WAY, LORD URO.
I AM VERY HAPPY, SIR.
I AWAIT YOUR ORDERS.
YOU HAVE GIVEN ME NO CHOICE BUT TO APPEAR BEFORE YOU.
YOU HAVE DISAPPOINTED ME.

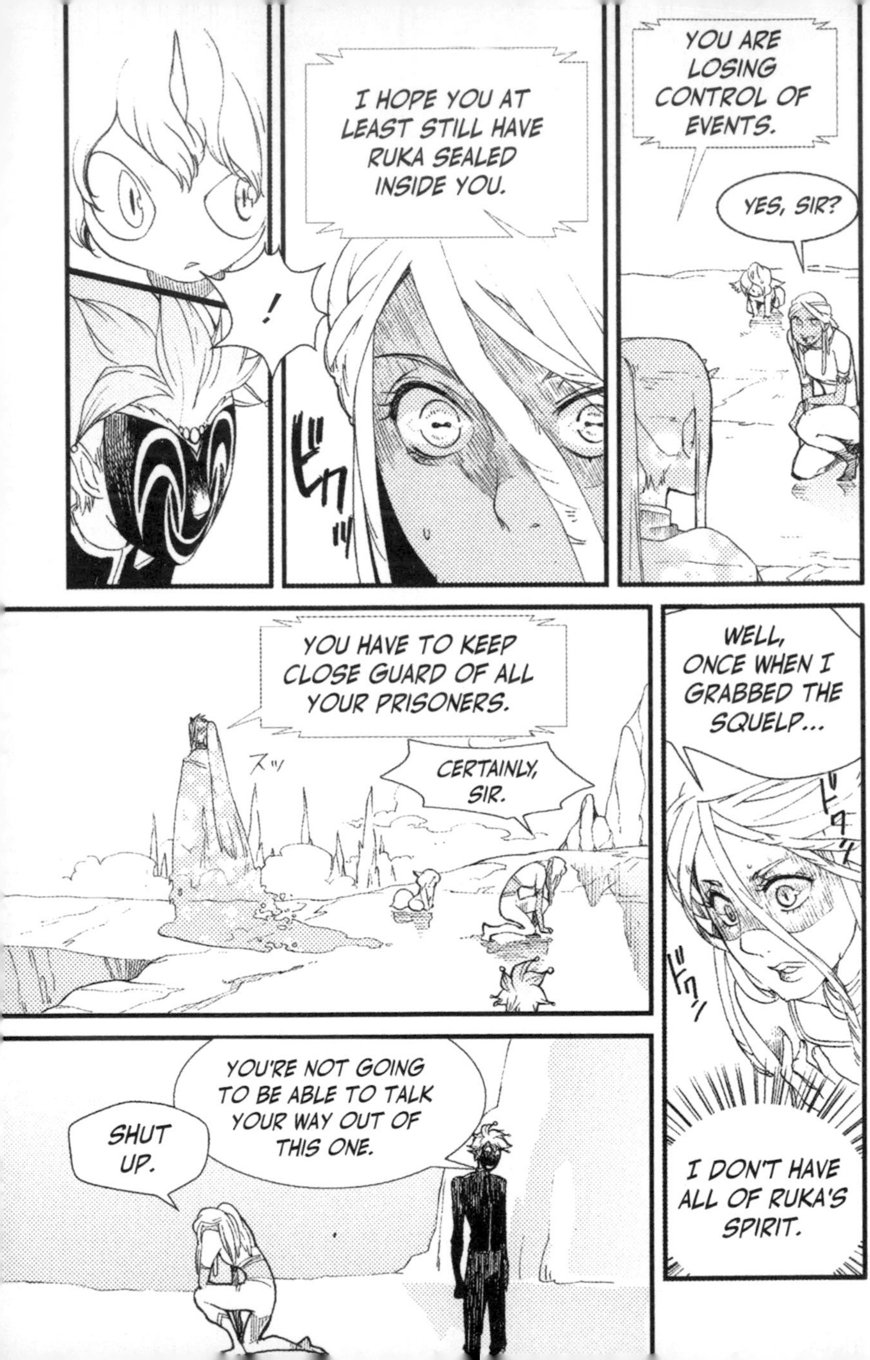
YOU ARE LOSING CONTROL OF EVENTS.
YES, SIR?
I HOPE YOU AT LEAST STILL HAVE RUKA SEALED INSIDE YOU.
ビクッ
!
WELL, ONCE WHEN I GRABBED THE SQUELP...
I DON'T HAVE ALL OF RUKA'S SPIRIT.
YOU HAVE TO KEEP CLOSE GUARD OF ALL YOUR PRISONERS.
ズッ
CERTAINLY, SIR.
YOU'RE NOT GOING TO BE ABLE TO TALK YOUR WAY OUT OF THIS ONE.
SHUT UP.

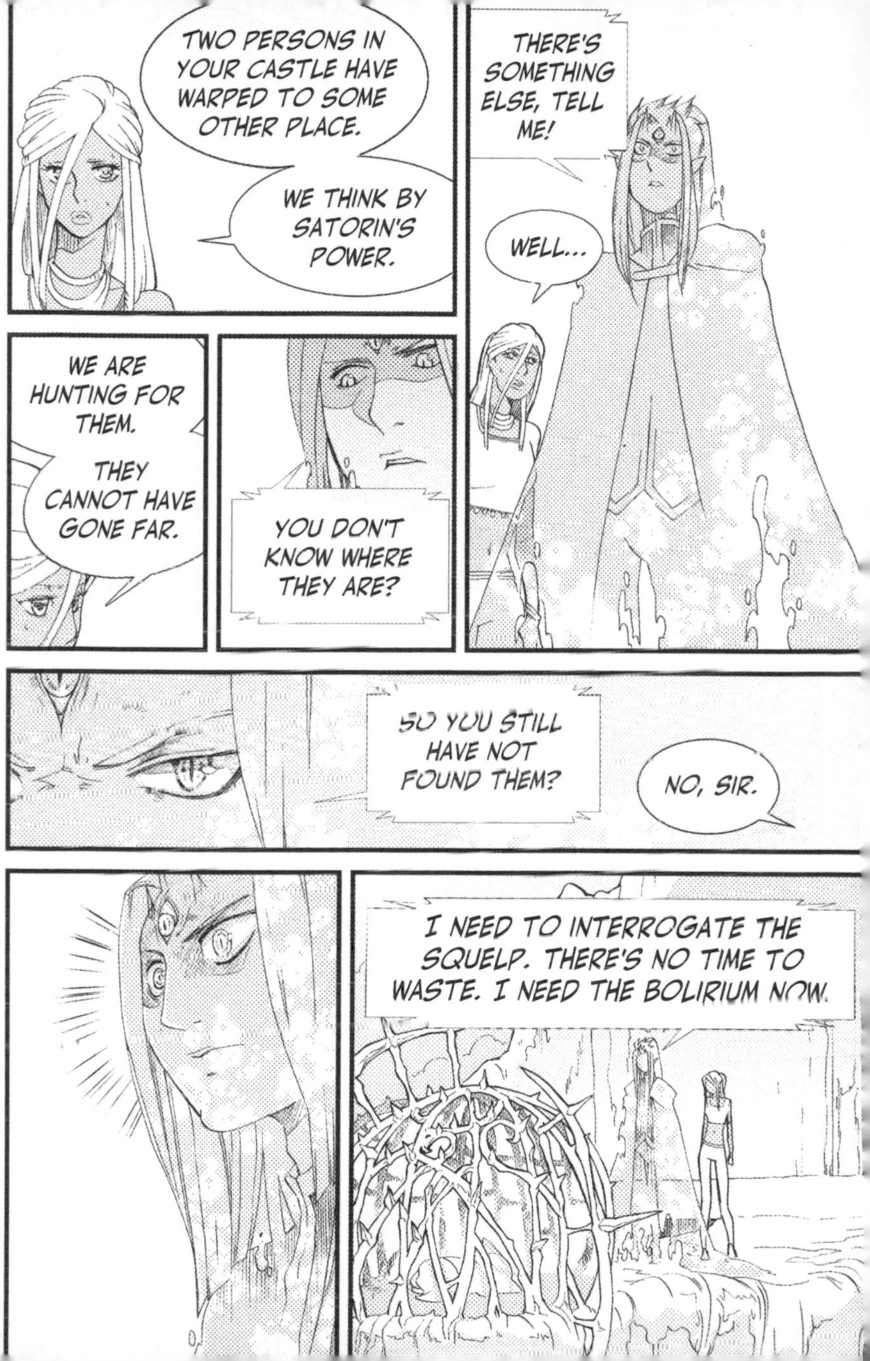
THERE'S SOMETHING ELSE, TELL ME!
WELL...
TWO PERSONS IN YOUR CASTLE HAVE WARPED TO SOME OTHER PLACE.
WE THINK BY SATORIN'S POWER.
YOU DON'T KNOW WHERE THEY ARE?
WE ARE HUNTING FOR THEM.
THEY CANNOT HAVE GONE FAR.
SO YOU STILL HAVE NOT FOUND THEM?
NO, SIR.
I NEED TO INTERROGATE THE SQUELP. THERE'S NO TIME TO WASTE. I NEED THE BOLIRIUM NOW.

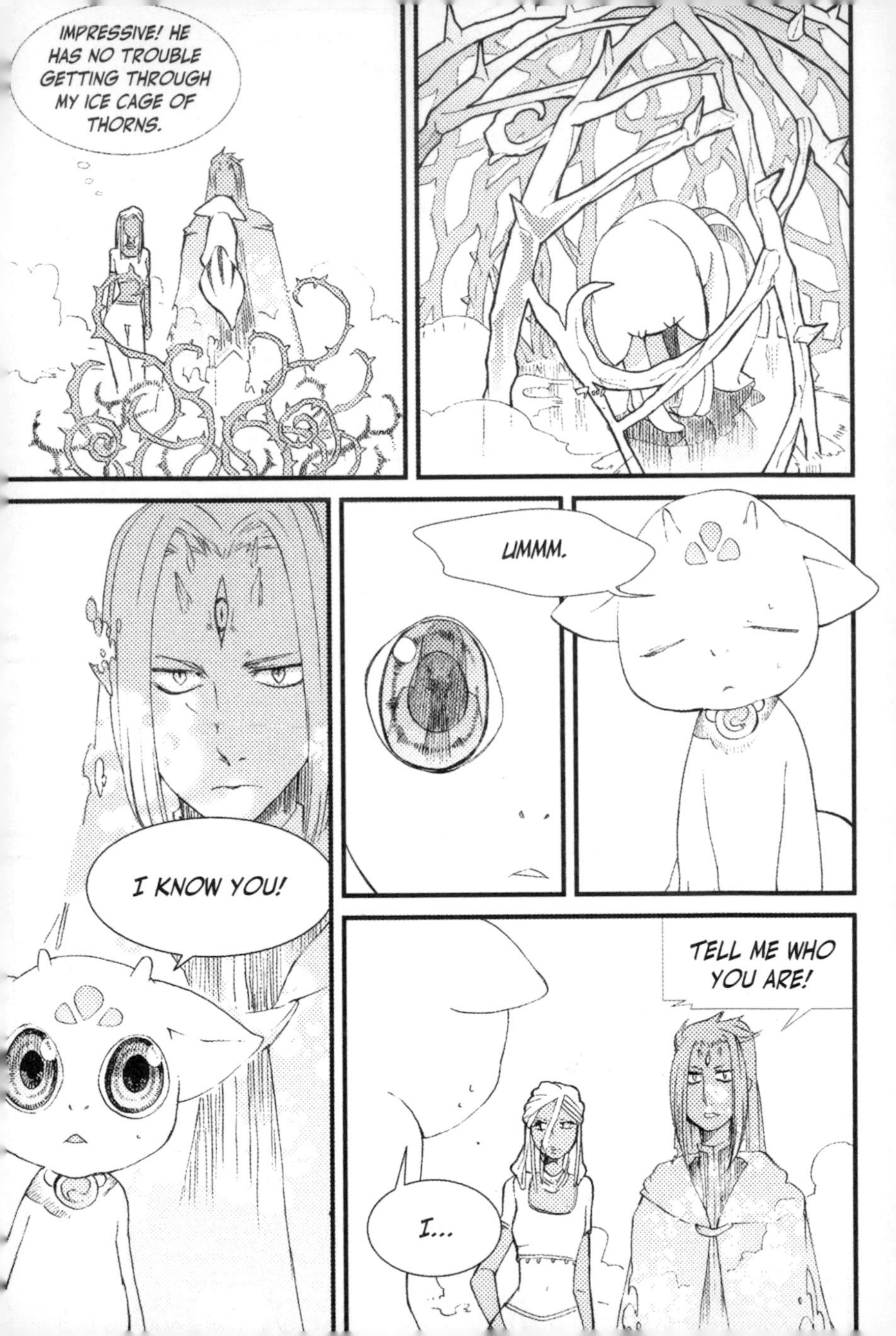
IMPRESSIVE! HE HAS NO TROUBLE GETTING THROUGH MY ICE CAGE OF THORNS.
I KNOW YOU!
UMMM.
TELL ME WHO YOU ARE!
I...

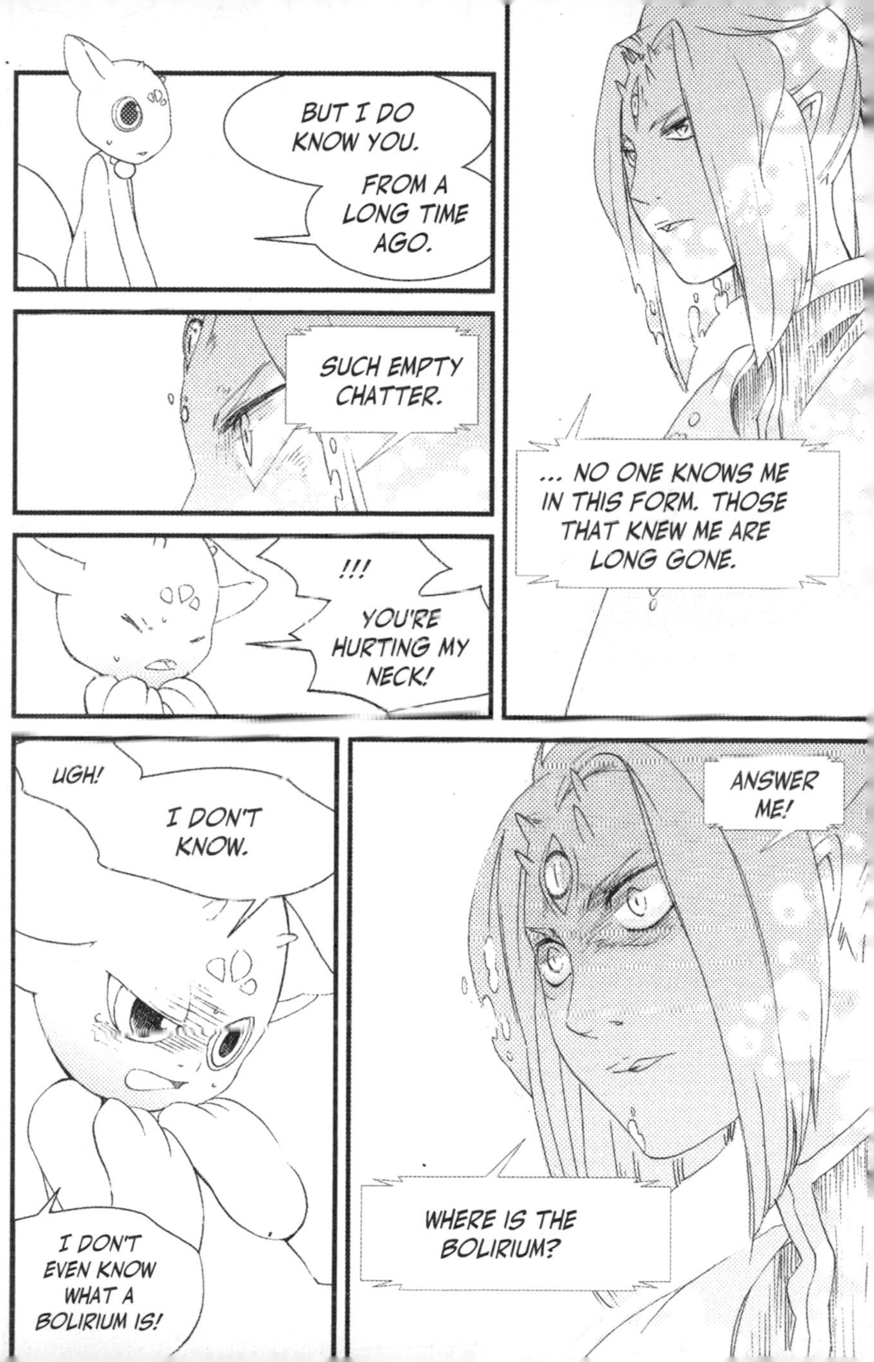
... NO ONE KNOWS ME IN THIS FORM. THOSE THAT KNEW ME ARE LONG GONE.
BUT I DO KNOW YOU.
FROM A LONG TIME AGO.
SUCH EMPTY CHATTER.
!!!
YOU'RE HURTING MY NECK!
ANSWER ME!
WHERE IS THE BOLIRIUM?
UGH!
I DON'T KNOW.
I DON'T EVEN KNOW WHAT A BOLIRIUM IS!

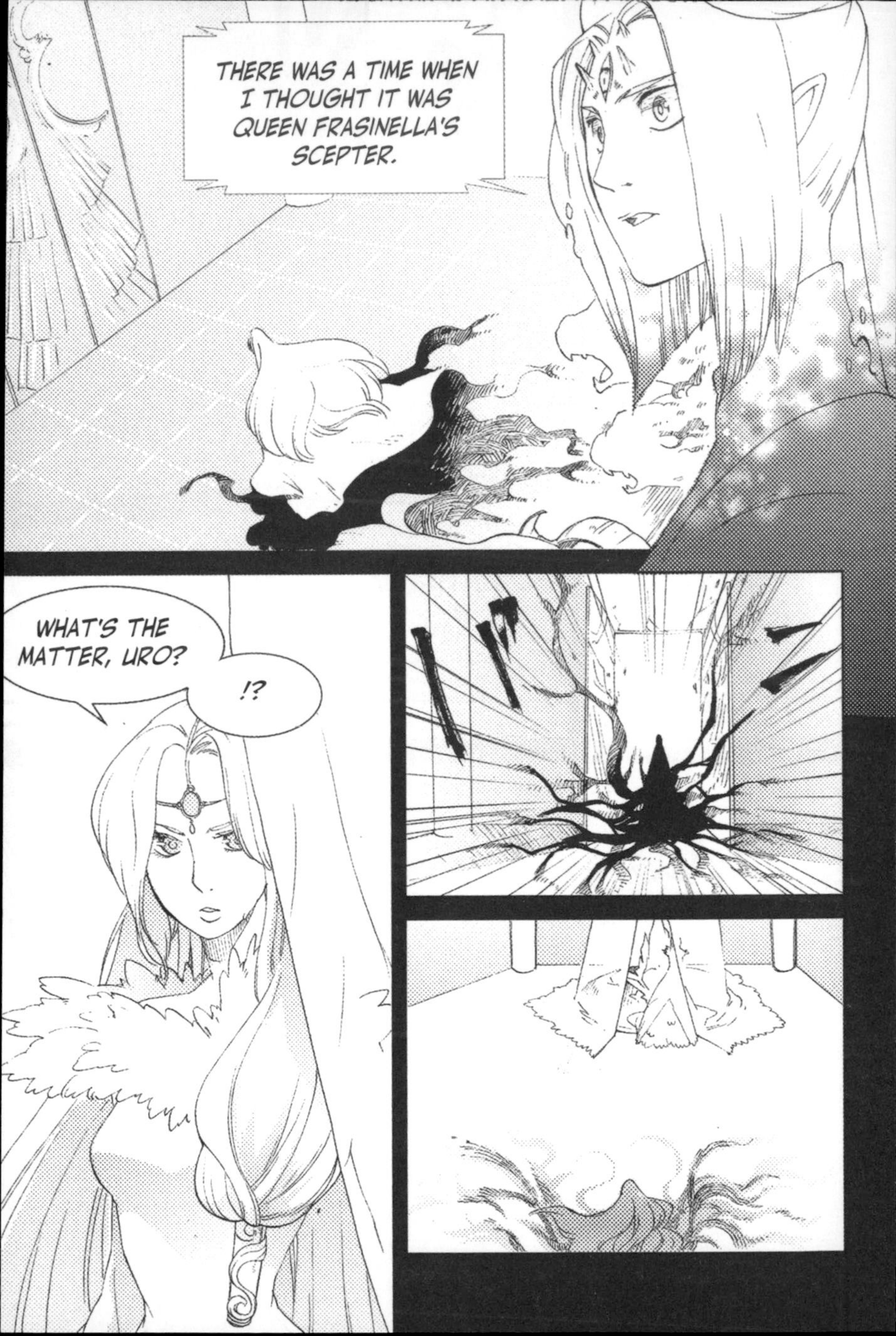
THERE WAS A TIME WHEN I THOUGHT IT WAS QUEEN FRASINELLA'S SCEPTER.
!?
WHAT'S THE MATTER, URO?

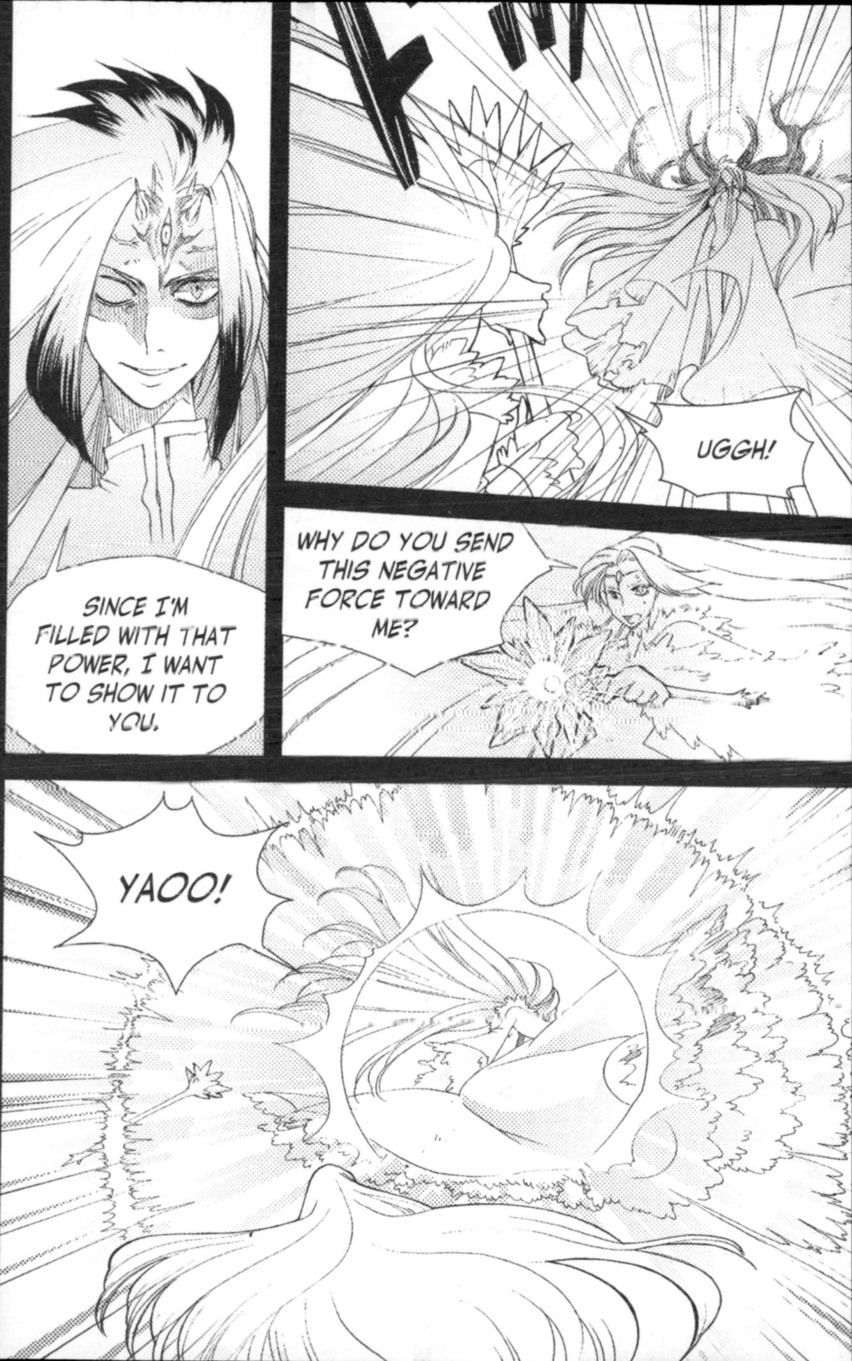
UGGH!
WHY DO YOU SEND THIS NEGATIVE FORCE TOWARD ME?
SINCE I'M FILLED WITH THAT POWER, I WANT TO SHOW IT TO YOU.
YAOO!

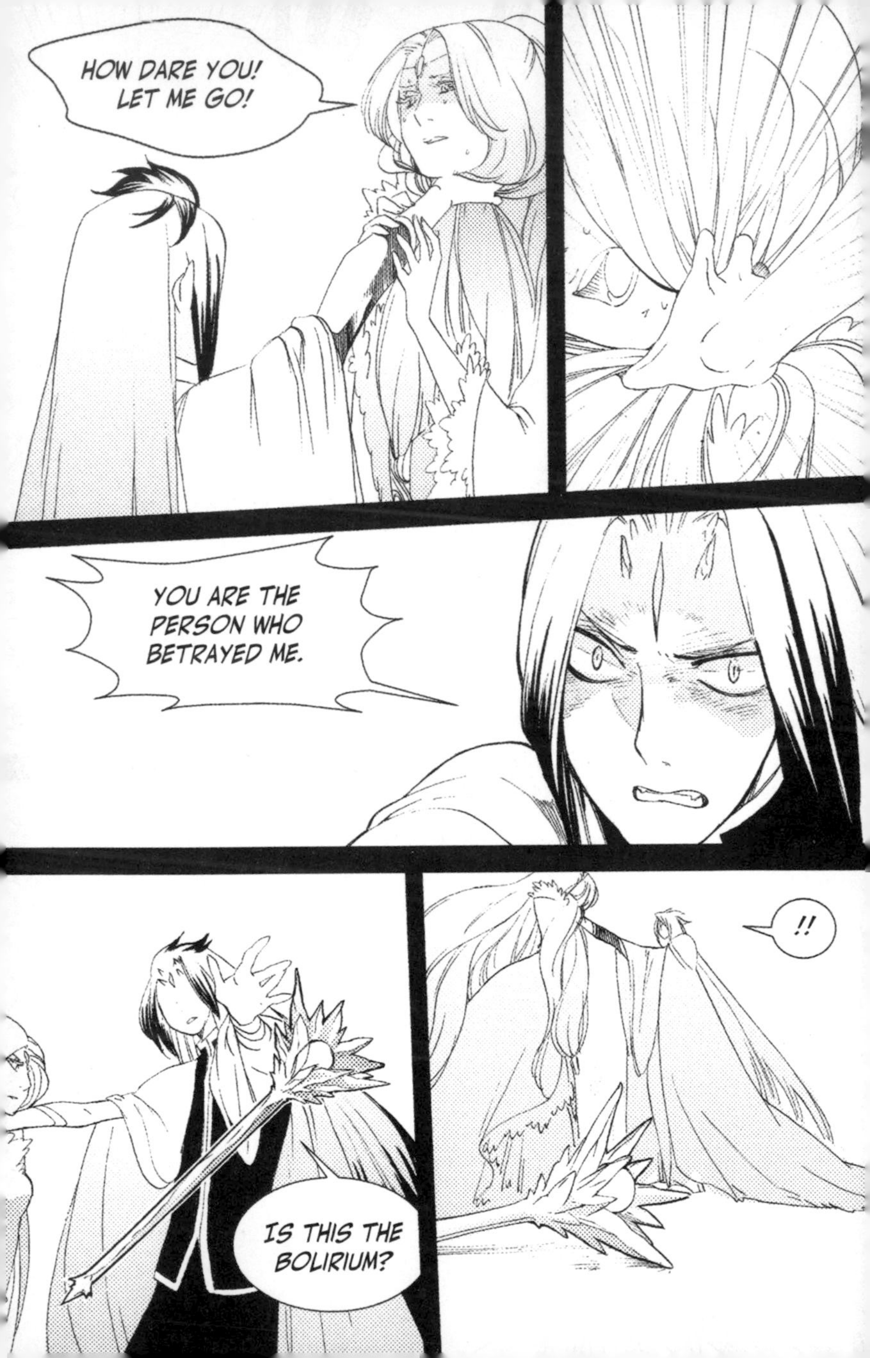
HOW DARE YOU! LET ME GO!
YOU ARE THE PERSON WHO BETRAYED ME.
!!
IS THIS THE BOLIRIUM?

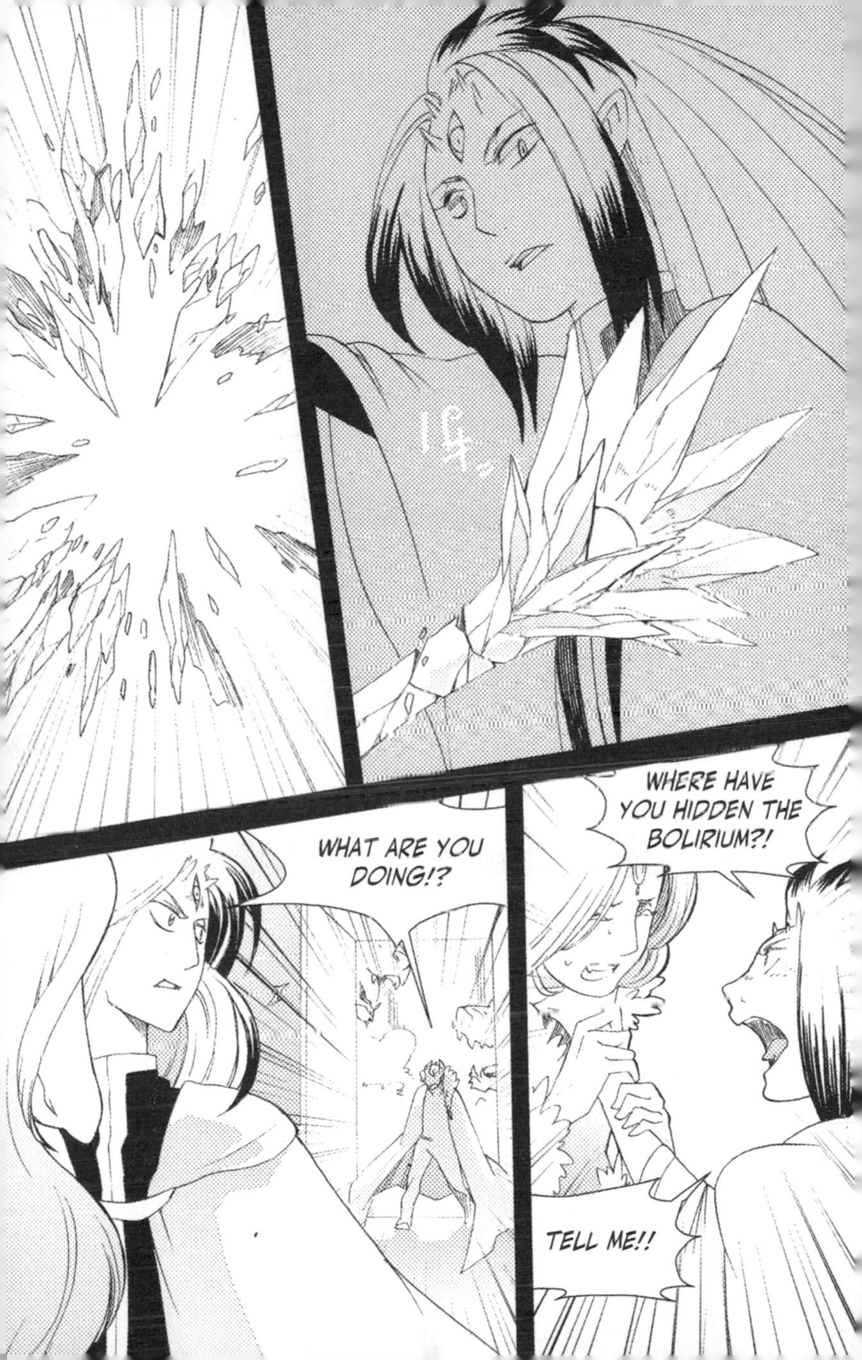
WHERE HAVE YOU HIDDEN THE BOLIRIUM?!
TELL ME!!
WHAT ARE YOU DOING!?

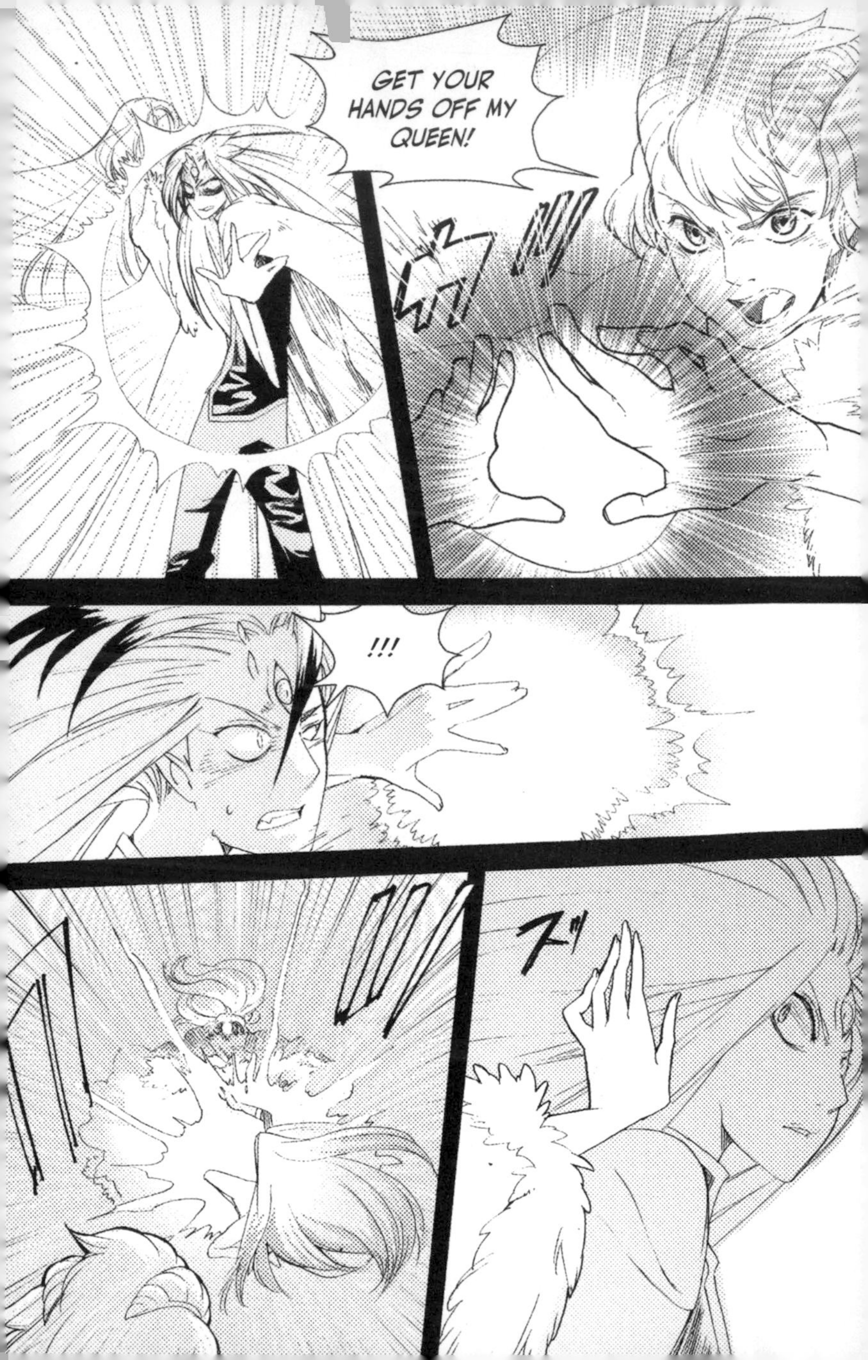
GET YOUR HANDS OFF MY QUEEN!
!!!

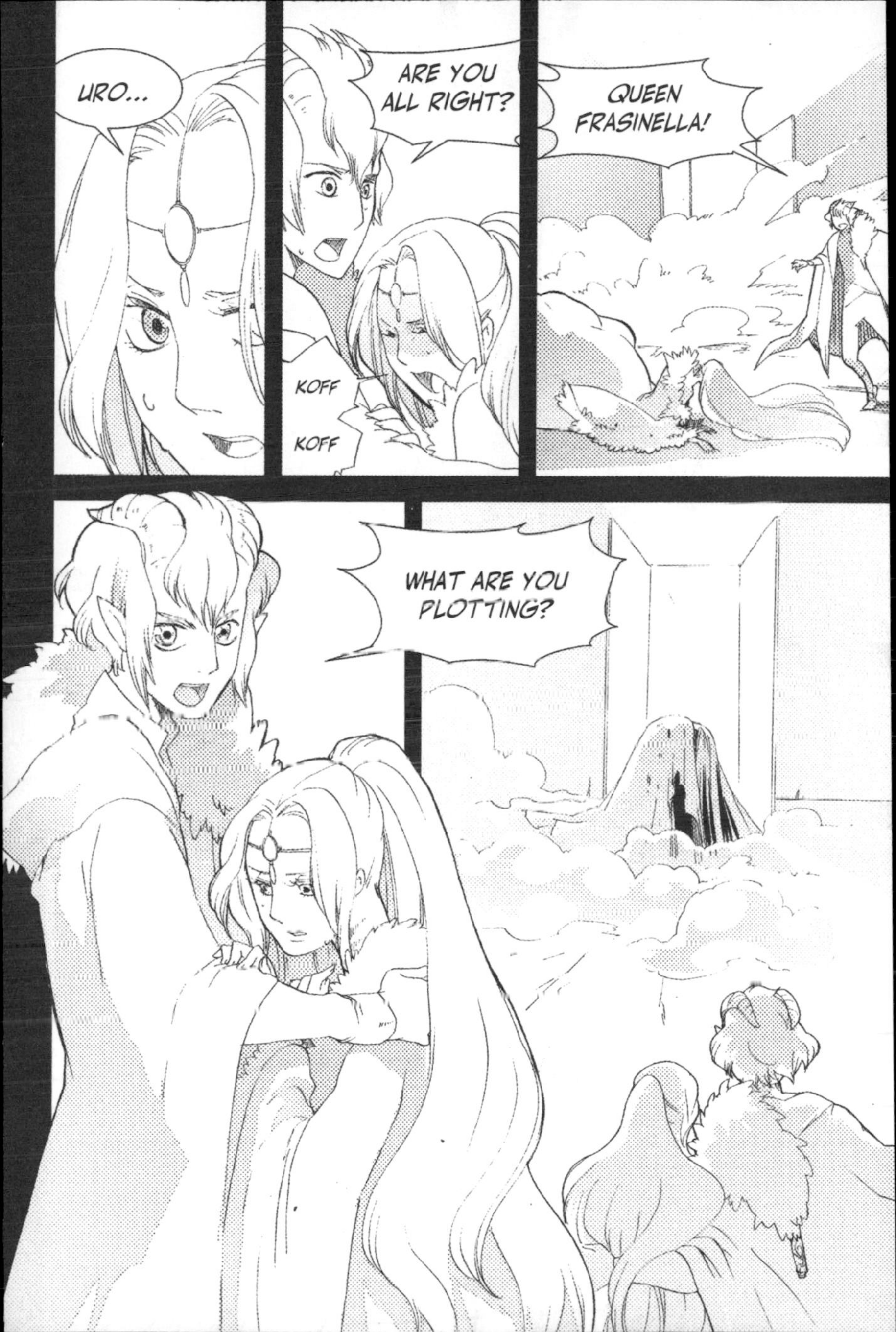
URO...
ARE YOU ALL RIGHT?
KOFF
KOFF
QUEEN FRASINELLA!
WHAT ARE YOU PLOTTING?

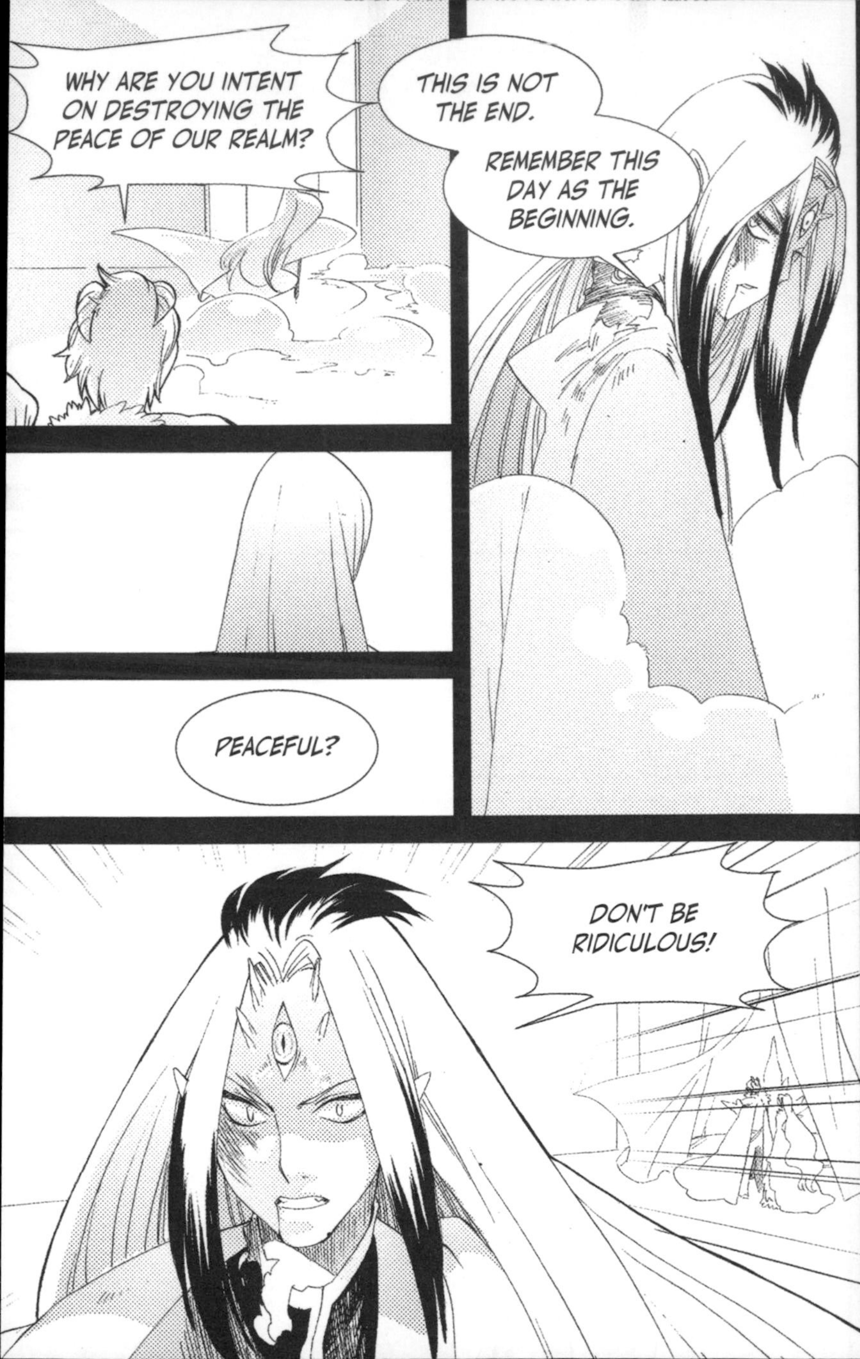
THIS IS NOT THE END.
REMEMBER THIS DAY AS THE BEGINNING.
WHY ARE YOU INTENT ON DESTROYING THE PEACE OF OUR REALM?
PEACEFUL?
DON'T BE RIDICULOUS!

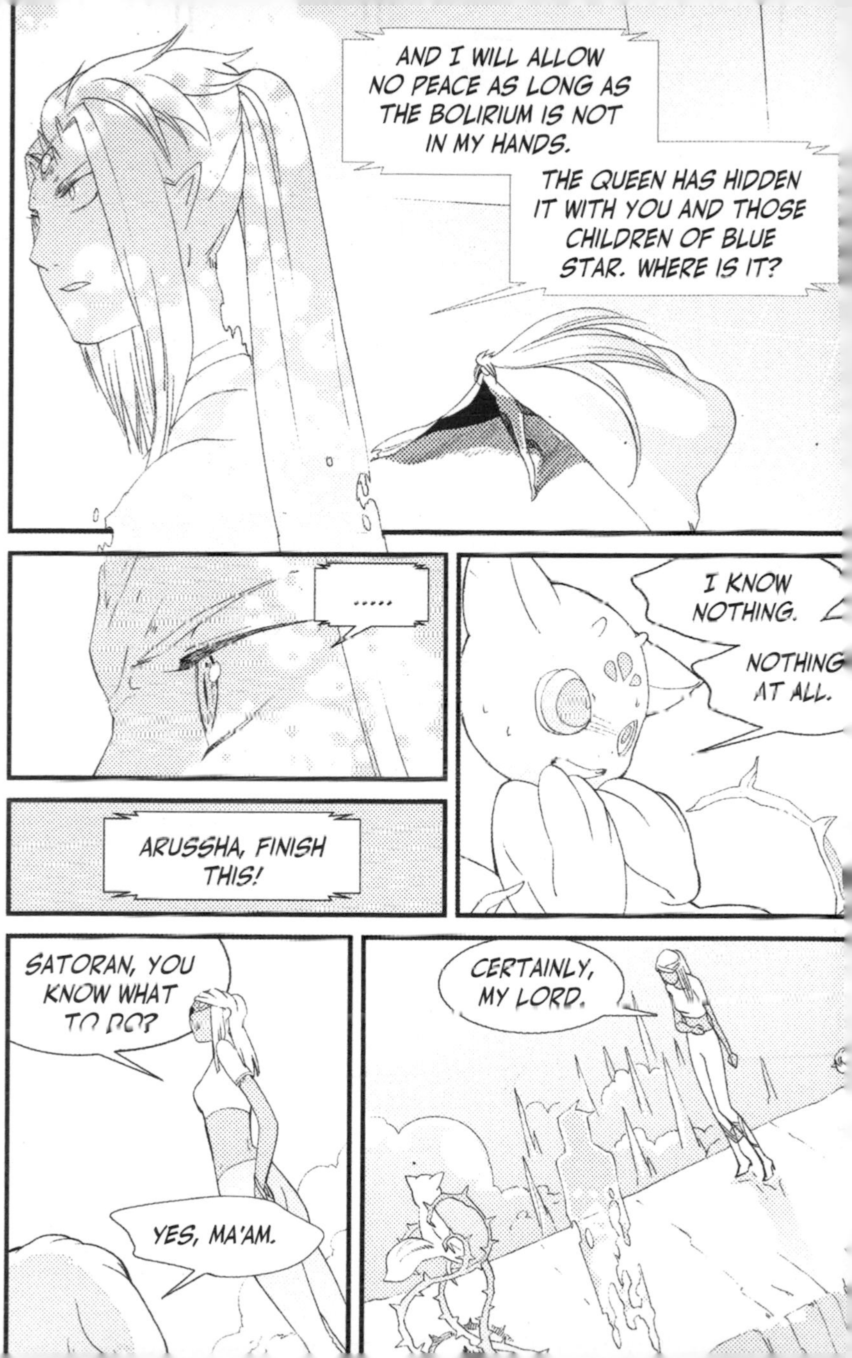
AND I WILL ALLOW NO PEACE AS LONG AS THE BOLIRIUM IS NOT IN MY HANDS.
THE QUEEN HAS HIDDEN IT WITH YOU AND THOSE CHILDREN OF BLUE STAR. WHERE IS IT?
I KNOW NOTHING.
NOTHING AT ALL.
......
ARUSSHA, FINISH THIS!
CERTAINLY, MY LORD.
SATORAN, YOU KNOW WHAT TO DO?
YES, MA'AM.

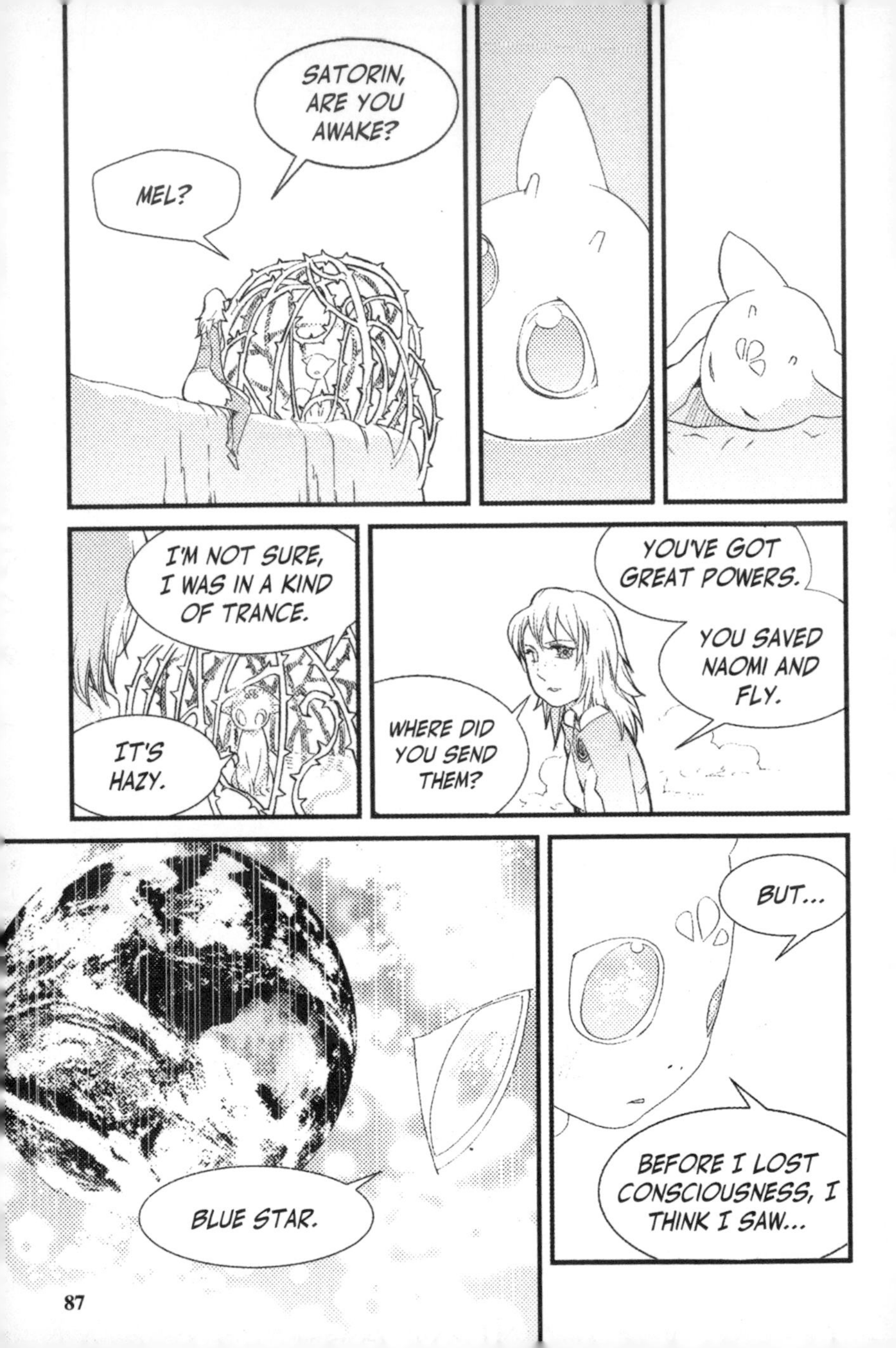
SATORIN, ARE YOU AWAKE?
MEL?
YOU'VE GOT GREAT POWERS.
YOU SAVED NAOMI AND FLY.
WHERE DID YOU SEND THEM?
I'M NOT SURE, I WAS IN A KIND OF TRANCE.
IT'S HAZY.
BUT...
BEFORE I LOST CONSCIOUSNESS, I THINK I SAW...
BLUE STAR.

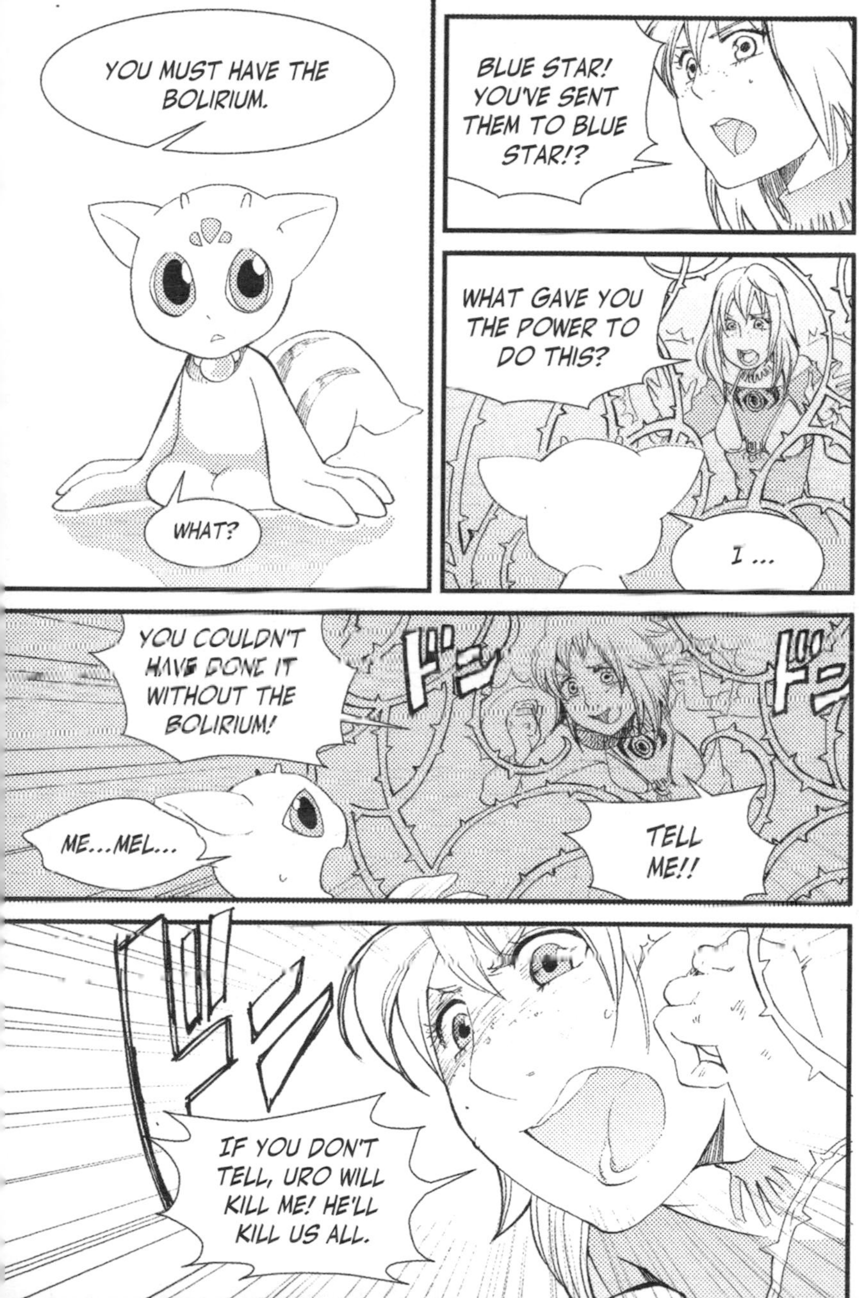

BLUE STAR! YOU'VE SENT THEM TO BLUE STAR!?
WHAT GAVE YOU THE POWER TO DO THIS?
I ...
YOU MUST HAVE THE BOLIRIUM.
WHAT?
ドン
ドン
YOU COULDN'T HAVE DONE IT WITHOUT THE BOLIRIUM!
TELL ME!!
ME...MEL...
IF YOU DON'T TELL, URO WILL KILL ME! HE'LL KILL US ALL.

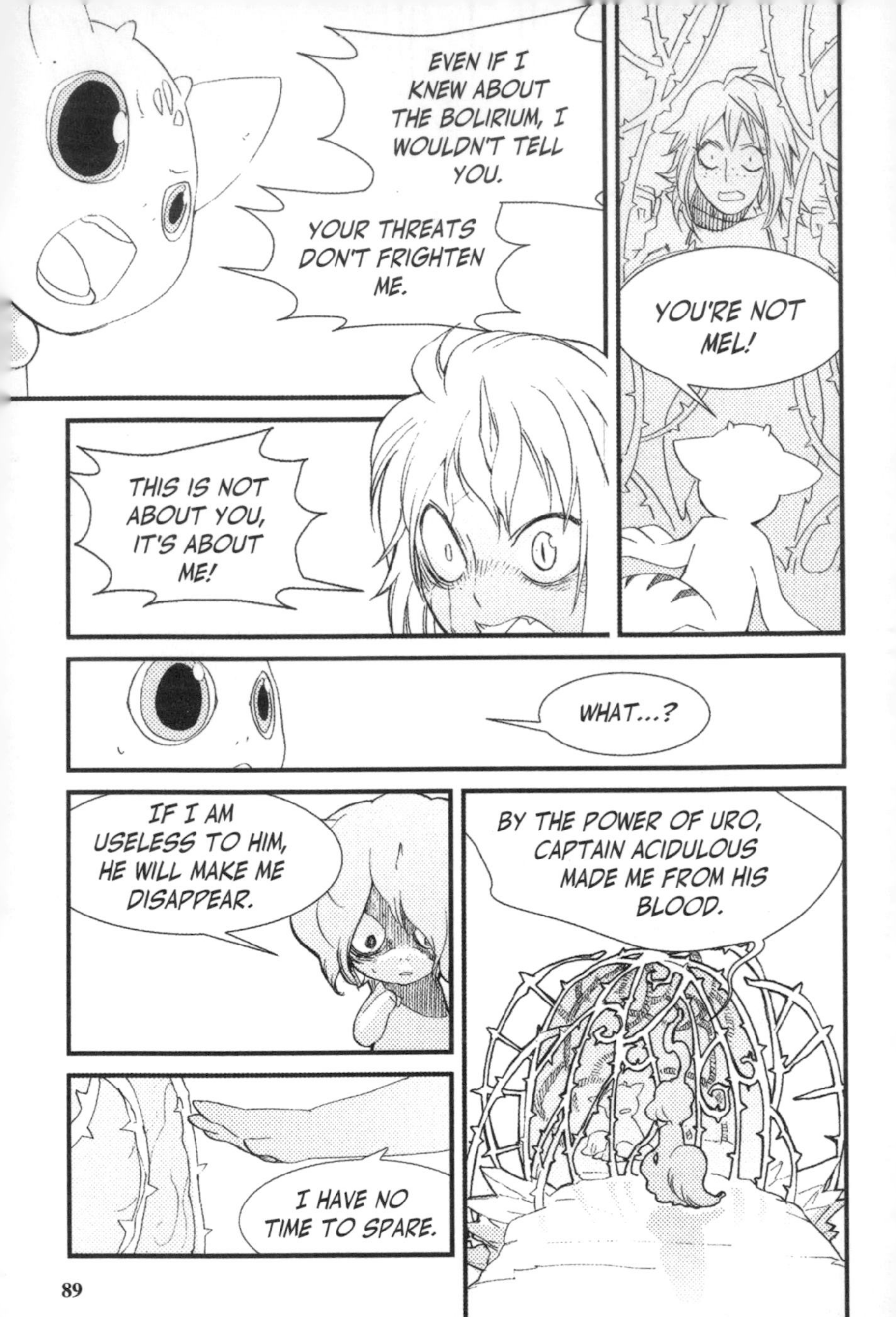
YOU'RE NOT MEL!
EVEN IF I KNEW ABOUT THE BOLIRIUM, I WOULDN'T TELL YOU.
YOUR THREATS DON'T FRIGHTEN ME.
THIS IS NOT ABOUT YOU, IT'S ABOUT ME!
WHAT...?
BY THE POWER OF URO, CAPTAIN ACIDULOUS MADE ME FROM HIS BLOOD.
IF I AM USELESS TO HIM, HE WILL MAKE ME DISAPPEAR.
I HAVE NO TIME TO SPARE.

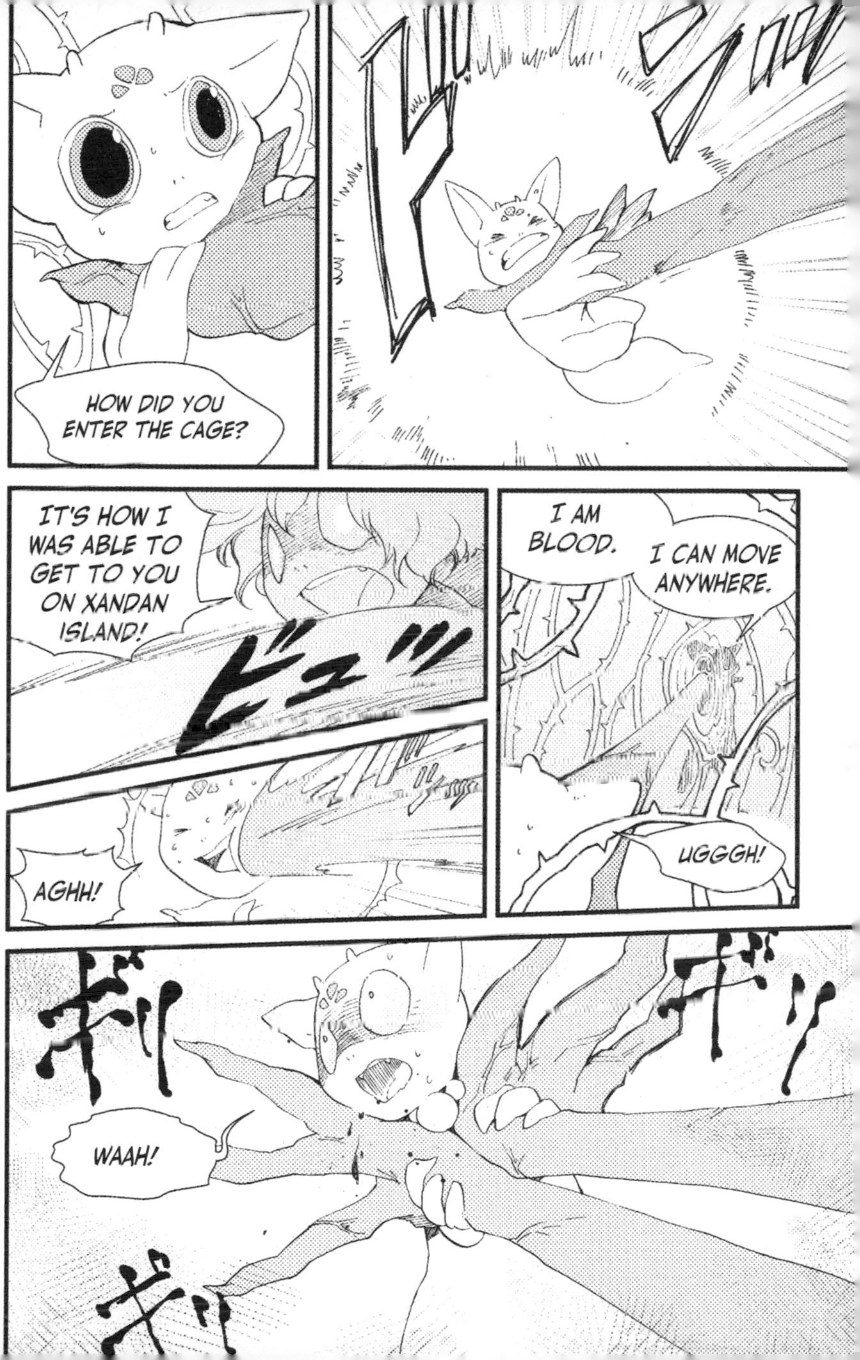
HOW DID YOU ENTER THE CAGE?
I AM BLOOD.
I CAN MOVE ANYWHERE.
IT'S HOW I WAS ABLE TO GET TO YOU ON XANDAN ISLAND!
ビュッ
AGHH!
UGGGH!
ギリ
ギリ
WAAH!
ギリ

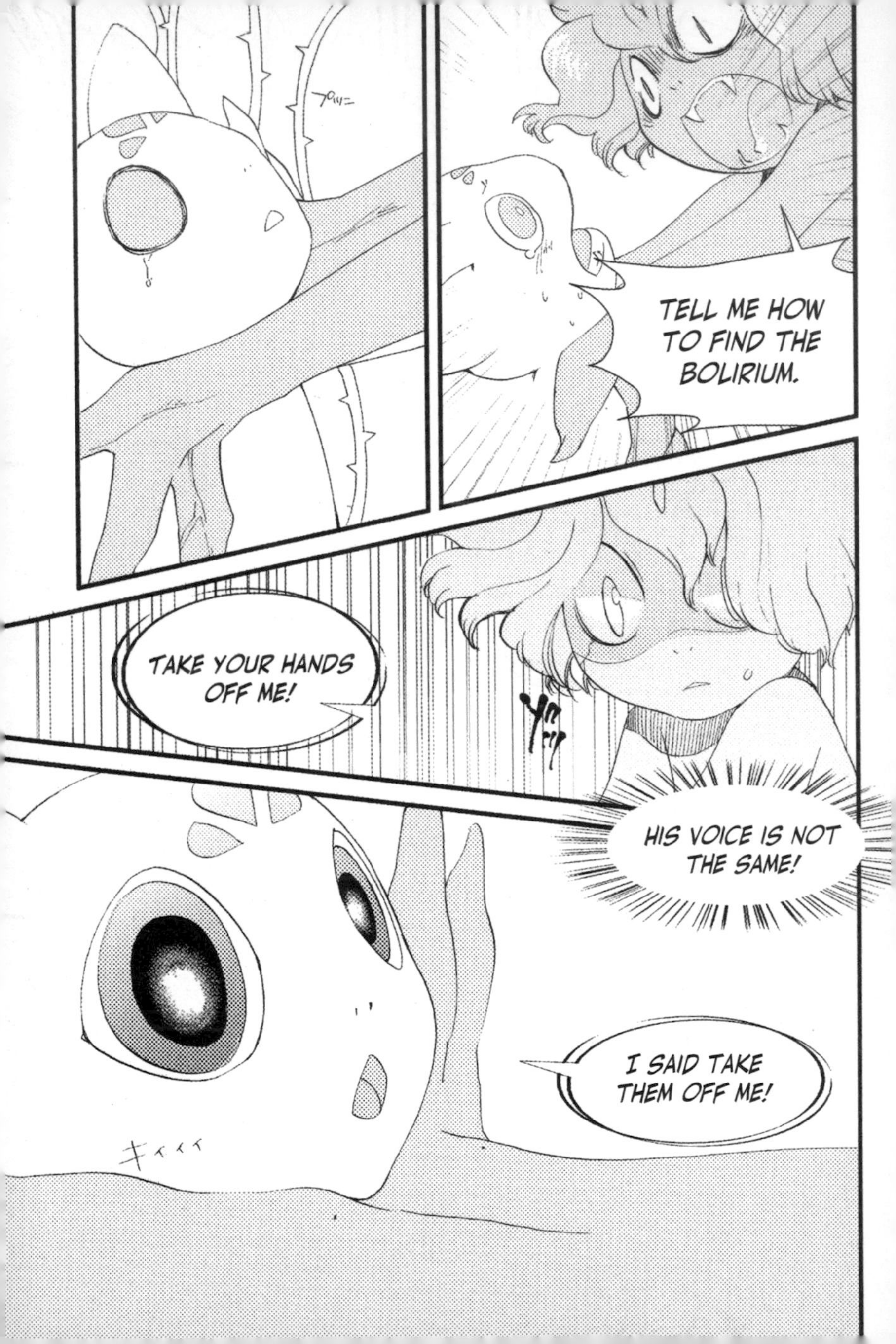
TELL ME HOW TO FIND THE BOLIRIUM.
TAKE YOUR HANDS OFF ME!
HIS VOICE IS NOT THE SAME!
I SAID TAKE THEM OFF ME!

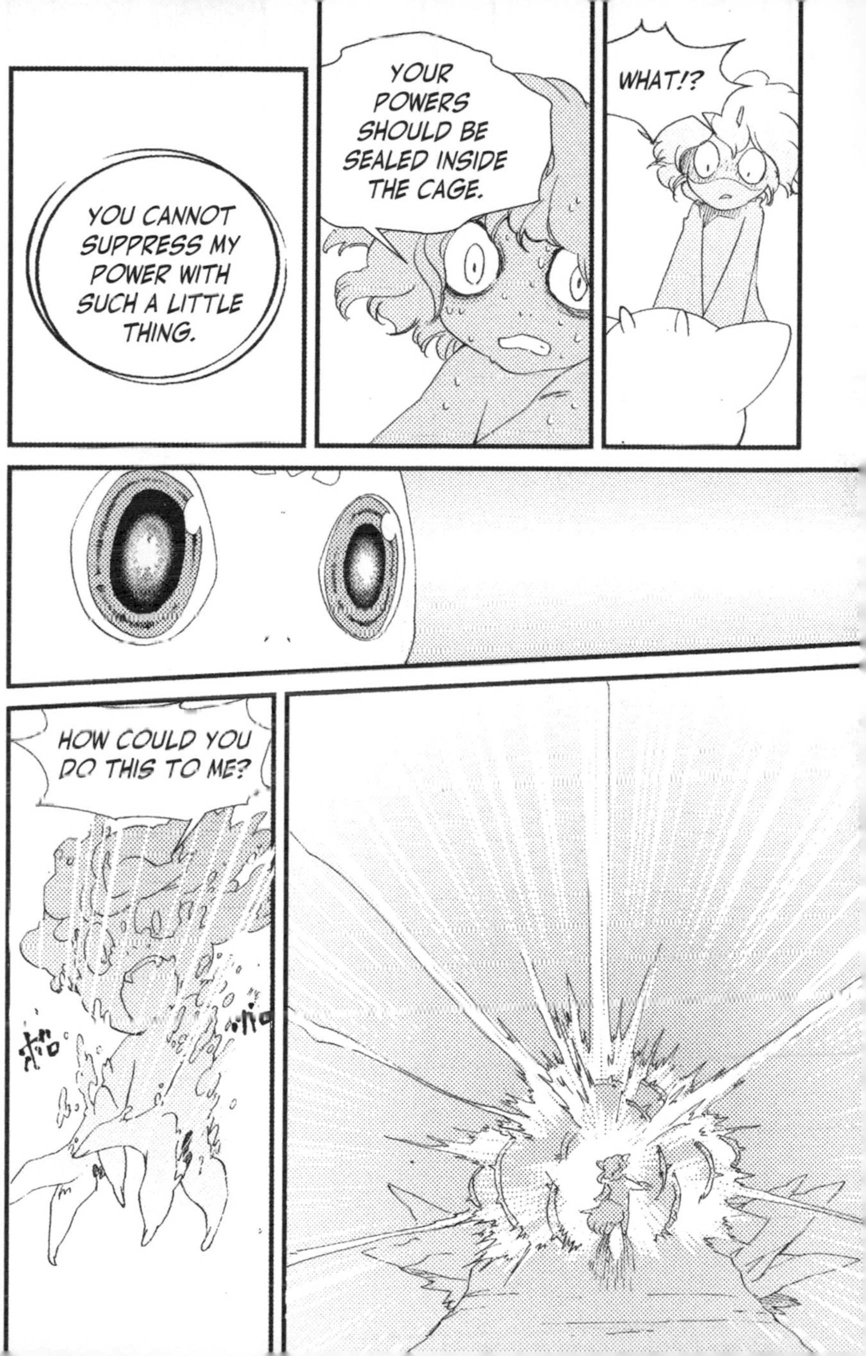
WHAT!?
YOUR POWERS SHOULD BE SEALED INSIDE THE CAGE.
YOU CANNOT SUPPRESS MY POWER WITH SUCH A LITTLE THING.
HOW COULD YOU DO THIS TO ME?

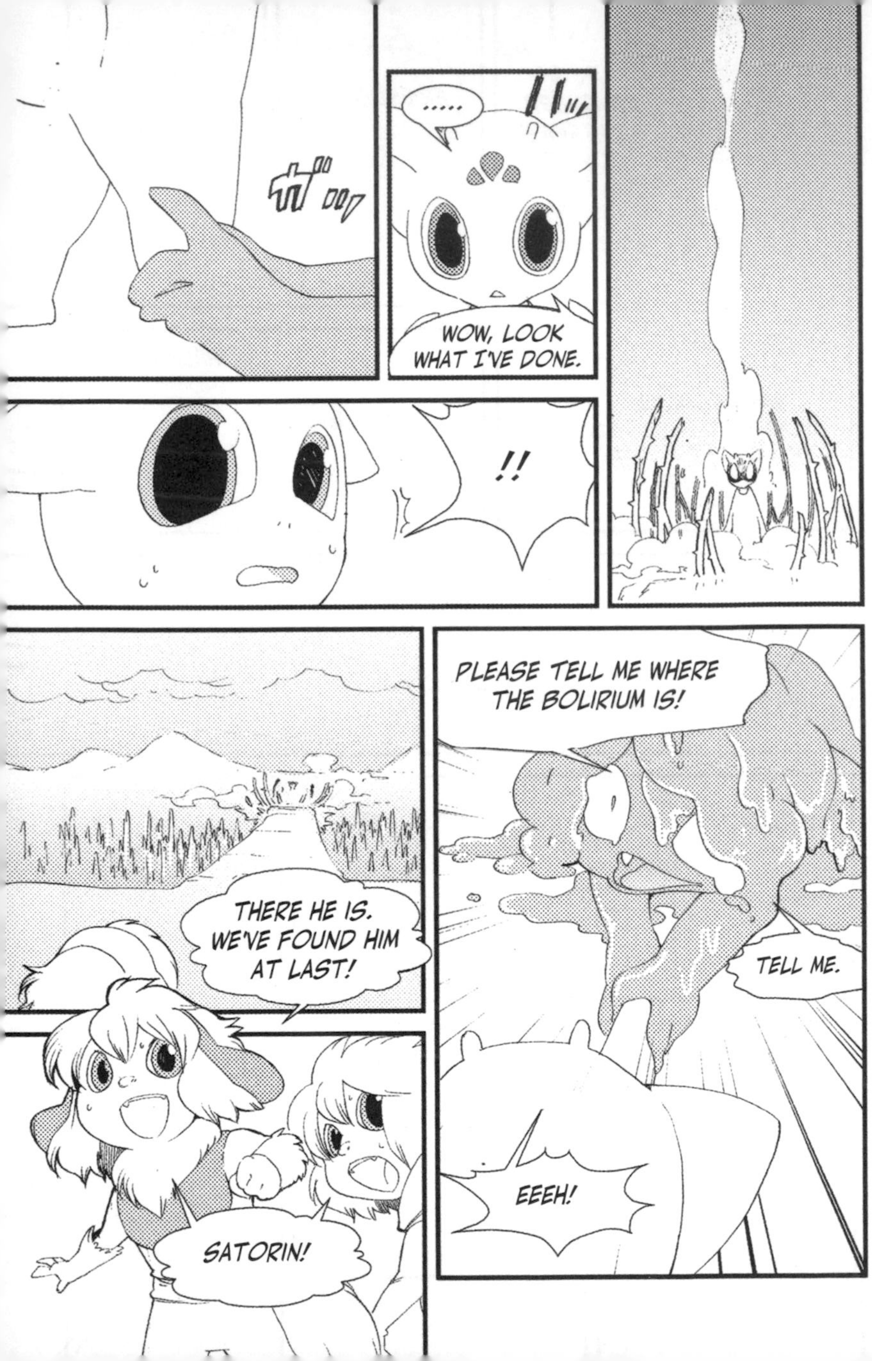
......
WOW, LOOK WHAT I'VE DONE.
!!
PLEASE TELL ME WHERE THE BOLIRIUM IS!
TELL ME.
EEEH!
THERE HE IS. WE'VE FOUND HIM AT LAST!
SATORIN!

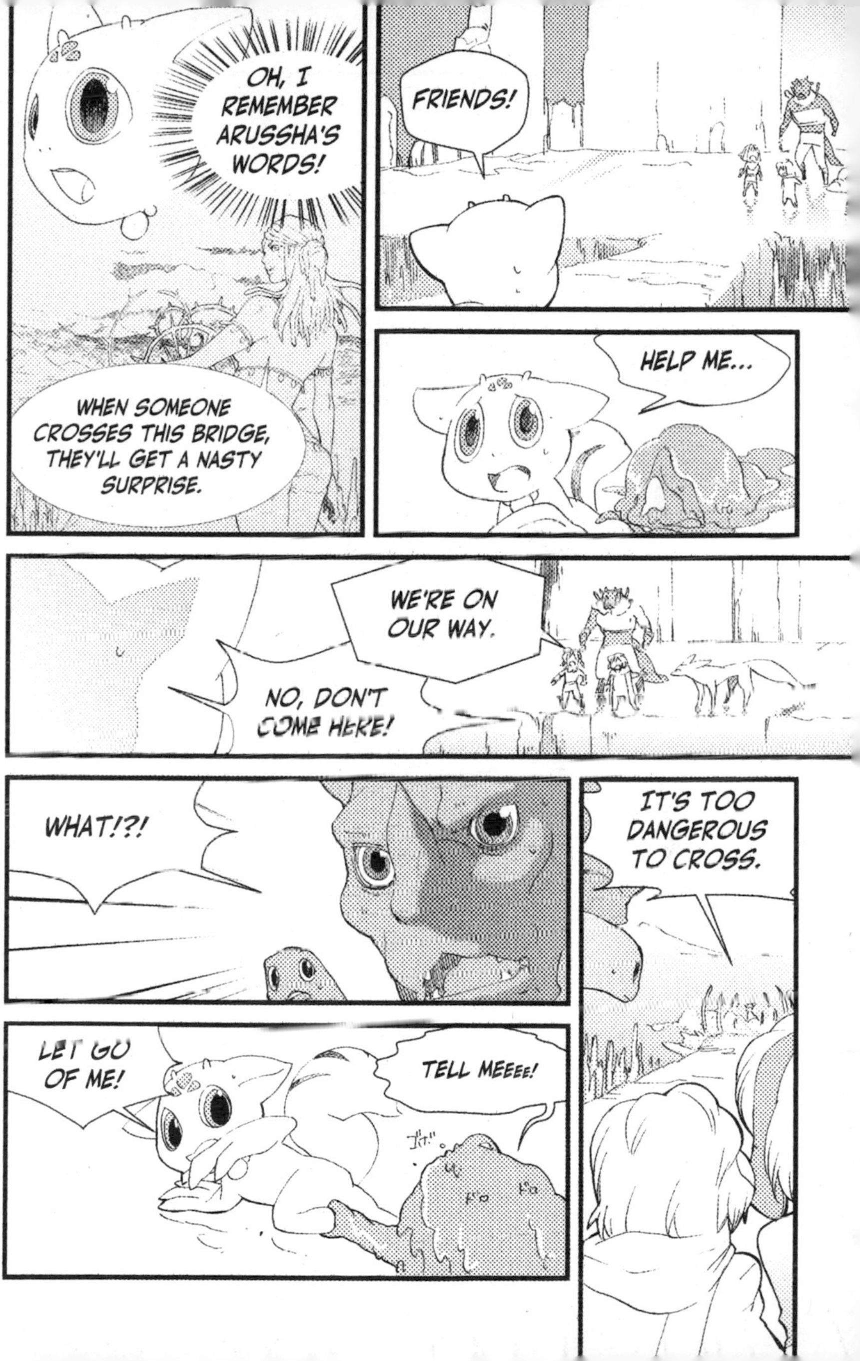
FRIENDS!
HELP ME...
OH, I REMEMBER ARUSSHA'S WORDS!
WHEN SOMEONE CROSSES THIS BRIDGE, THEY'LL GET A NASTY SURPRISE.
WE'RE ON OUR WAY.
NO, DON'T COME HERE!
IT'S TOO DANGEROUS TO CROSS.
WHAT!?!
TELL MEEEEE!
LET GO OF ME!

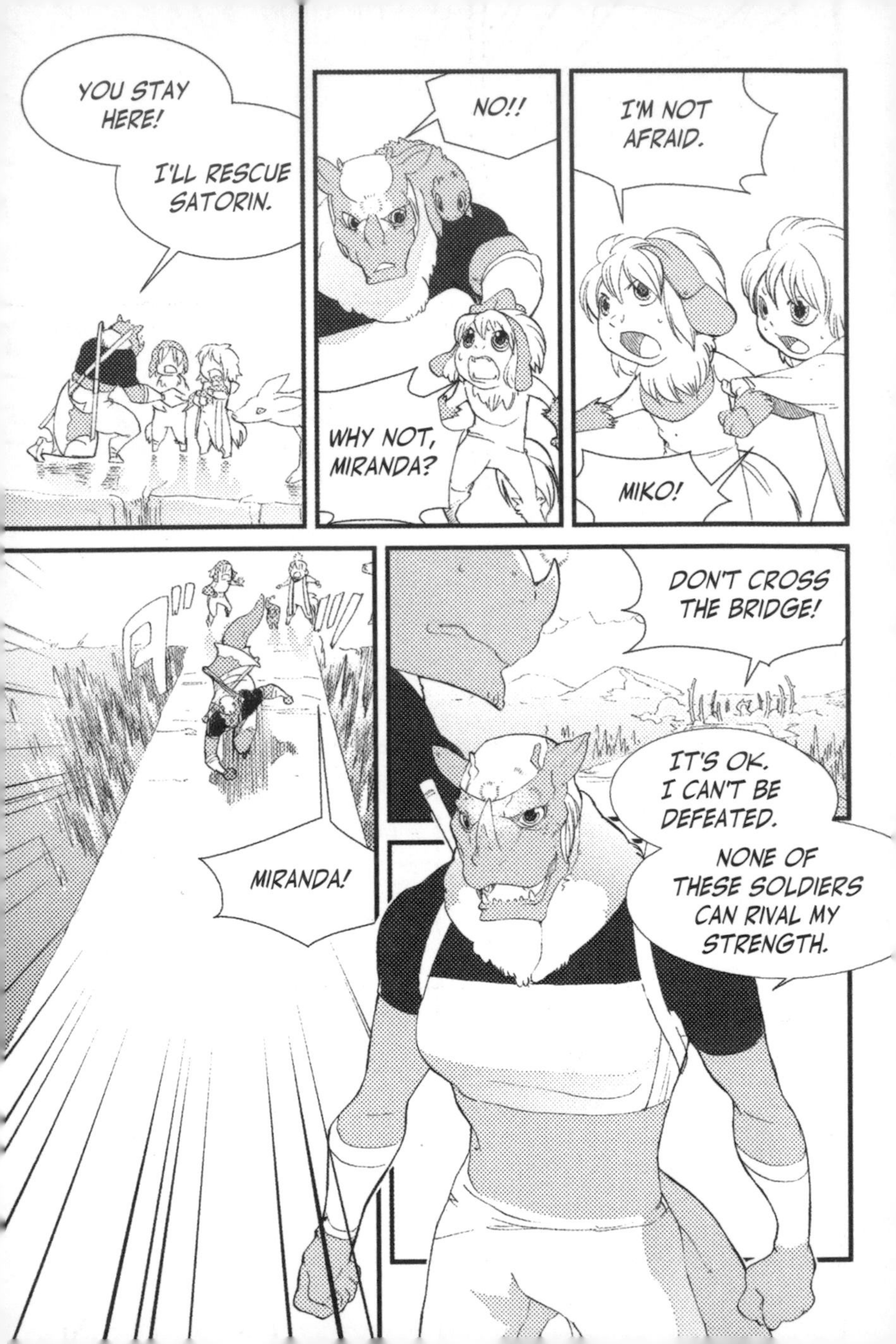
YOU STAY HERE!
I'LL RESCUE SATORIN.
NO!!
WHY NOT, MIRANDA?
I'M NOT AFRAID.
MIKO!
MIRANDA!
DON'T CROSS THE BRIDGE!
IT'S OK. I CAN'T BE DEFEATED.
NONE OF THESE SOLDIERS CAN RIVAL MY STRENGTH.

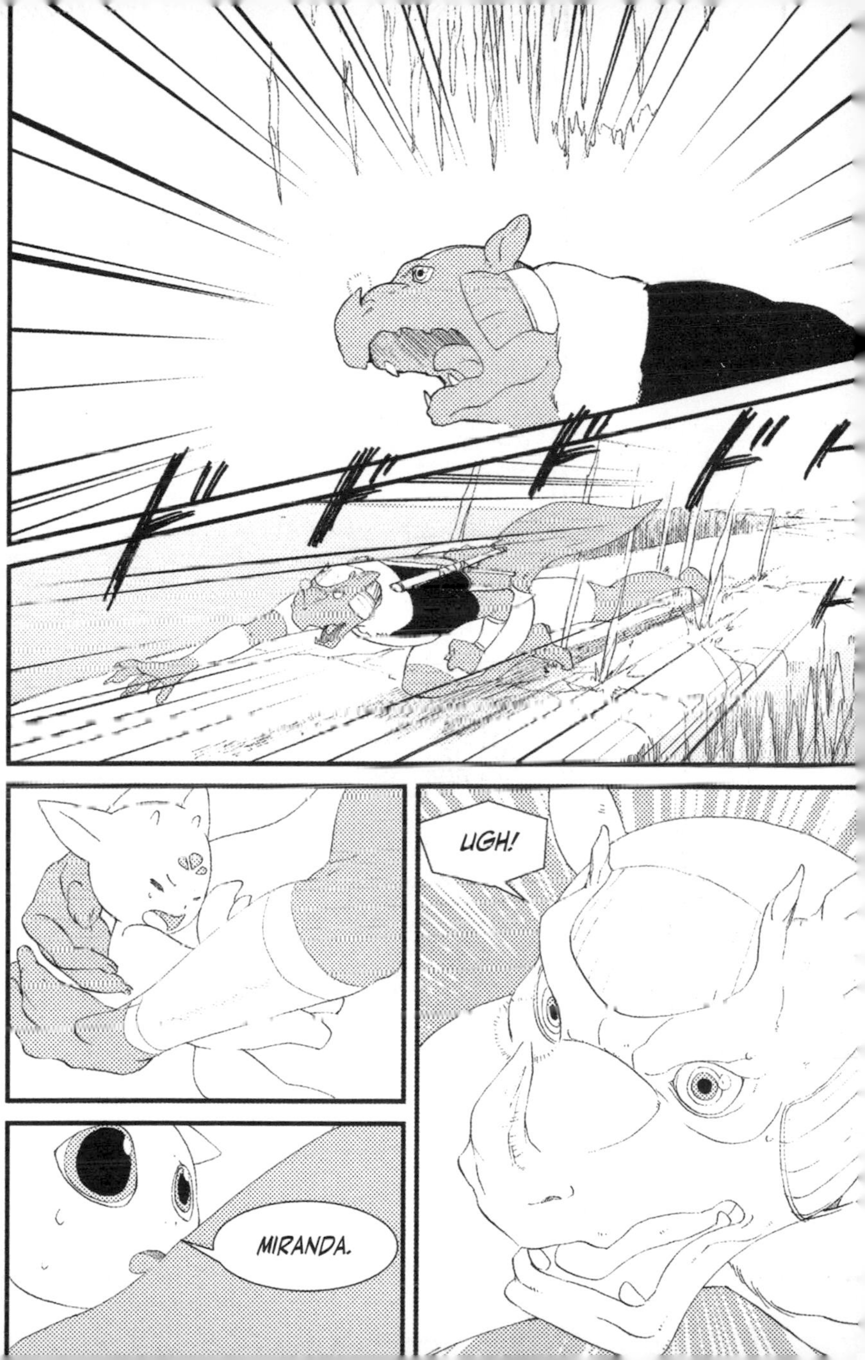
UGH!
MIRANDA.

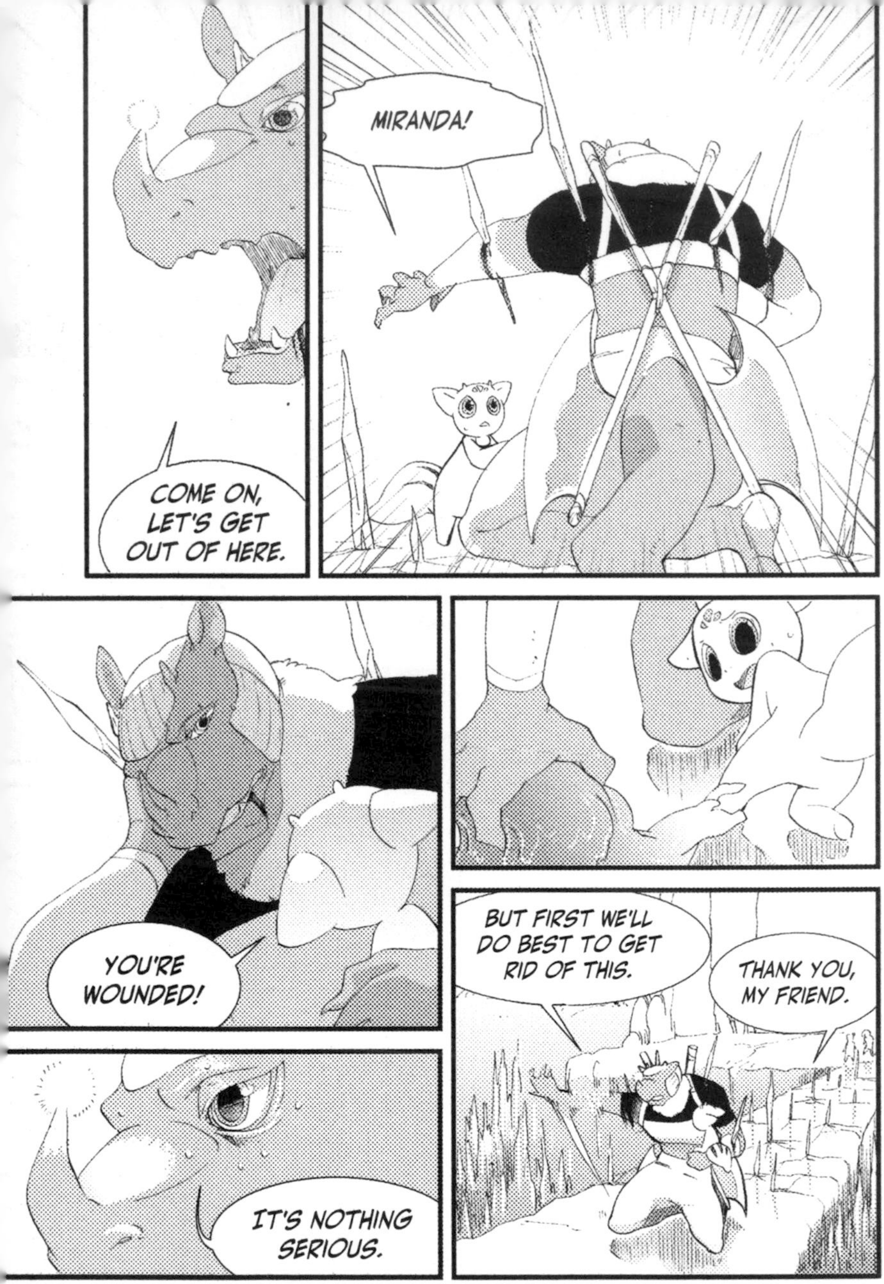
MIRANDA!
COME ON, LET'S GET OUT OF HERE.
YOU'RE WOUNDED!
IT'S NOTHING SERIOUS.
THANK YOU, MY FRIEND.
BUT FIRST WE'LL DO BEST TO GET RID OF THIS.

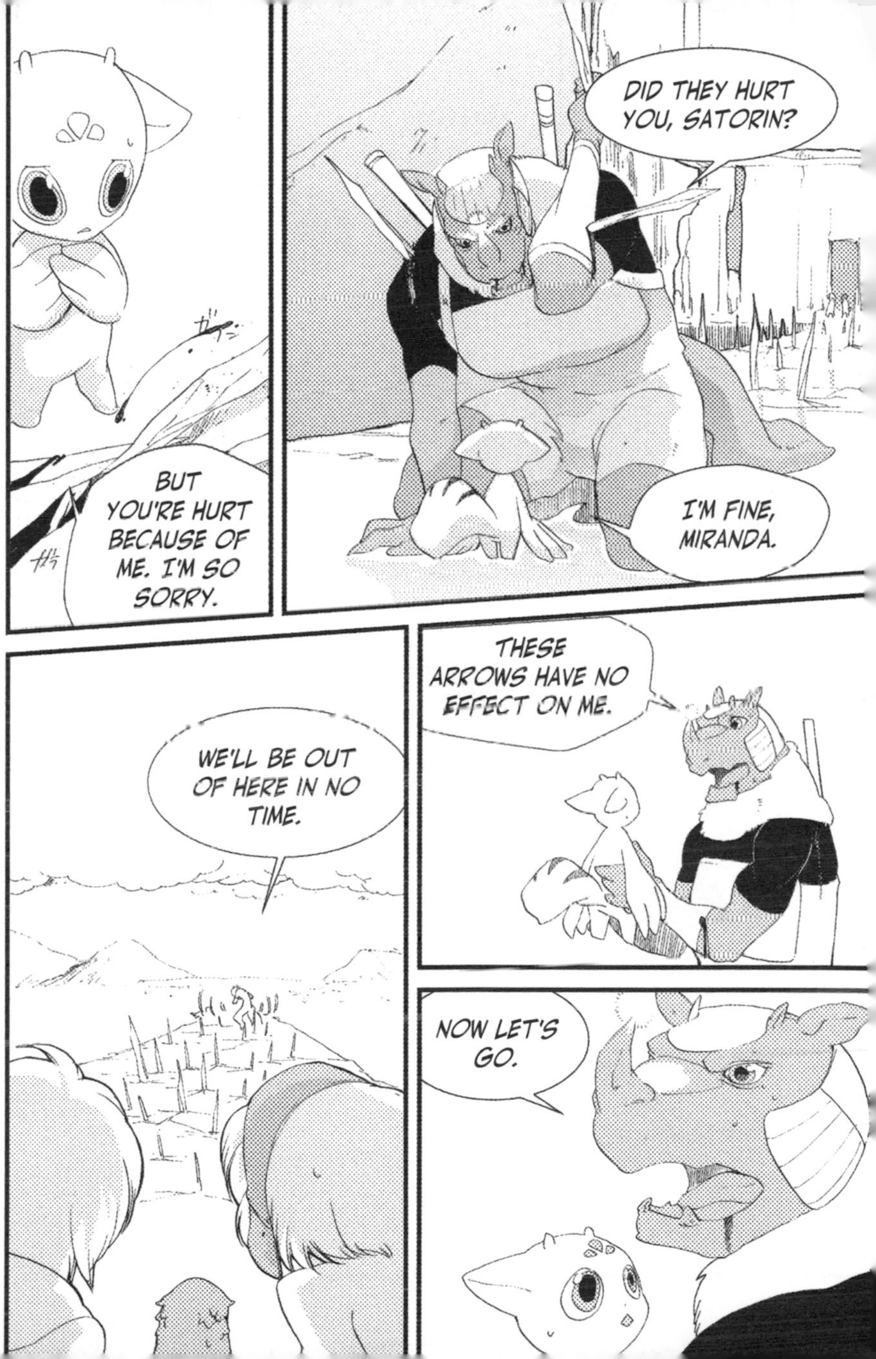
DID THEY HURT YOU, SATORIN?
I'M FINE, MIRANDA.
BUT YOU'RE HURT BECAUSE OF ME. I'M SO SORRY.
THESE ARROWS HAVE NO EFFECT ON ME.
NOW LET'S GO.
WE'LL BE OUT OF HERE IN NO TIME.

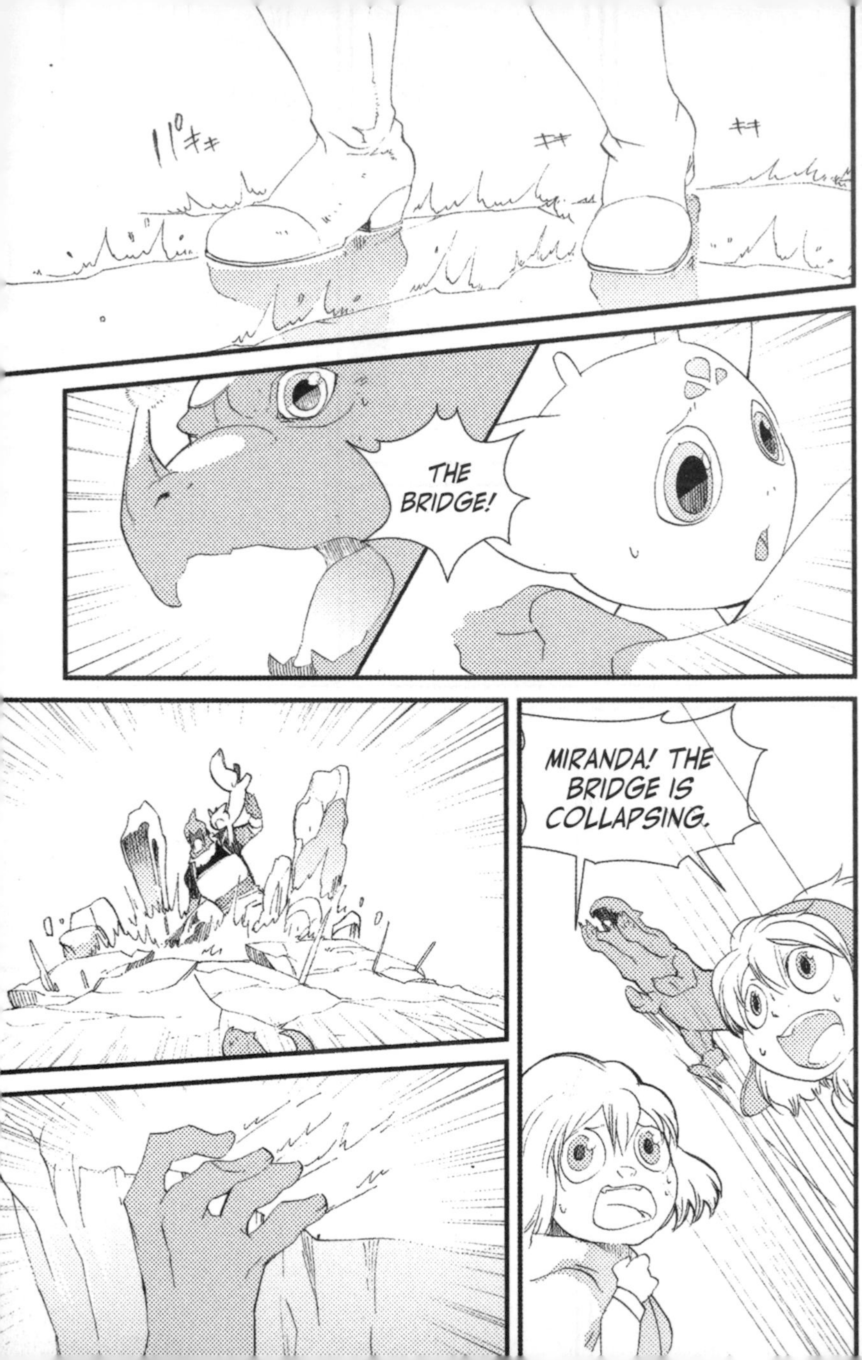
キキ
キキ
パキキ
THE BRIDGE!
MIRANDA! THE BRIDGE IS COLLAPSING.

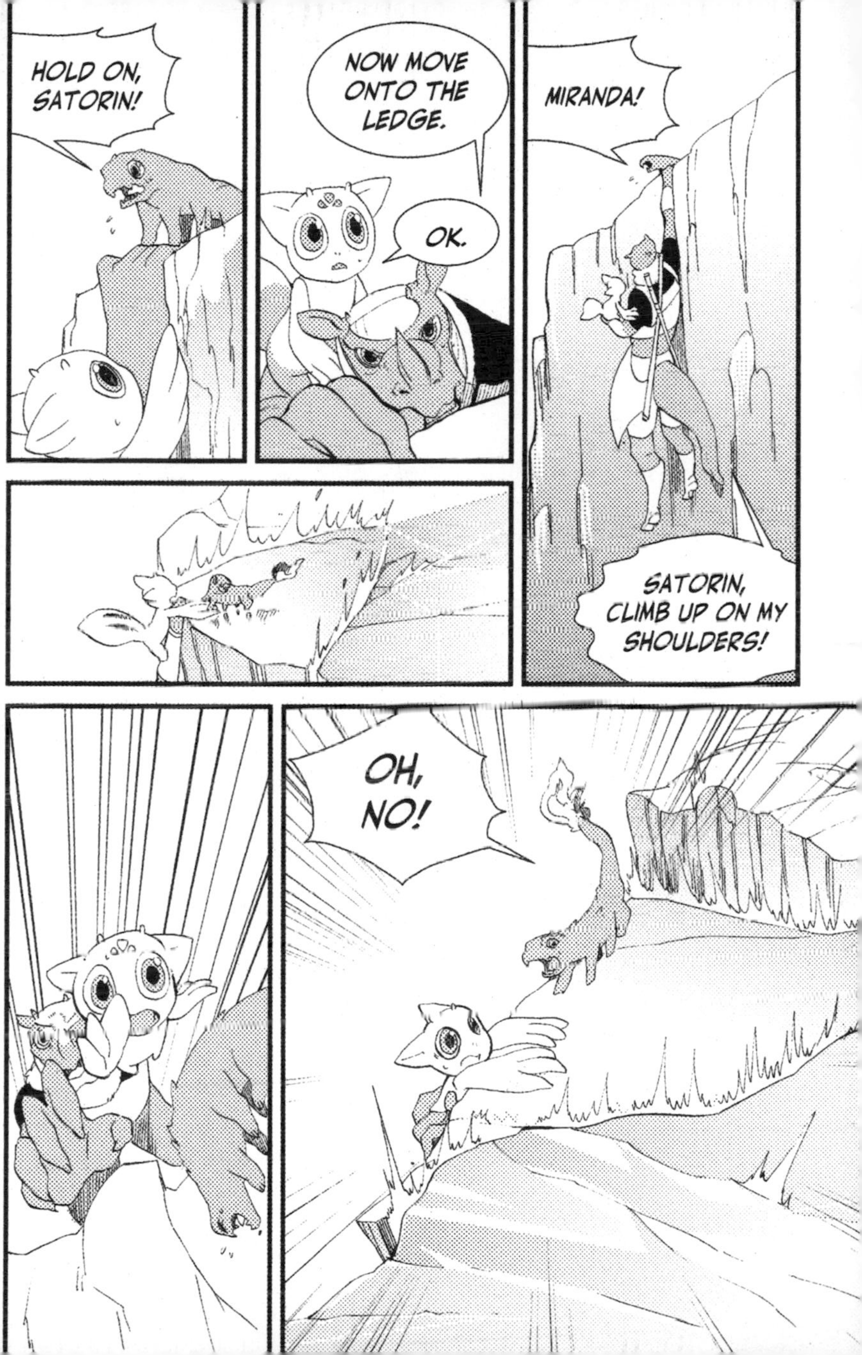
HOLD ON, SATORIN!
NOW MOVE ONTO THE LEDGE.
OK.
MIRANDA!
SATORIN, CLIMB UP ON MY SHOULDERS!
OH, NO!

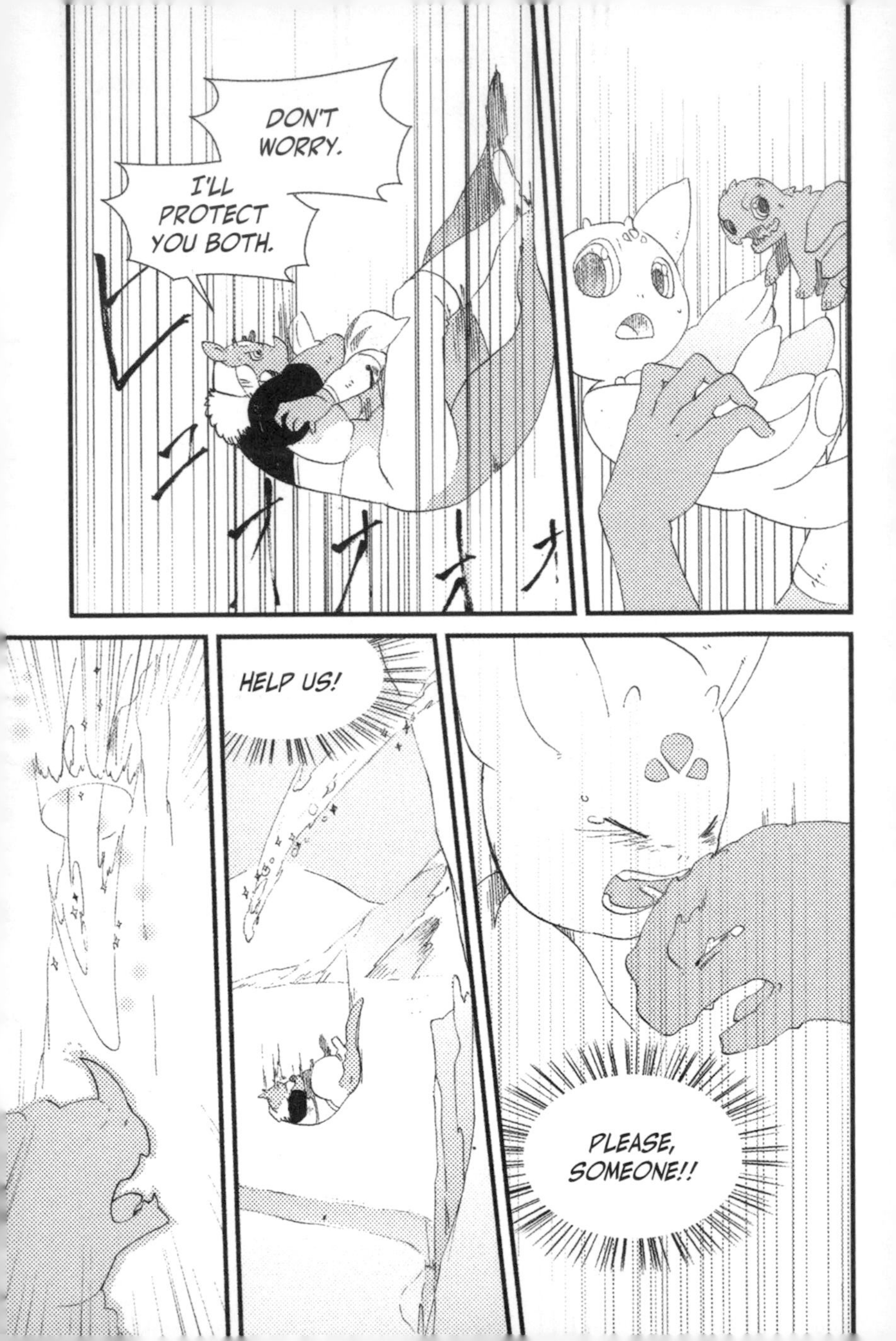
DON'T WORRY.
I'LL PROTECT YOU BOTH.
PLEASE, SOMEONE!!
HELP US!

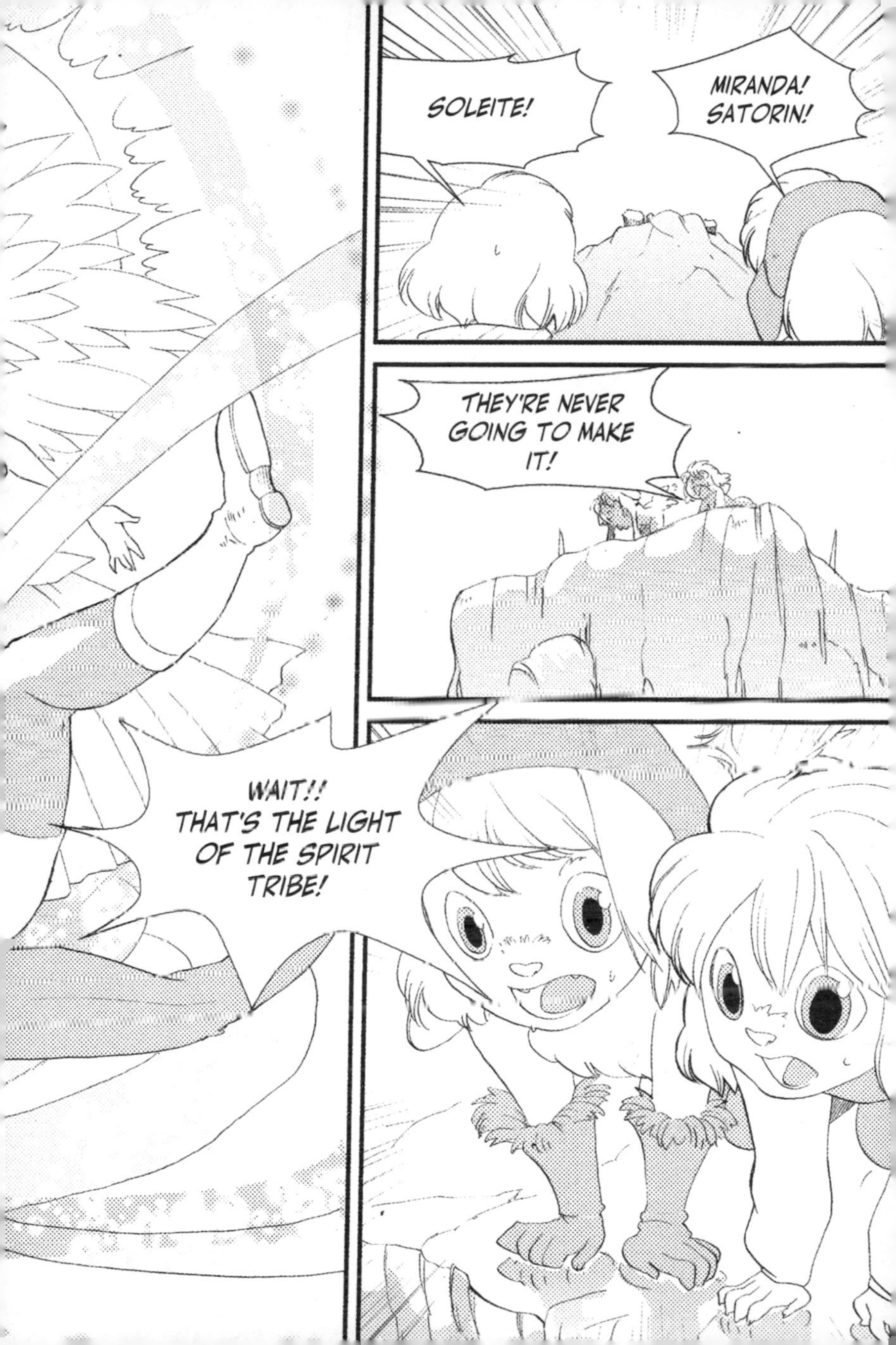
MIRANDA! SATORIN!
SOLEITE!
THEY'RE NEVER GOING TO MAKE IT!
WAIT!! THAT'S THE LIGHT OF THE SPIRIT TRIBE!

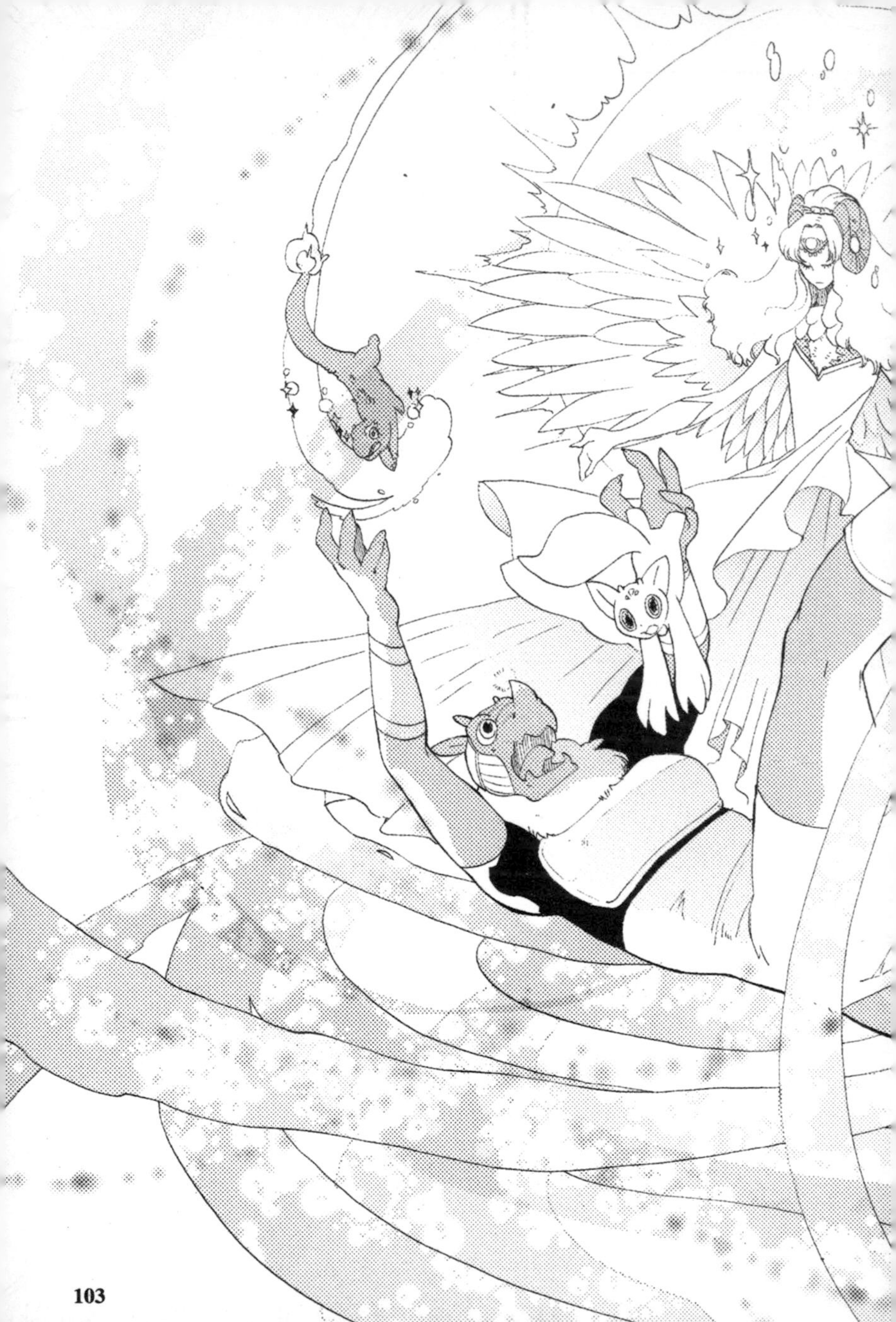

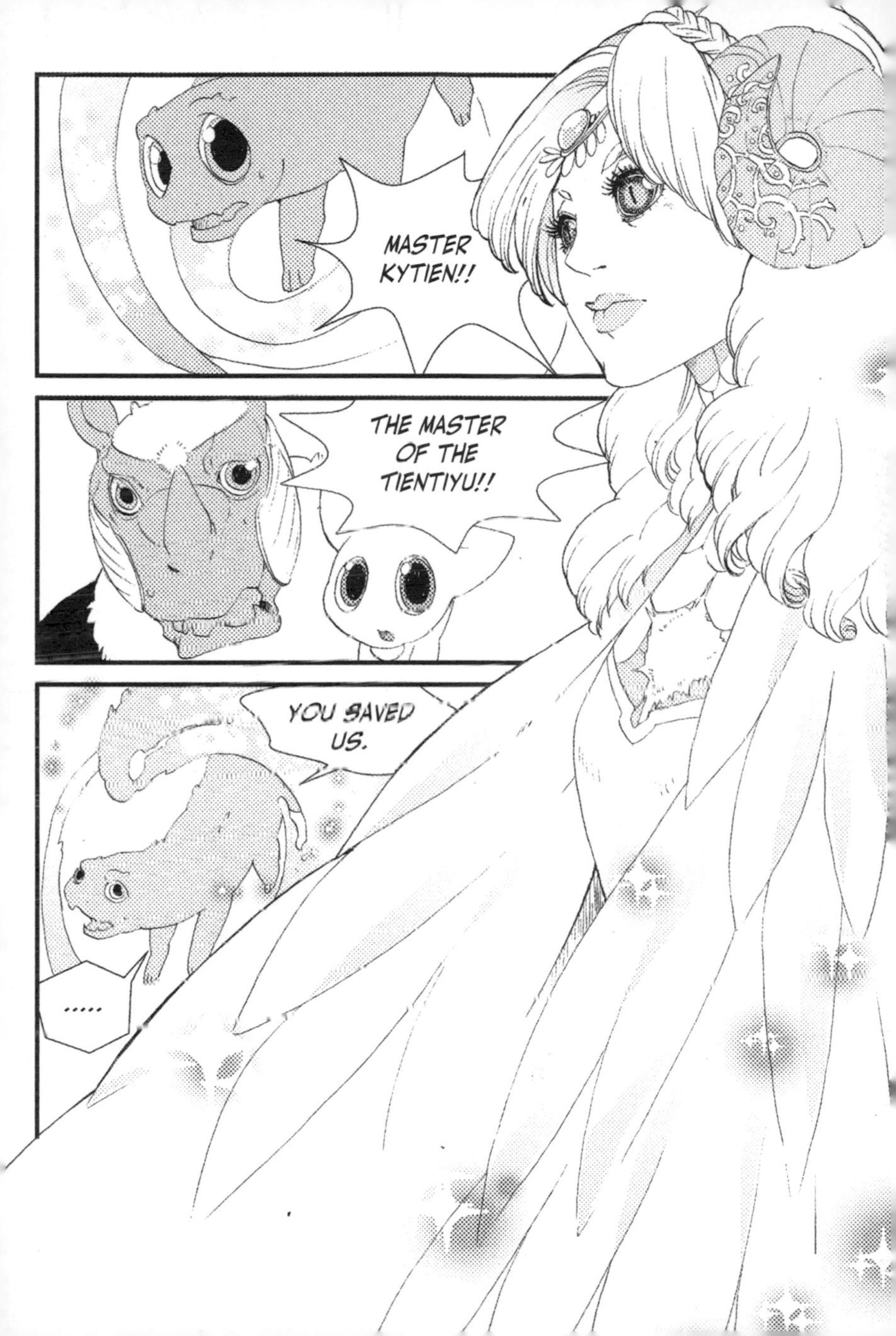
MASTER KYTIEN!!
THE MASTER OF THE TIENTIYU!!
YOU SAVED US.
......

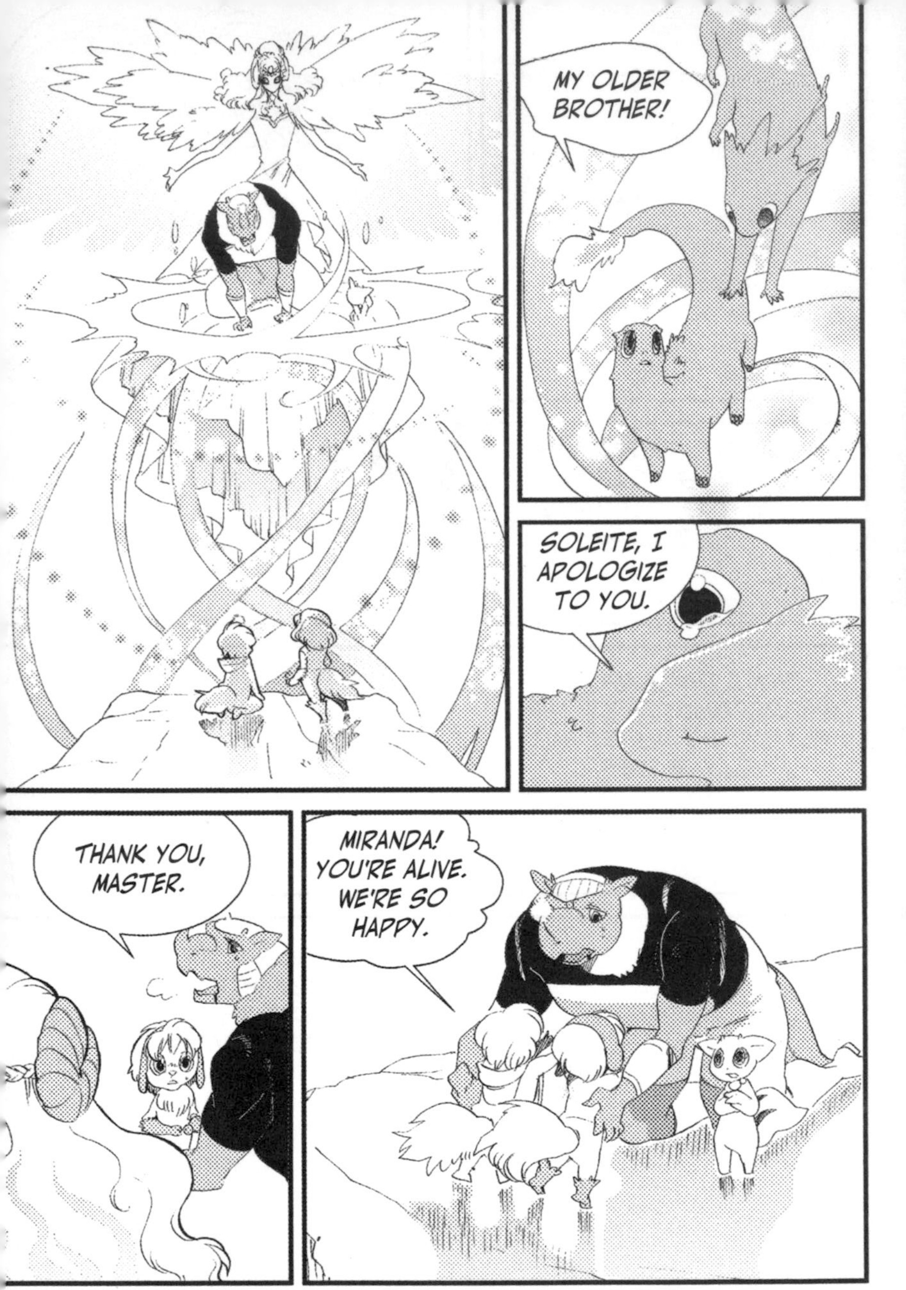
MY OLDER BROTHER!
SOLEITE, I APOLOGIZE TO YOU.
MIRANDA! YOU'RE ALIVE. WE'RE SO HAPPY.
THANK YOU, MASTER.

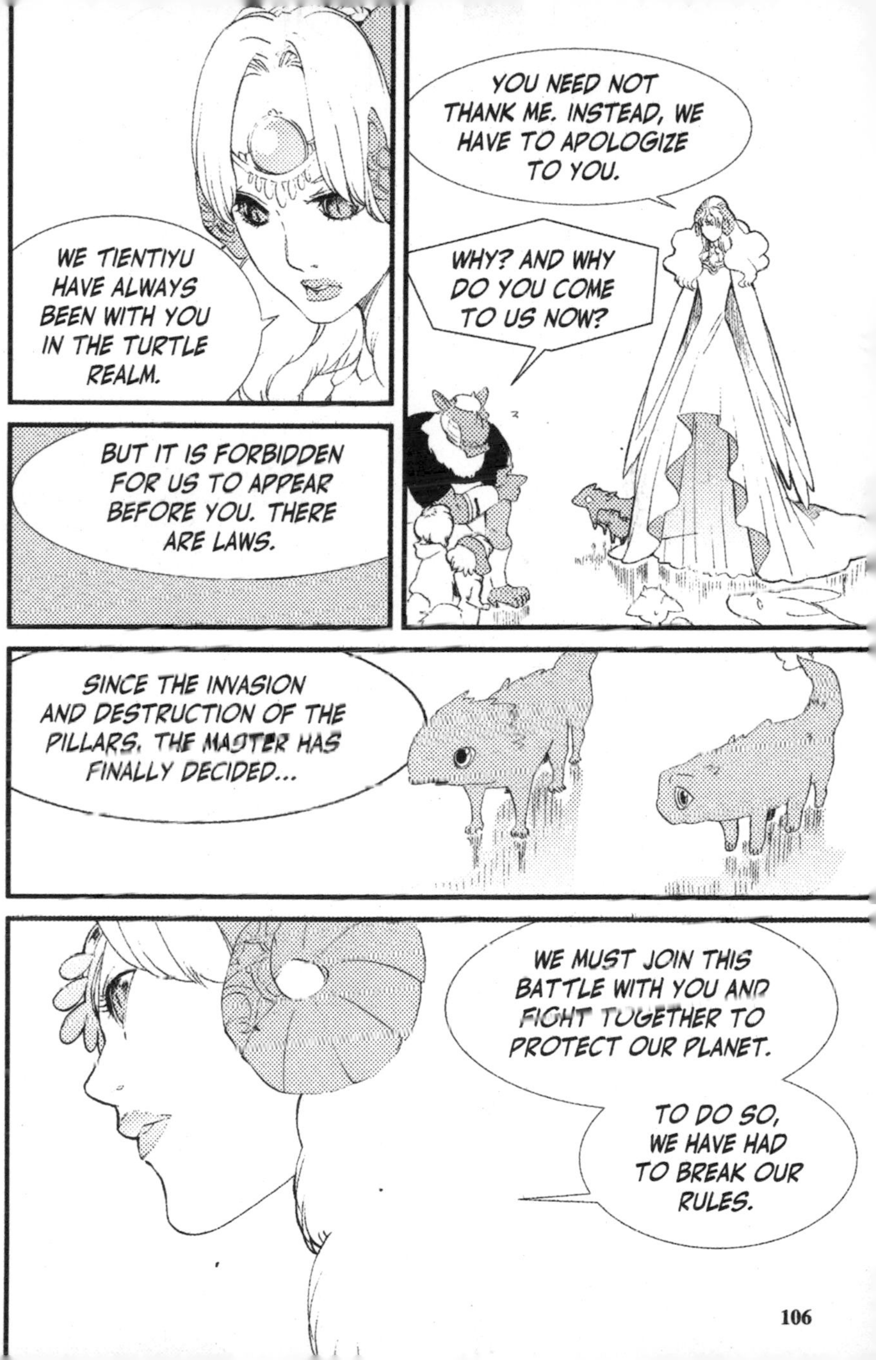
YOU NEED NOT THANK ME. INSTEAD, WE HAVE TO APOLOGIZE TO YOU.
WHY? AND WHY DO YOU COME TO US NOW?
WE TIENTIYU HAVE ALWAYS BEEN WITH YOU IN THE TURTLE REALM.
BUT IT IS FORBIDDEN FOR US TO APPEAR BEFORE YOU. THERE ARE LAWS.
SINCE THE INVASION AND DESTRUCTION OF THE PILLARS, THE MASTER HAS FINALLY DECIDED...
WE MUST JOIN THIS BATTLE WITH YOU AND FIGHT TOGETHER TO PROTECT OUR PLANET.
TO DO SO, WE HAVE HAD TO BREAK OUR RULES.

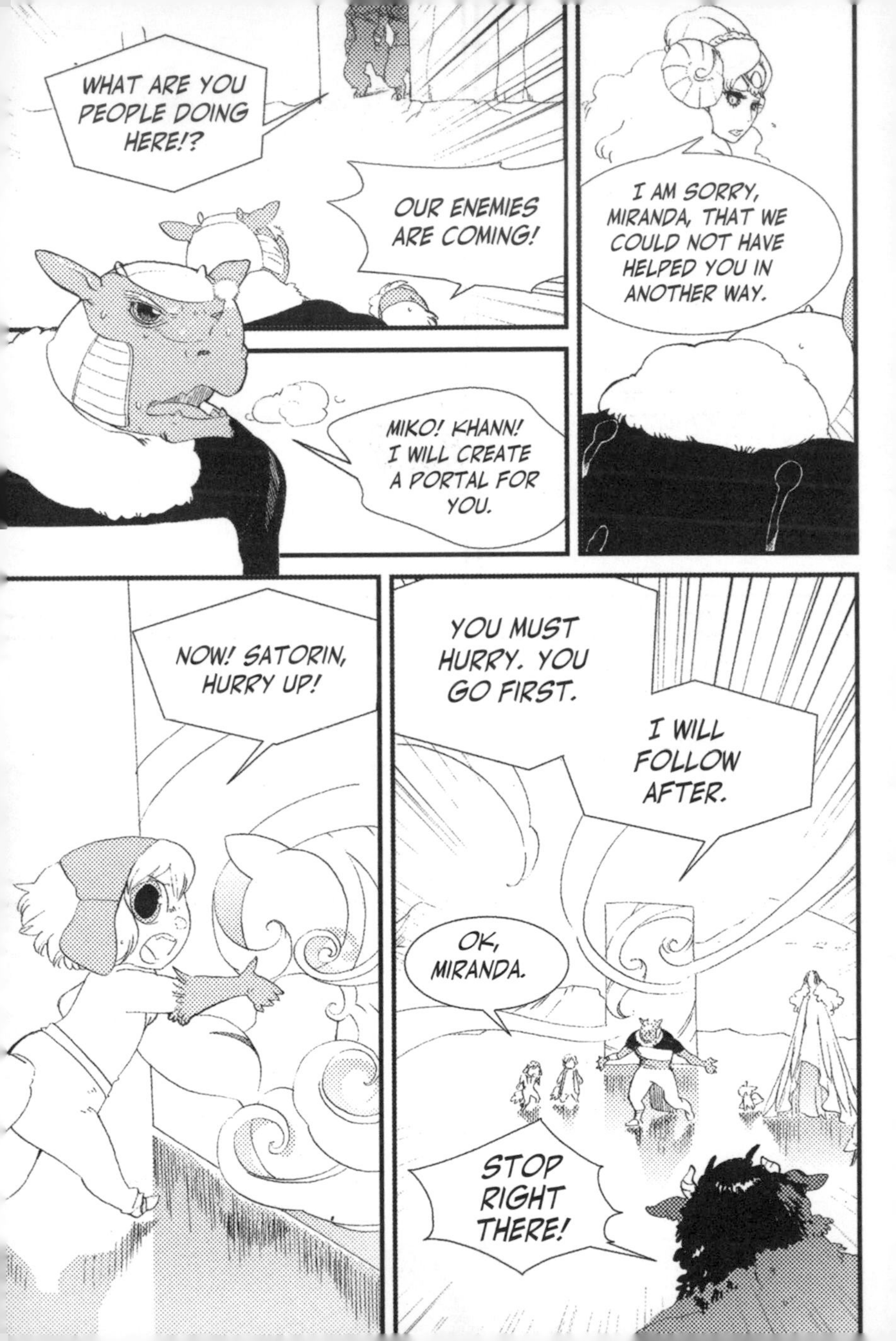
WHAT ARE YOU PEOPLE DOING HERE!?
OUR ENEMIES ARE COMING!
MIKO! KHANN! I WILL CREATE A PORTAL FOR YOU.
I AM SORRY, MIRANDA, THAT WE COULD NOT HAVE HELPED YOU IN ANOTHER WAY.
NOW! SATORIN, HURRY UP!
YOU MUST HURRY. YOU GO FIRST.
I WILL FOLLOW AFTER.
OK, MIRANDA.
STOP RIGHT THERE!

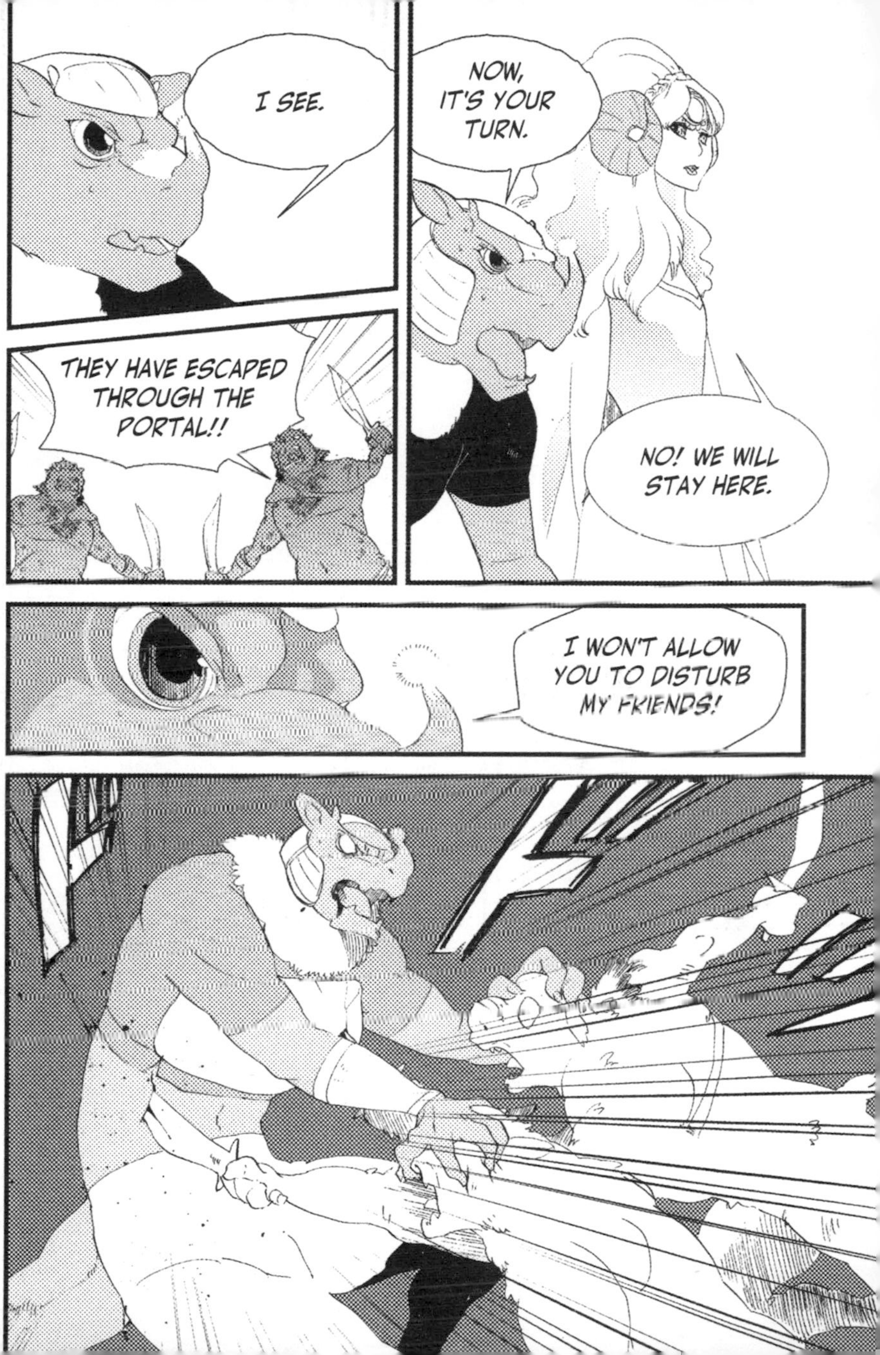
NOW, IT'S YOUR TURN.
NO! WE WILL STAY HERE.
I SEE.
THEY HAVE ESCAPED THROUGH THE PORTAL!!
I WON'T ALLOW YOU TO DISTURB MY FRIENDS!

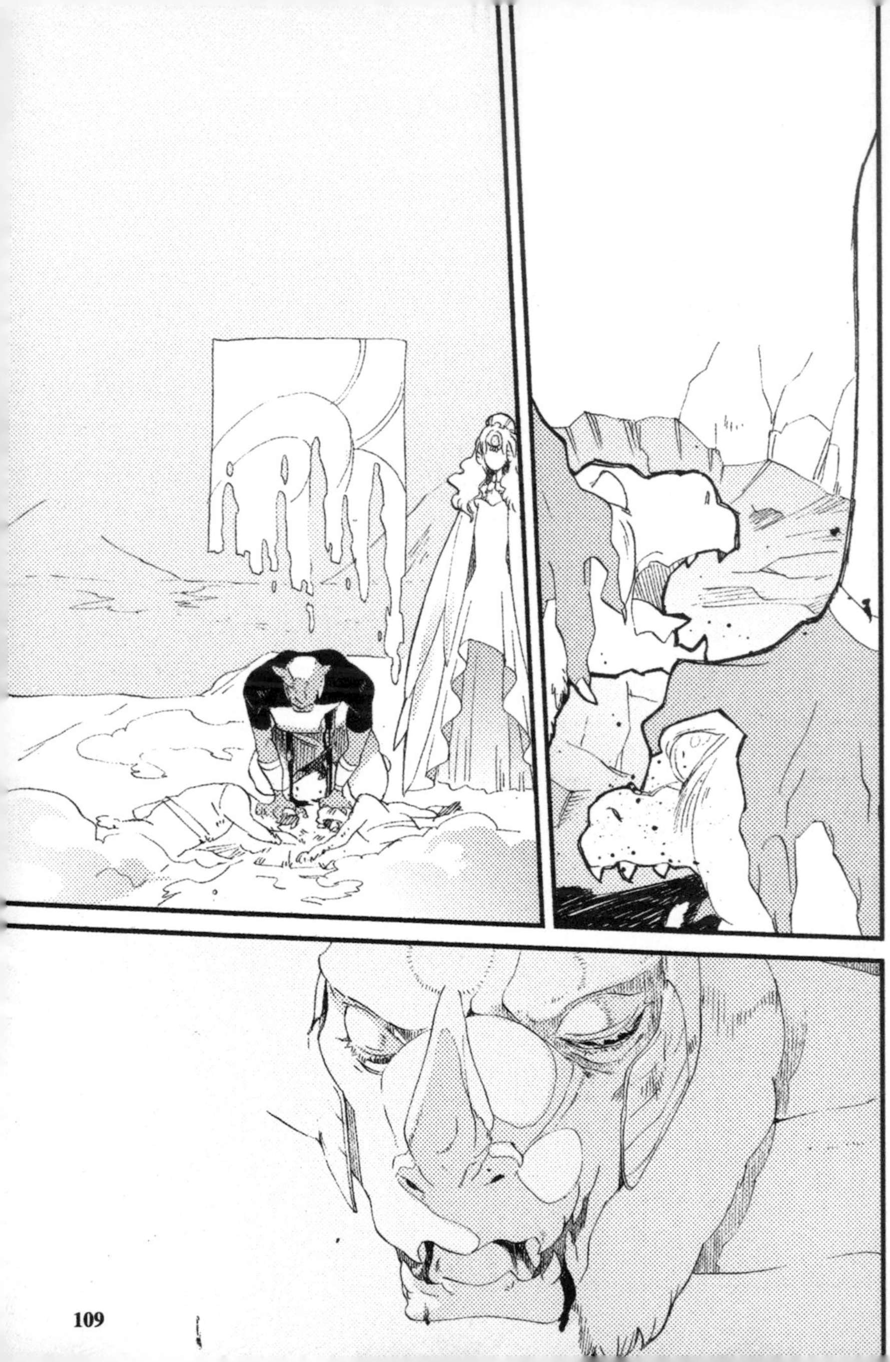

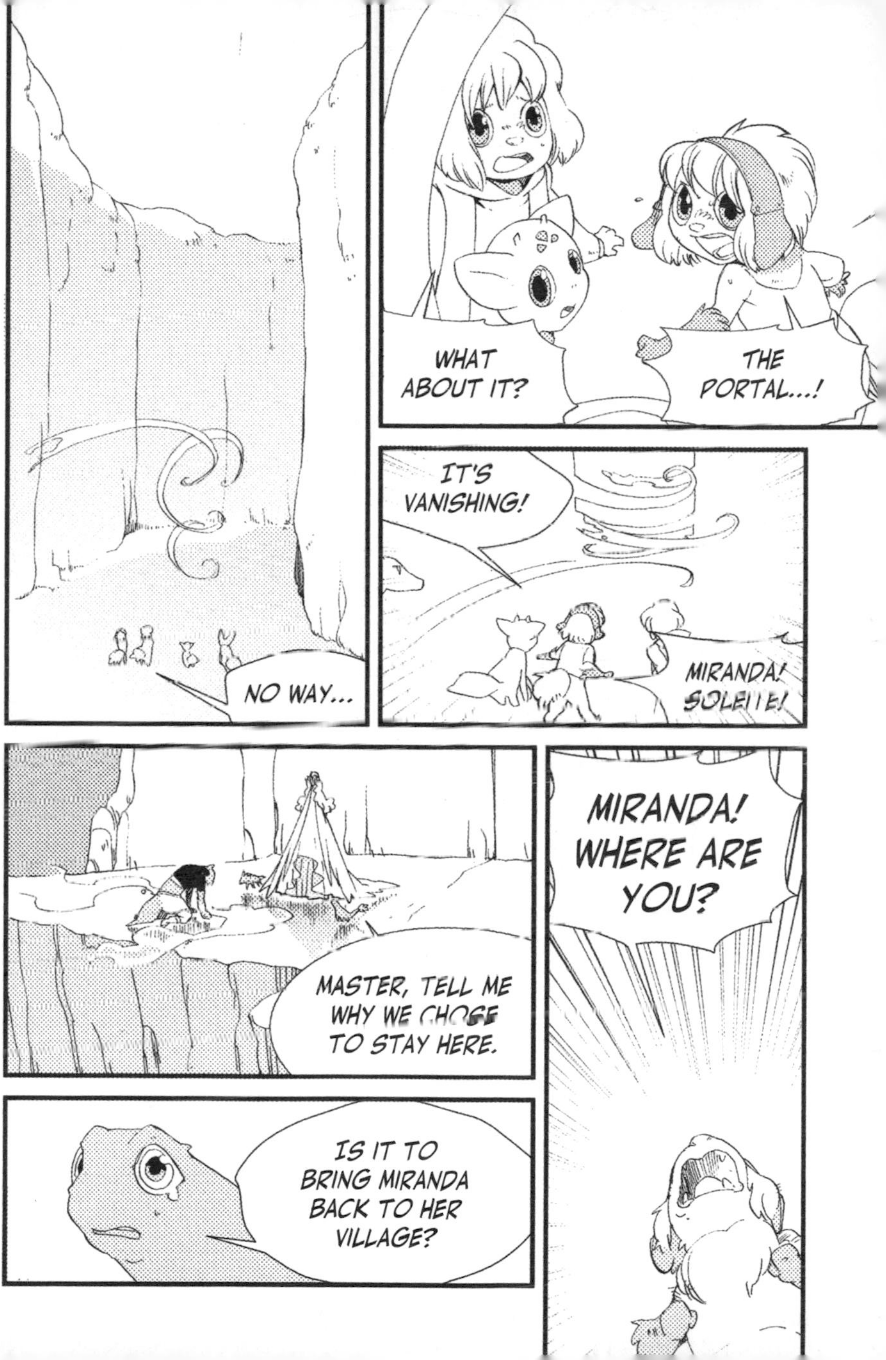
THE PORTAL...!
WHAT ABOUT IT?
IT'S VANISHING!
MIRANDA! SOLETTE!
NO WAY...
MIRANDA! WHERE ARE YOU?
MASTER, TELL ME WHY WE CHOSE TO STAY HERE.
IS IT TO BRING MIRANDA BACK TO HER VILLAGE?

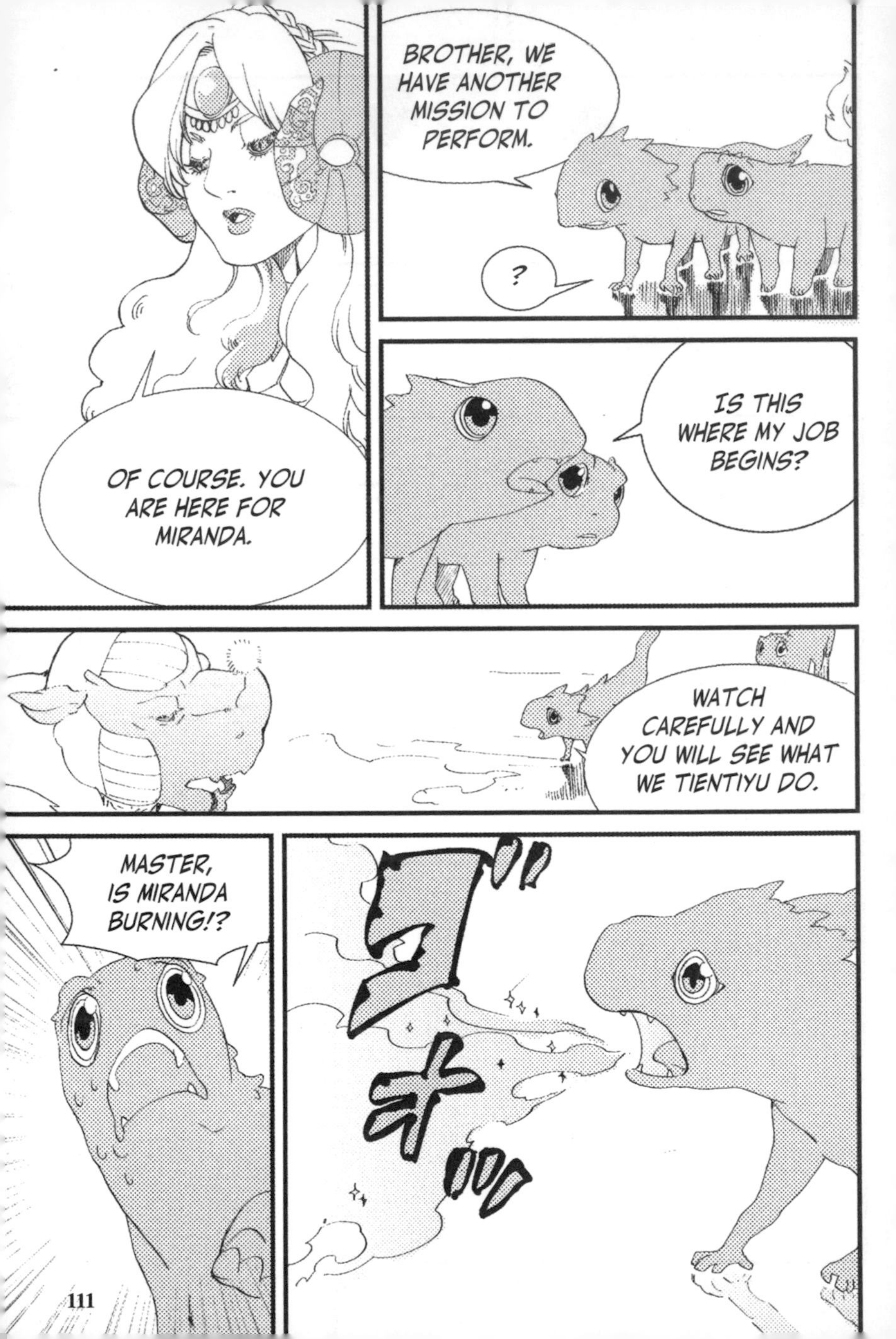
BROTHER, WE HAVE ANOTHER MISSION TO PERFORM.
?
IS THIS WHERE MY JOB BEGINS?
OF COURSE. YOU ARE HERE FOR MIRANDA.
WATCH CAREFULLY AND YOU WILL SEE WHAT WE TIENTIYU DO.
MASTER, IS MIRANDA BURNING!?

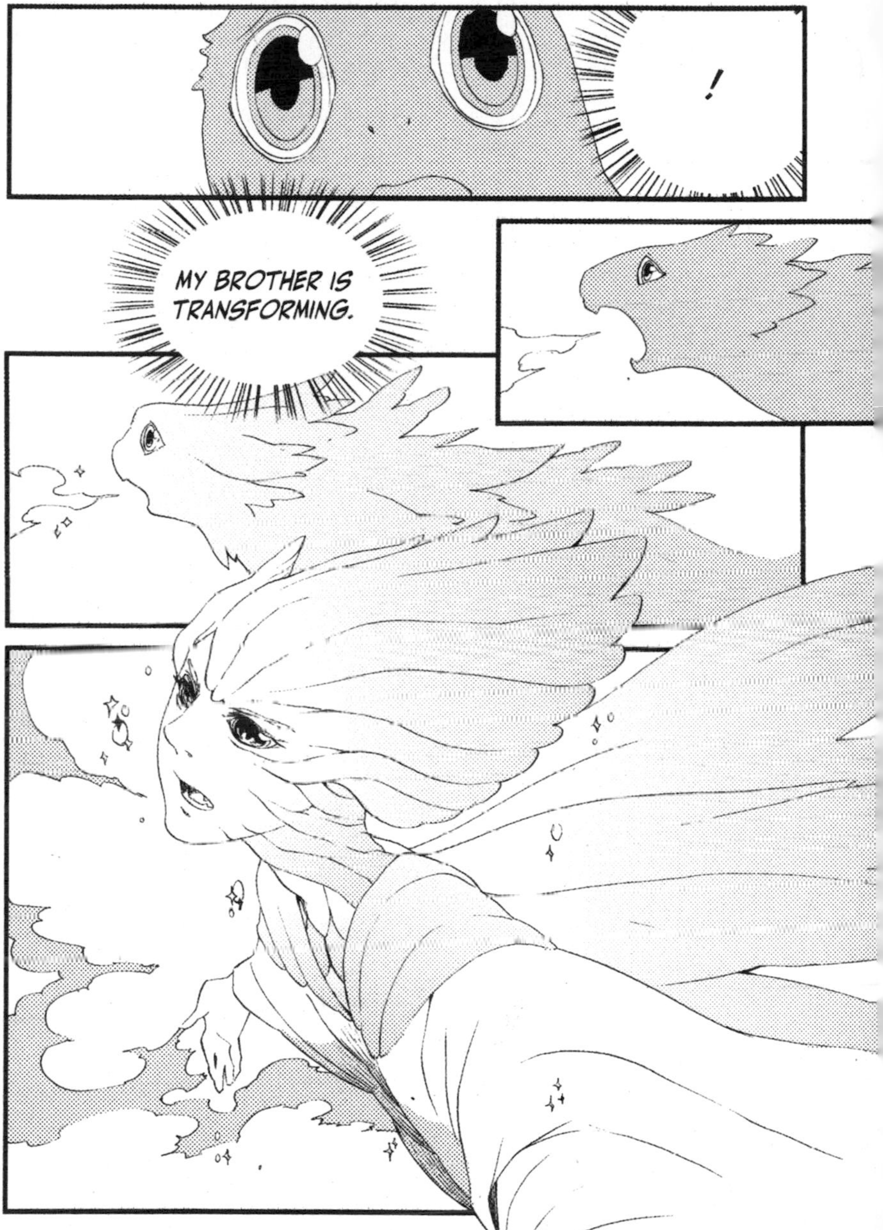
!
MY BROTHER IS TRANSFORMING.

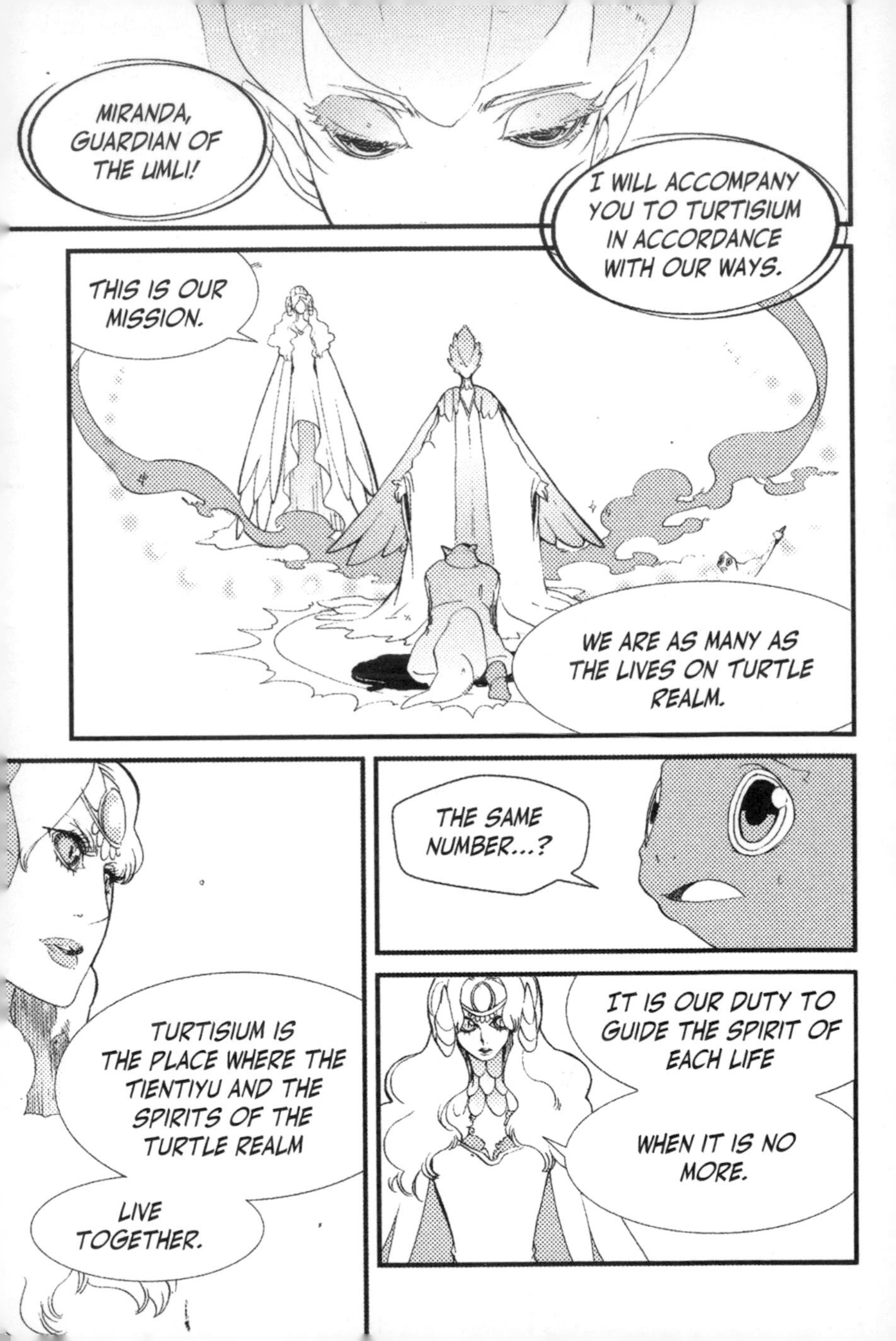
MIRANDA, GUARDIAN OF THE UMLI!
I WILL ACCOMPANY YOU TO TURTISIUM IN ACCORDANCE WITH OUR WAYS.
THIS IS OUR MISSION.
WE ARE AS MANY AS THE LIVES ON TURTLE REALM.
THE SAME NUMBER...?
IT IS OUR DUTY TO GUIDE THE SPIRIT OF EACH LIFE
WHEN IT IS NO MORE.
TURTISIUM IS THE PLACE WHERE THE TIENTIYU AND THE SPIRITS OF THE TURTLE REALM
LIVE TOGETHER.

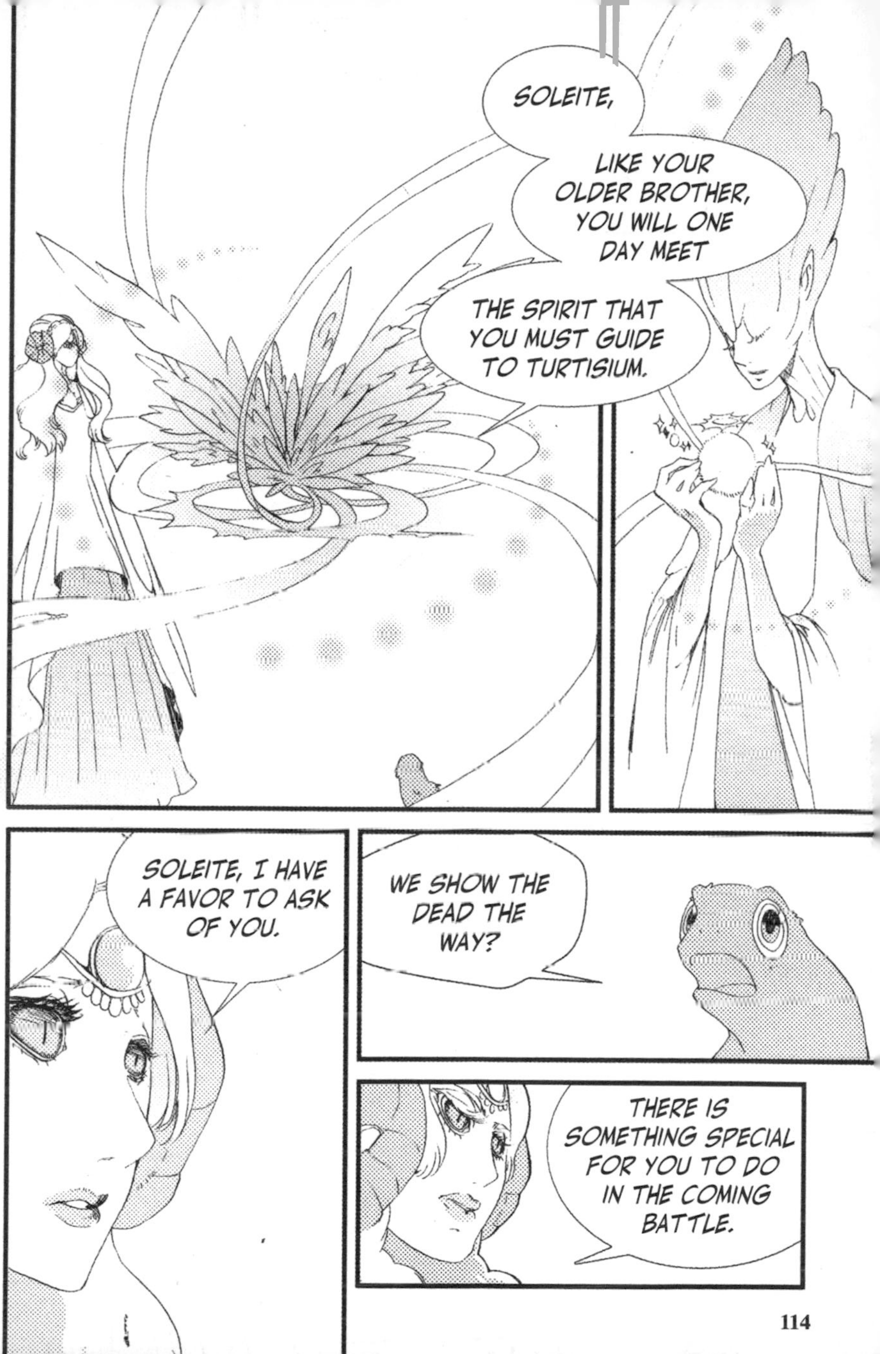

SOLEITE,
LIKE YOUR OLDER BROTHER, YOU WILL ONE DAY MEET
THE SPIRIT THAT YOU MUST GUIDE TO TURTISIUM.
SOLEITE, I HAVE A FAVOR TO ASK OF YOU.
WE SHOW THE DEAD THE WAY?
THERE IS SOMETHING SPECIAL FOR YOU TO DO IN THE COMING BATTLE.

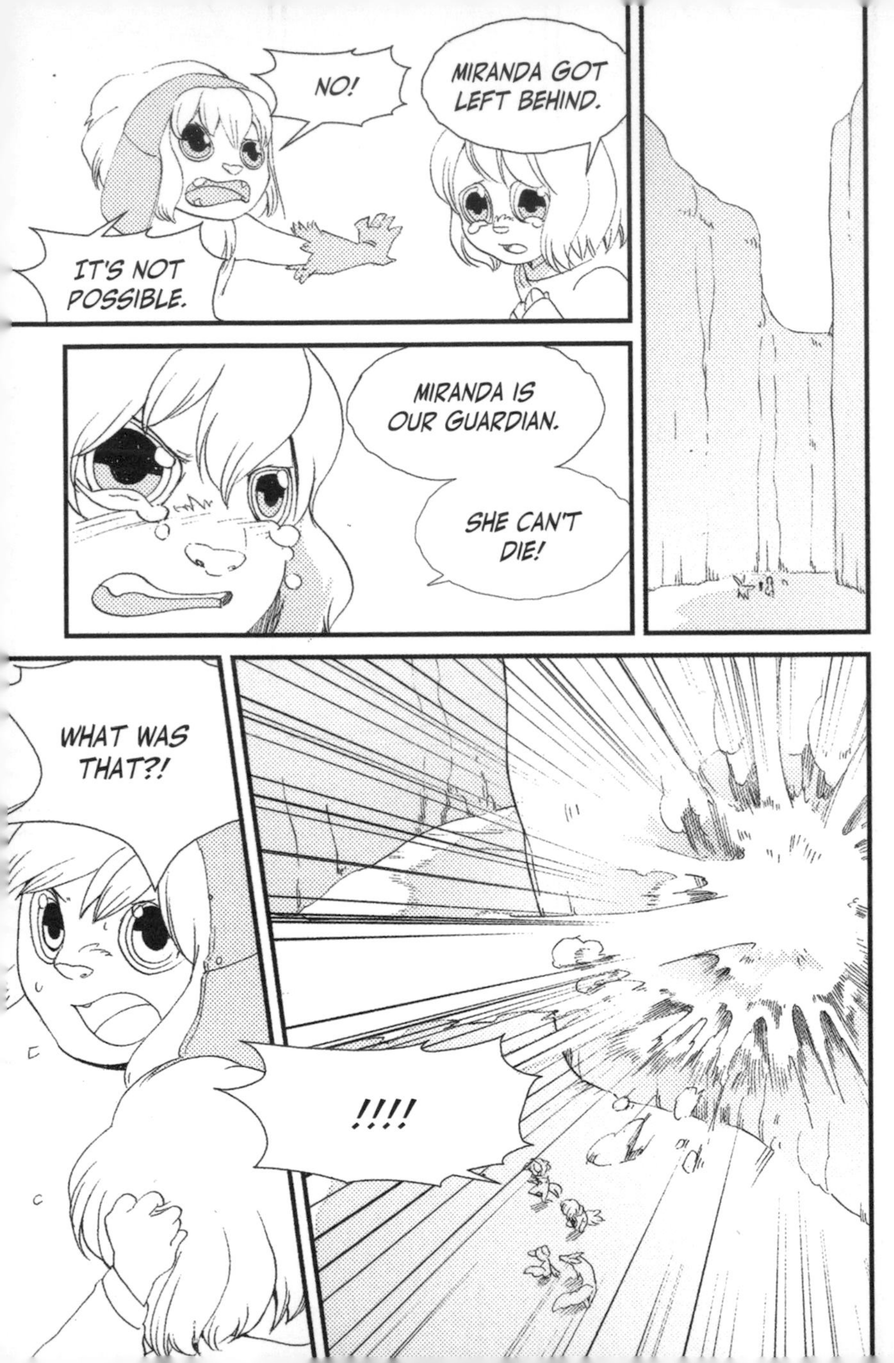
MIRANDA GOT LEFT BEHIND.
NO!
IT'S NOT POSSIBLE.
MIRANDA IS OUR GUARDIAN.
SHE CAN'T DIE!
!!!!
WHAT WAS THAT?!

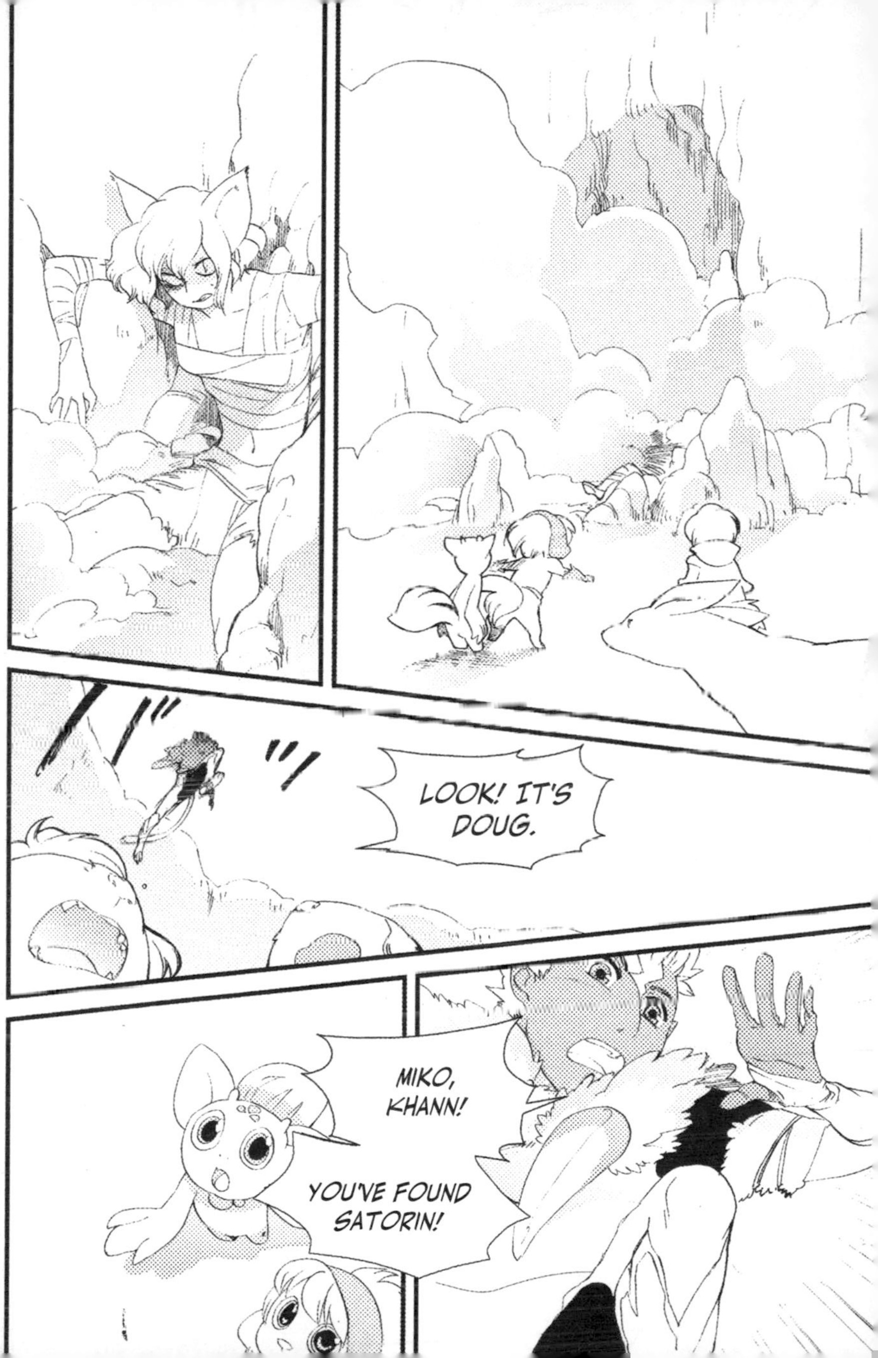
LOOK! IT'S DOUG.
MIKO, KHANN!
YOU'VE FOUND SATORIN!

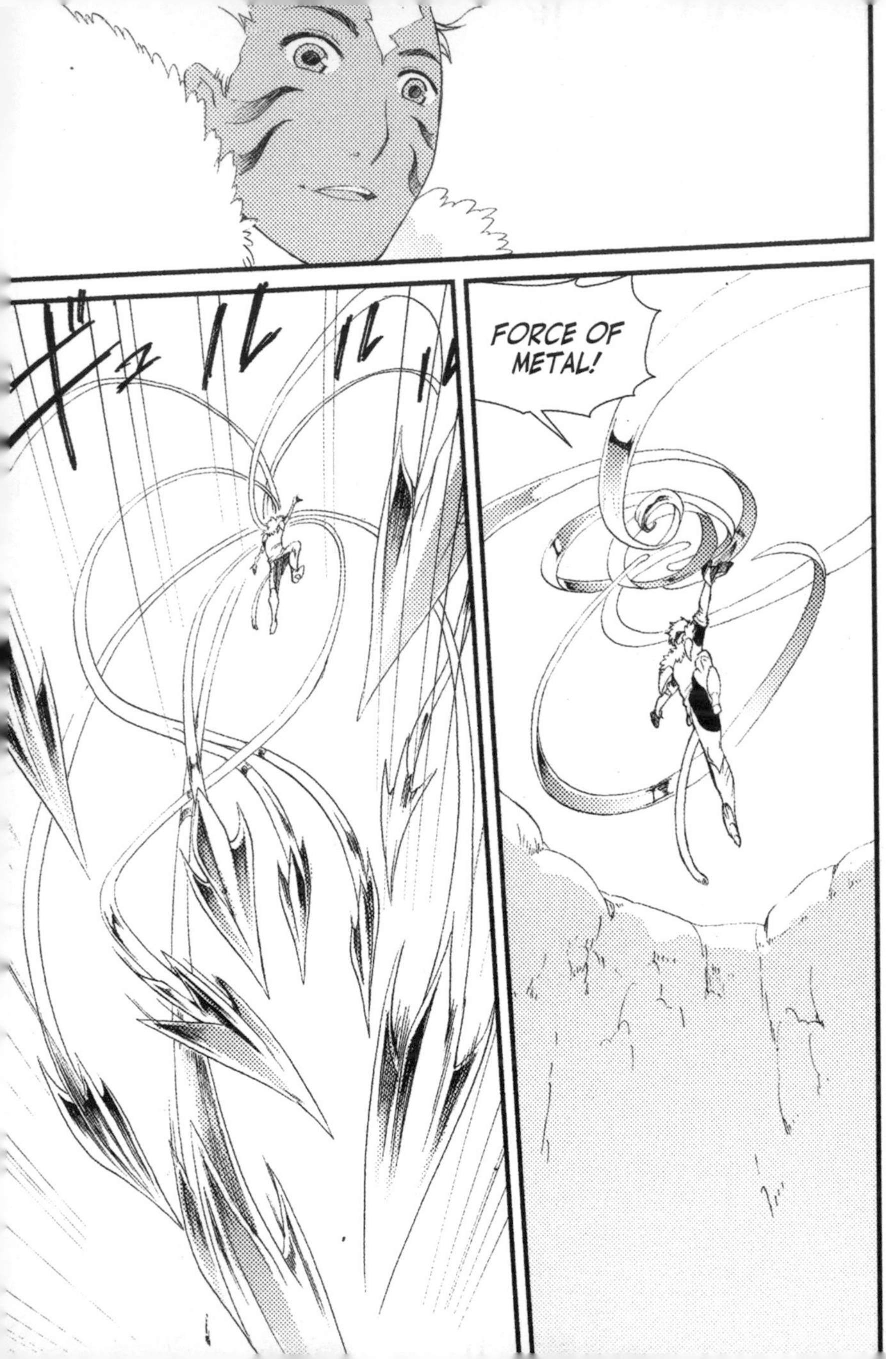
FORCE OF METAL!
ギュルルル

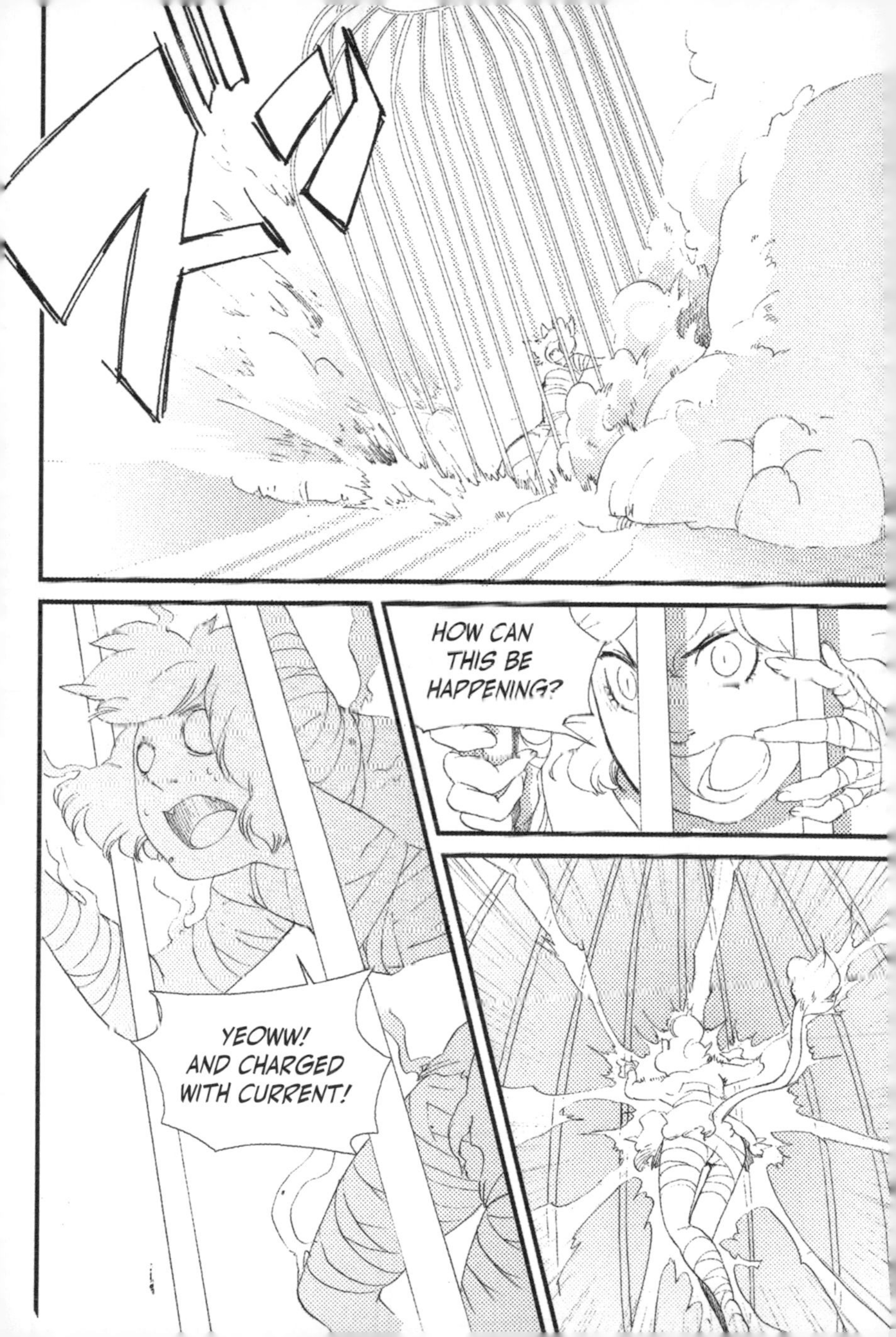
HOW CAN THIS BE HAPPENING?
YEOWW! AND CHARGED WITH CURRENT!

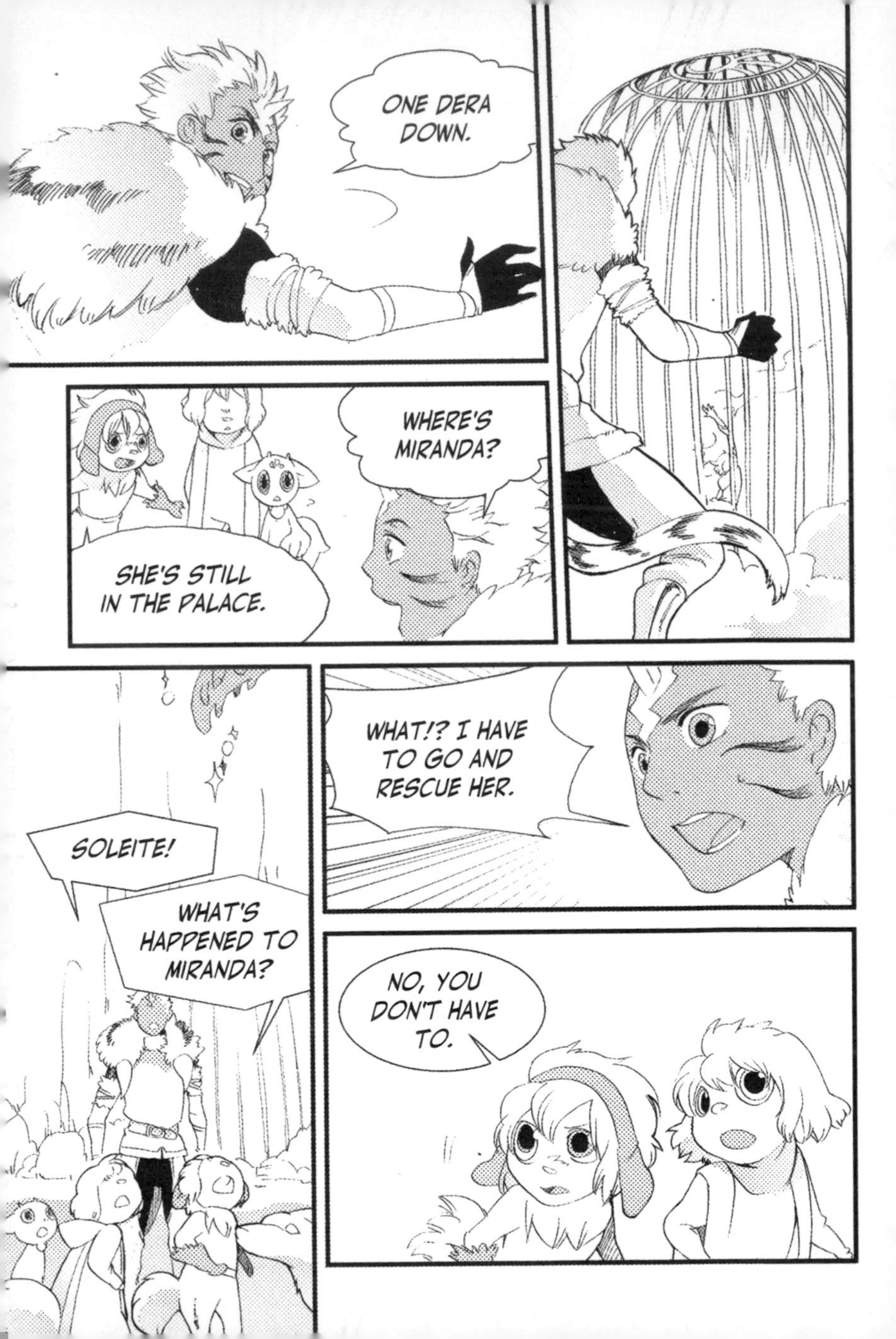
ONE DERA DOWN.
WHERE'S MIRANDA?
SHE'S STILL IN THE PALACE.
SOLEITE!
WHAT'S HAPPENED TO MIRANDA?
WHAT!? I HAVE TO GO AND RESCUE HER.
NO, YOU DON'T HAVE TO.

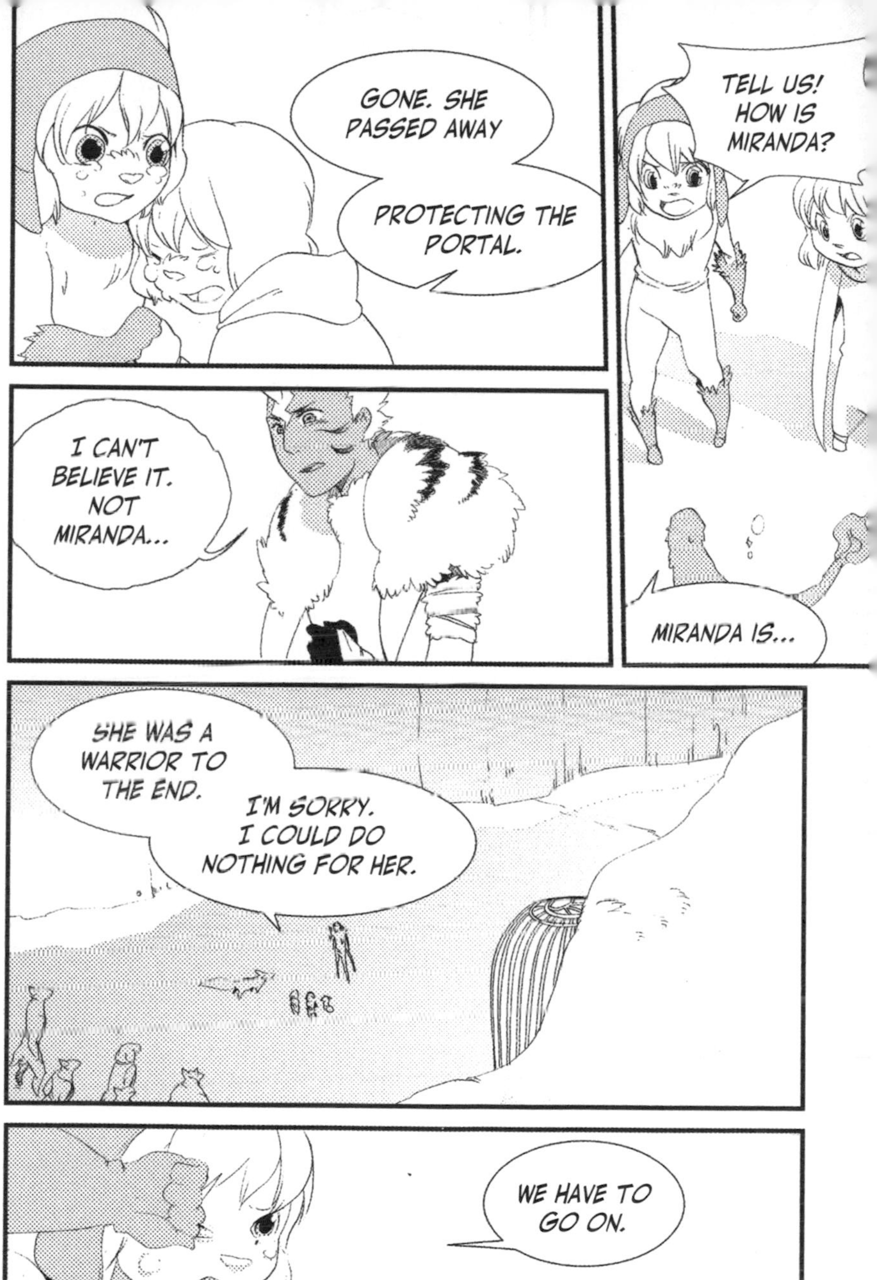
TELL US! HOW IS MIRANDA?
MIRANDA IS...
GONE. SHE PASSED AWAY
PROTECTING THE PORTAL.
I CAN'T BELIEVE IT. NOT MIRANDA...
SHE WAS A WARRIOR TO THE END.
I'M SORRY. I COULD DO NOTHING FOR HER.
WE HAVE TO GO ON.

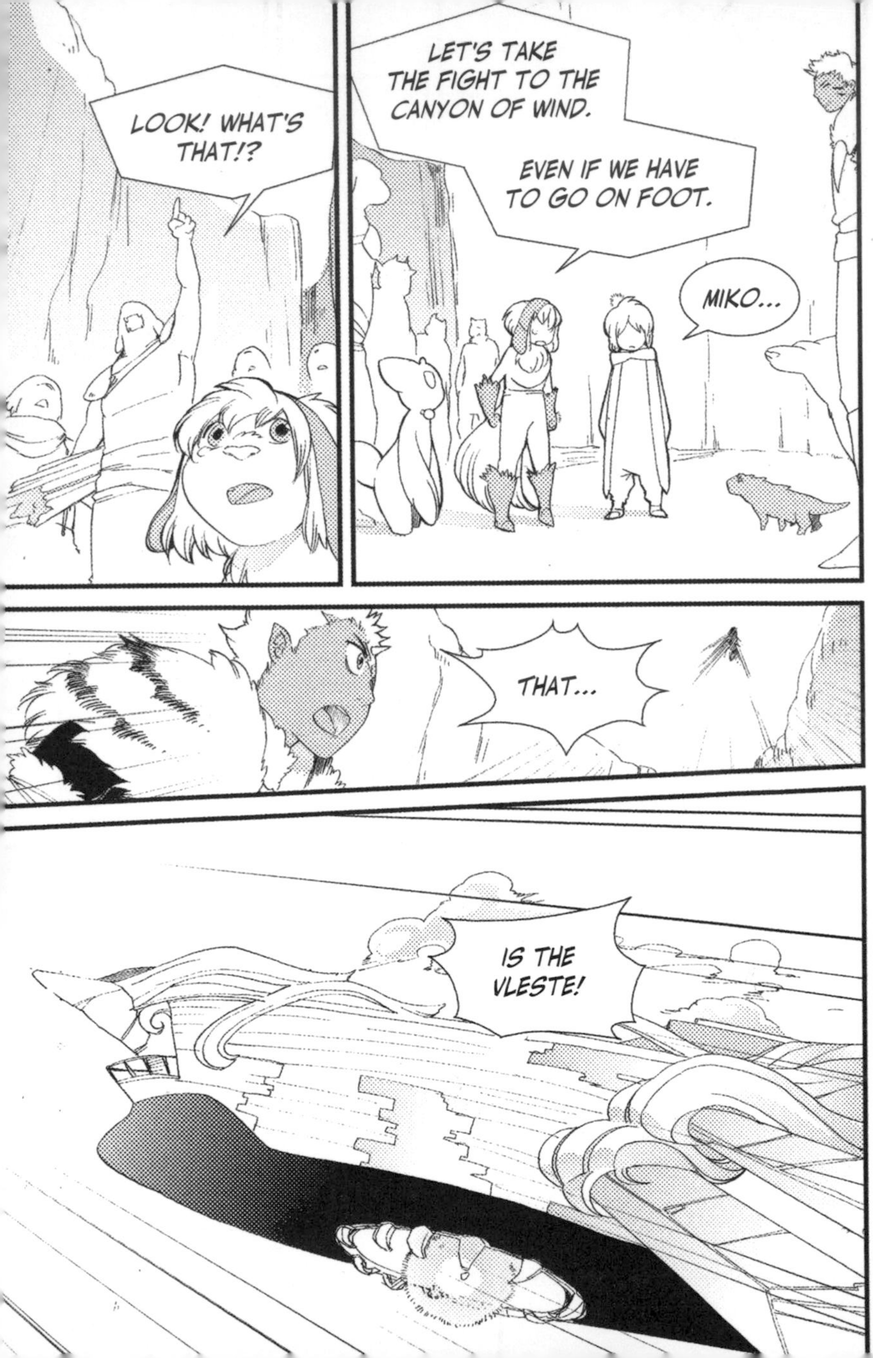
LET'S TAKE THE FIGHT TO THE CANYON OF WIND.
EVEN IF WE HAVE TO GO ON FOOT.
MIKO...
LOOK! WHAT'S THAT!?
THAT...
IS THE VLESTE!

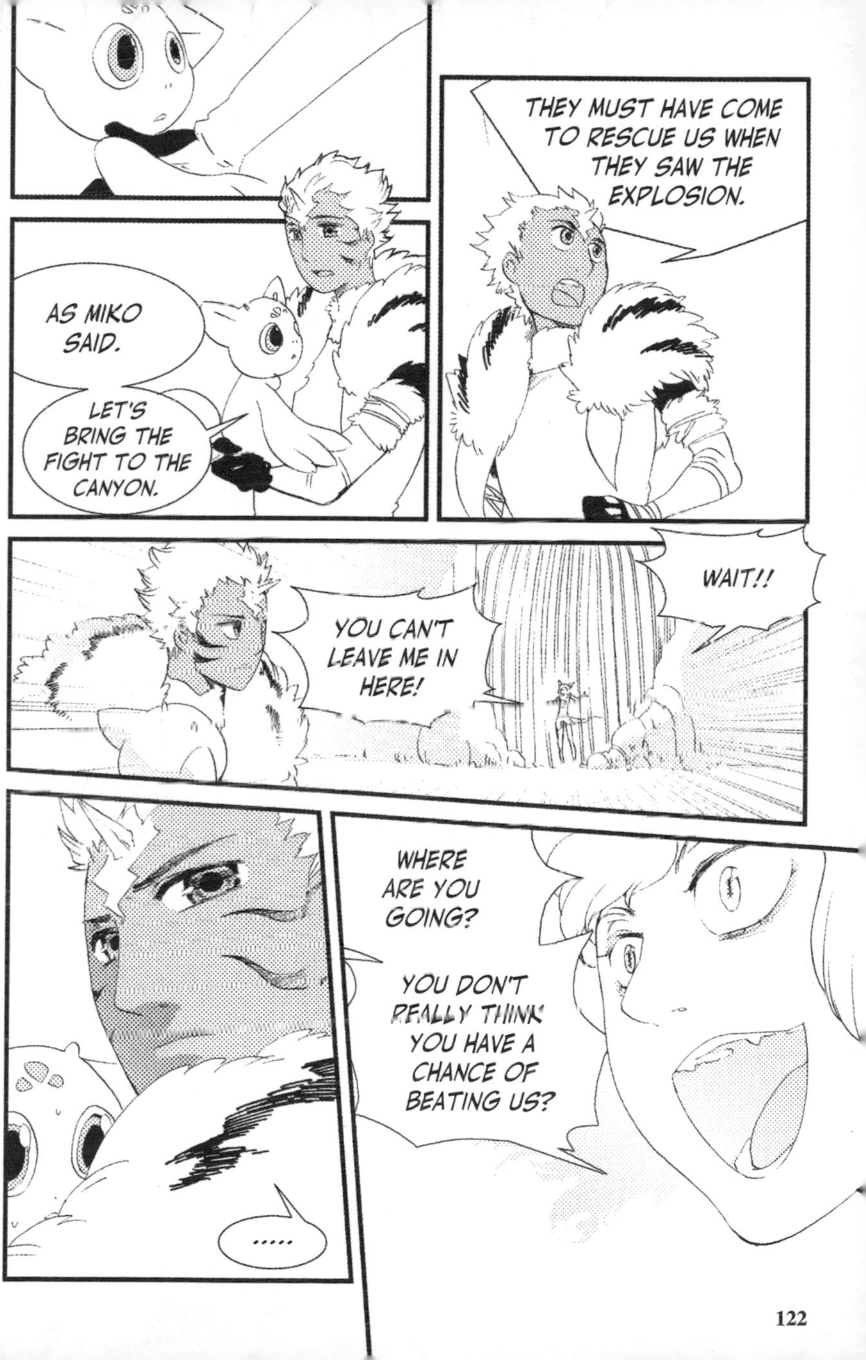
THEY MUST HAVE COME TO RESCUE US WHEN THEY SAW THE EXPLOSION.
AS MIKO SAID.
LET'S BRING THE FIGHT TO THE CANYON.
WAIT!!
YOU CAN'T LEAVE ME IN HERE!
WHERE ARE YOU GOING?
YOU DON'T REALLY THINK YOU HAVE A CHANCE OF BEATING US?
......

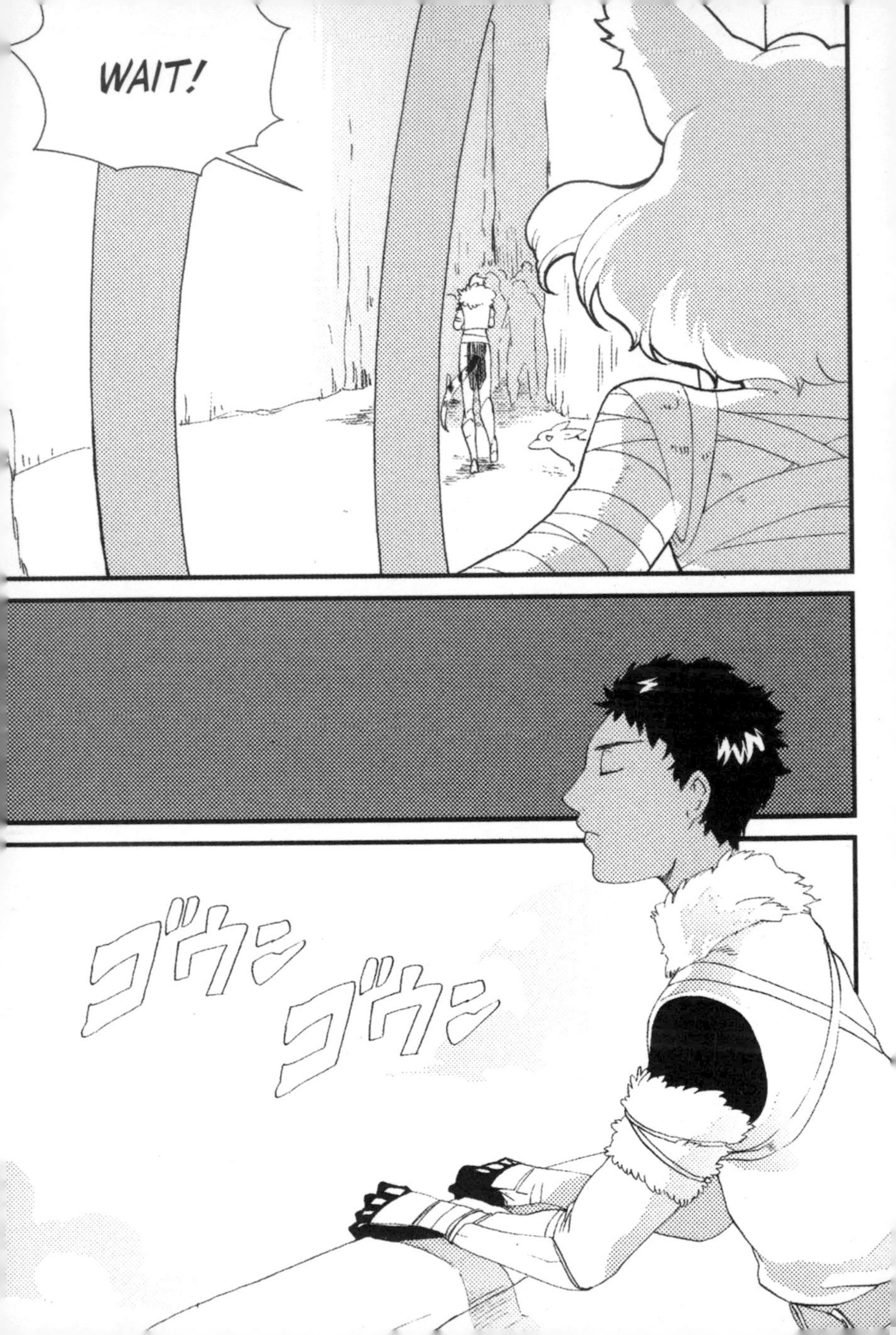
WAIT!
ゴウン
ゴウン

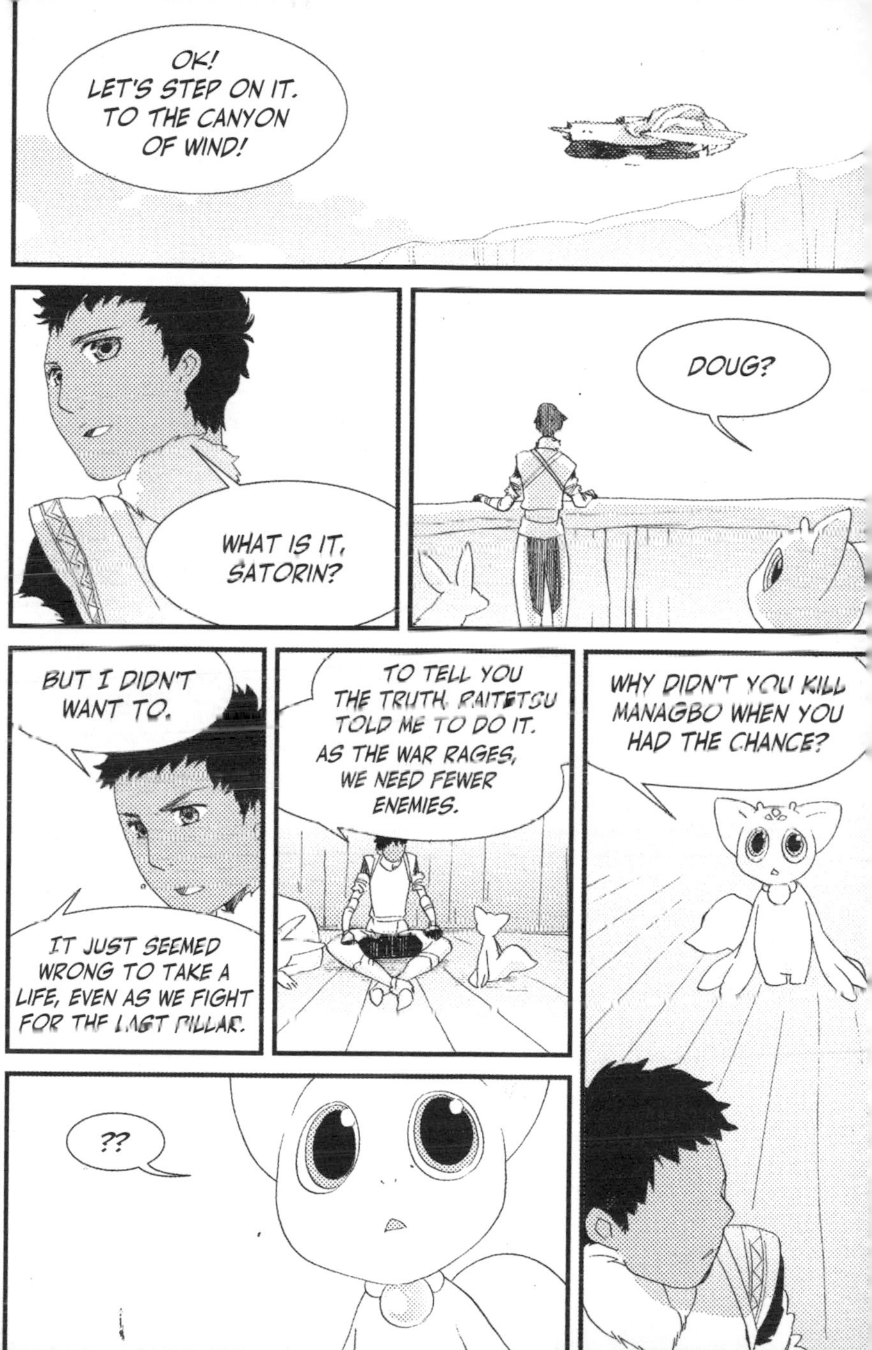
OK!
LET'S STEP ON IT.
TO THE CANYON
OF WIND!
DOUG?
WHAT IS IT,
SATORIN?
WHY DIDN'T YOU KILL MANAGBO WHEN YOU HAD THE CHANCE?
TO TELL YOU THE TRUTH, RAITETSU TOLD ME TO DO IT.
AS THE WAR RAGES, WE NEED FEWER ENEMIES.
BUT I DIDN'T WANT TO.
IT JUST SEEMED WRONG TO TAKE A LIFE, EVEN AS WE FIGHT FOR THE LAST PILLAR.
??

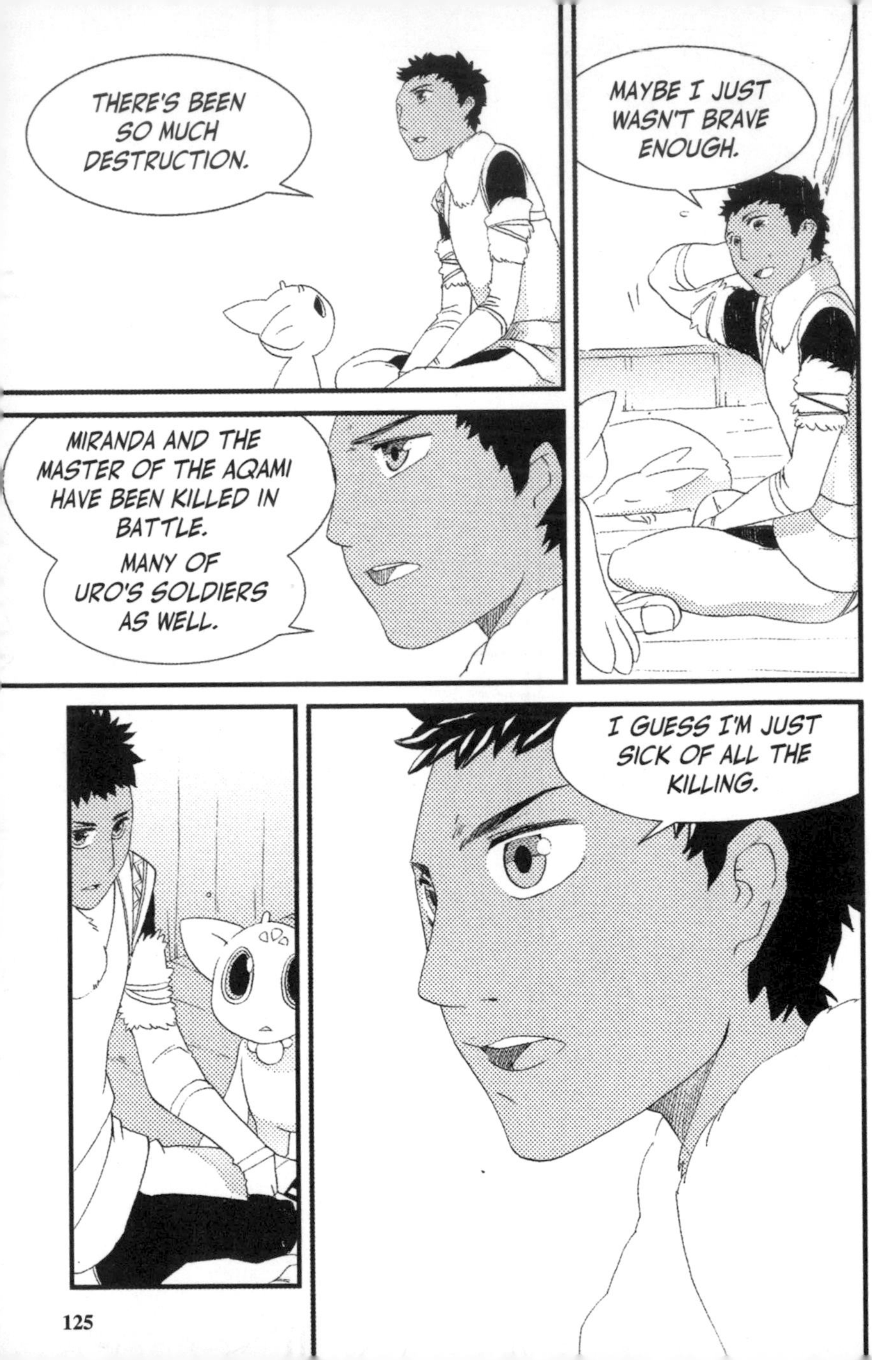
THERE'S BEEN SO MUCH DESTRUCTION.
MIRANDA AND THE MASTER OF THE AQAMI HAVE BEEN KILLED IN BATTLE.
MANY OF URO'S SOLDIERS AS WELL.
MAYBE I JUST WASN'T BRAVE ENOUGH.
I GUESS I'M JUST SICK OF ALL THE KILLING.

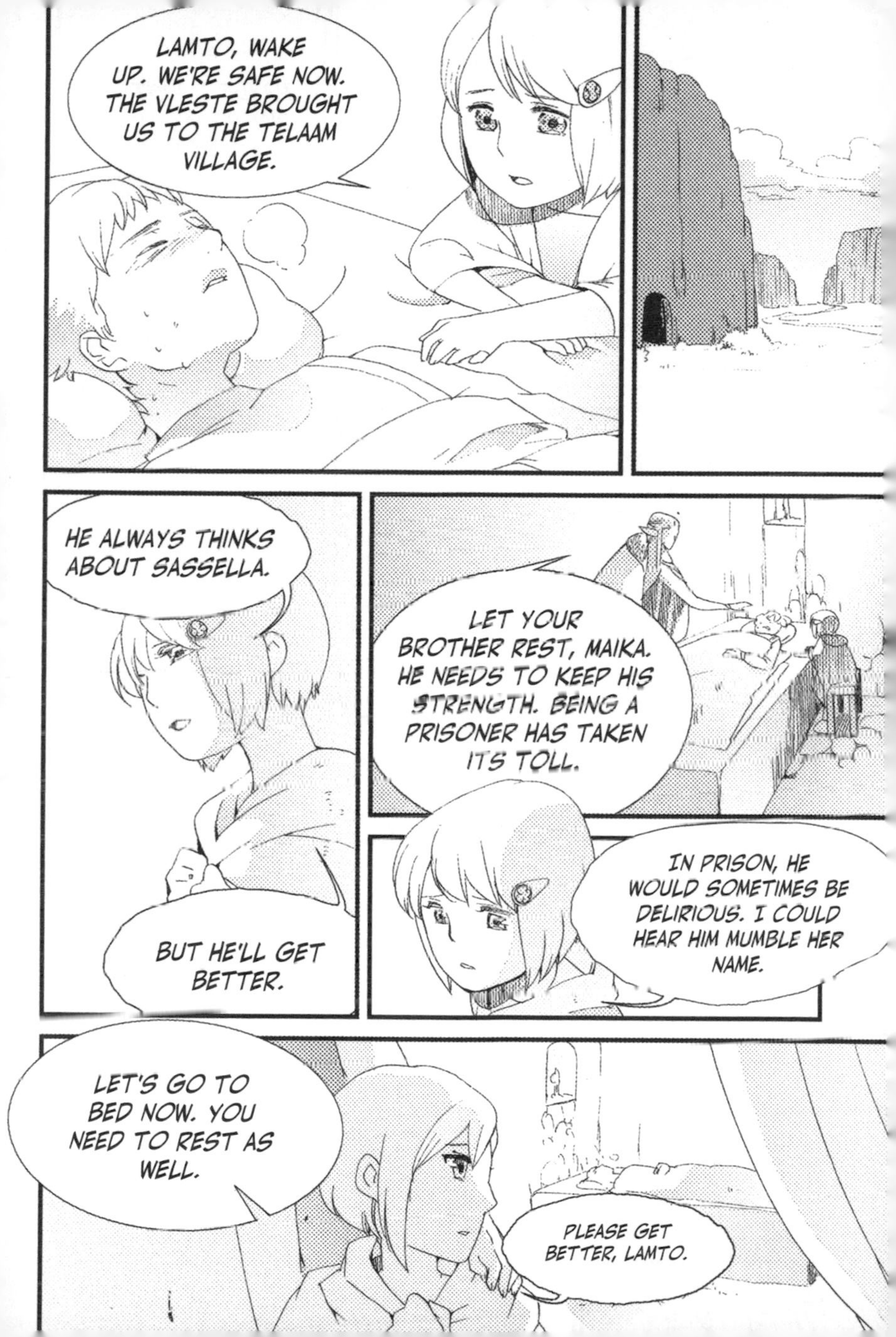
LAMTO, WAKE UP. WE'RE SAFE NOW. THE VLESTE BROUGHT US TO THE TELAAM VILLAGE.
LET YOUR BROTHER REST, MAIKA. HE NEEDS TO KEEP HIS STRENGTH. BEING A PRISONER HAS TAKEN ITS TOLL.
IN PRISON, HE WOULD SOMETIMES BE DELIRIOUS. I COULD HEAR HIM MUMBLE HER NAME.
HE ALWAYS THINKS ABOUT SASSELLA.
BUT HE'LL GET BETTER.
LET'S GO TO BED NOW. YOU NEED TO REST AS WELL.
PLEASE GET BETTER, LAMTO.

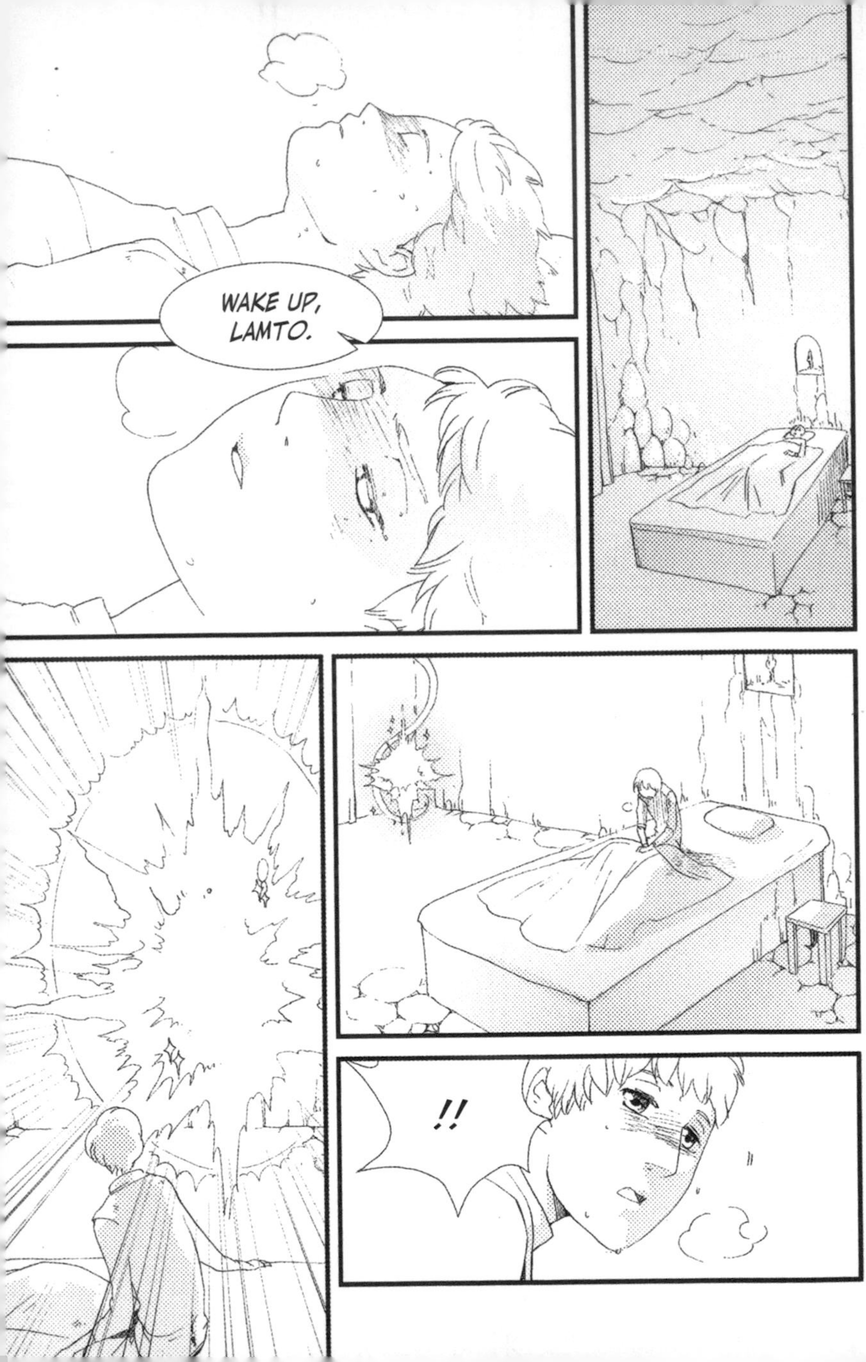
WAKE UP, LAMTO.
!!

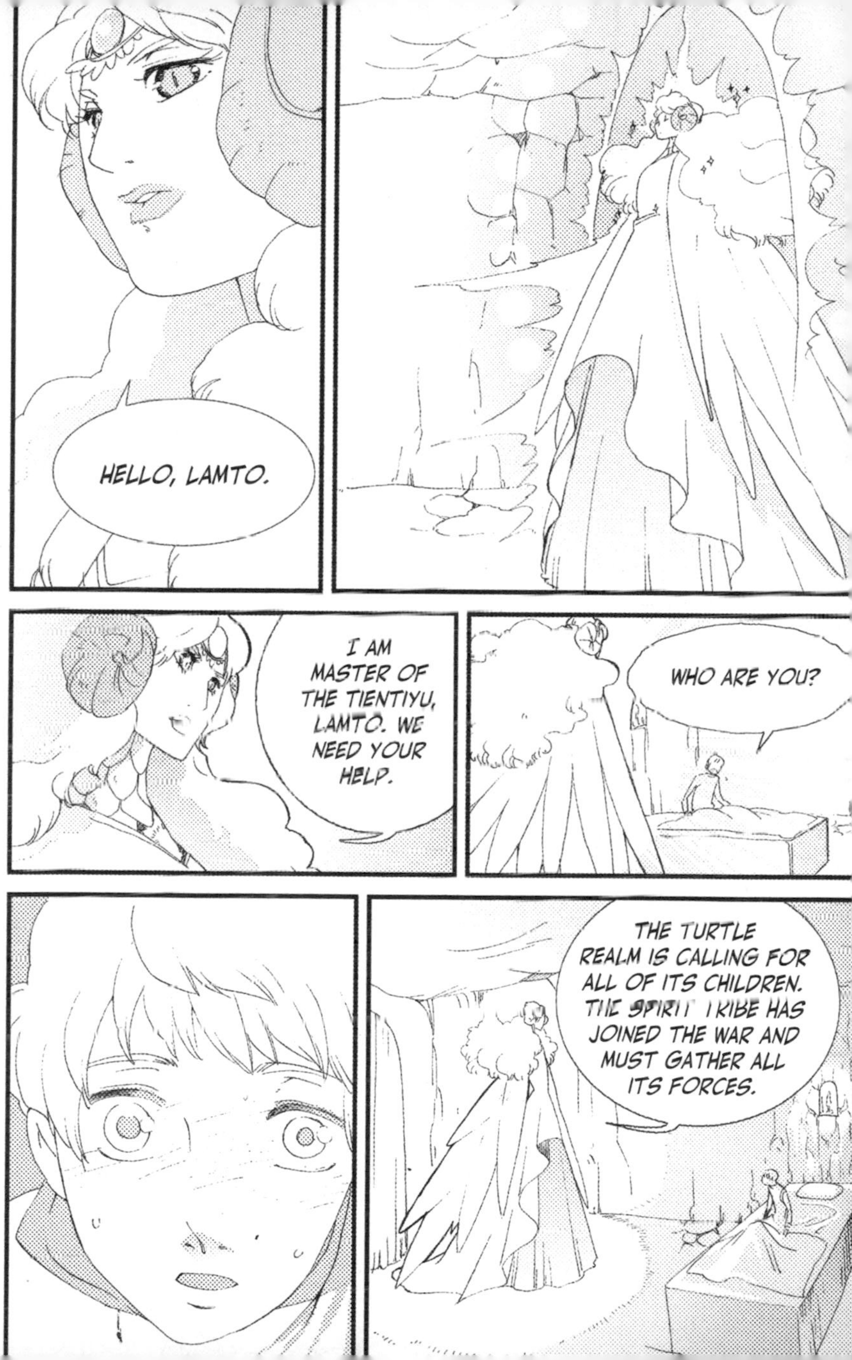
HELLO, LAMTO.
WHO ARE YOU?
I AM MASTER OF THE TIENTIYU, LAMTO. WE NEED YOUR HELP.
THE TURTLE REALM IS CALLING FOR ALL OF ITS CHILDREN. THE SPIRIT TRIBE HAS JOINED THE WAR AND MUST GATHER ALL ITS FORCES.

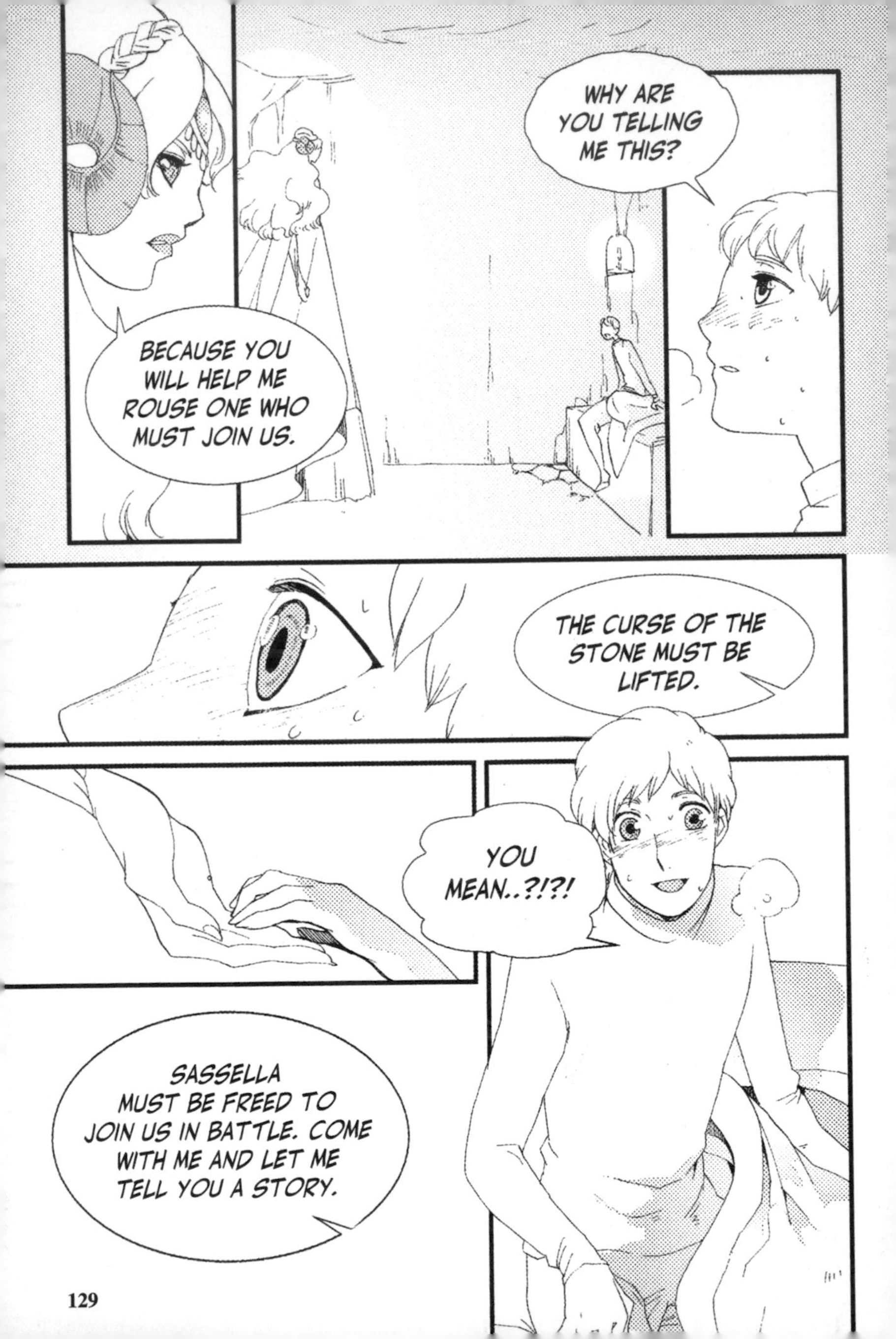
WHY ARE YOU TELLING ME THIS?
BECAUSE YOU WILL HELP ME ROUSE ONE WHO MUST JOIN US.
THE CURSE OF THE STONE MUST BE LIFTED.
YOU MEAN..?!?!
SASSELLA MUST BE FREED TO JOIN US IN BATTLE. COME WITH ME AND LET ME TELL YOU A STORY.

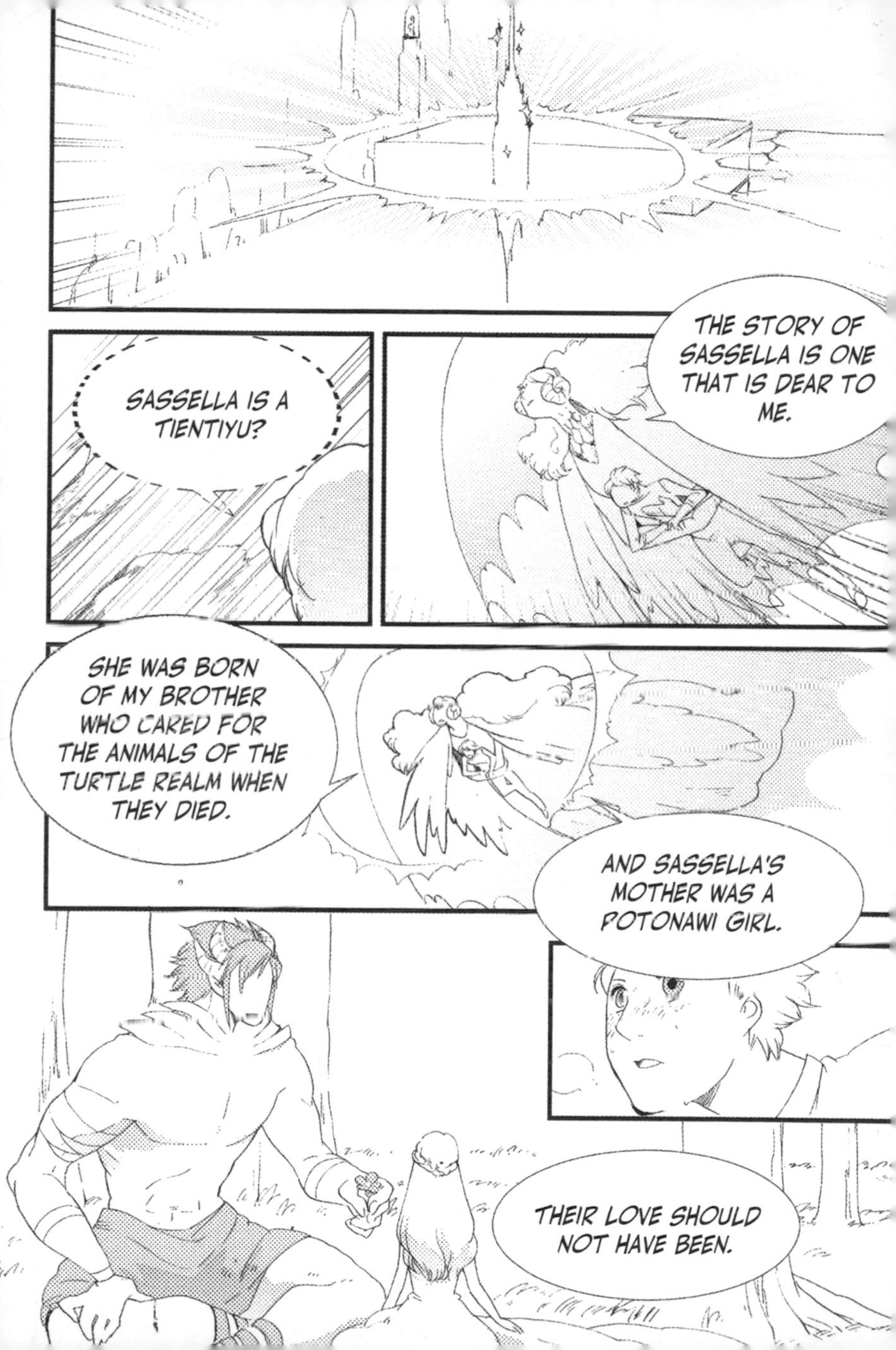
SASSELLA IS A TIENTIYU?
THE STORY OF SASSELLA IS ONE THAT IS DEAR TO ME.
SHE WAS BORN OF MY BROTHER WHO CARED FOR THE ANIMALS OF THE TURTLE REALM WHEN THEY DIED.
AND SASSELLA'S MOTHER WAS A POTONAWI GIRL.
THEIR LOVE SHOULD NOT HAVE BEEN.

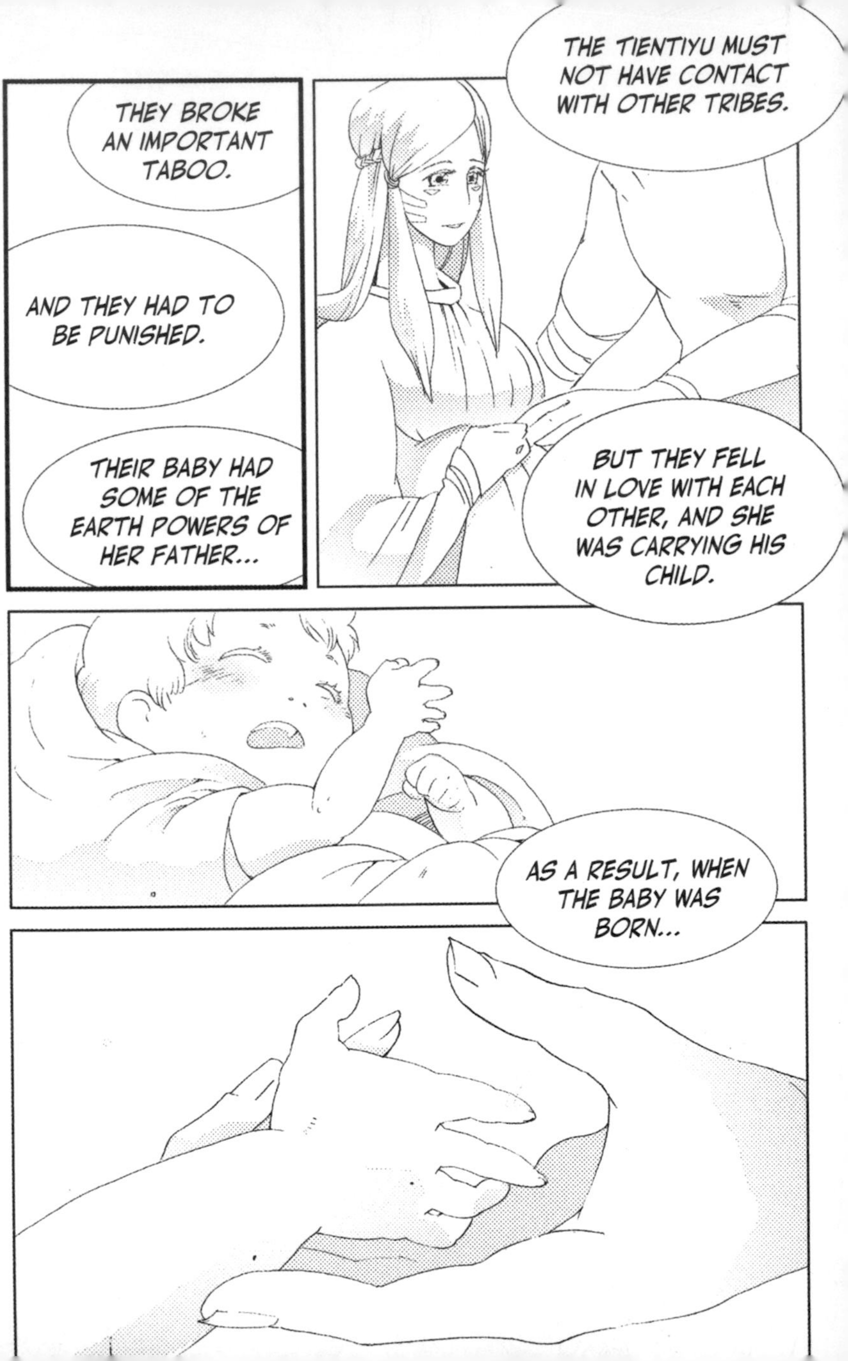
THE TIENTIYU MUST NOT HAVE CONTACT WITH OTHER TRIBES.
BUT THEY FELL IN LOVE WITH EACH OTHER, AND SHE WAS CARRYING HIS CHILD.
THEY BROKE AN IMPORTANT TABOO.
AND THEY HAD TO BE PUNISHED.
THEIR BABY HAD SOME OF THE EARTH POWERS OF HER FATHER...
AS A RESULT, WHEN THE BABY WAS BORN...

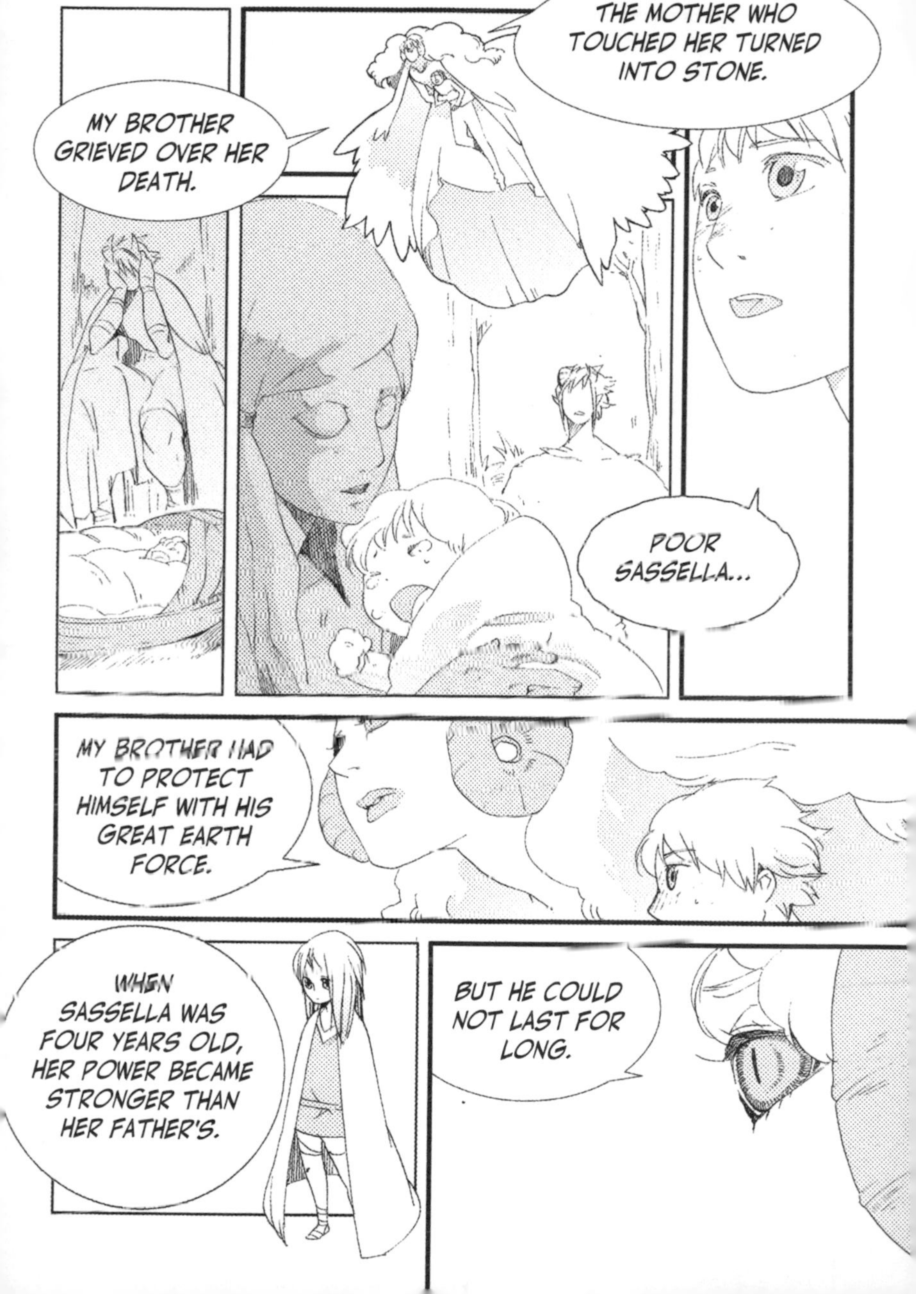
MY BROTHER GRIEVED OVER HER DEATH.
THE MOTHER WHO TOUCHED HER TURNED INTO STONE.
POOR SASSELLA...
MY BROTHER HAD TO PROTECT HIMSELF WITH HIS GREAT EARTH FORCE.
WHEN SASSELLA WAS FOUR YEARS OLD, HER POWER BECAME STRONGER THAN HER FATHER'S.
BUT HE COULD NOT LAST FOR LONG.

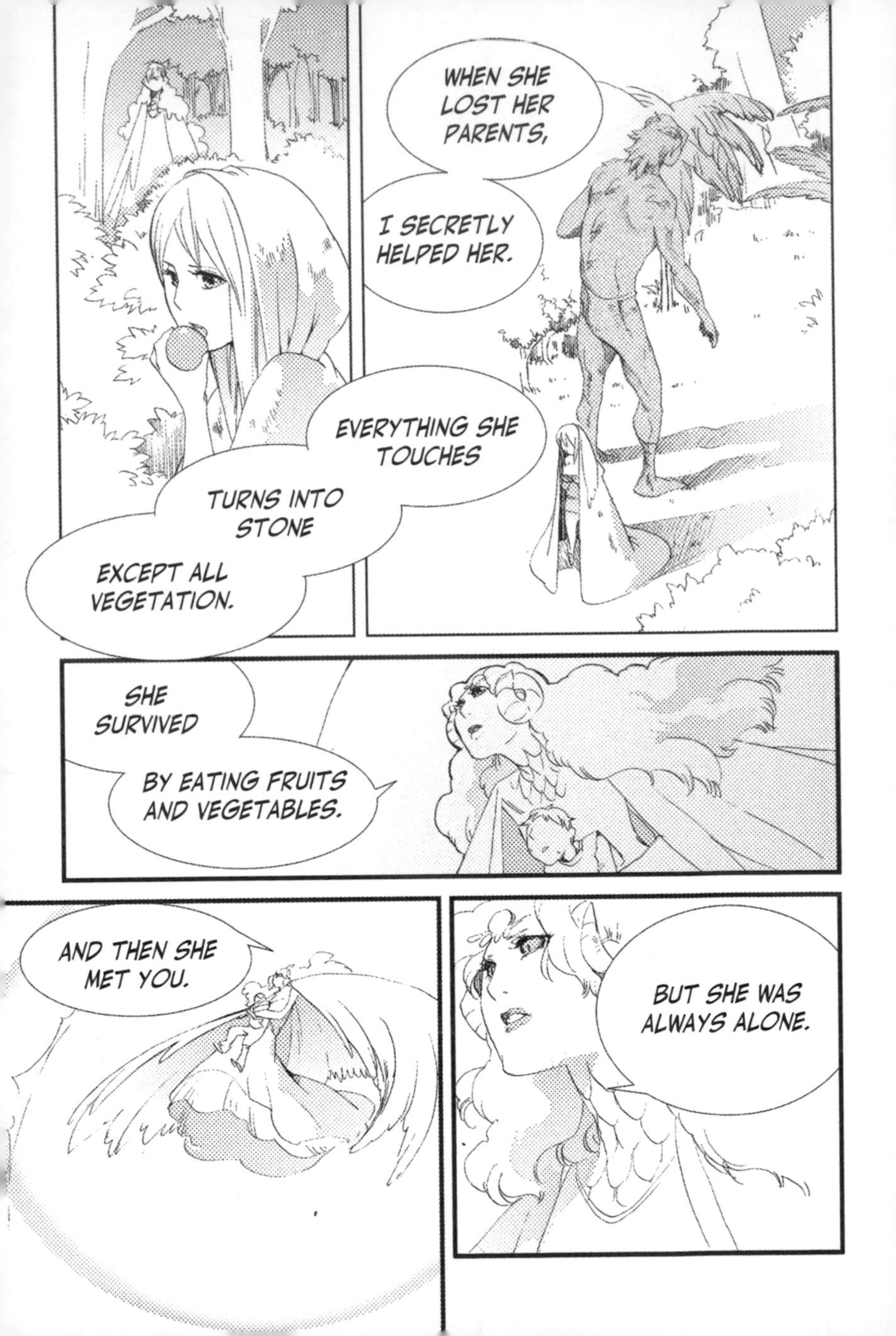
WHEN SHE LOST HER PARENTS,
I SECRETLY HELPED HER.
EVERYTHING SHE TOUCHES
TURNS INTO STONE
EXCEPT ALL VEGETATION.
SHE SURVIVED
BY EATING FRUITS AND VEGETABLES.
BUT SHE WAS ALWAYS ALONE.
AND THEN SHE MET YOU.

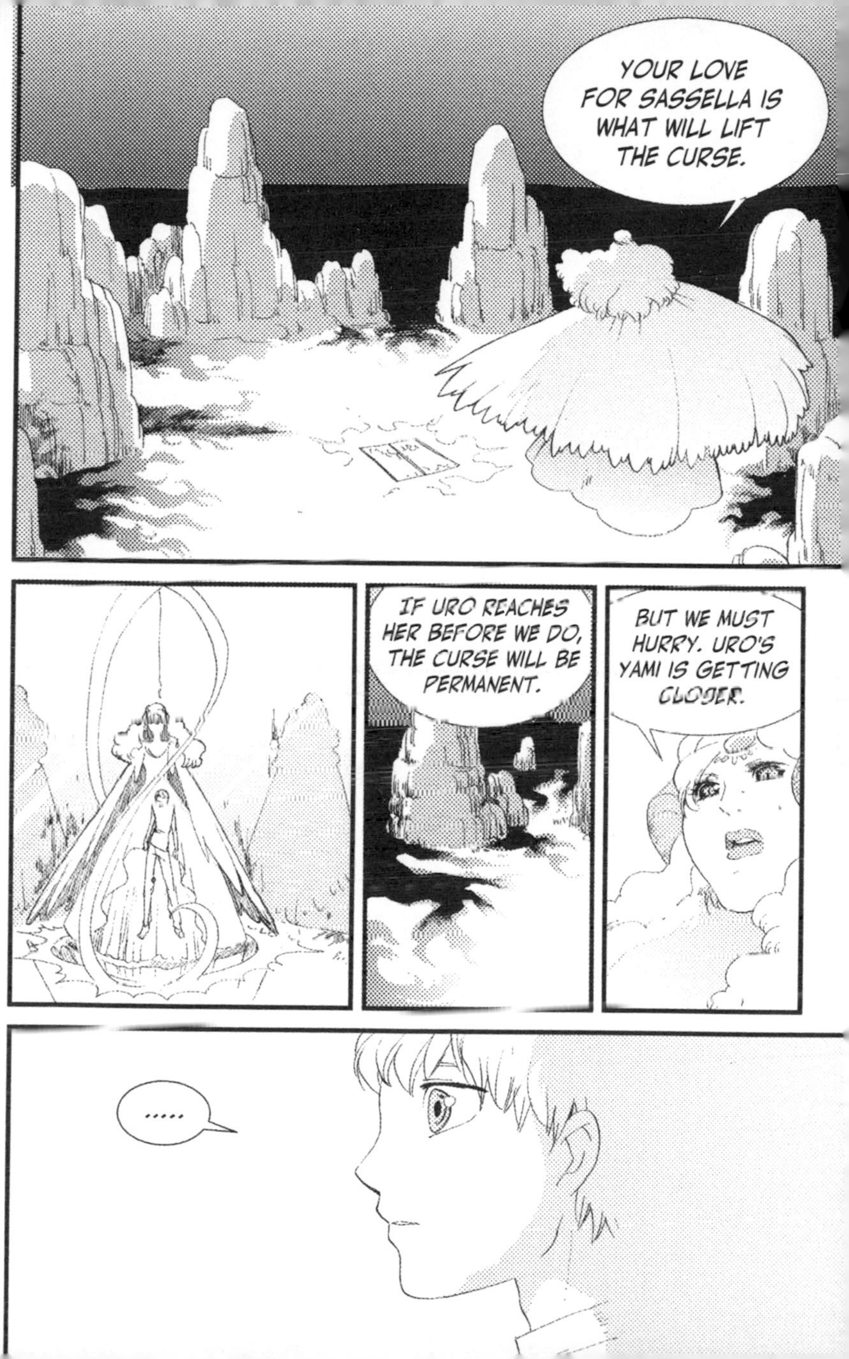
YOUR LOVE FOR SASSELLA IS WHAT WILL LIFT THE CURSE.
IF URO REACHES HER BEFORE WE DO, THE CURSE WILL BE PERMANENT.
BUT WE MUST HURRY. URO'S YAMI IS GETTING CLOSER.
......

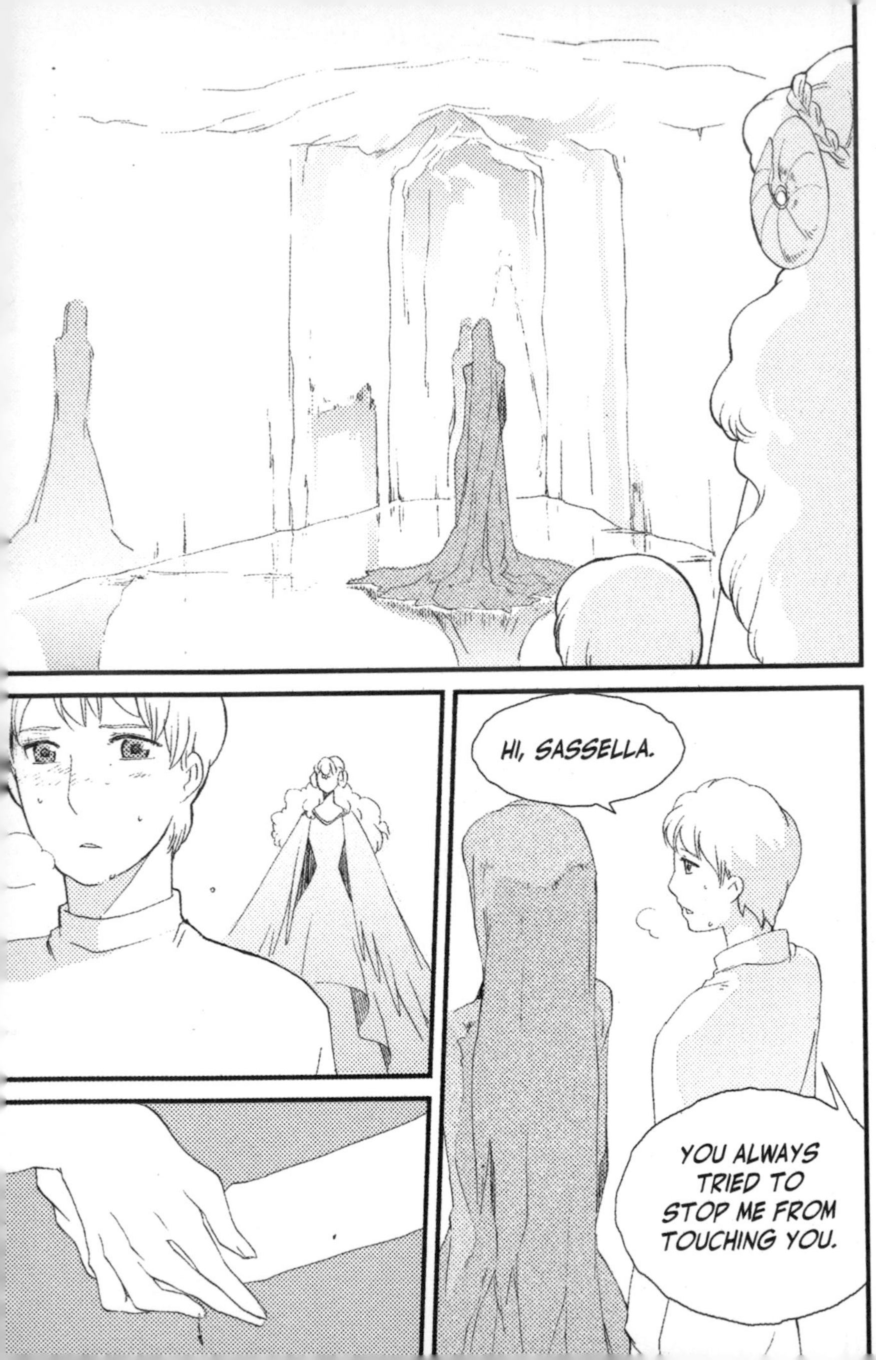
HI, SASSELLA.
YOU ALWAYS TRIED TO STOP ME FROM TOUCHING YOU.

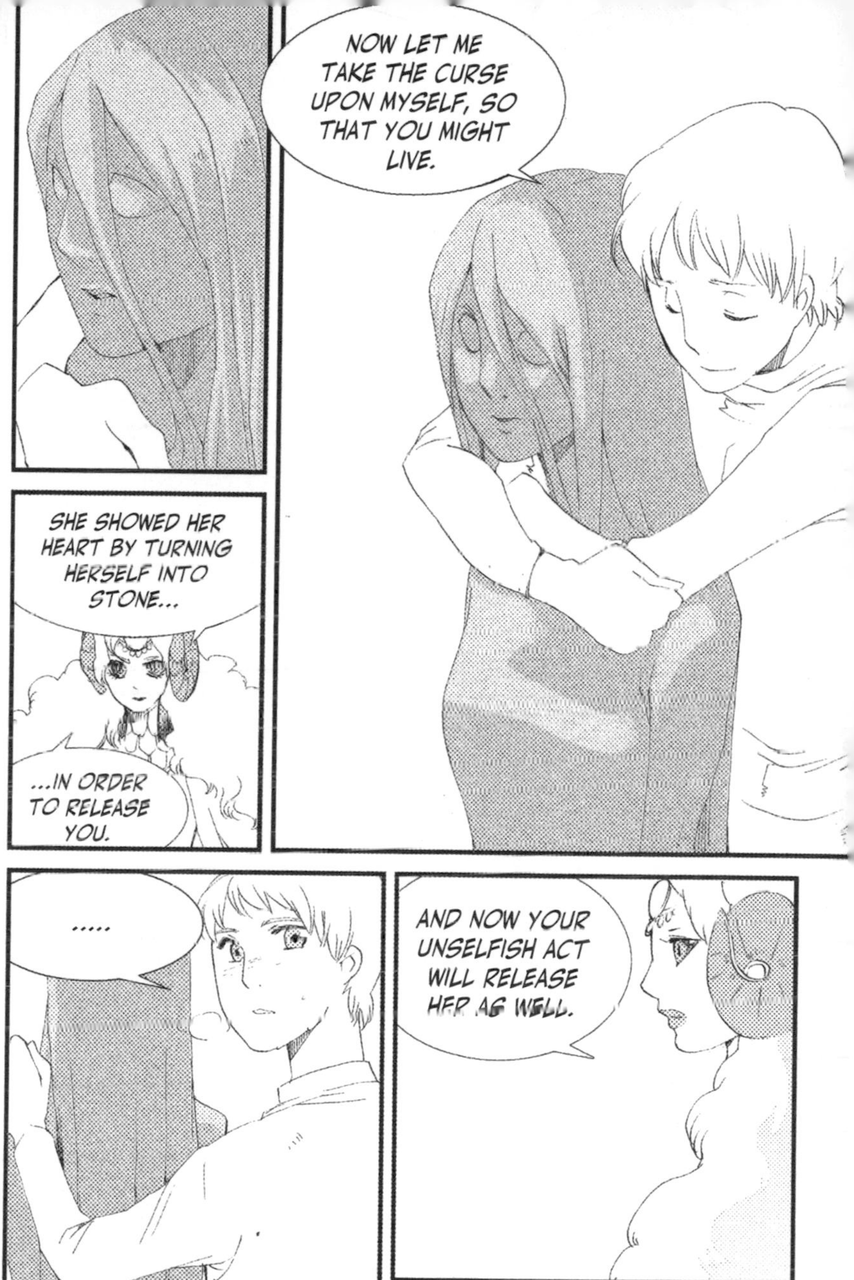
NOW LET ME TAKE THE CURSE UPON MYSELF, SO THAT YOU MIGHT LIVE.
SHE SHOWED HER HEART BY TURNING HERSELF INTO STONE...
...IN ORDER TO RELEASE YOU.
AND NOW YOUR UNSELFISH ACT WILL RELEASE HER AS WELL.
.....

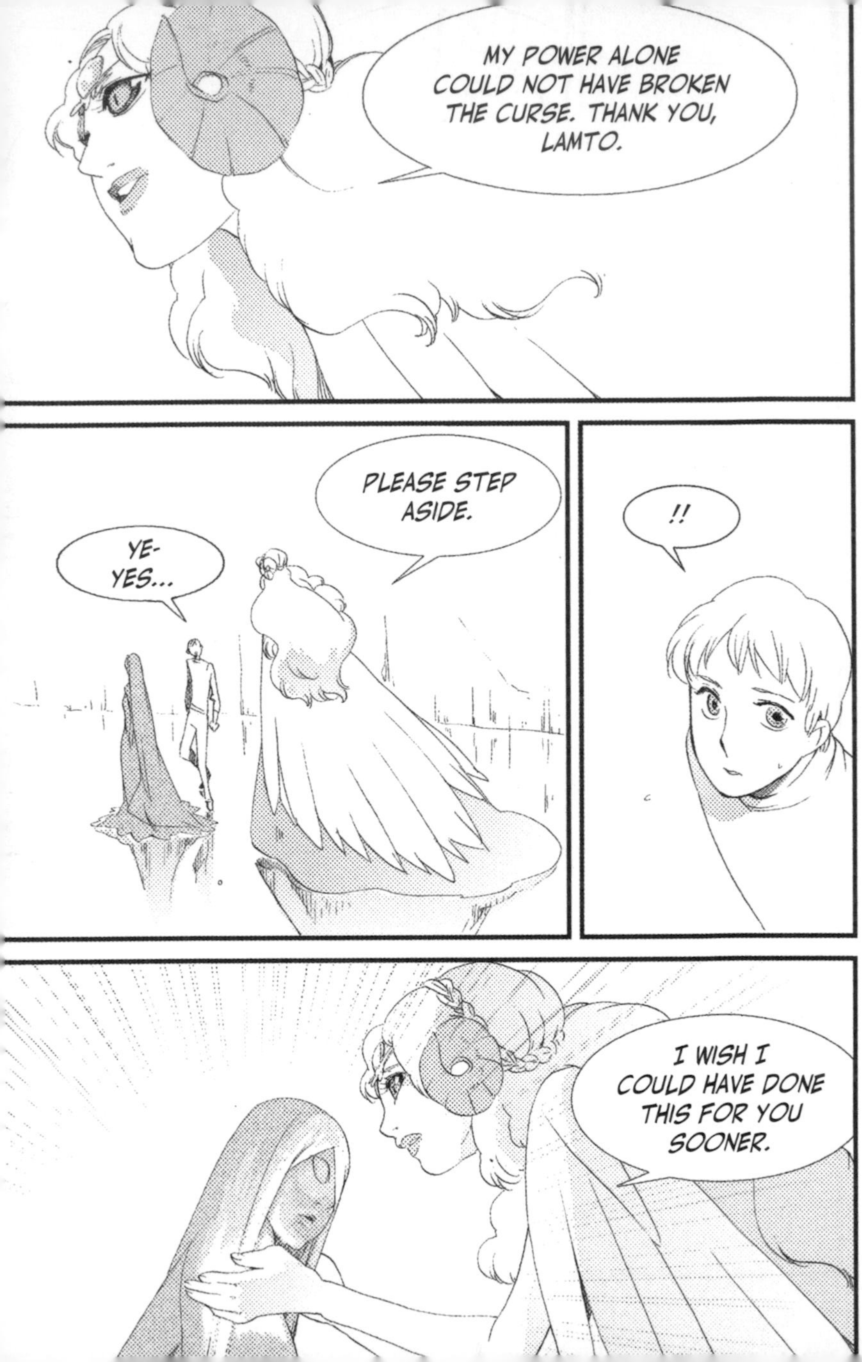
MY POWER ALONE COULD NOT HAVE BROKEN THE CURSE. THANK YOU, LAMTO.
!!
PLEASE STEP ASIDE.
YE- YES...
I WISH I COULD HAVE DONE THIS FOR YOU SOONER.

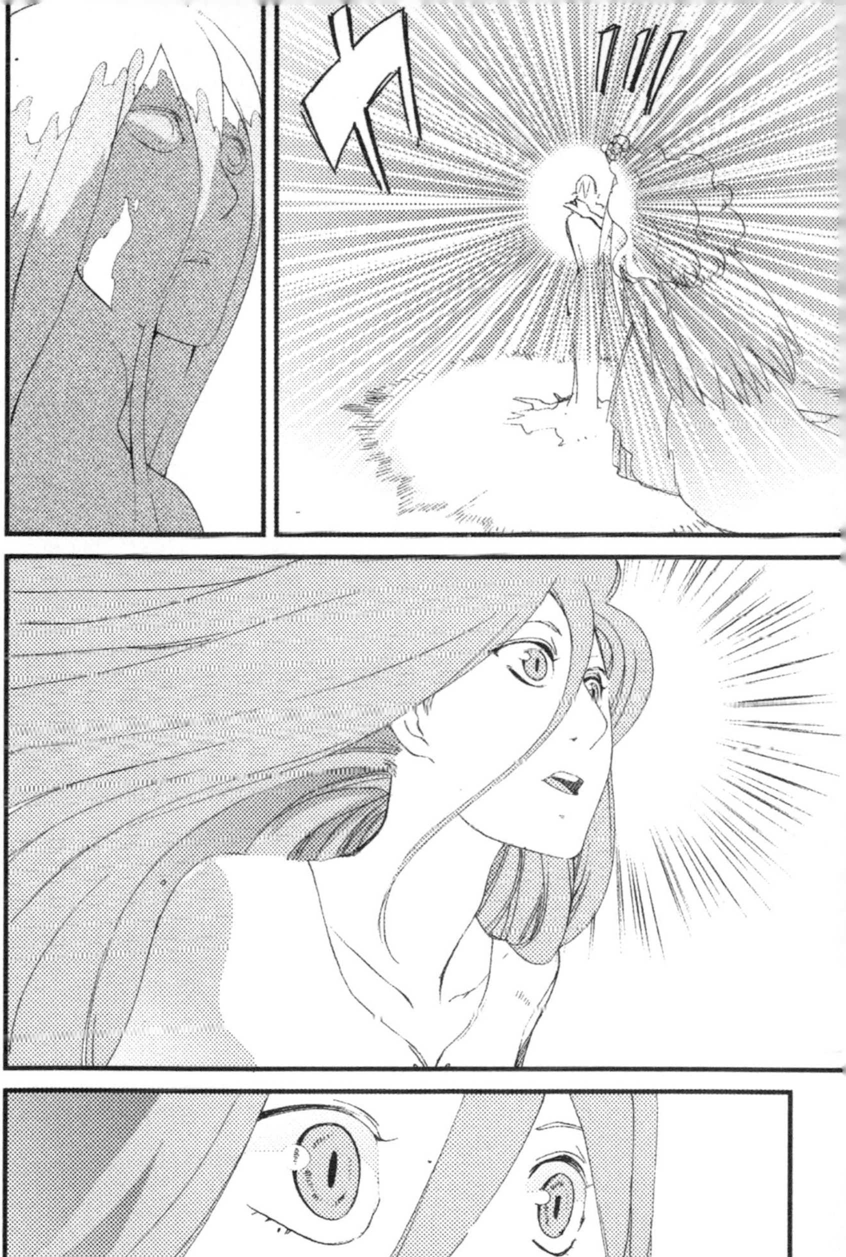

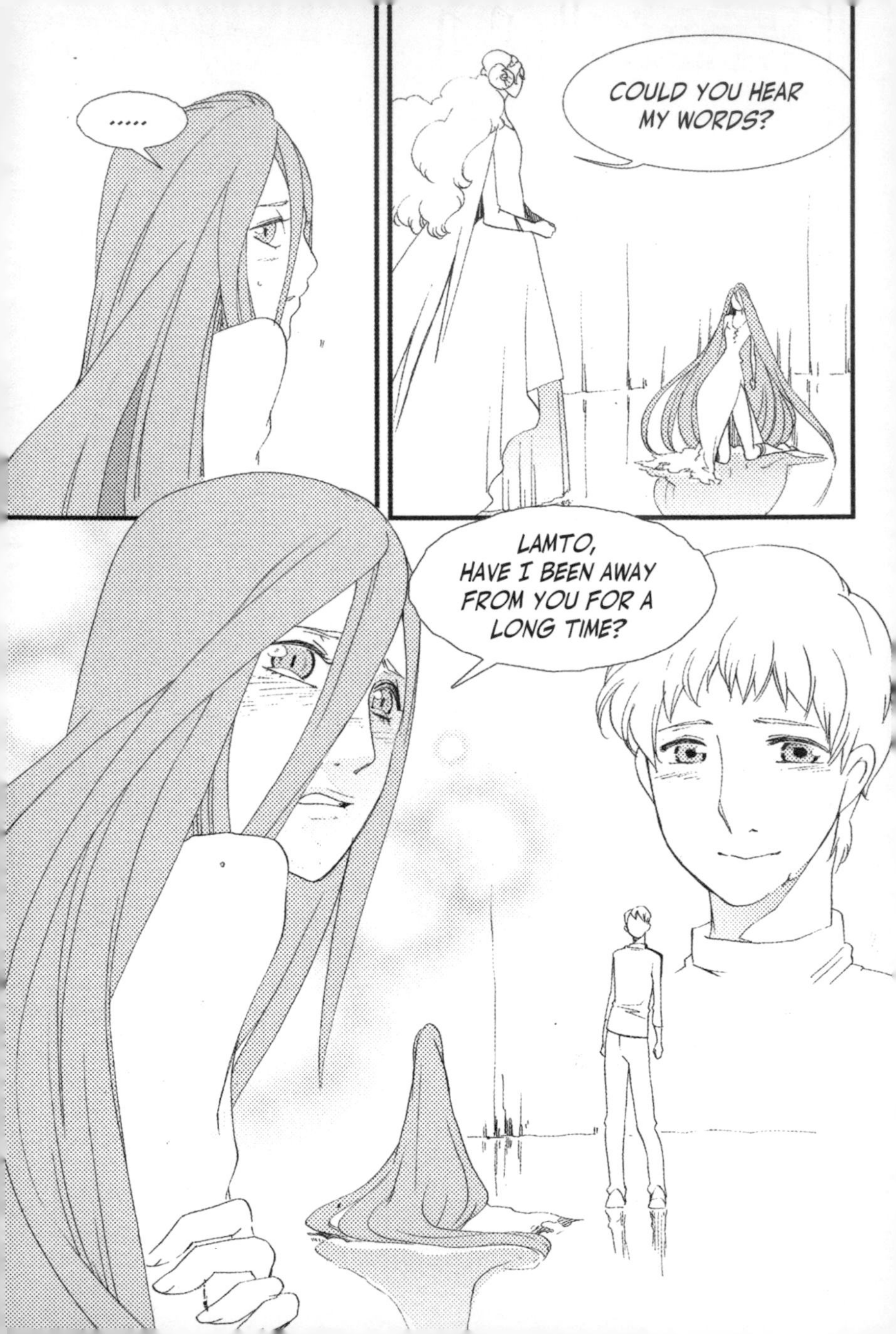
COULD YOU HEAR MY WORDS?
......
LAMTO, HAVE I BEEN AWAY FROM YOU FOR A LONG TIME?

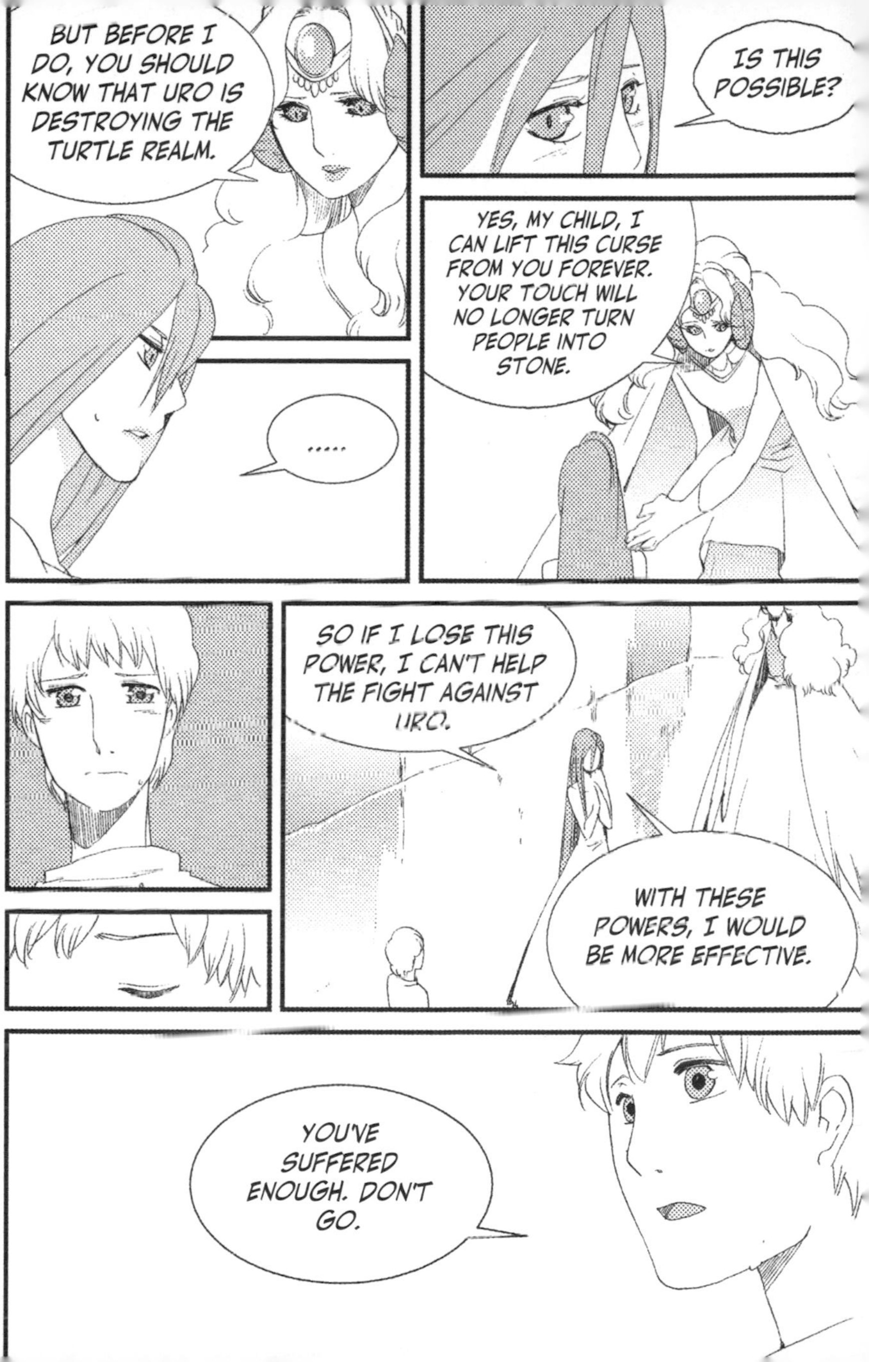
IS THIS POSSIBLE?
YES, MY CHILD, I CAN LIFT THIS CURSE FROM YOU FOREVER. YOUR TOUCH WILL NO LONGER TURN PEOPLE INTO STONE.
BUT BEFORE I DO, YOU SHOULD KNOW THAT URO IS DESTROYING THE TURTLE REALM.
.....
SO IF I LOSE THIS POWER, I CAN'T HELP THE FIGHT AGAINST URO.
WITH THESE POWERS, I WOULD BE MORE EFFECTIVE.
YOU'VE SUFFERED ENOUGH. DON'T GO.

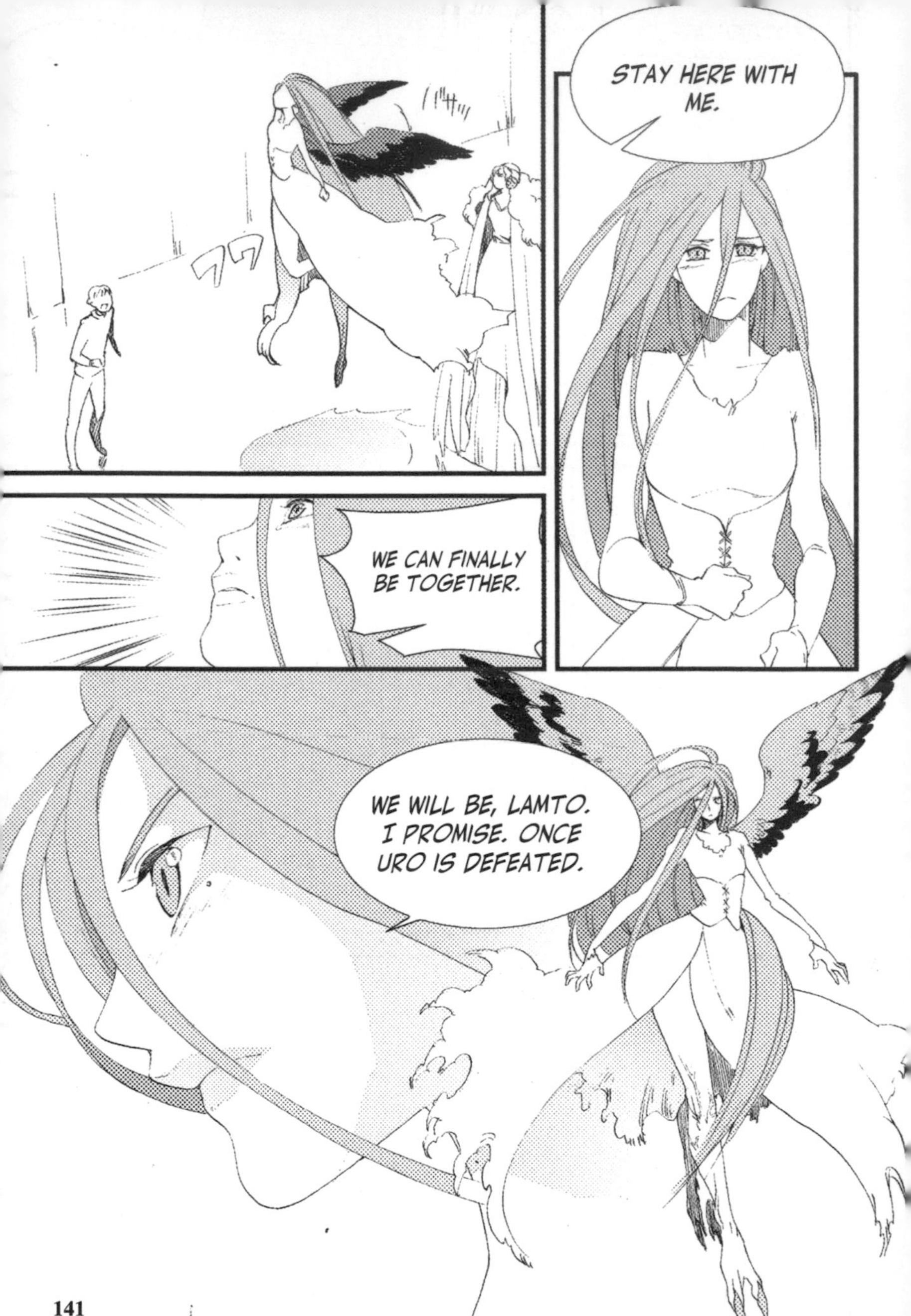
STAY HERE WITH ME.
フワ
WE CAN FINALLY BE TOGETHER.
WE WILL BE, LAMTO. I PROMISE. ONCE URO IS DEFEATED.

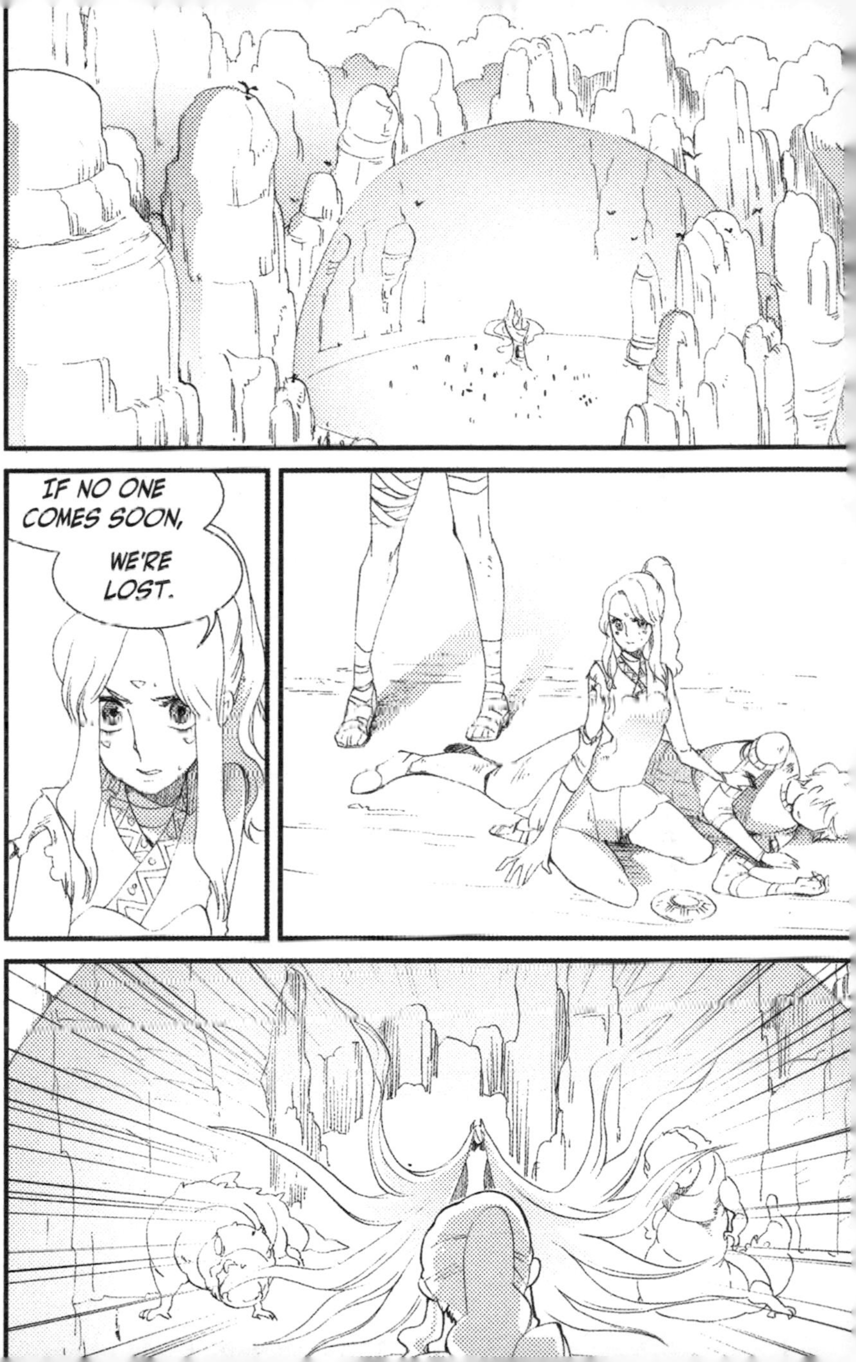
IF NO ONE COMES SOON, WE'RE LOST.

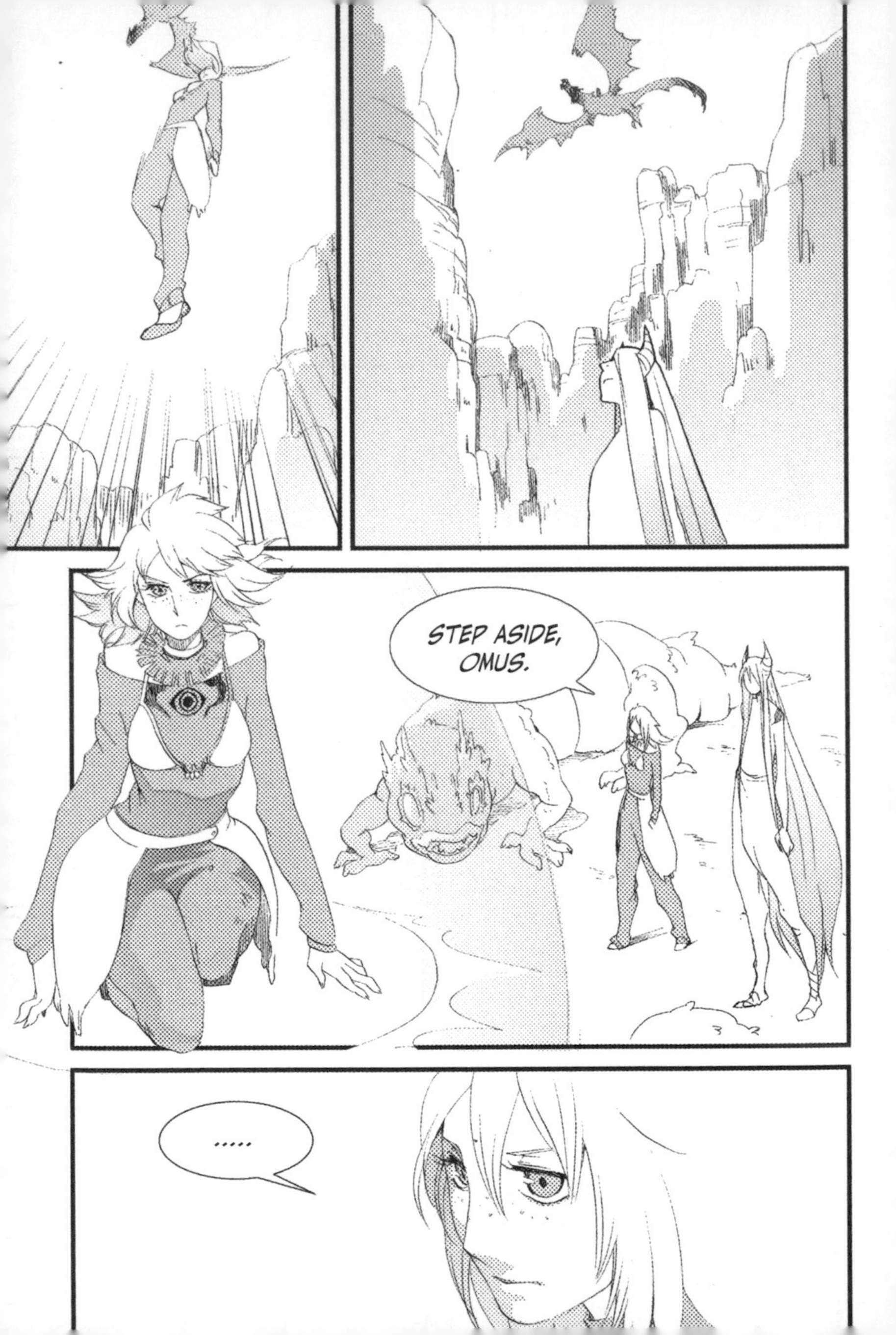
STEP ASIDE, OMUS.
......

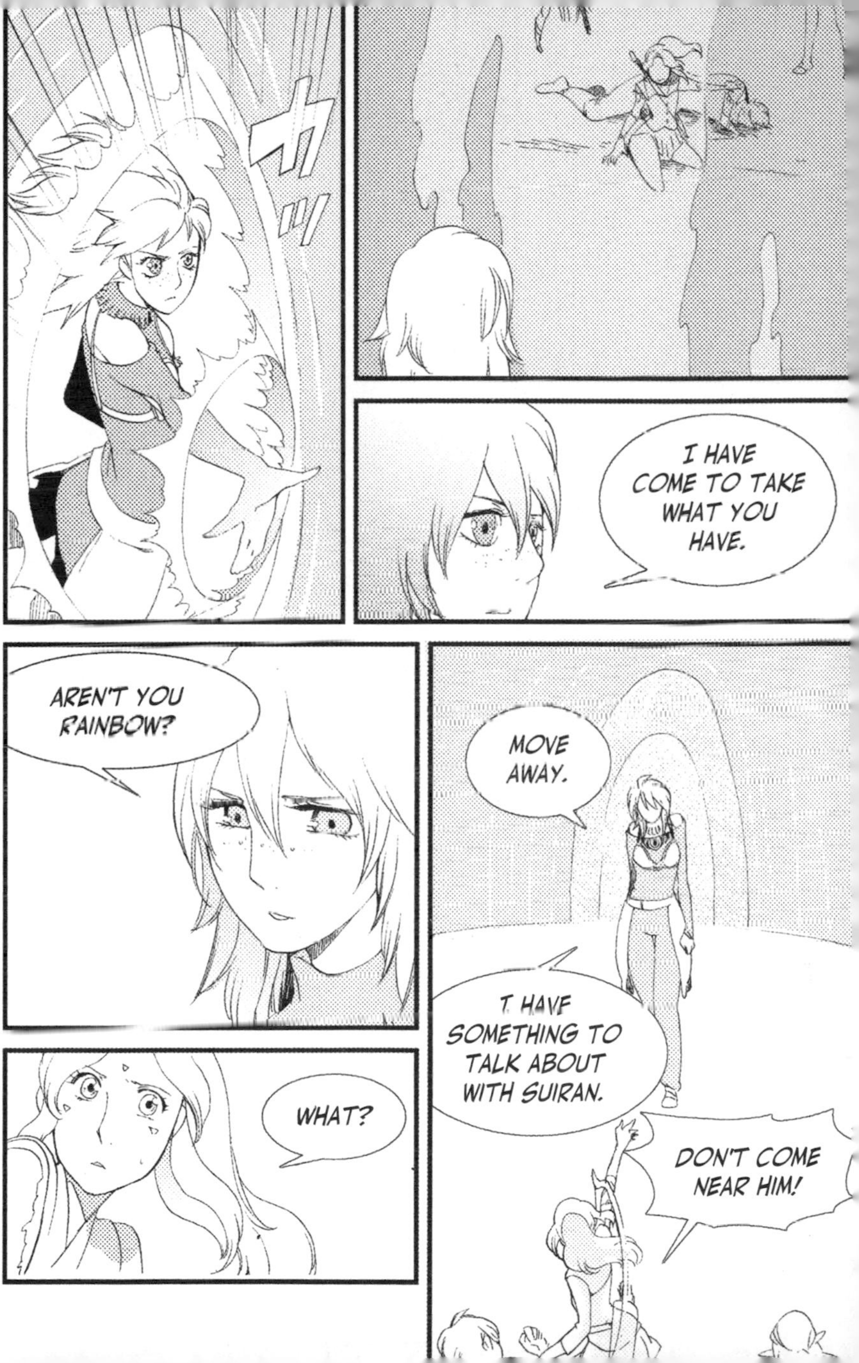
I HAVE COME TO TAKE WHAT YOU HAVE.
カッ
MOVE AWAY.
I HAVE SOMETHING TO TALK ABOUT WITH SUIRAN.
DON'T COME NEAR HIM!
AREN'T YOU RAINBOW?
WHAT?

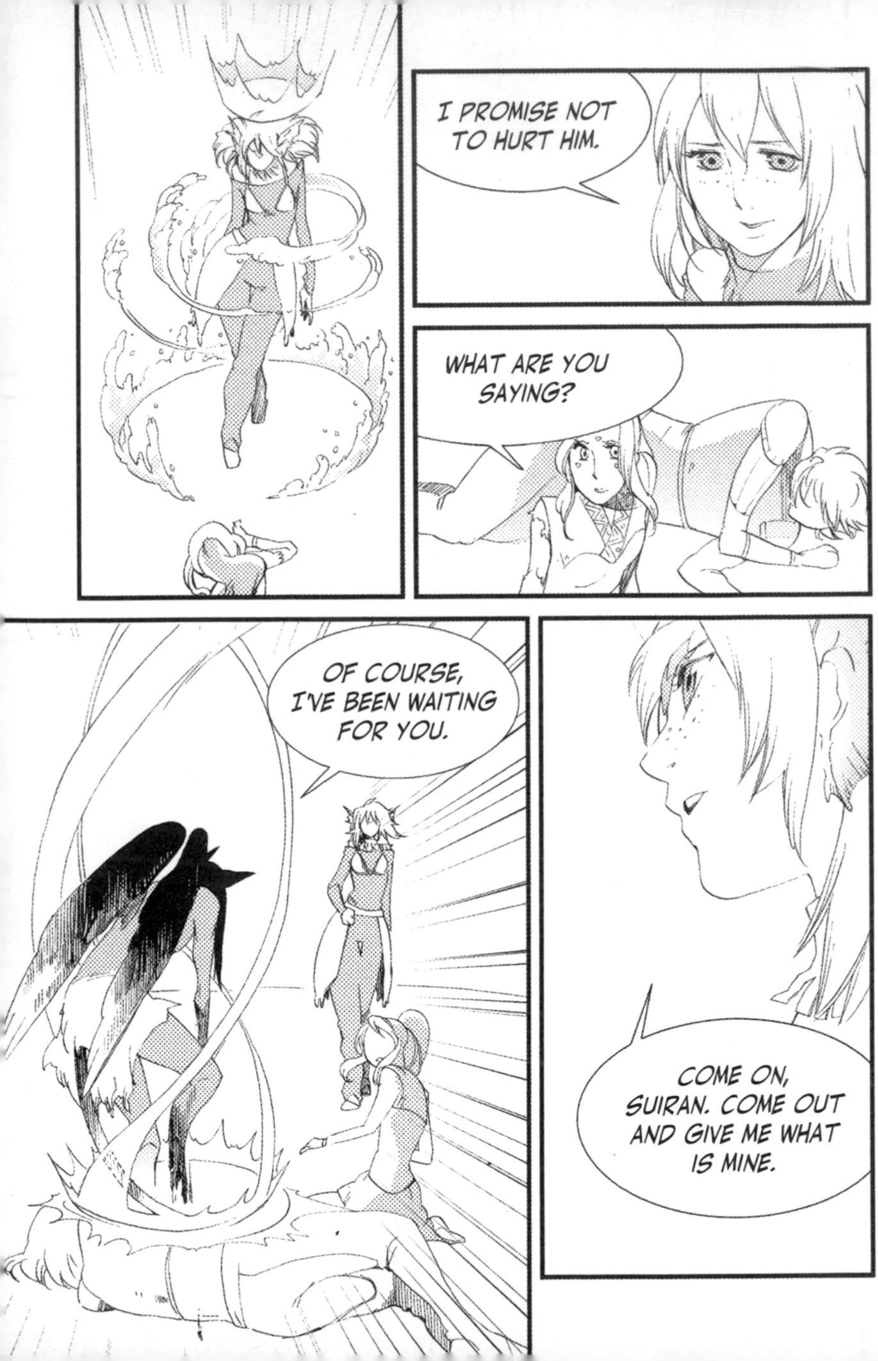
I PROMISE NOT TO HURT HIM.
WHAT ARE YOU SAYING?
COME ON, SUIRAN. COME OUT AND GIVE ME WHAT IS MINE.
OF COURSE, I'VE BEEN WAITING FOR YOU.

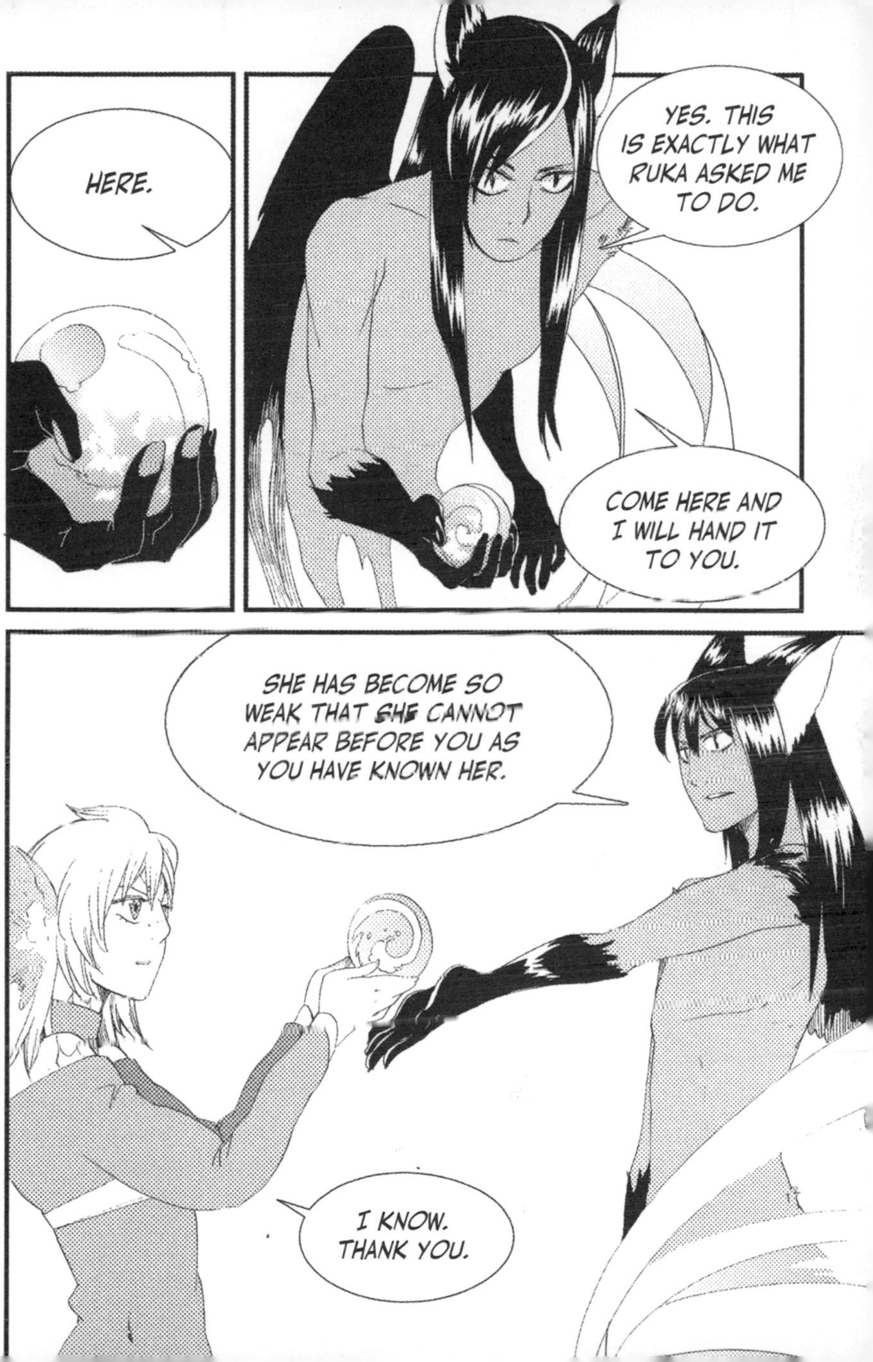
YES. THIS IS EXACTLY WHAT RUKA ASKED ME TO DO.
COME HERE AND I WILL HAND IT TO YOU.
HERE.
SHE HAS BECOME SO WEAK THAT SHE CANNOT APPEAR BEFORE YOU AS YOU HAVE KNOWN HER.
I KNOW. THANK YOU.

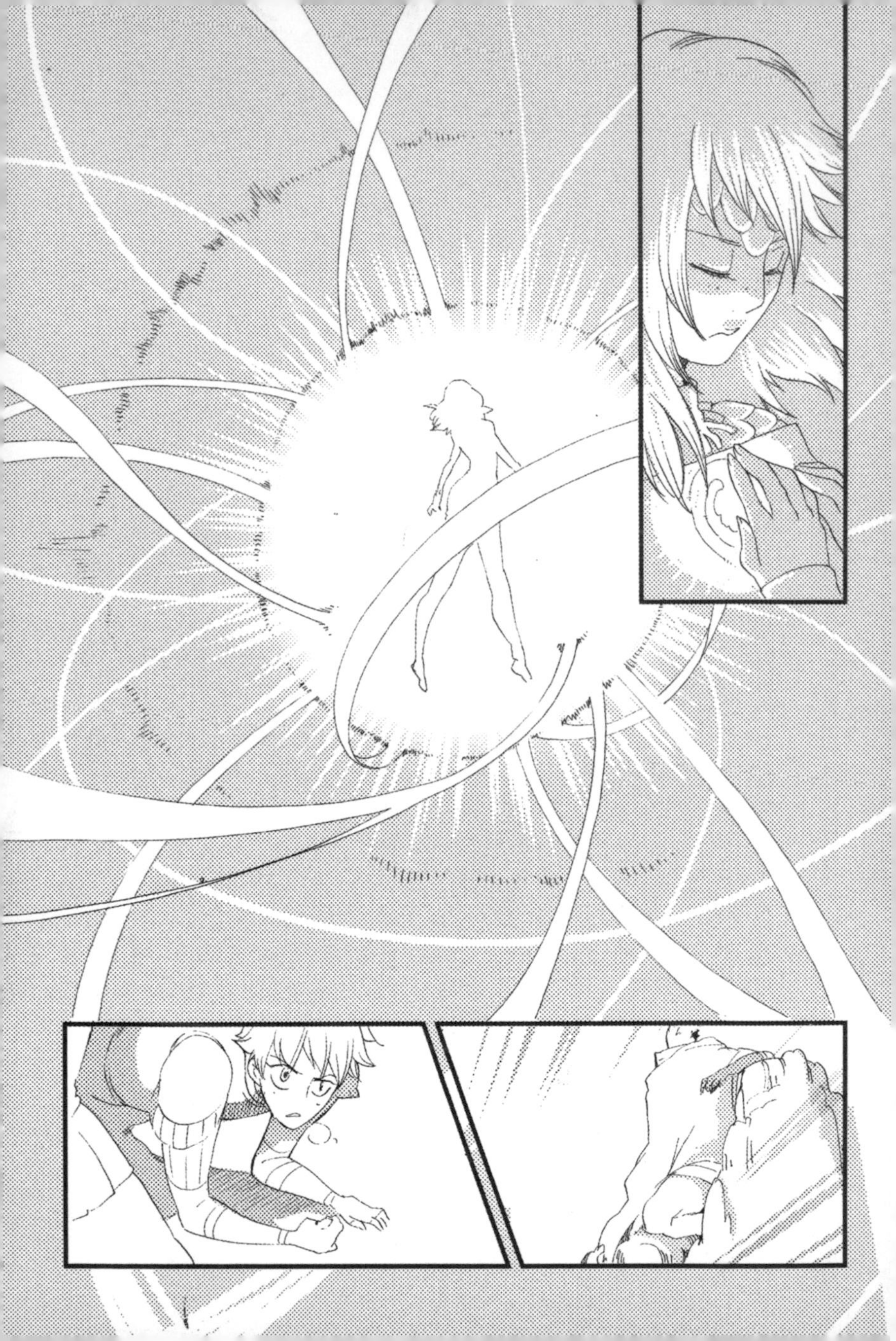

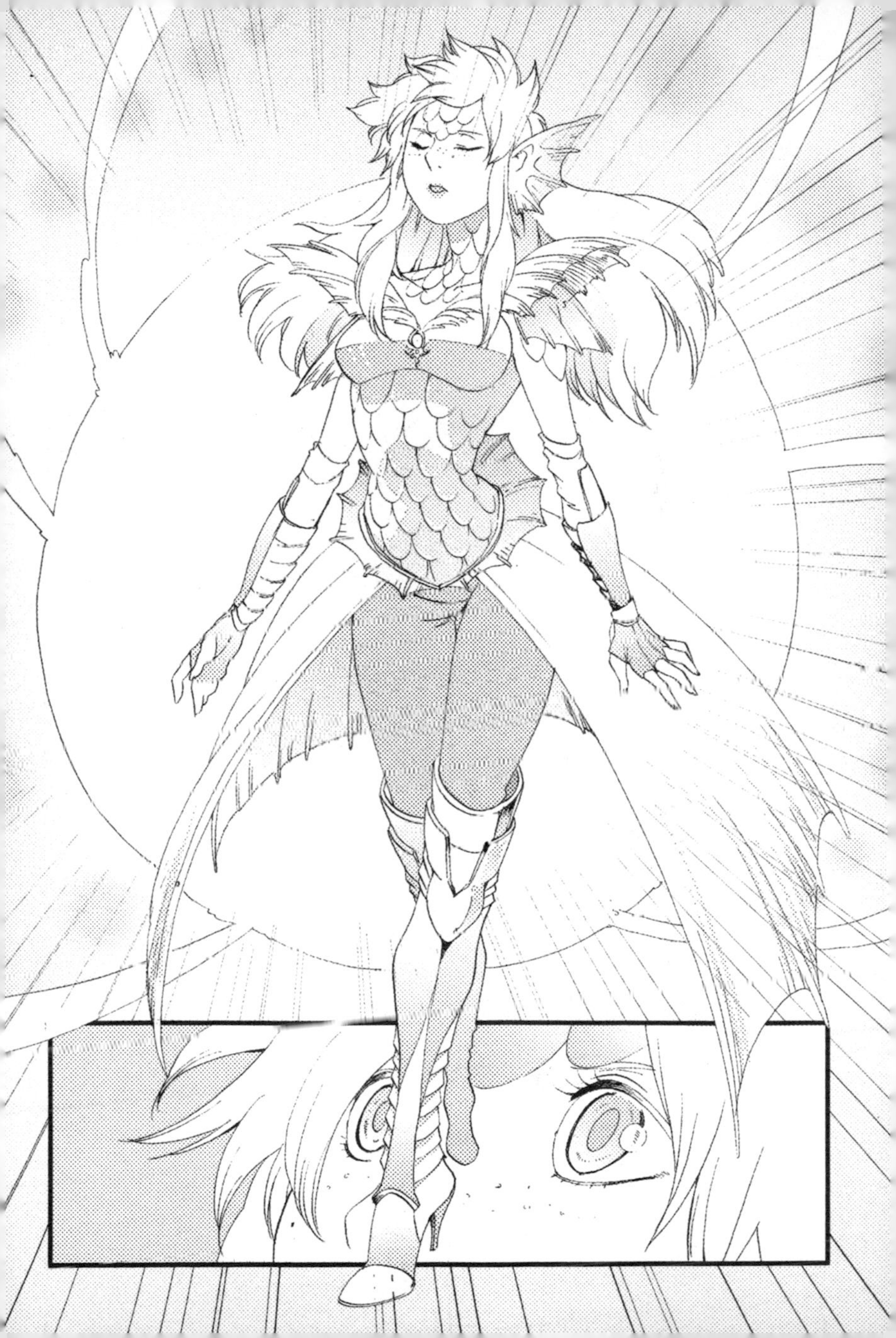

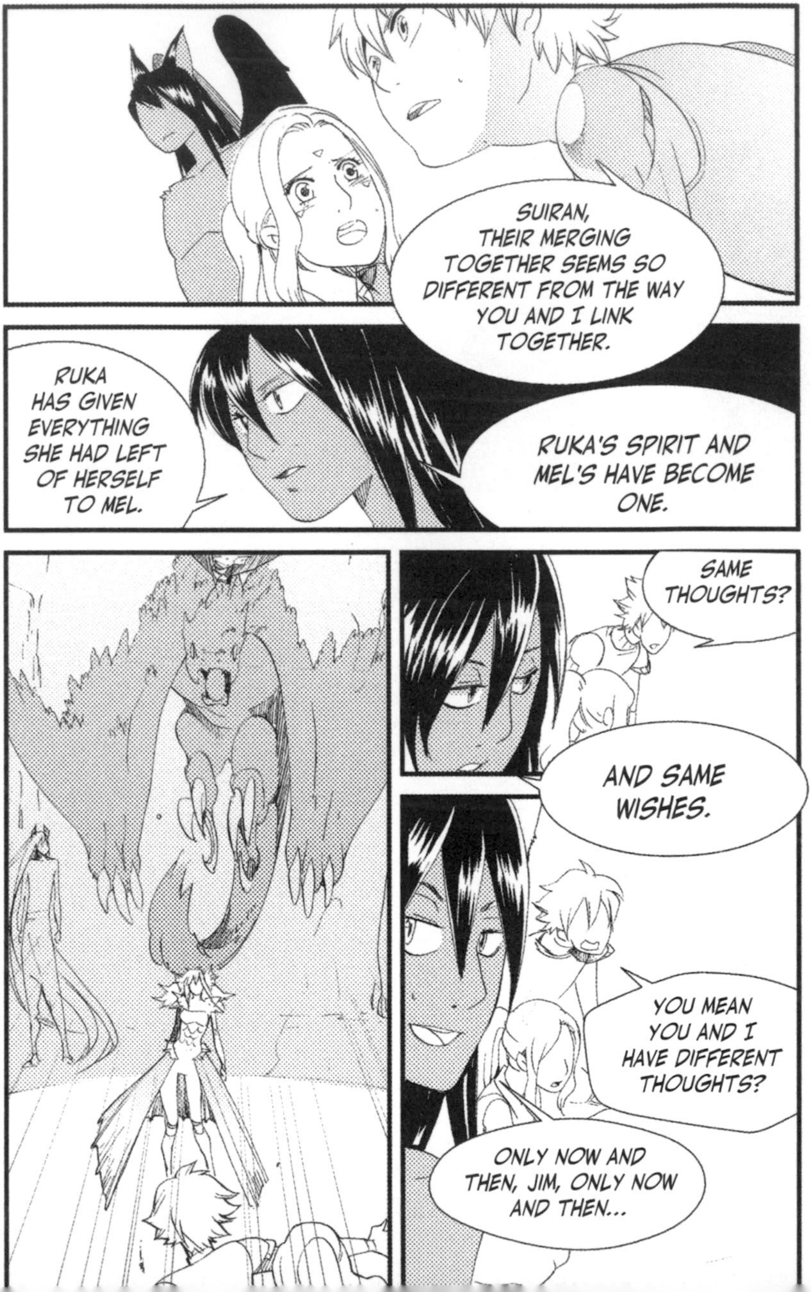
SUIRAN, THEIR MERGING TOGETHER SEEMS SO DIFFERENT FROM THE WAY YOU AND I LINK TOGETHER.
RUKA'S SPIRIT AND MEL'S HAVE BECOME ONE.
RUKA HAS GIVEN EVERYTHING SHE HAD LEFT OF HERSELF TO MEL.
SAME THOUGHTS?
AND SAME WISHES.
YOU MEAN YOU AND I HAVE DIFFERENT THOUGHTS?
ONLY NOW AND THEN, JIM, ONLY NOW AND THEN...

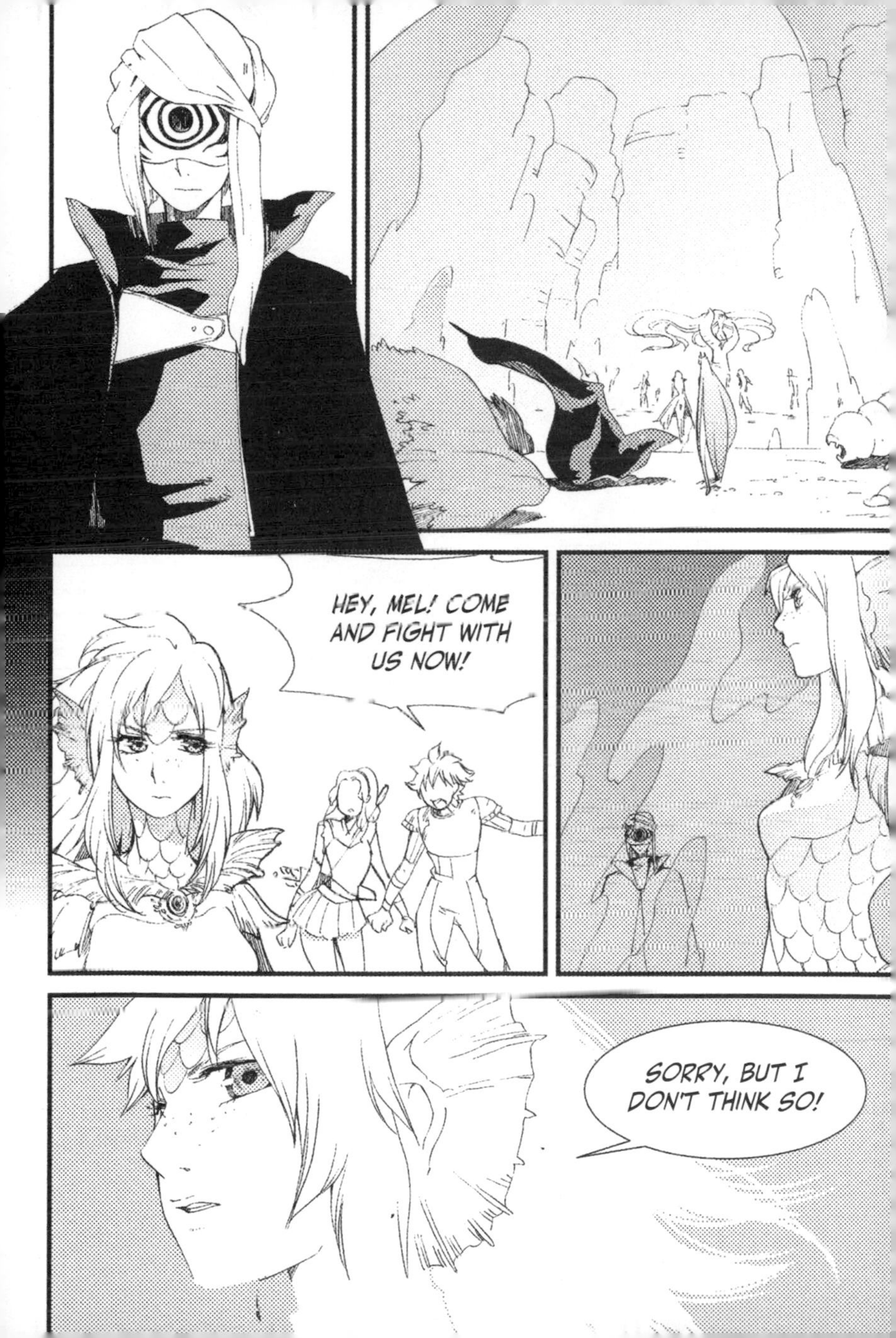
HEY, MEL! COME AND FIGHT WITH US NOW!
SORRY, BUT I DON'T THINK SO!

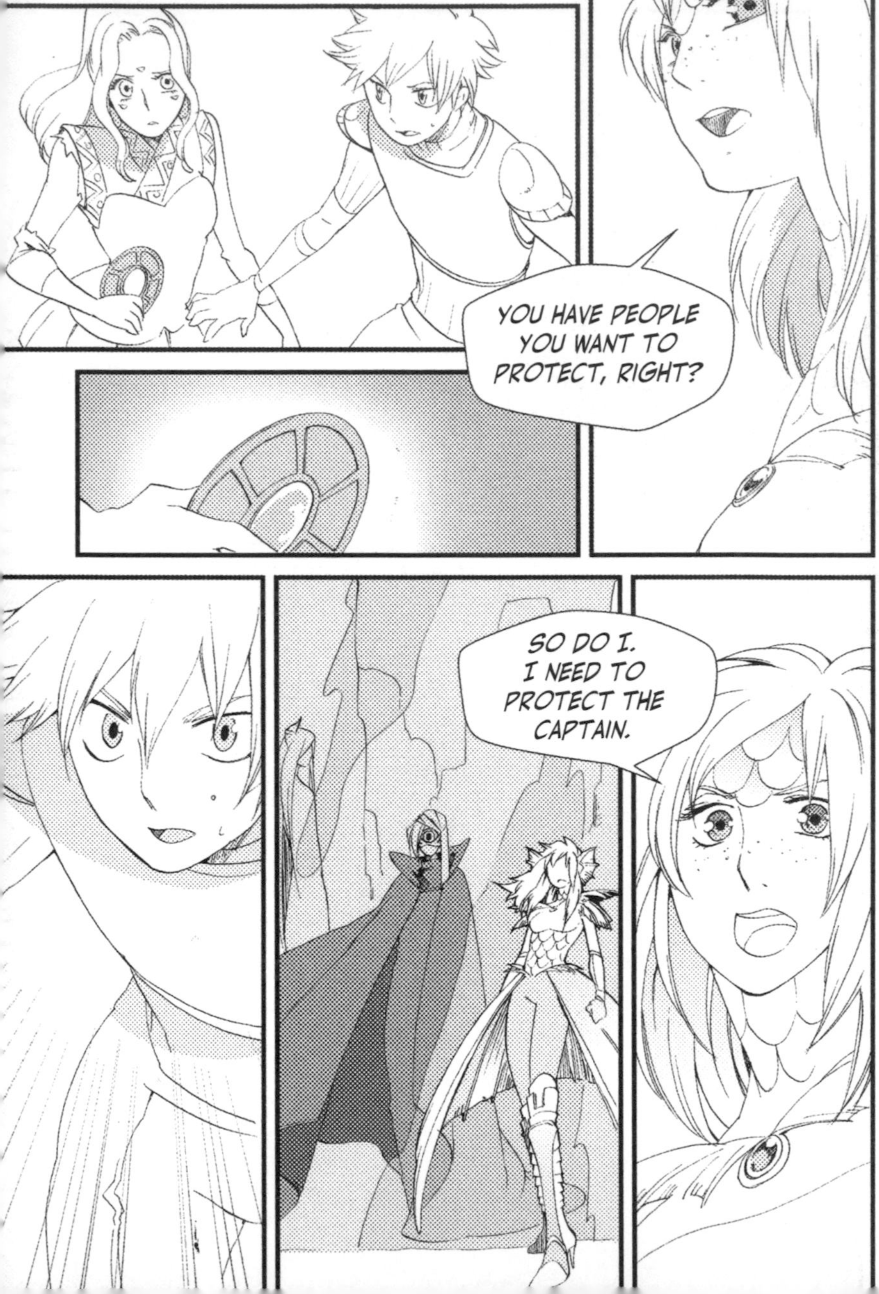
YOU HAVE PEOPLE YOU WANT TO PROTECT, RIGHT?
SO DO I. I NEED TO PROTECT THE CAPTAIN.

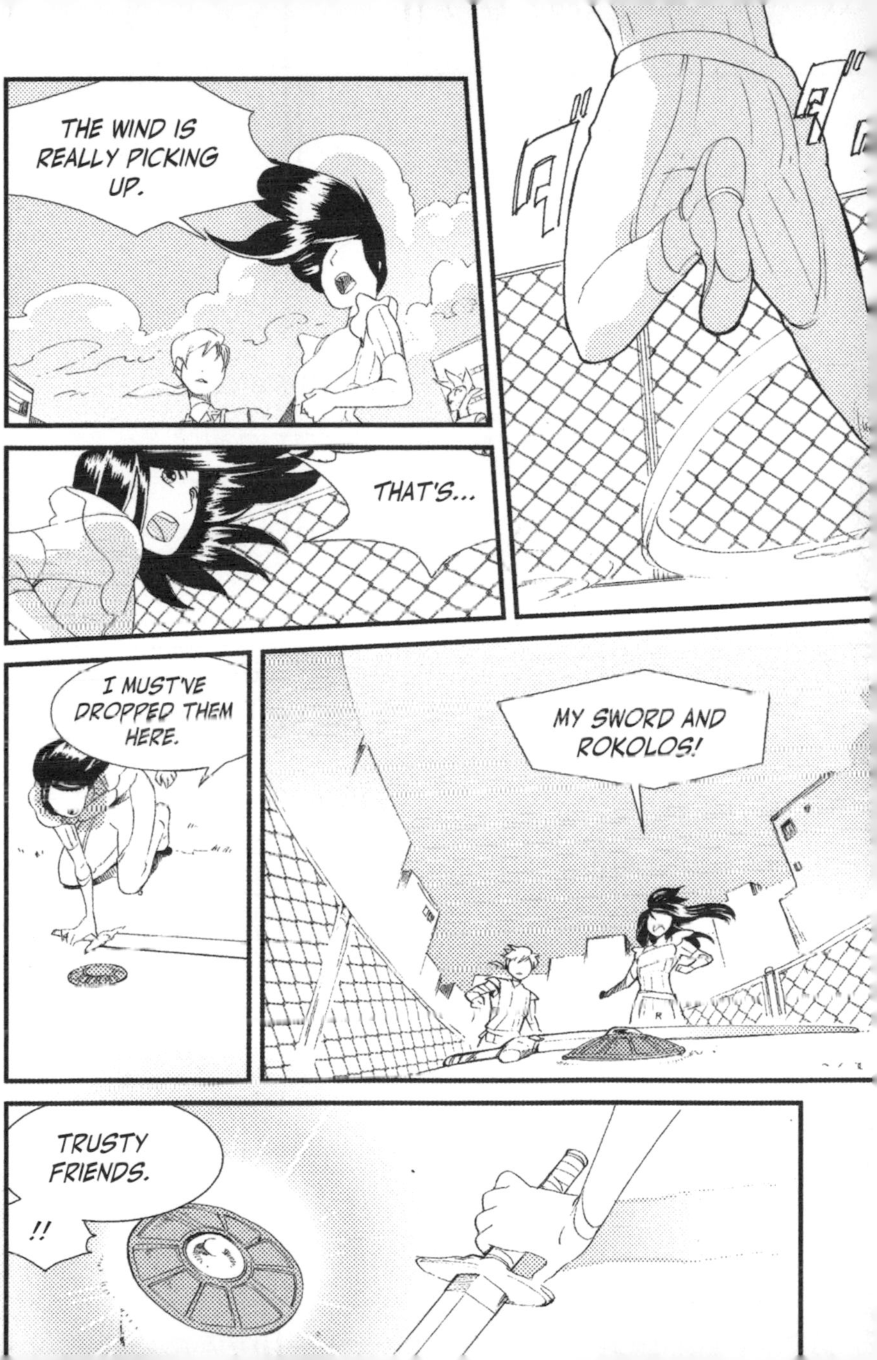
THE WIND IS REALLY PICKING UP.
THAT'S...
MY SWORD AND ROKOLOS!
I MUST'VE DROPPED THEM HERE.
TRUSTY FRIENDS.
!!

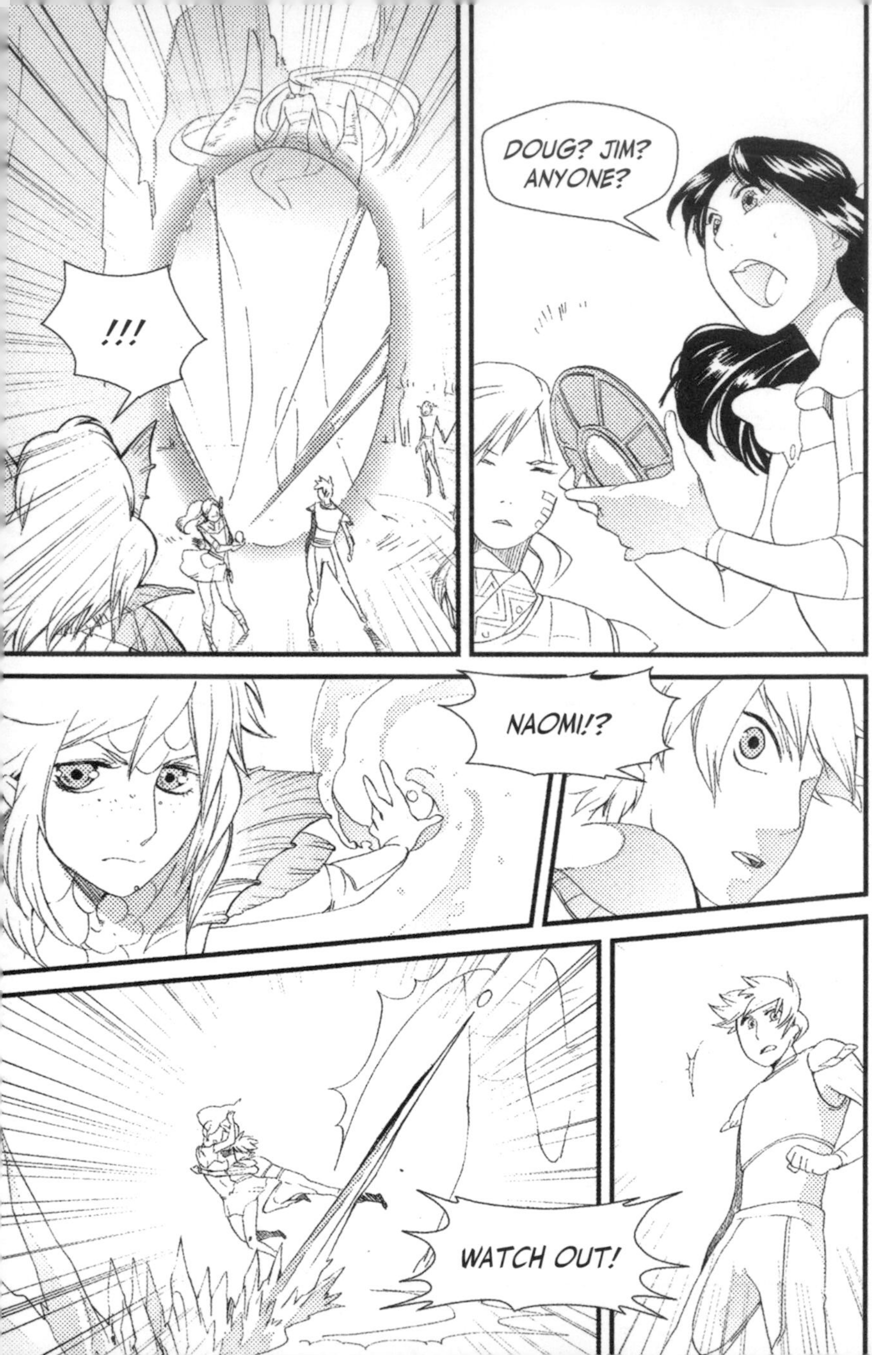
DOUG? JIM? ANYONE?
!!!
NAOMI!?
WATCH OUT!

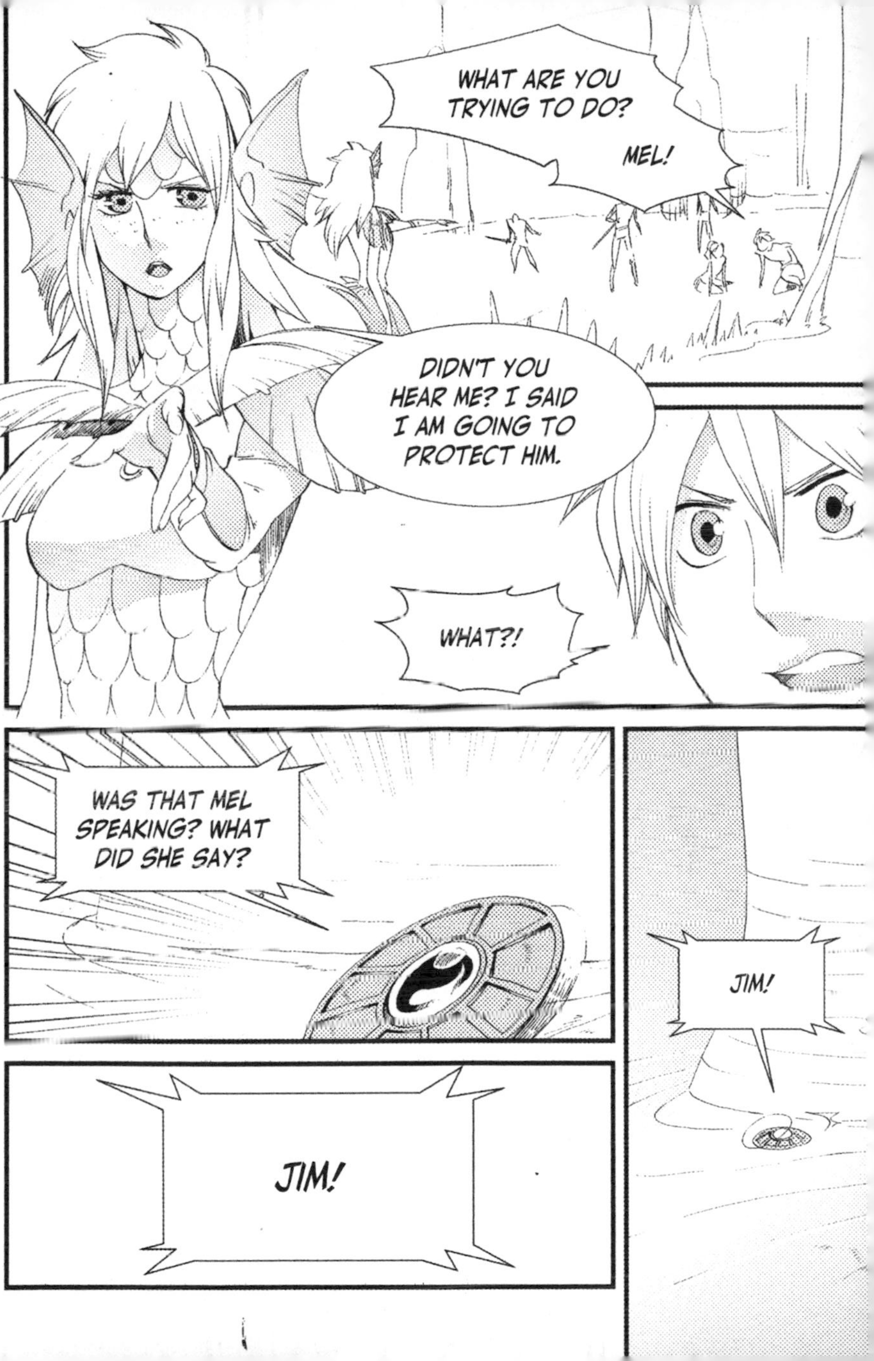
WHAT ARE YOU TRYING TO DO?
MEL!
DIDN'T YOU HEAR ME? I SAID I AM GOING TO PROTECT HIM.
WHAT?!
WAS THAT MEL SPEAKING? WHAT DID SHE SAY?
JIM!
JIM!

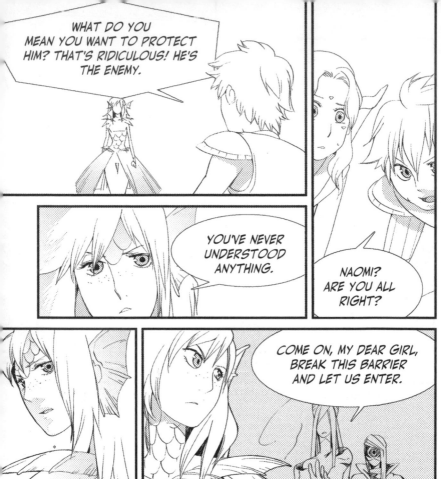

WHAT DO YOU MEAN YOU WANT TO PROTECT HIM? THAT'S RIDICULOUS! HE'S THE ENEMY.

YOU'VE NEVER UNDERSTOOD ANYTHING.

NAOMI? ARE YOU ALL RIGHT?

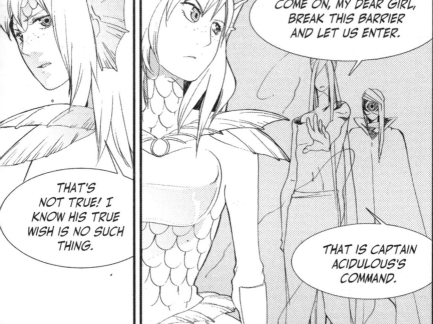

THAT'S NOT TRUE! I KNOW HIS TRUE WISH IS NO SUCH THING.

COME ON, MY DEAR GIRL, BREAK THIS BARRIER AND LET US ENTER.

THAT IS CAPTAIN ACIDULOUS'S COMMAND.

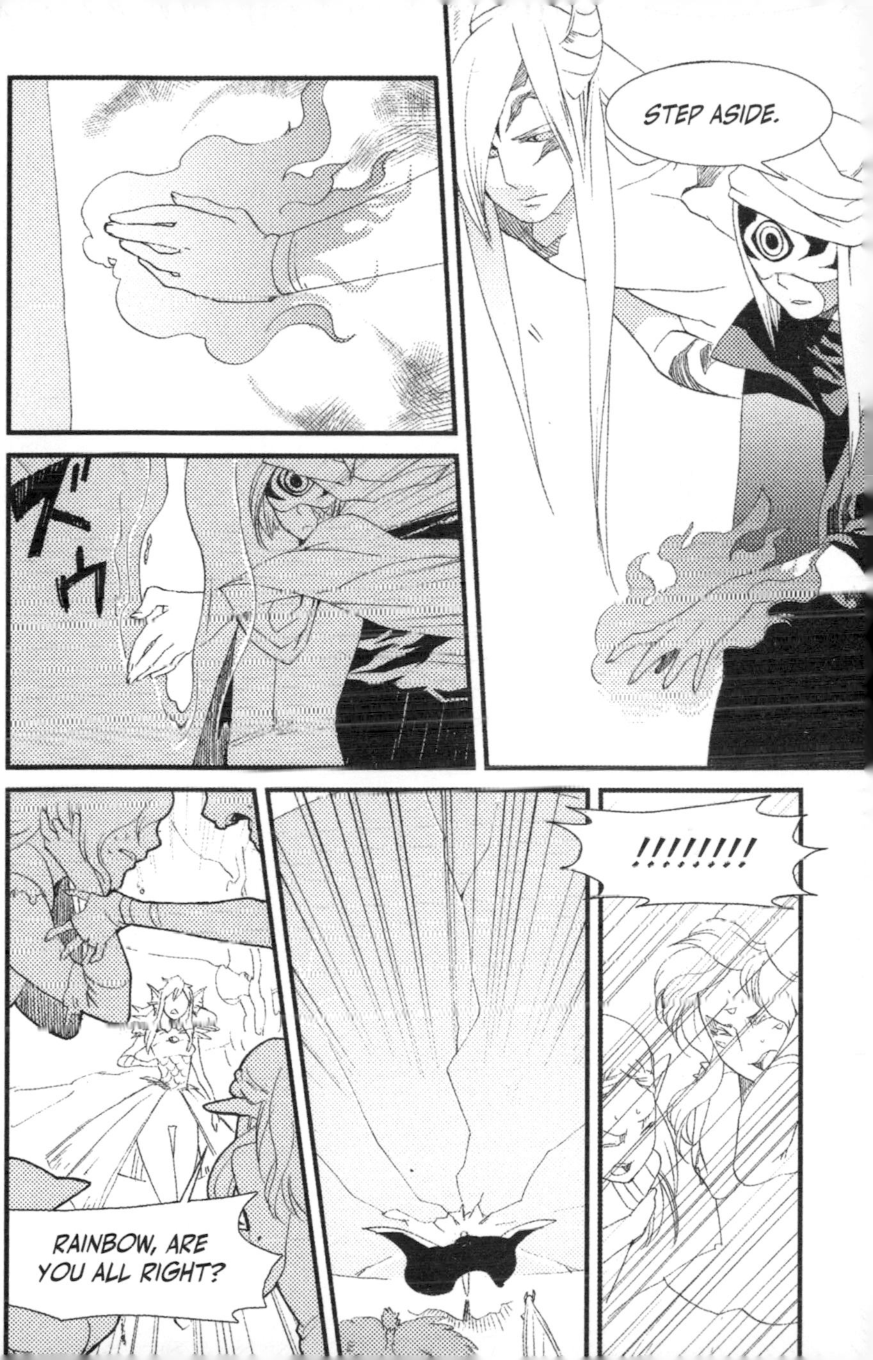
STEP ASIDE.
!!!!!!!!
RAINBOW, ARE YOU ALL RIGHT?

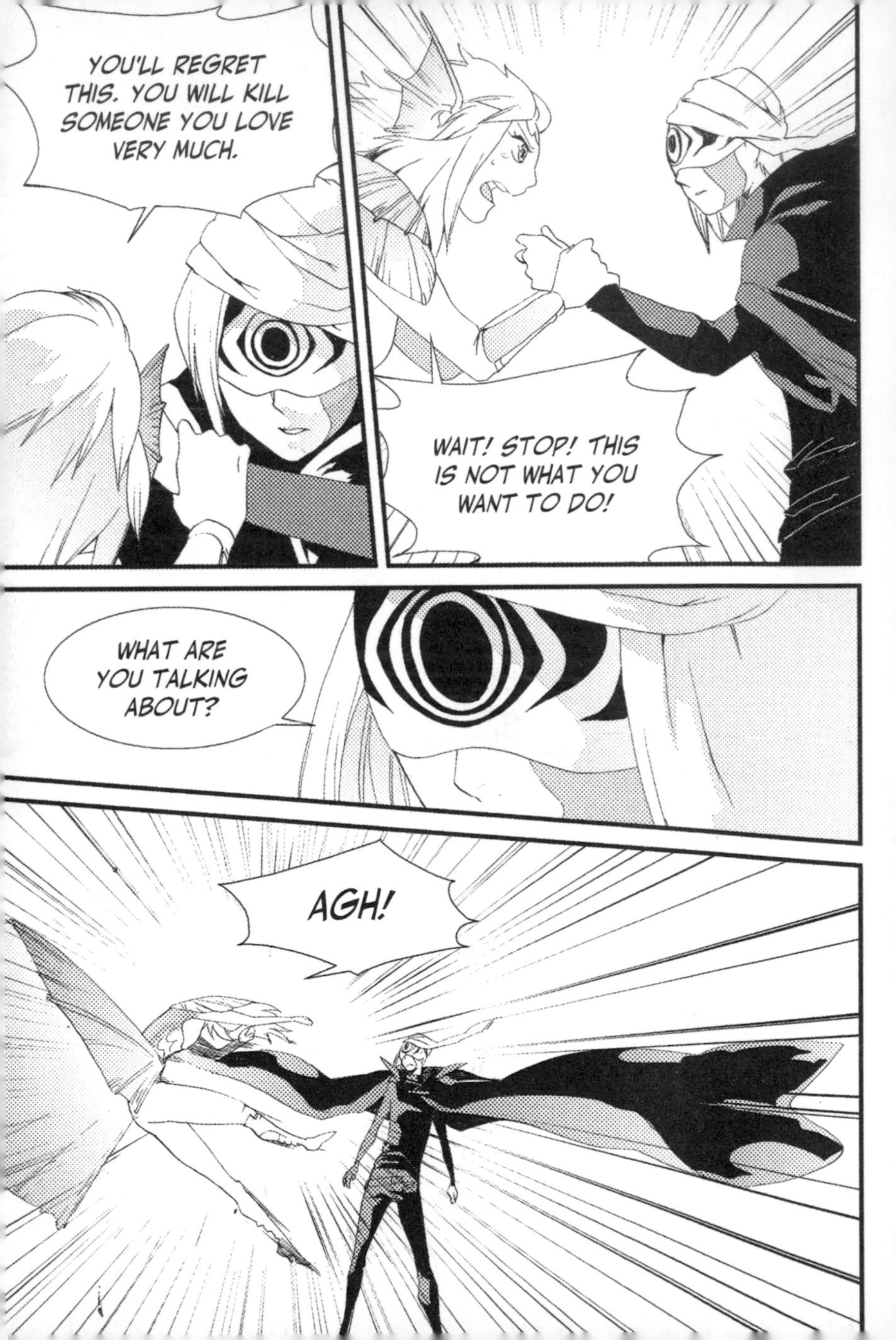
WAIT! STOP! THIS IS NOT WHAT YOU WANT TO DO!
YOU'LL REGRET THIS. YOU WILL KILL SOMEONE YOU LOVE VERY MUCH.
WHAT ARE YOU TALKING ABOUT?
AGH!

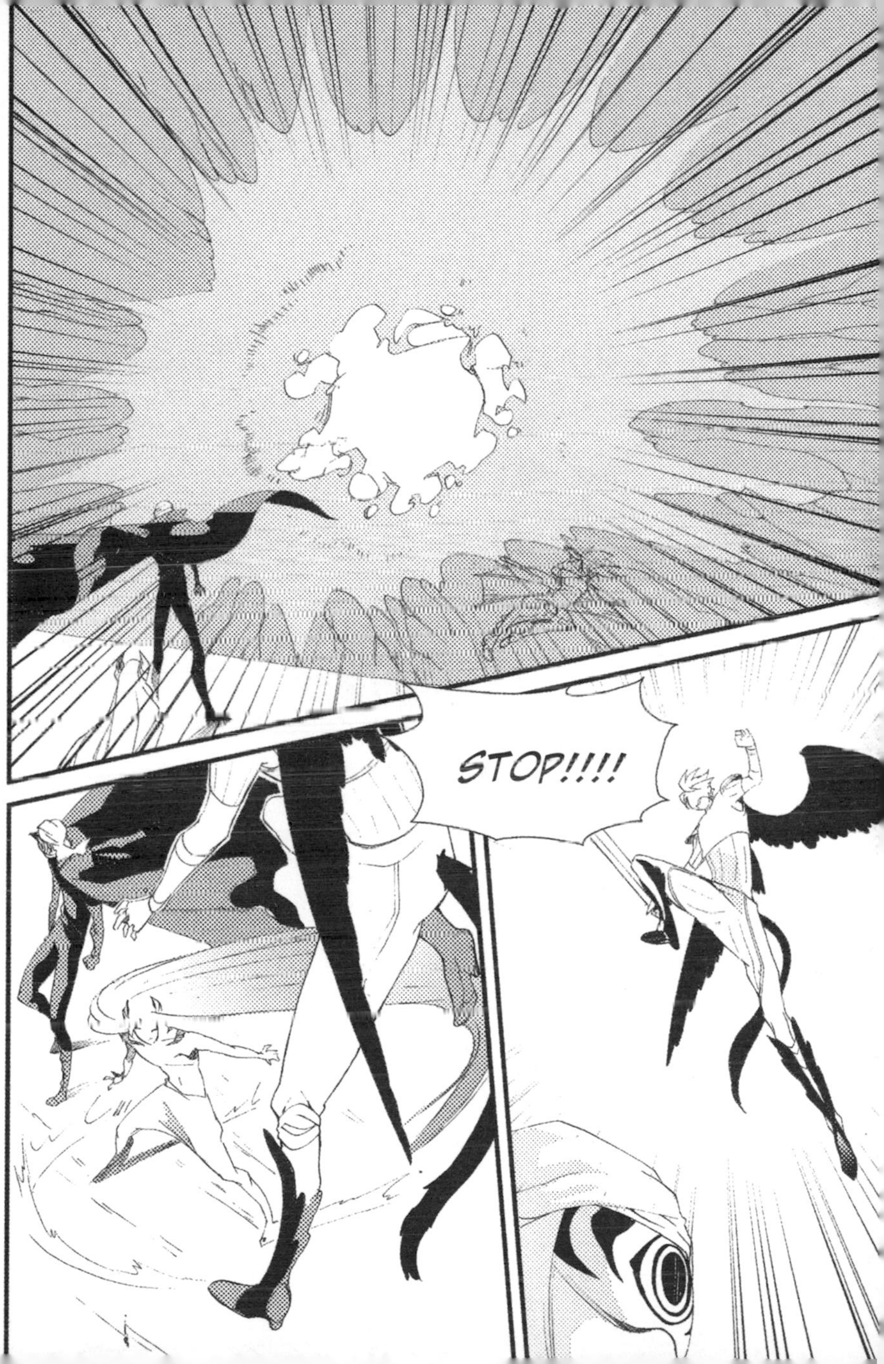
STOP!!!!

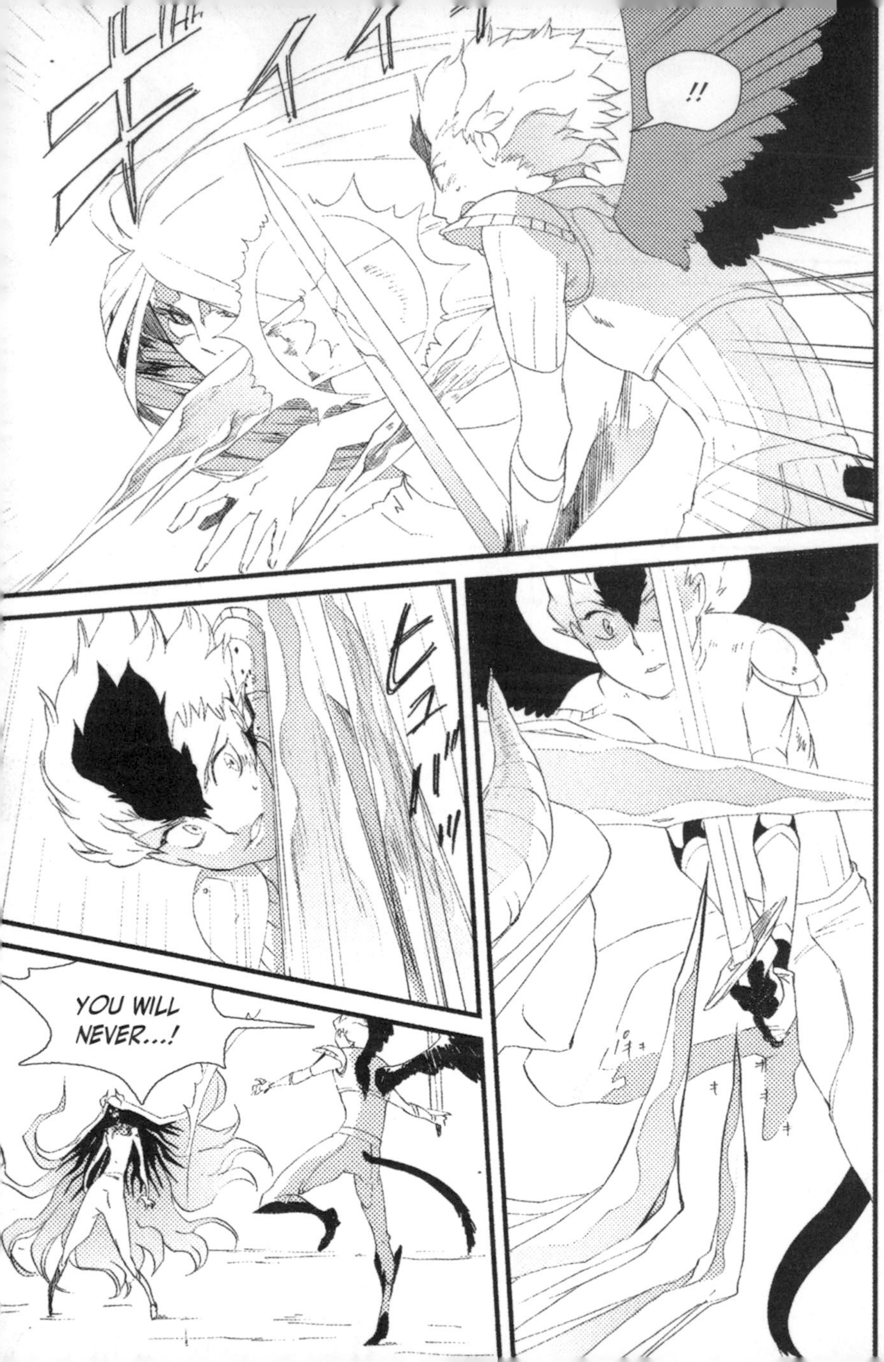
!!
YOU WILL NEVER...!

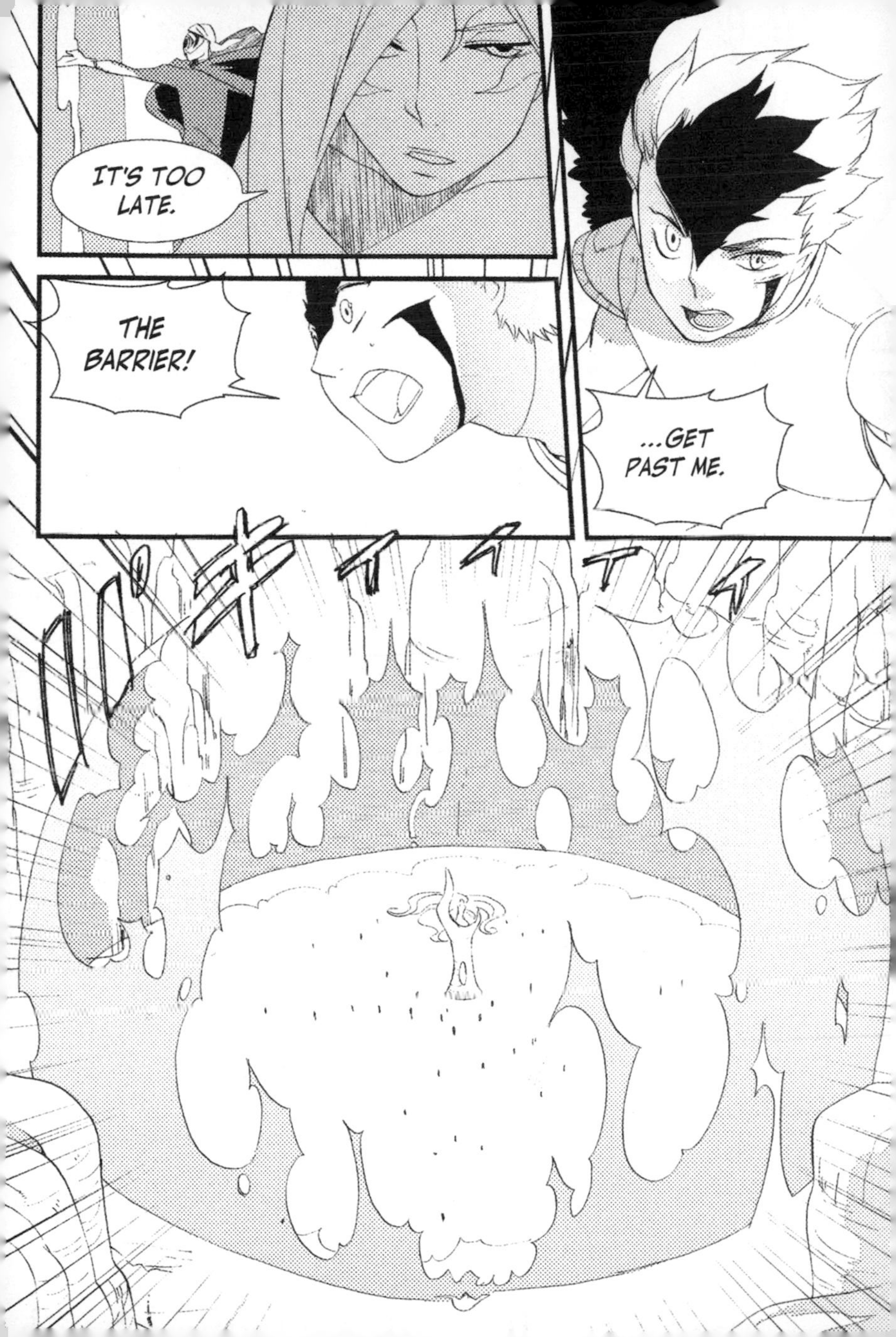
...GET PAST ME.
IT'S TOO LATE.
THE BARRIER!

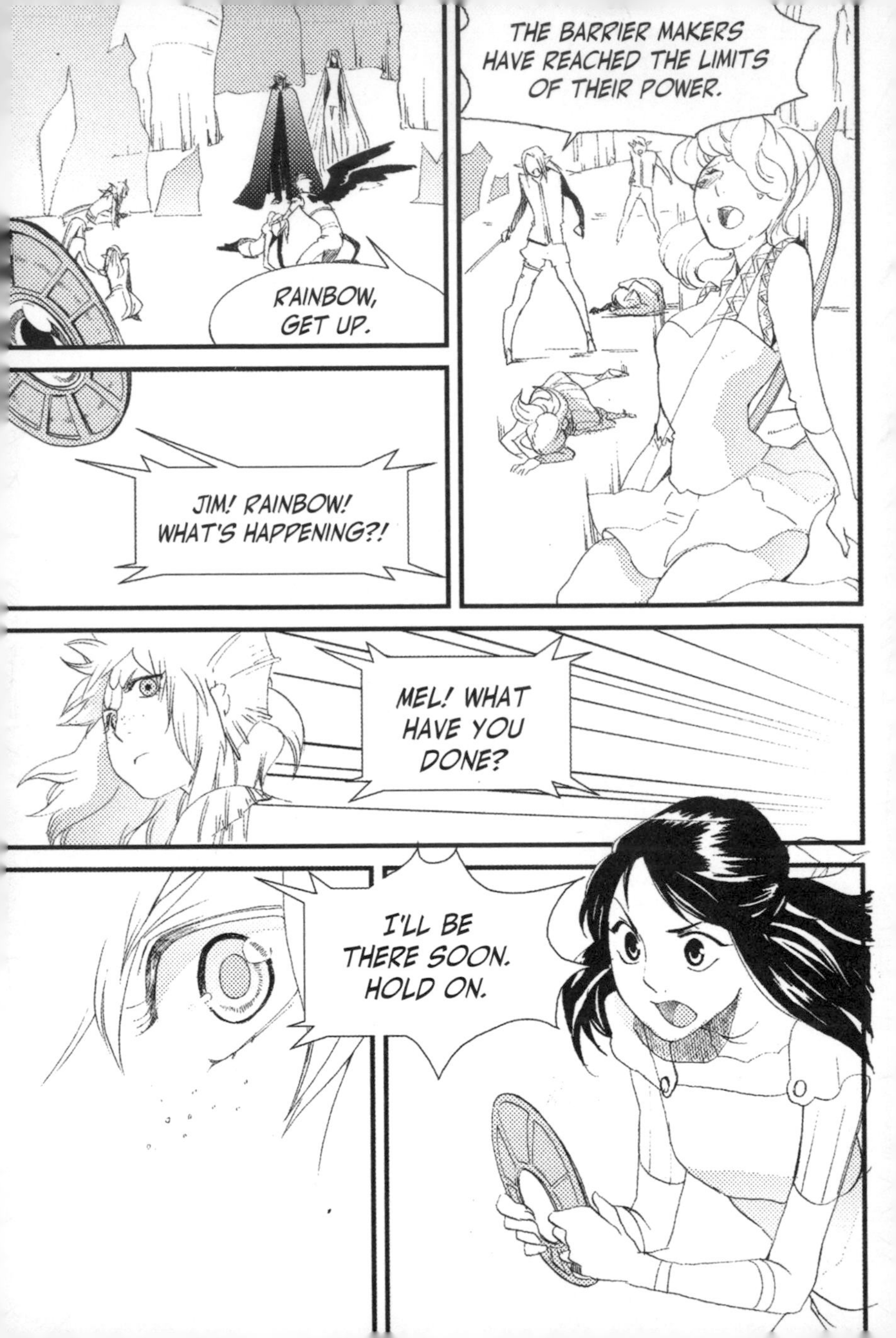
THE BARRIER MAKERS HAVE REACHED THE LIMITS OF THEIR POWER.
RAINBOW, GET UP.
JIM! RAINBOW! WHAT'S HAPPENING?!
MEL! WHAT HAVE YOU DONE?
I'LL BE THERE SOON. HOLD ON.

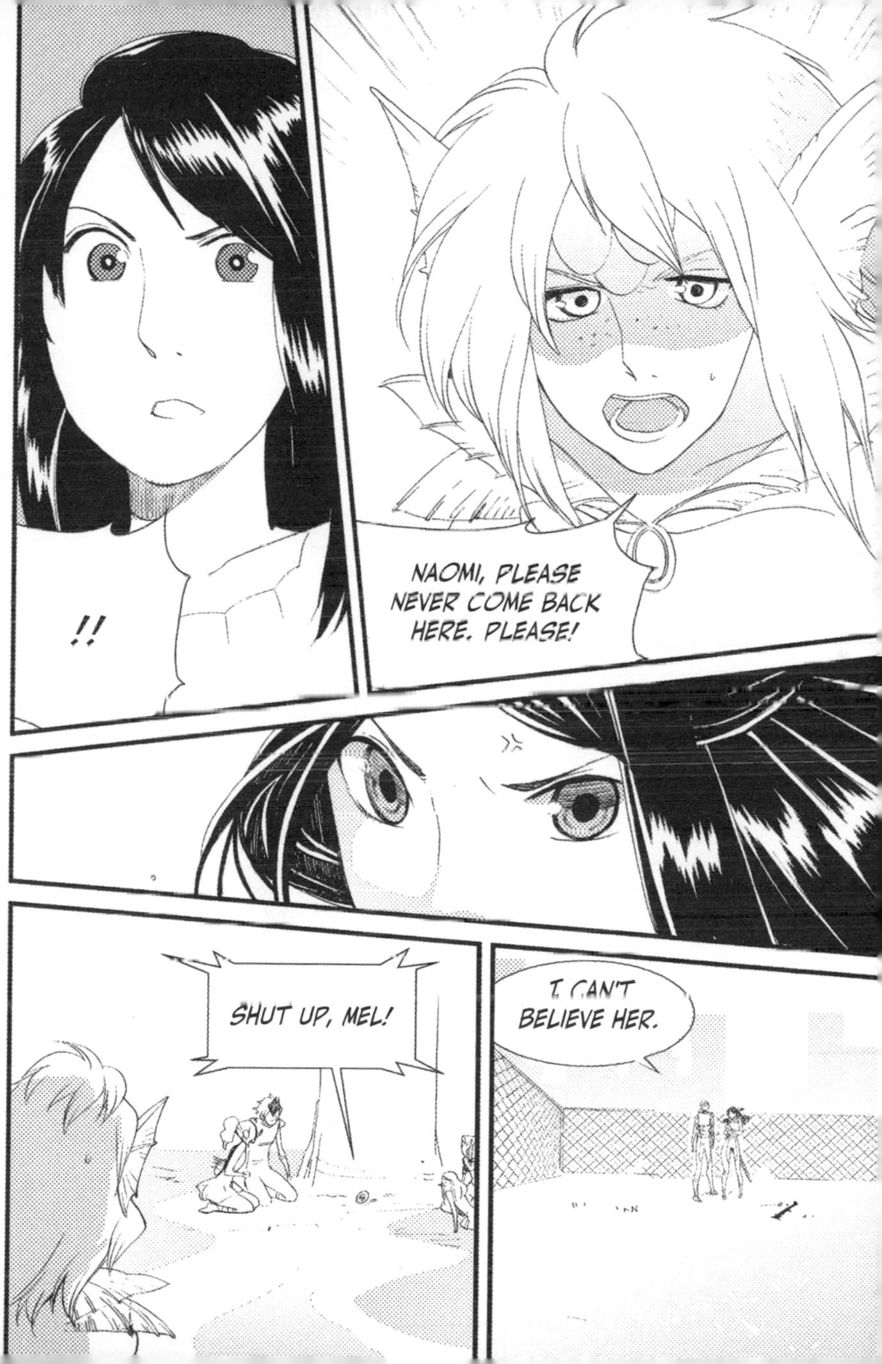
NAOMI, PLEASE NEVER COME BACK HERE. PLEASE!
!!
I CAN'T BELIEVE HER.
SHUT UP, MEL!

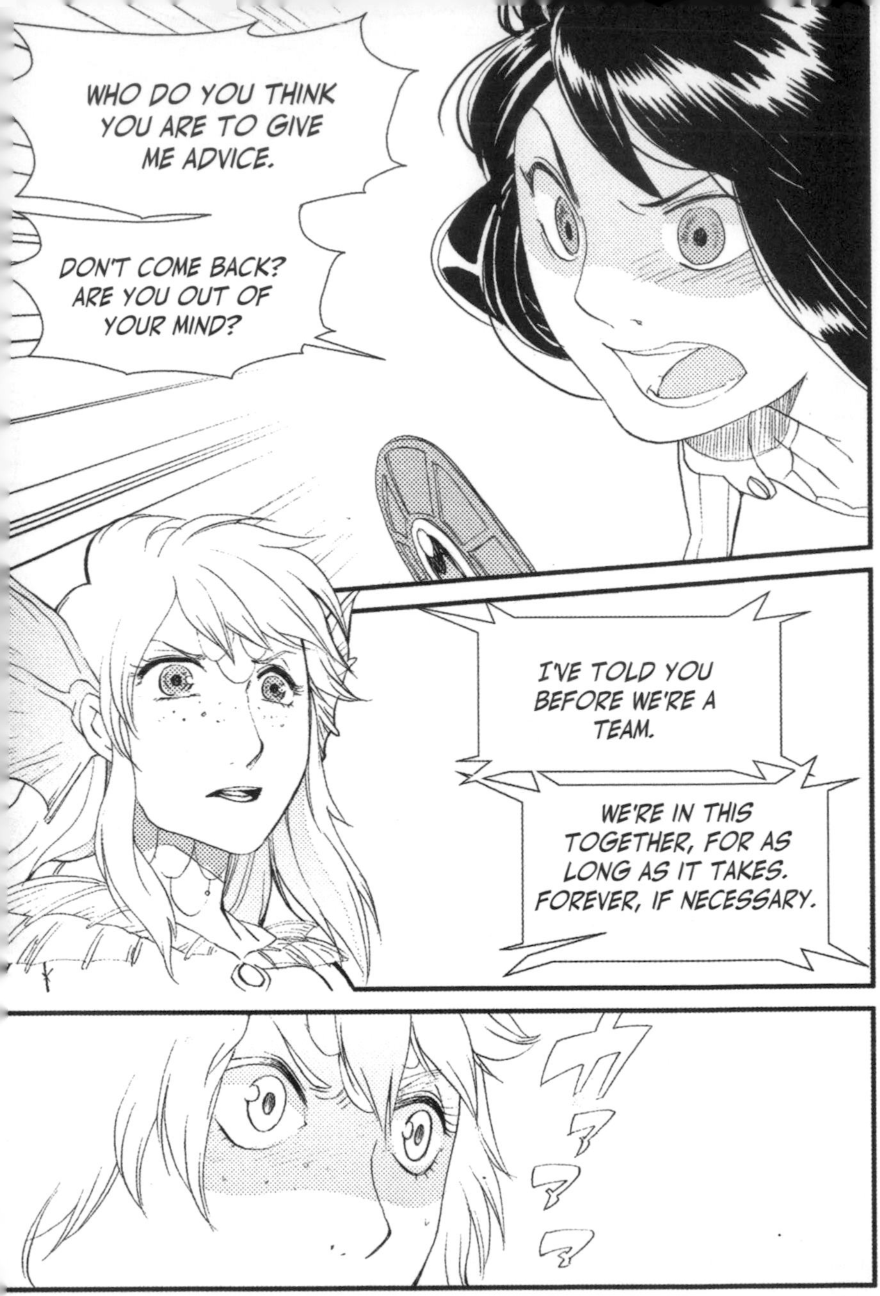
WHO DO YOU THINK YOU ARE TO GIVE ME ADVICE.
DON'T COME BACK? ARE YOU OUT OF YOUR MIND?
I'VE TOLD YOU BEFORE WE'RE A TEAM.
WE'RE IN THIS TOGETHER, FOR AS LONG AS IT TAKES. FOREVER, IF NECESSARY.

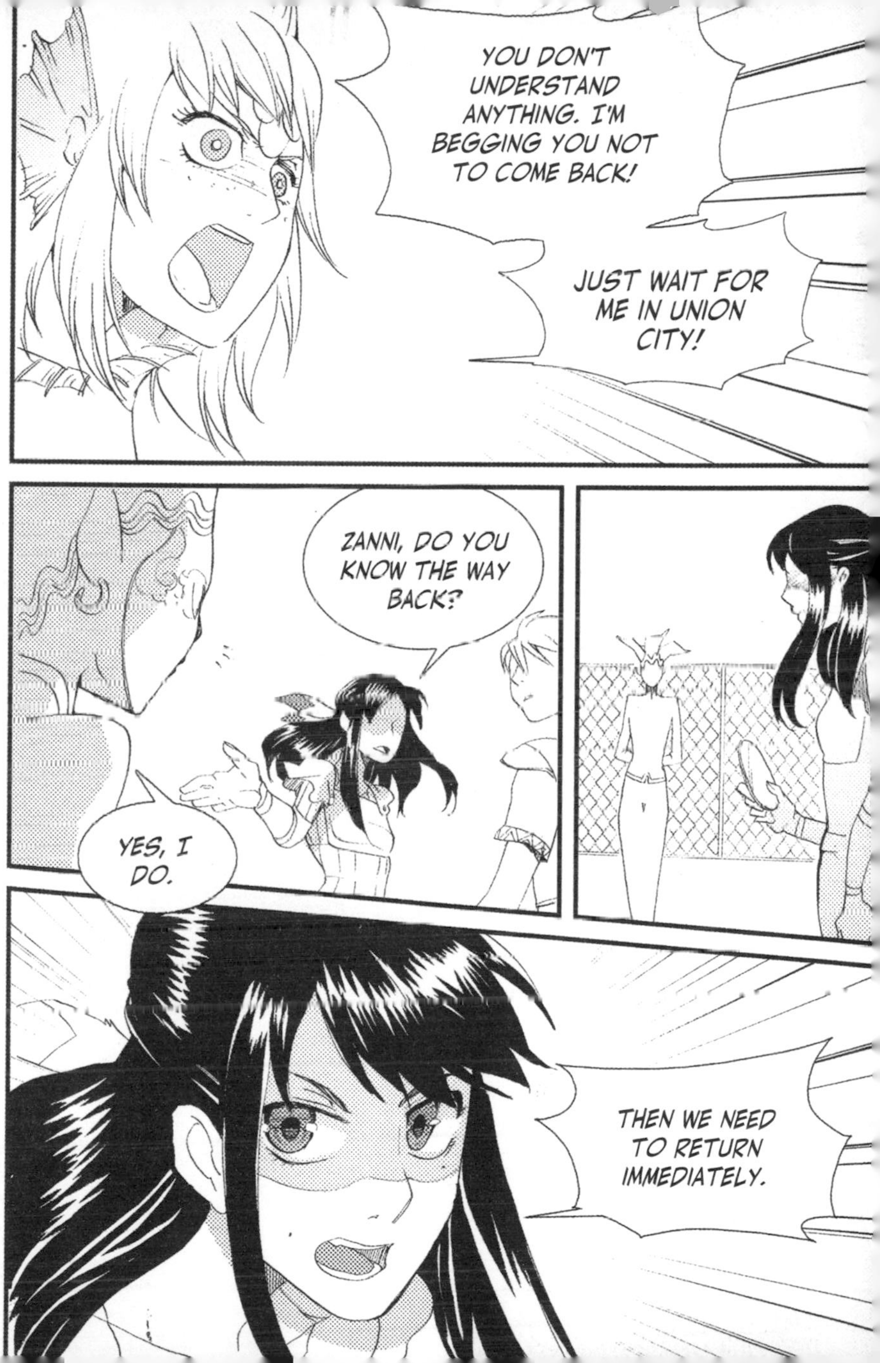
YOU DON'T UNDERSTAND ANYTHING. I'M BEGGING YOU NOT TO COME BACK!
JUST WAIT FOR ME IN UNION CITY!
ZANNI, DO YOU KNOW THE WAY BACK?
YES, I DO.
THEN WE NEED TO RETURN IMMEDIATELY.

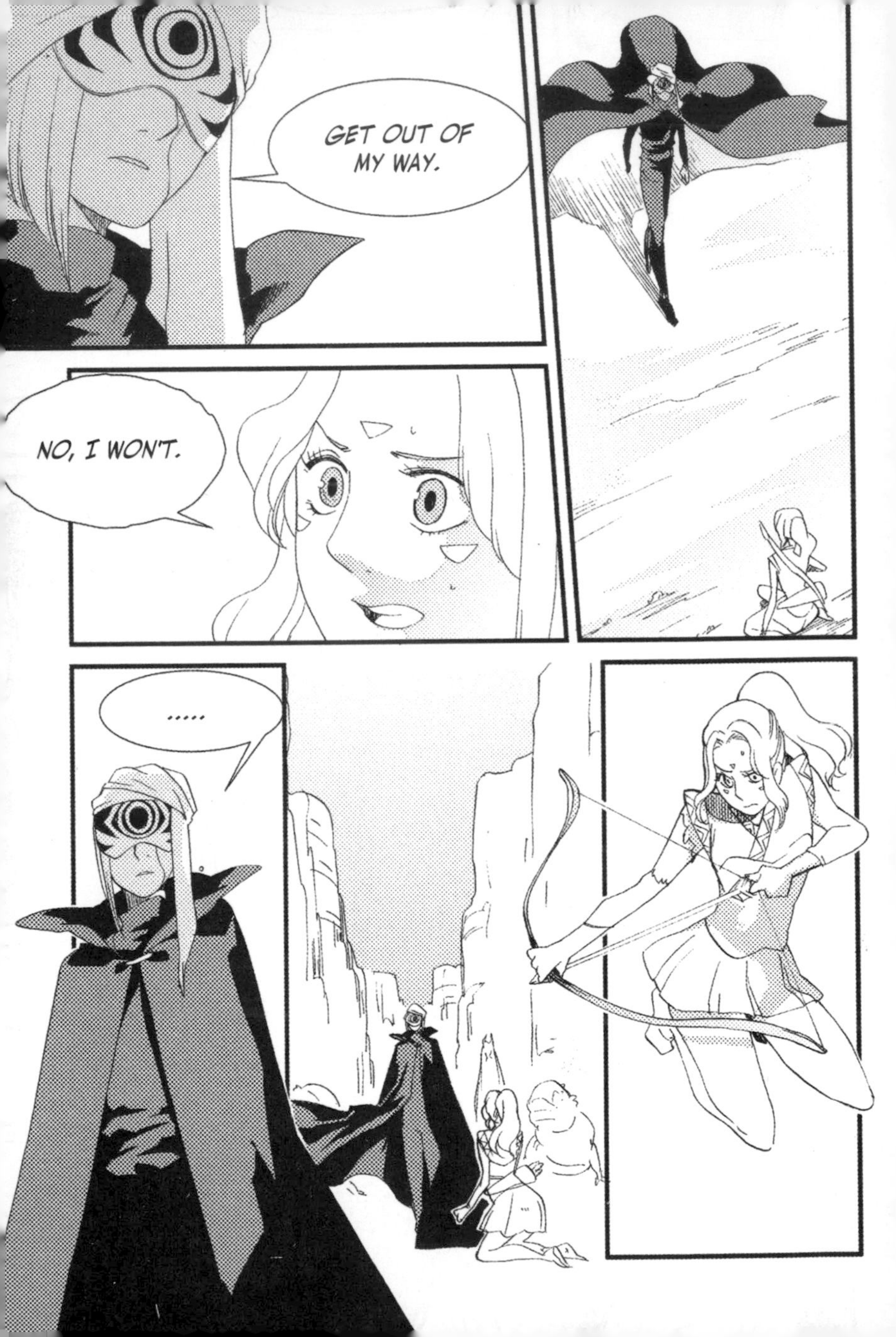
GET OUT OF MY WAY.
NO, I WON'T.
.....

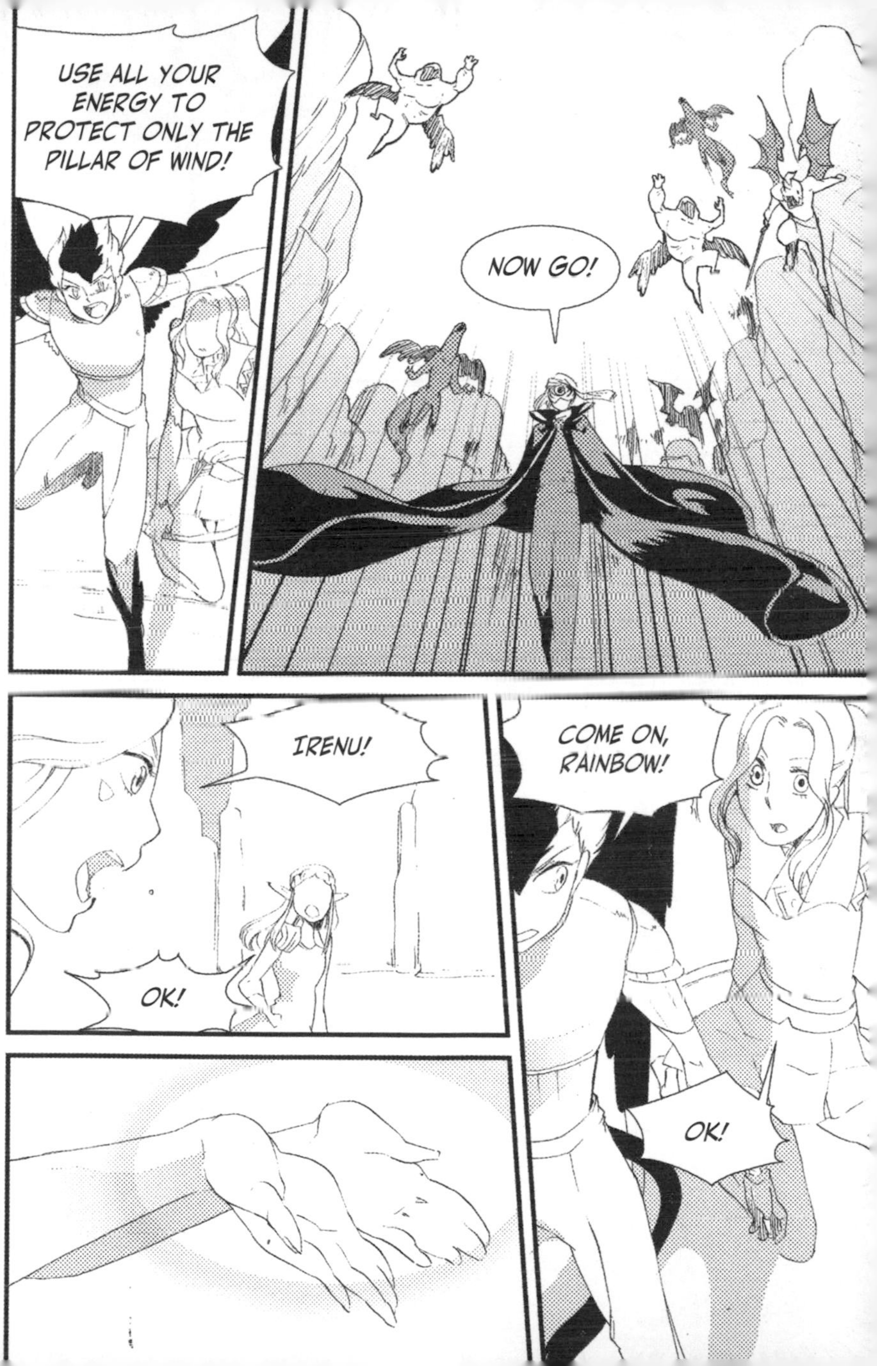
NOW GO!
USE ALL YOUR ENERGY TO PROTECT ONLY THE PILLAR OF WIND!
COME ON, RAINBOW!
OK!
IRENU!
OK!

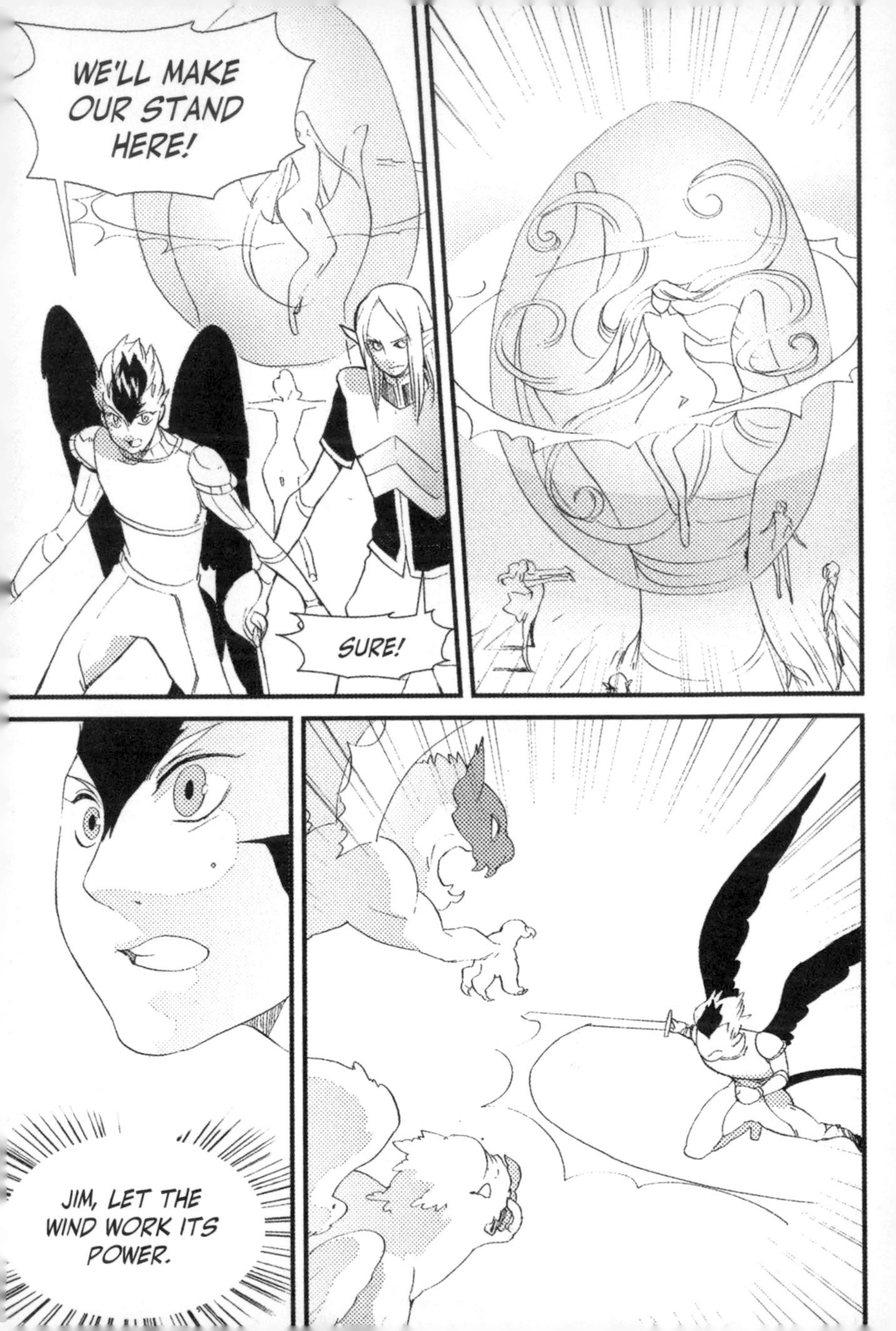
WE'LL MAKE OUR STAND HERE!
SURE!
JIM, LET THE WIND WORK ITS POWER.

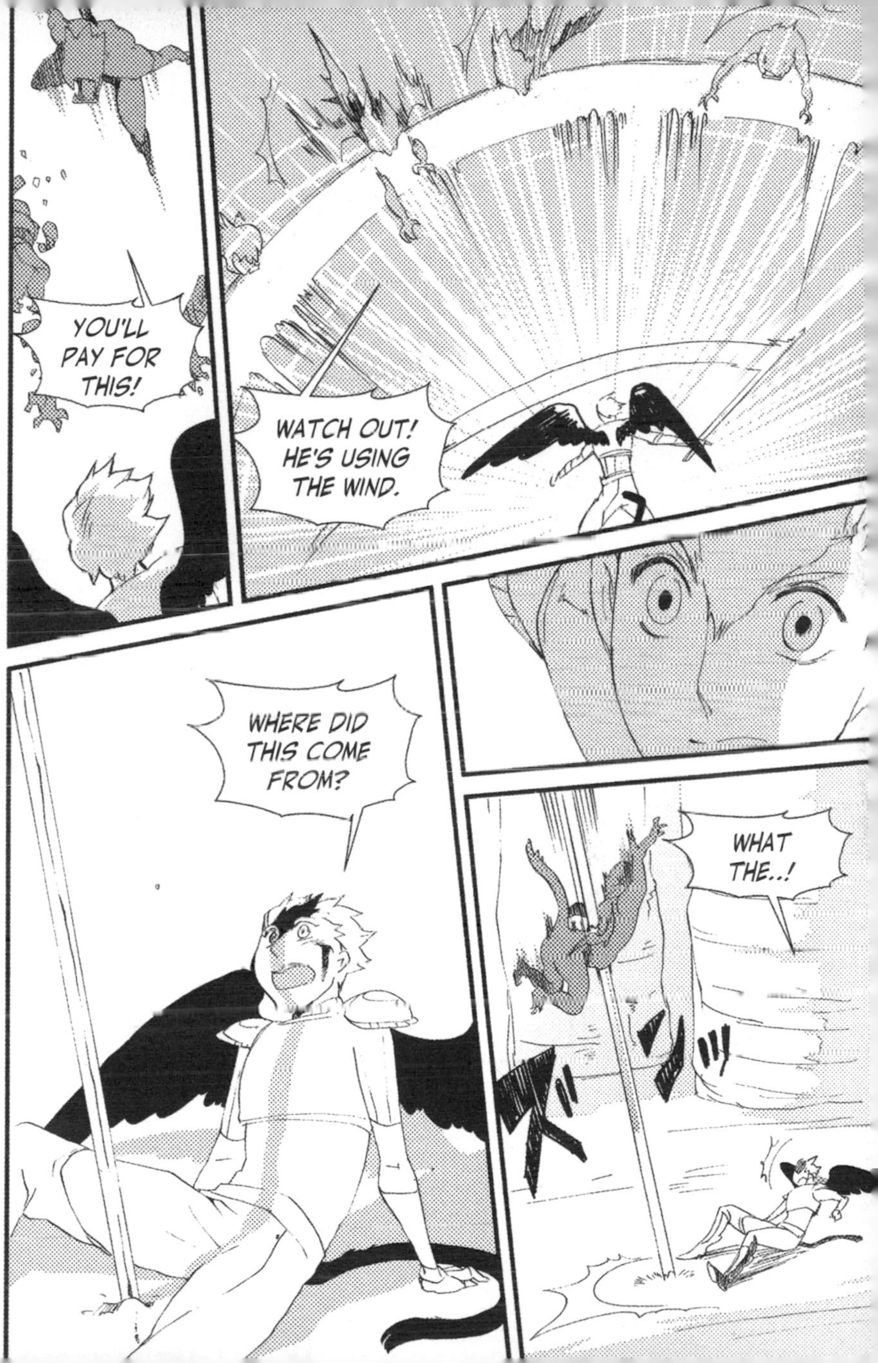
WATCH OUT! HE'S USING THE WIND.
YOU'LL PAY FOR THIS!
WHAT THE..!
WHERE DID THIS COME FROM?

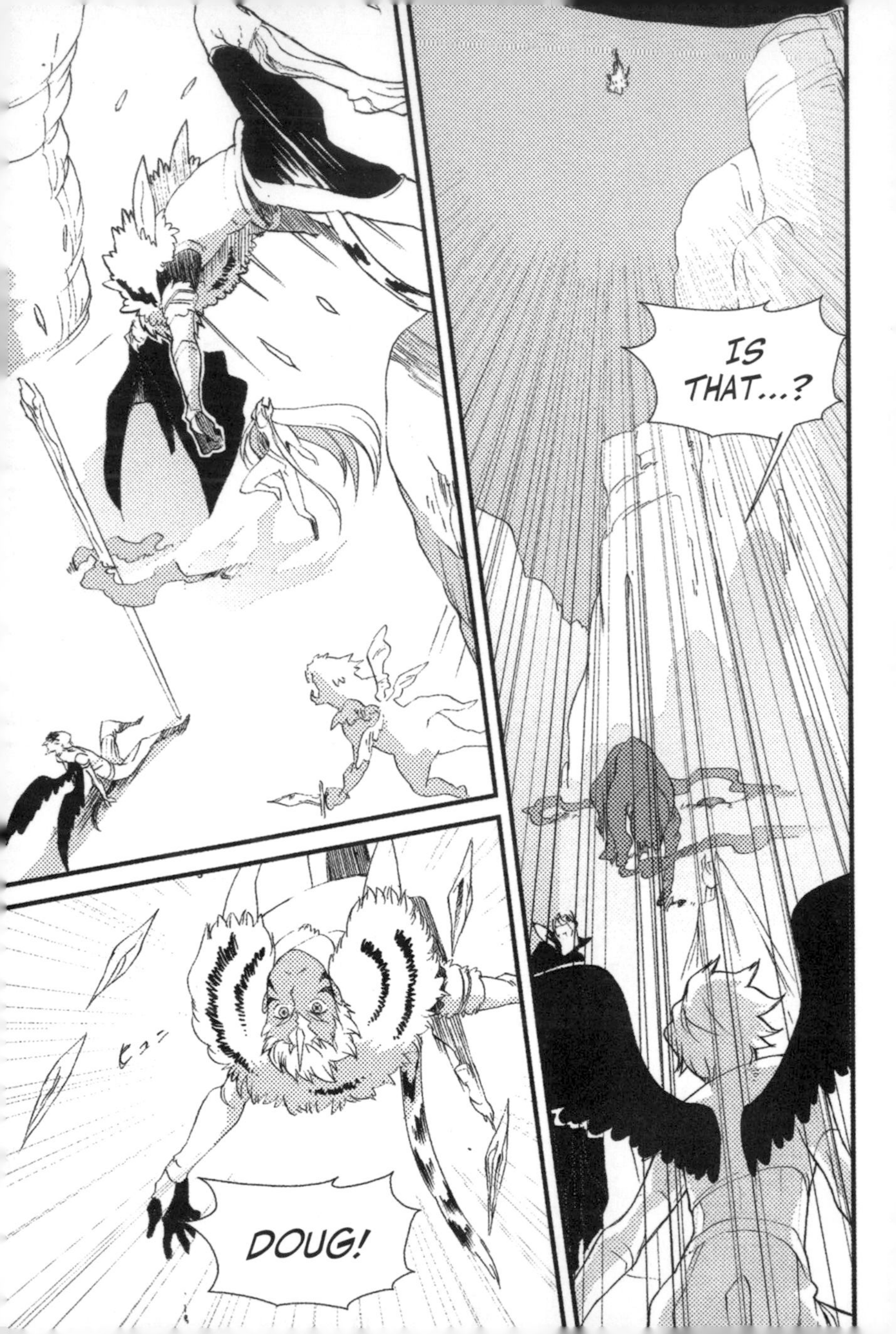
IS THAT...?
DOUG!

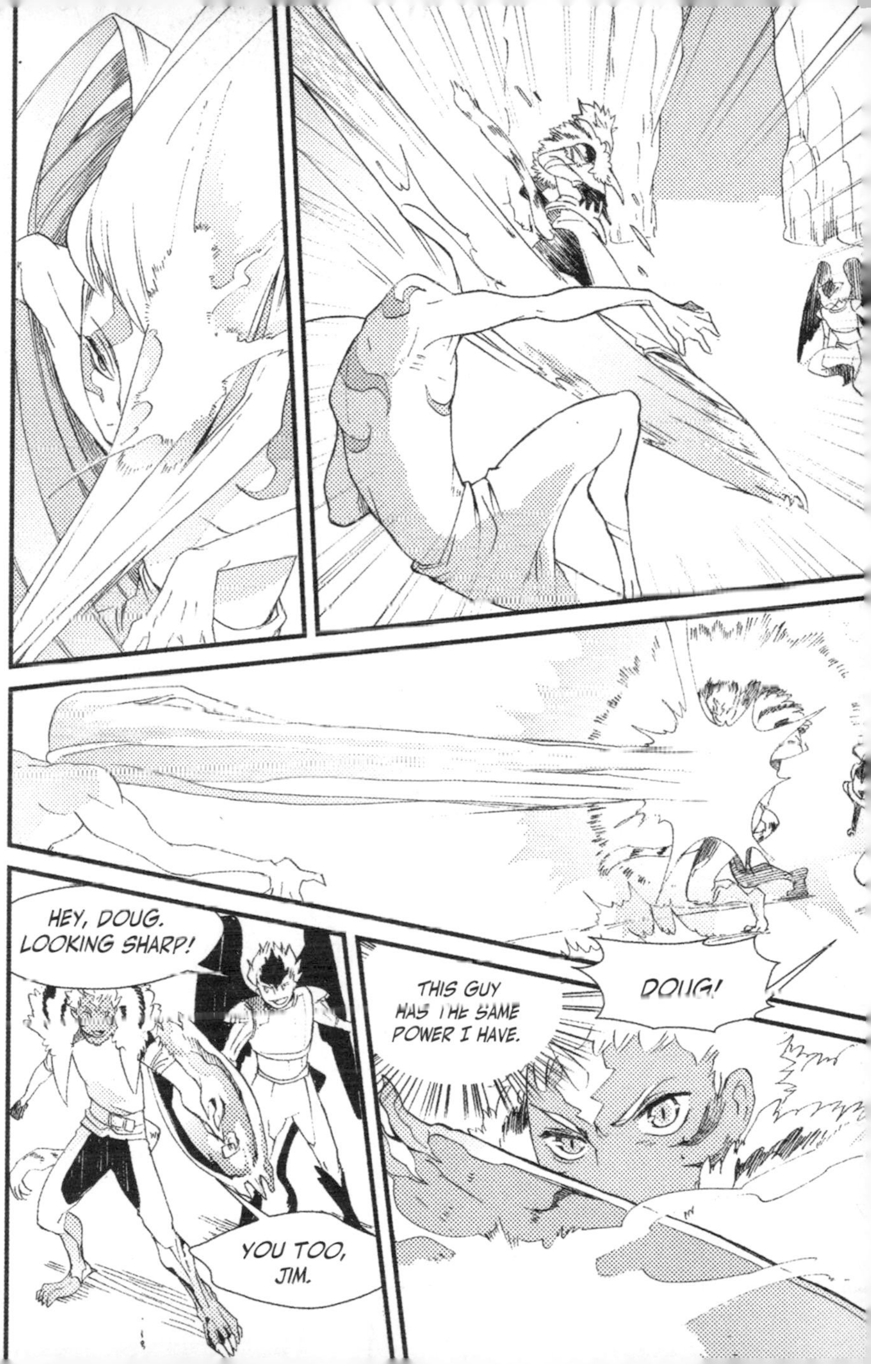
DOUG!
THIS GUY HAS THE SAME POWER I HAVE.
HEY, DOUG. LOOKING SHARP!
YOU TOO, JIM.

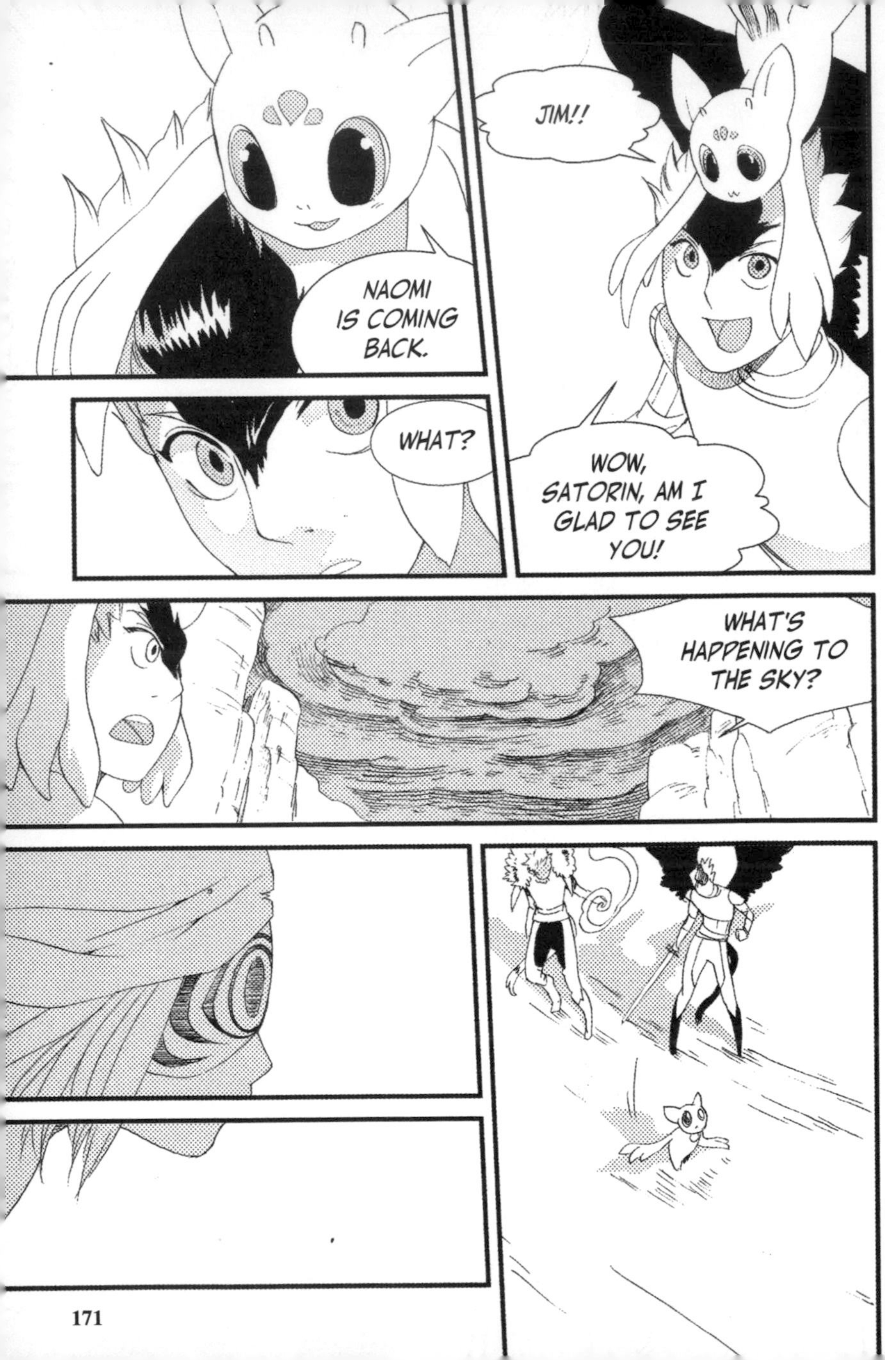
JIM!!
WOW, SATORIN, AM I GLAD TO SEE YOU!
NAOMI IS COMING BACK.
WHAT?
WHAT'S HAPPENING TO THE SKY?

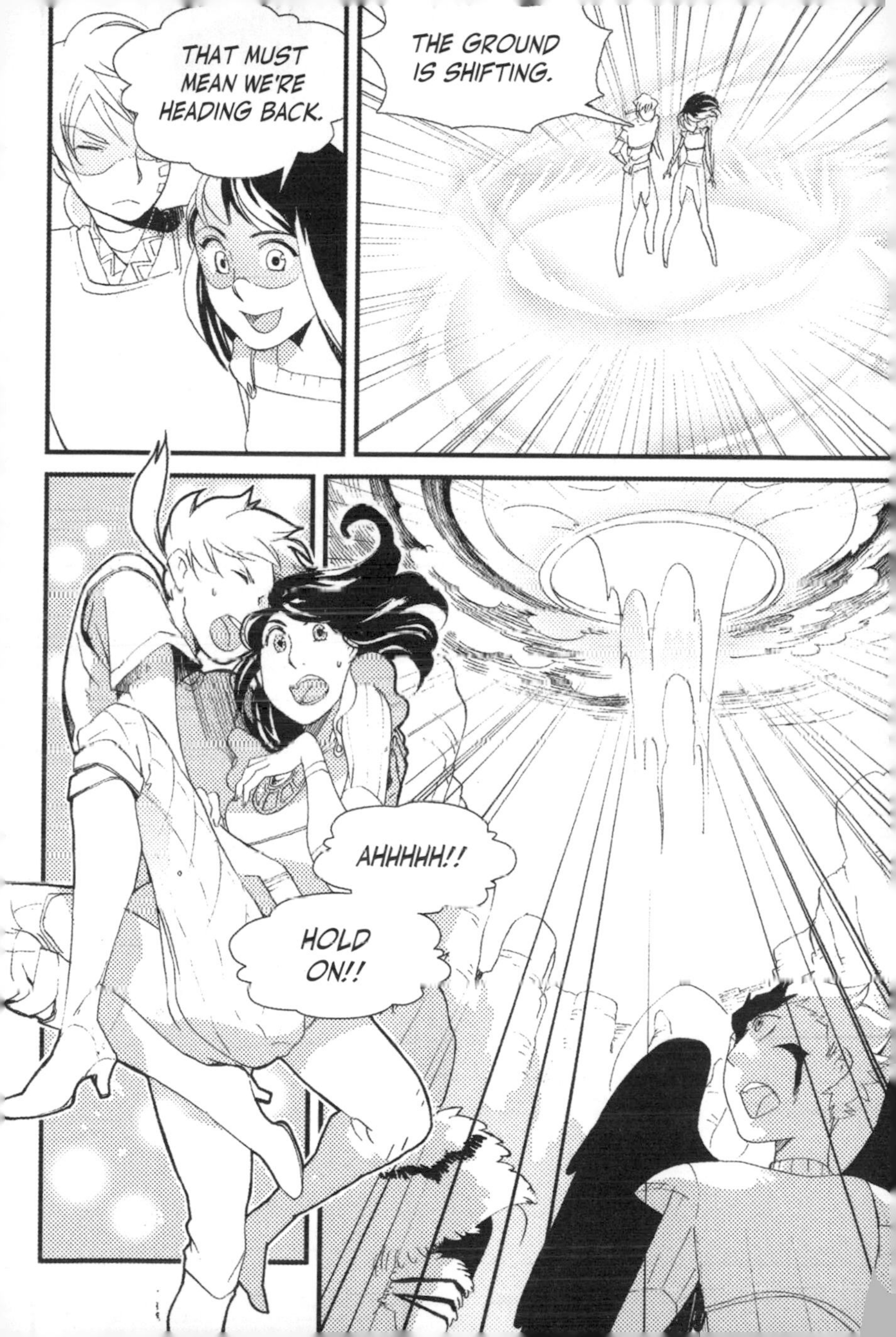
THE GROUND IS SHIFTING.
THAT MUST MEAN WE'RE HEADING BACK.
AHHHHH!!
HOLD ON!!

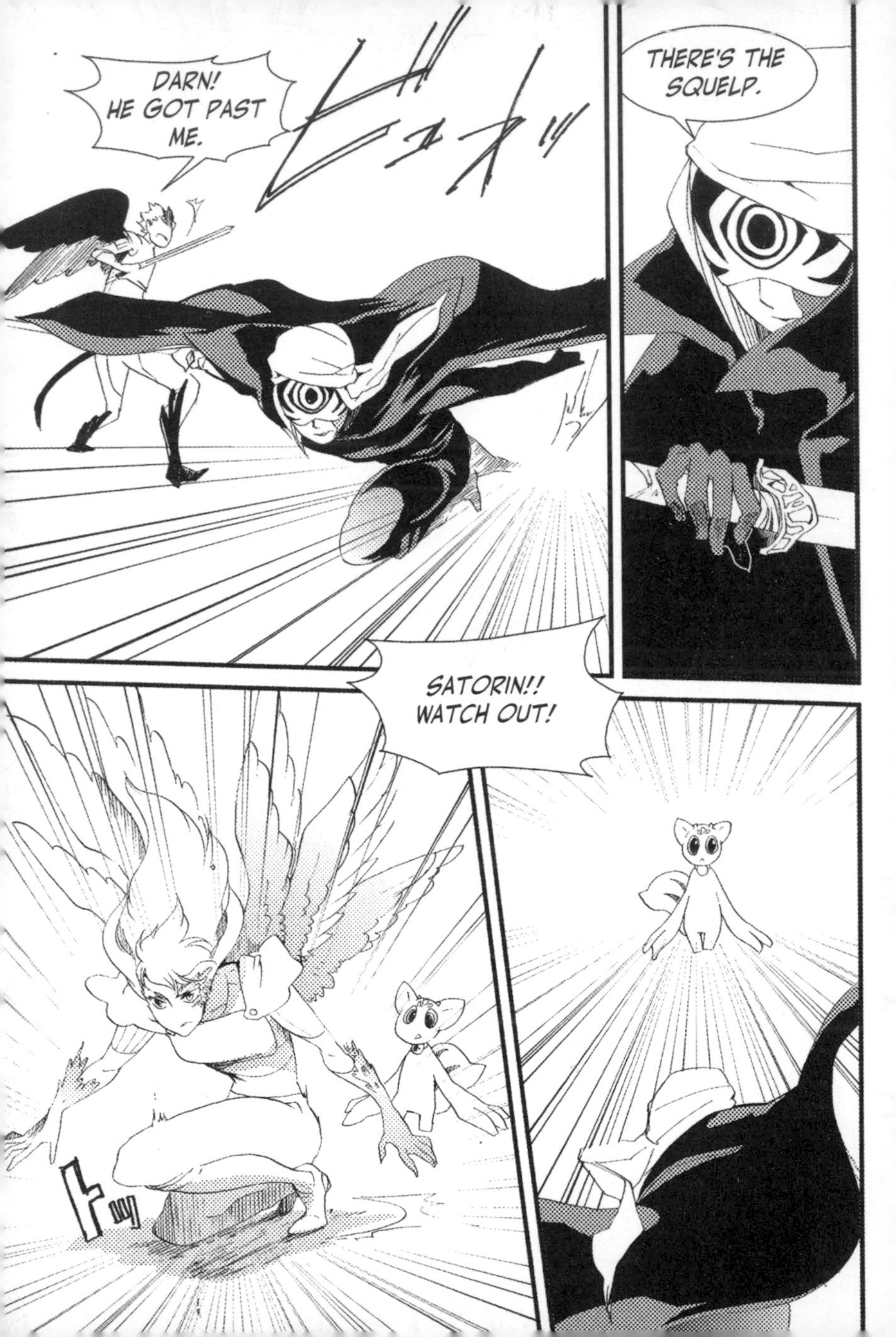
THERE'S THE SQUELP.
DARN! HE GOT PAST ME.
ビュオッ
SATORIN!! WATCH OUT!
トッ

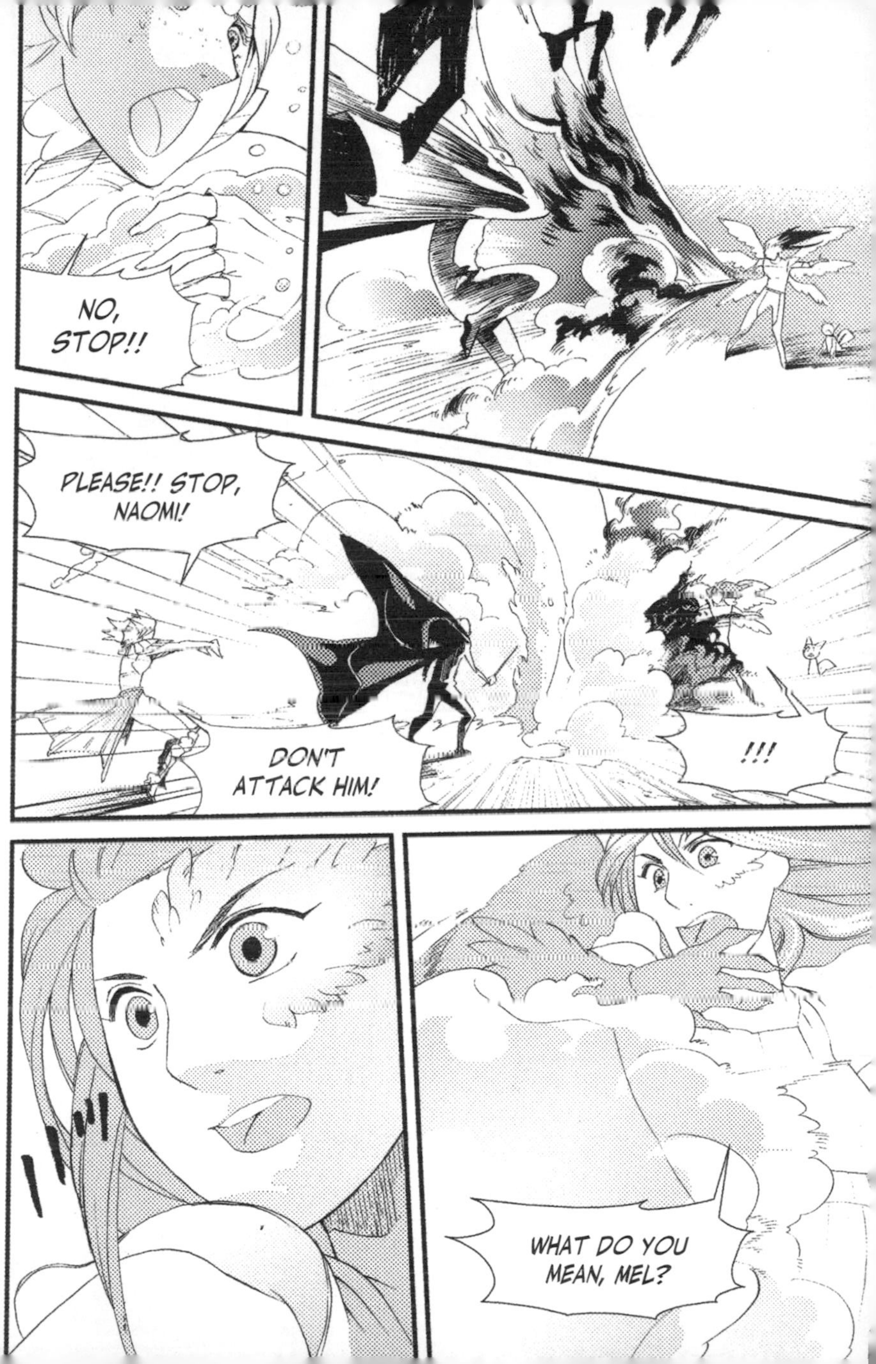
NO, STOP!!
PLEASE!! STOP, NAOMI!
DON'T ATTACK HIM!
!!!
WHAT DO YOU MEAN, MEL?

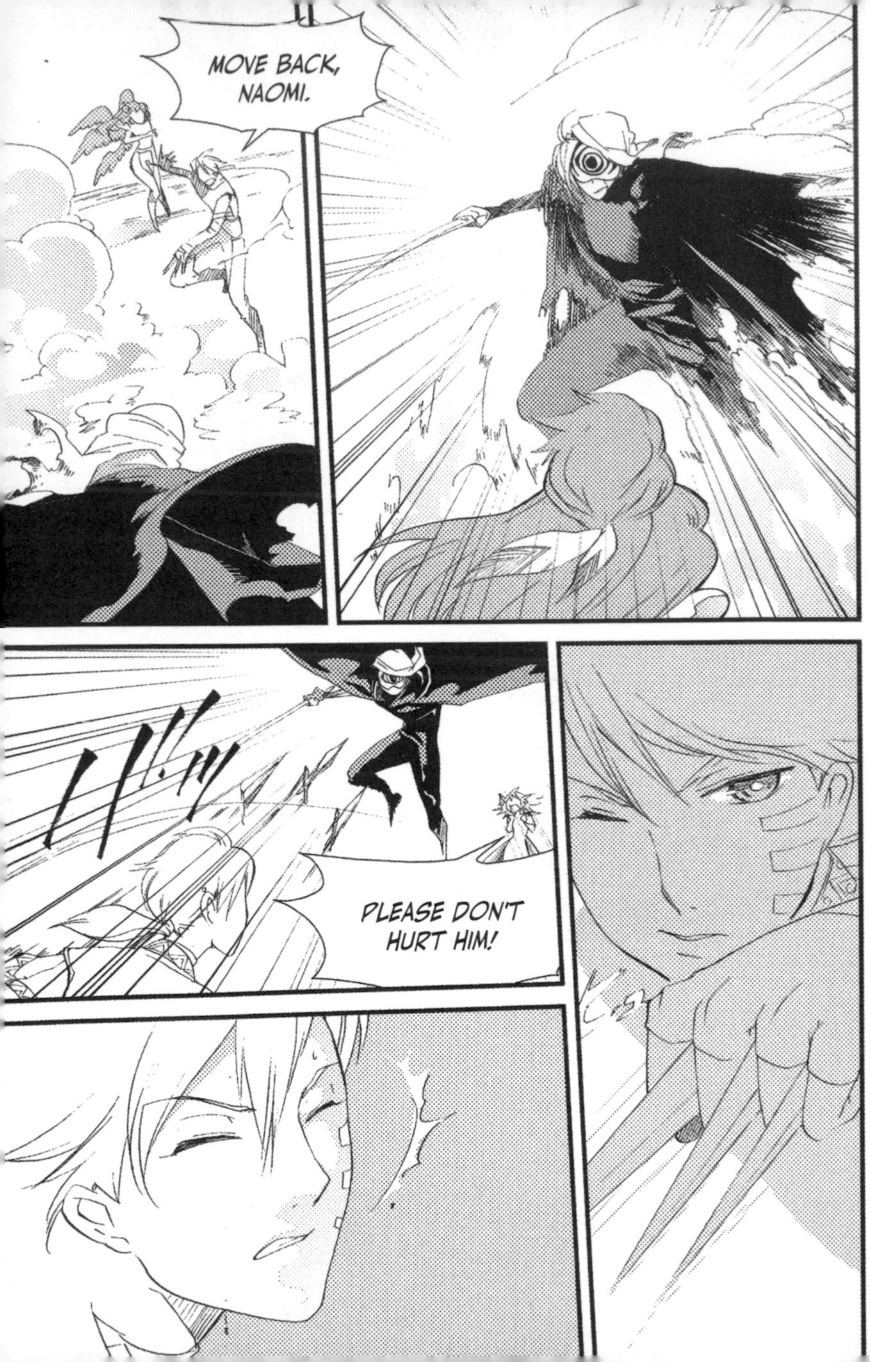
MOVE BACK, NAOMI.
PLEASE DON'T HURT HIM!

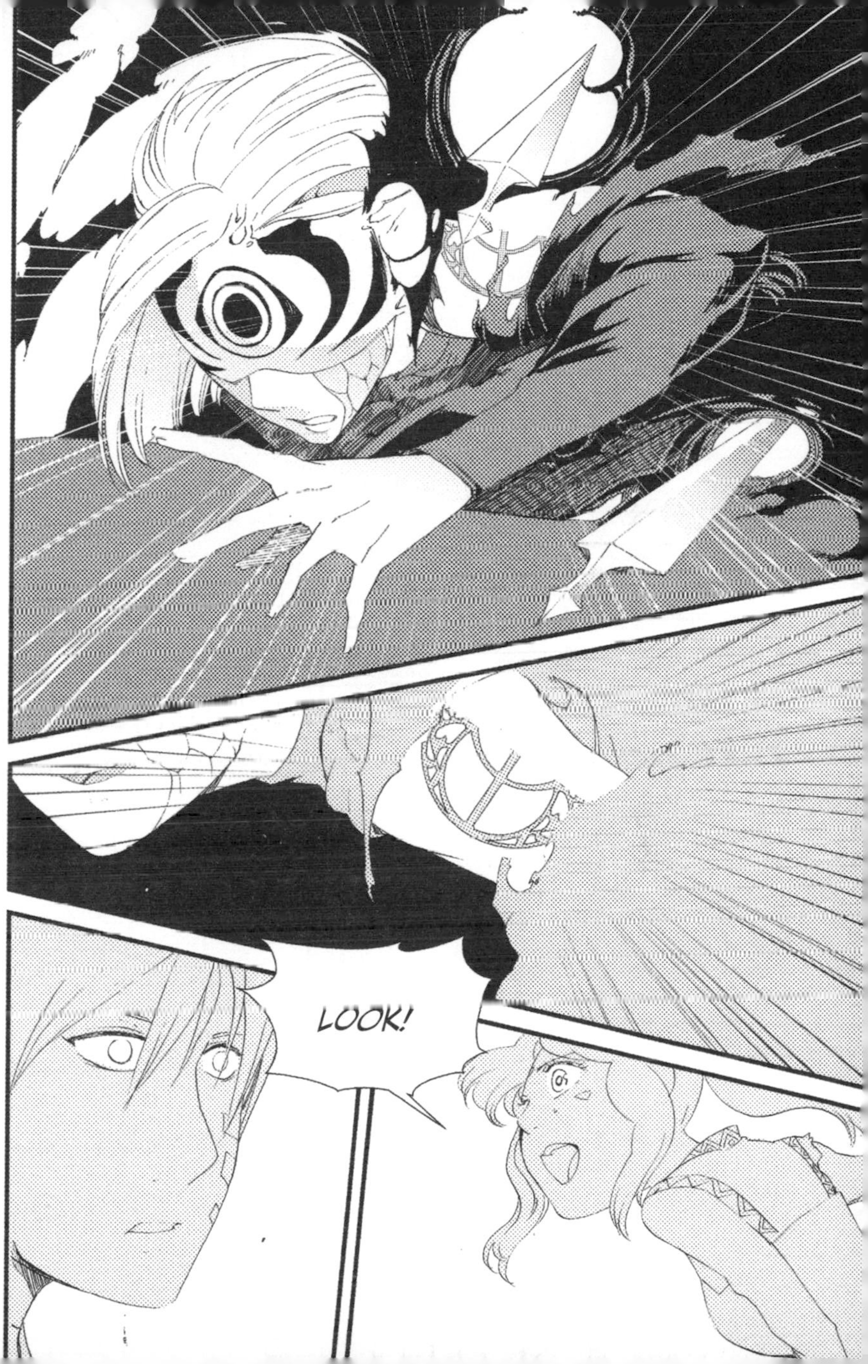
LOOK!

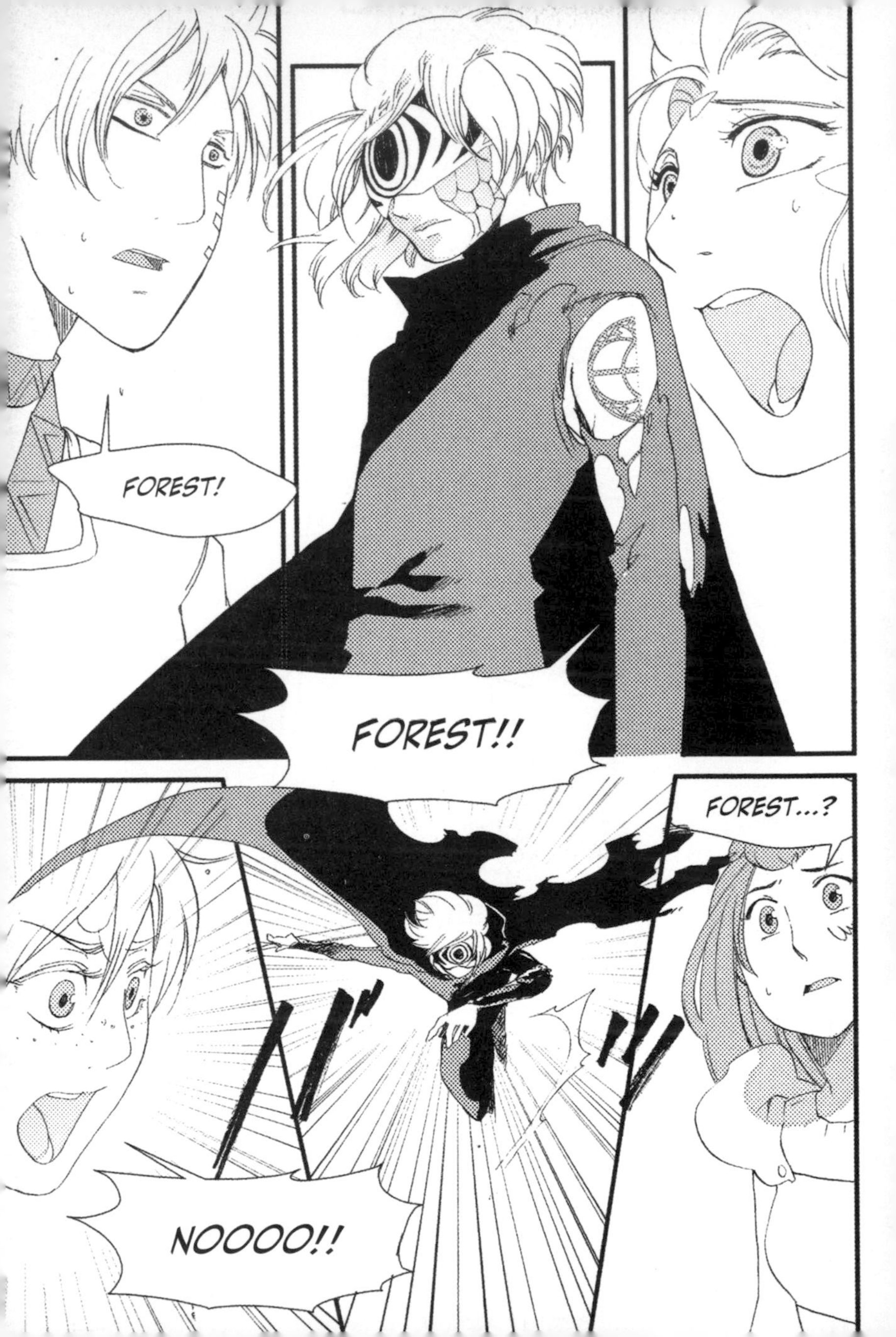
FOREST!
FOREST!!
FOREST...?
NOOOO!!

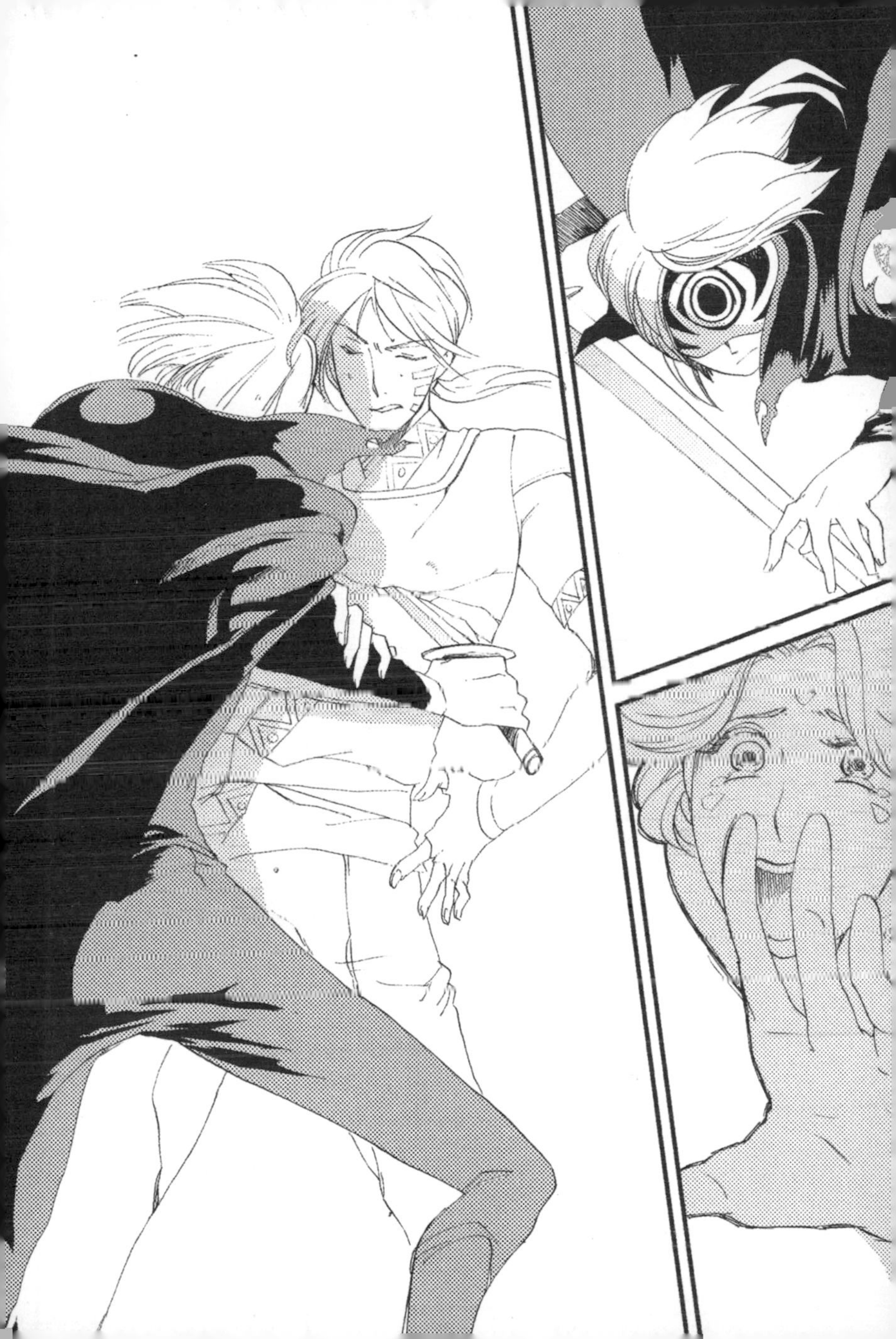

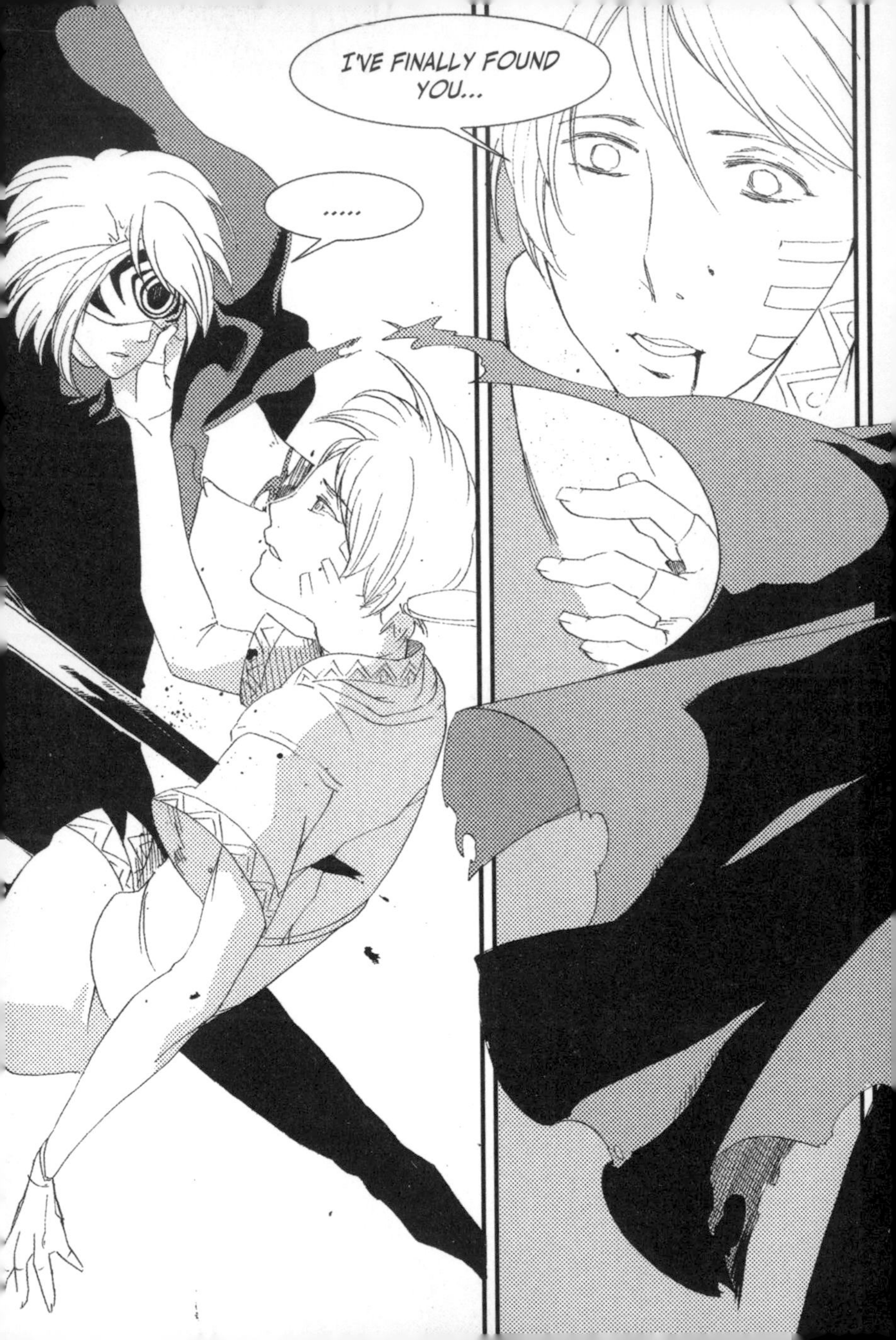
I'VE FINALLY FOUND YOU...
.....

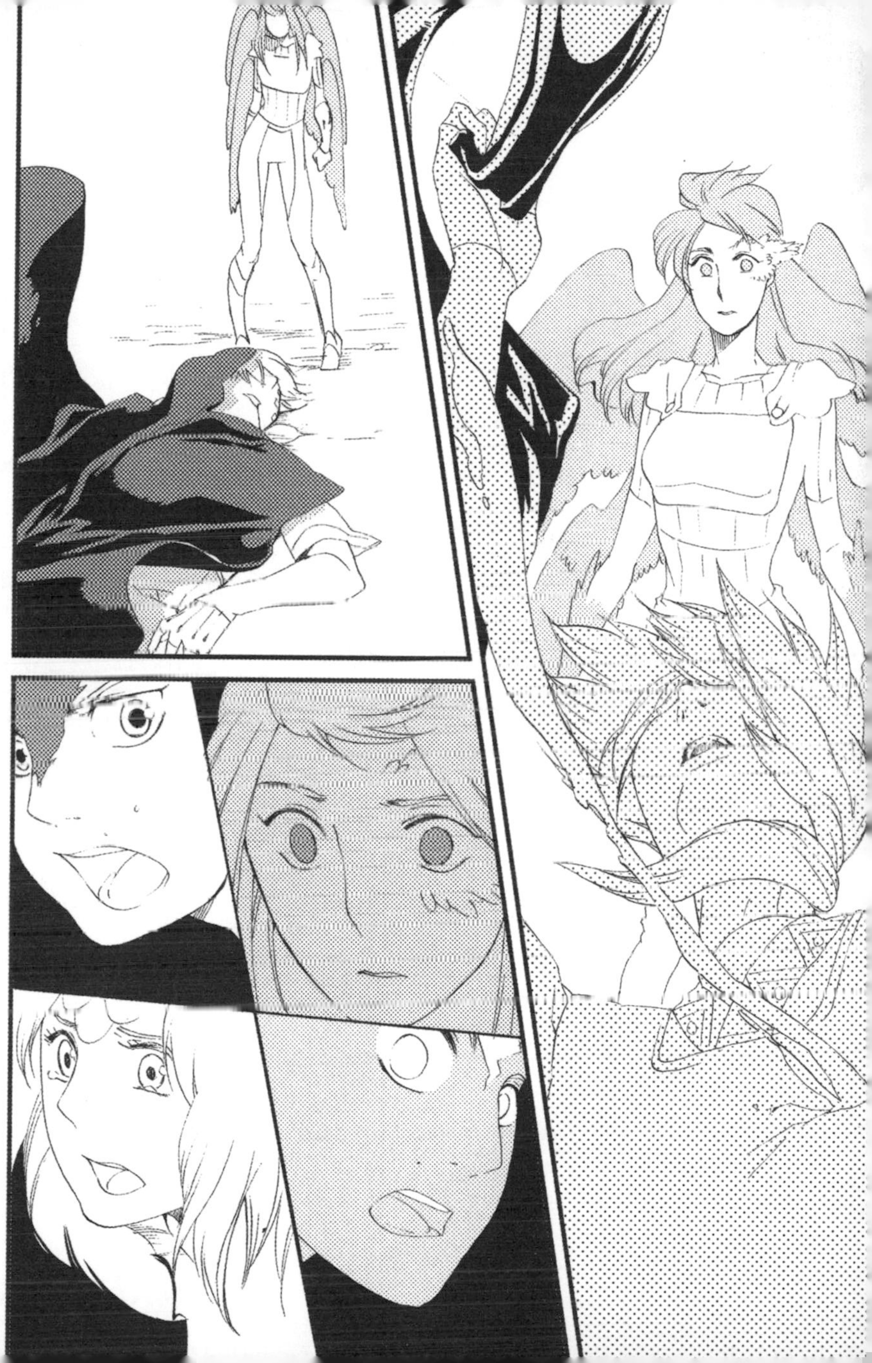

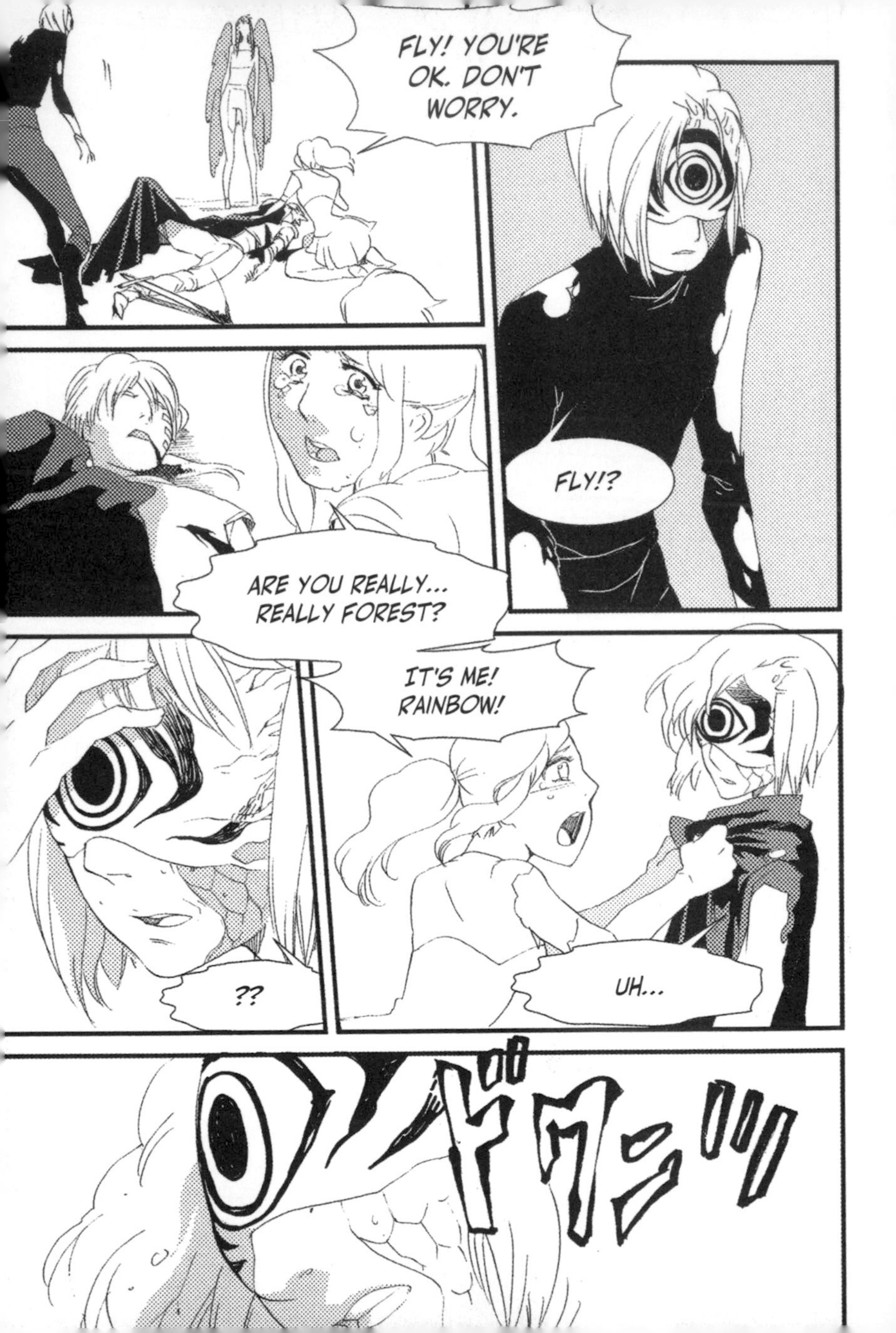
FLY!?
FLY! YOU'RE OK. DON'T WORRY.
ARE YOU REALLY... REALLY FOREST?
IT'S ME! RAINBOW!
UH...
??
ドクンッ

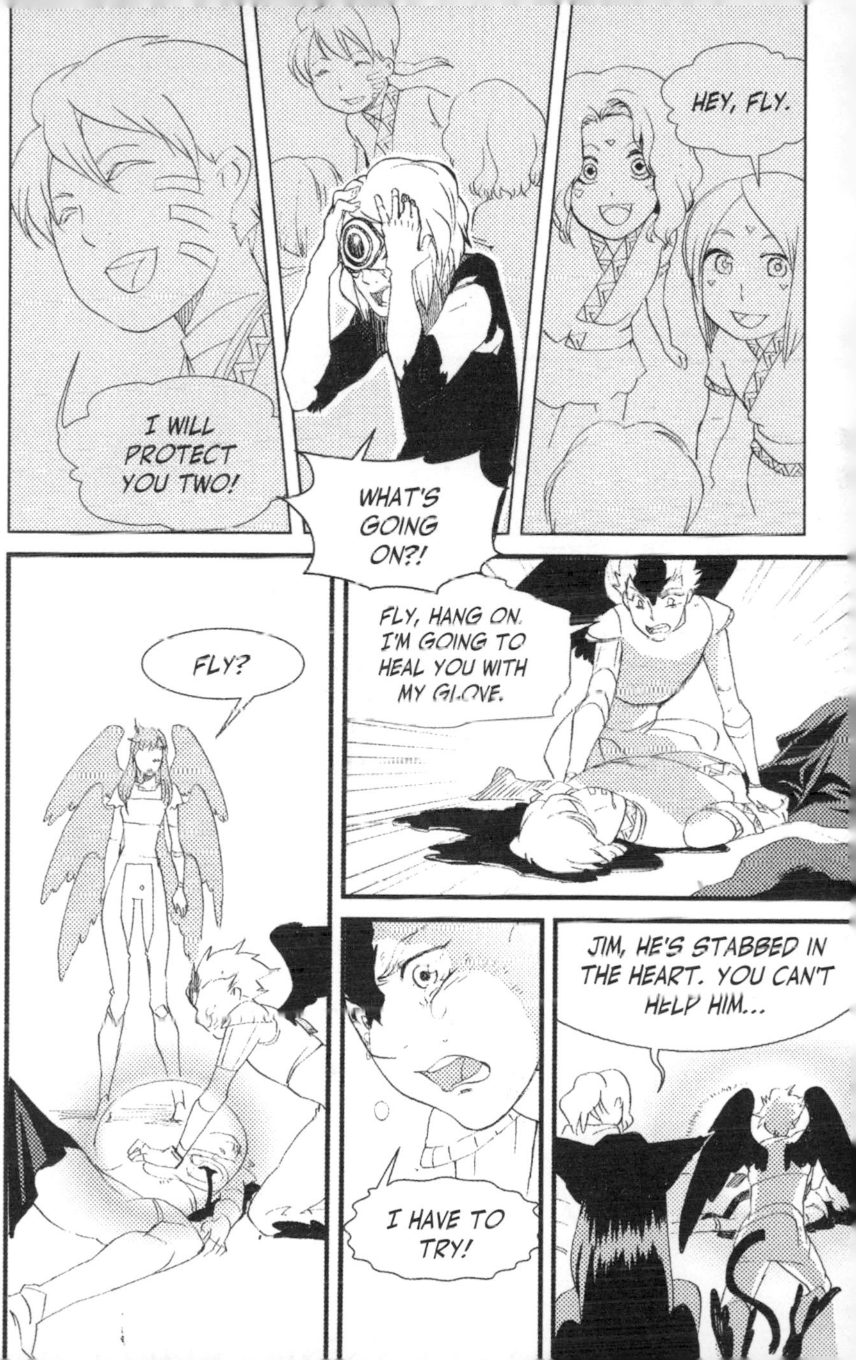
HEY, FLY.
WHAT'S GOING ON?!
I WILL PROTECT YOU TWO!
FLY, HANG ON. I'M GOING TO HEAL YOU WITH MY GLOVE.
JIM, HE'S STABBED IN THE HEART. YOU CAN'T HELP HIM...
I HAVE TO TRY!
FLY?

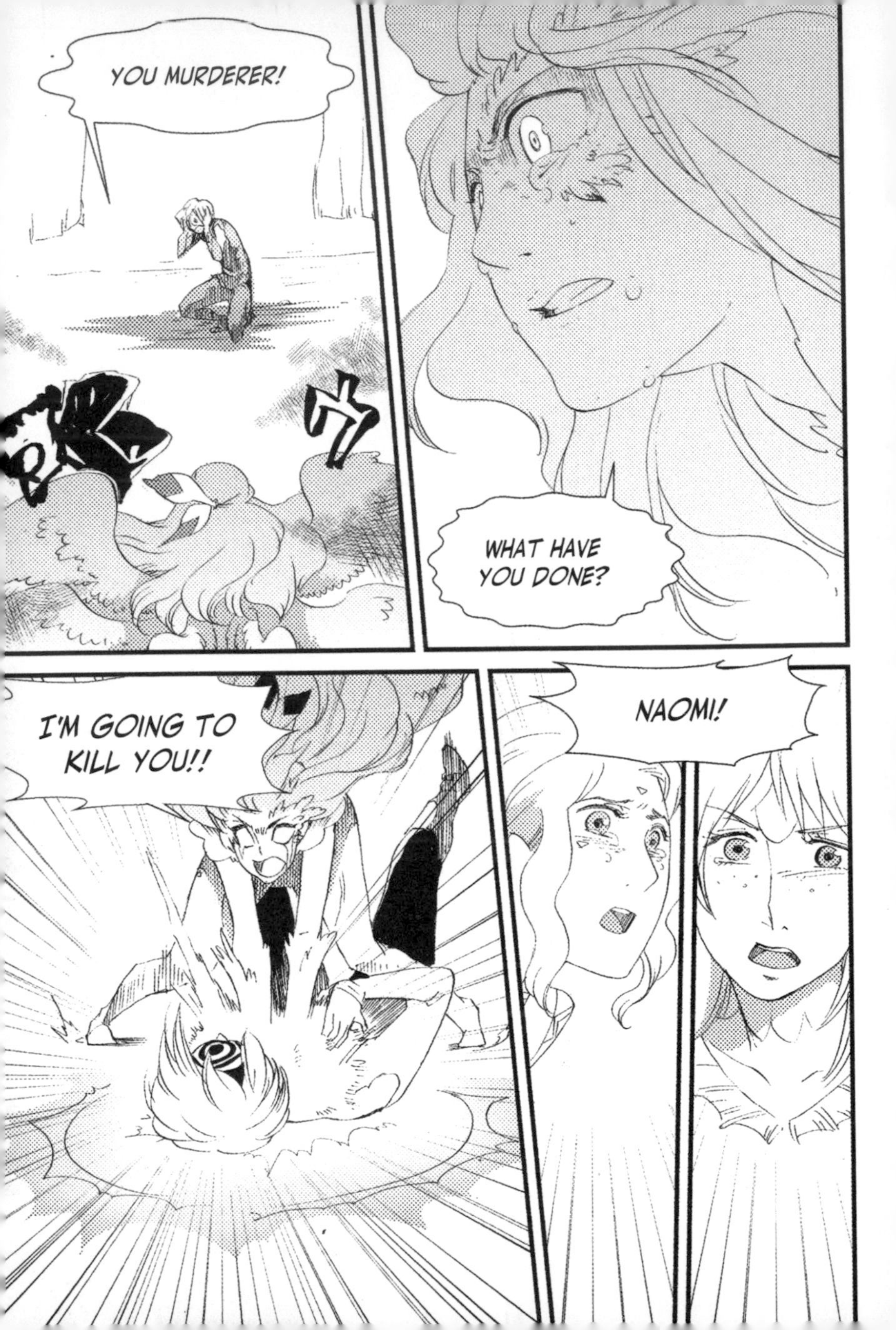
WHAT HAVE YOU DONE?
YOU MURDERER!
NAOMI!
I'M GOING TO KILL YOU!!

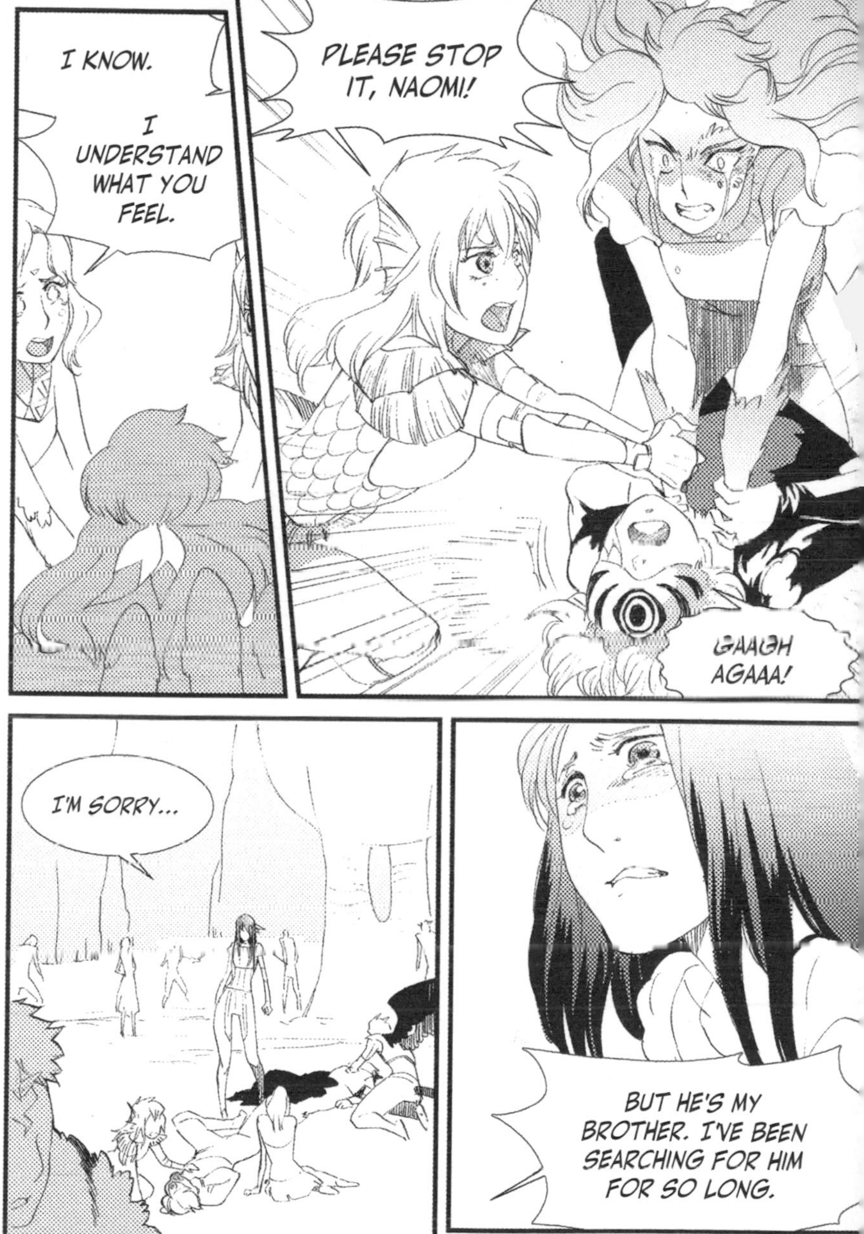
PLEASE STOP IT, NAOMI!
GAAGH AGAAA!
I KNOW.
I UNDERSTAND WHAT YOU FEEL.
BUT HE'S MY BROTHER. I'VE BEEN SEARCHING FOR HIM FOR SO LONG.
I'M SORRY...

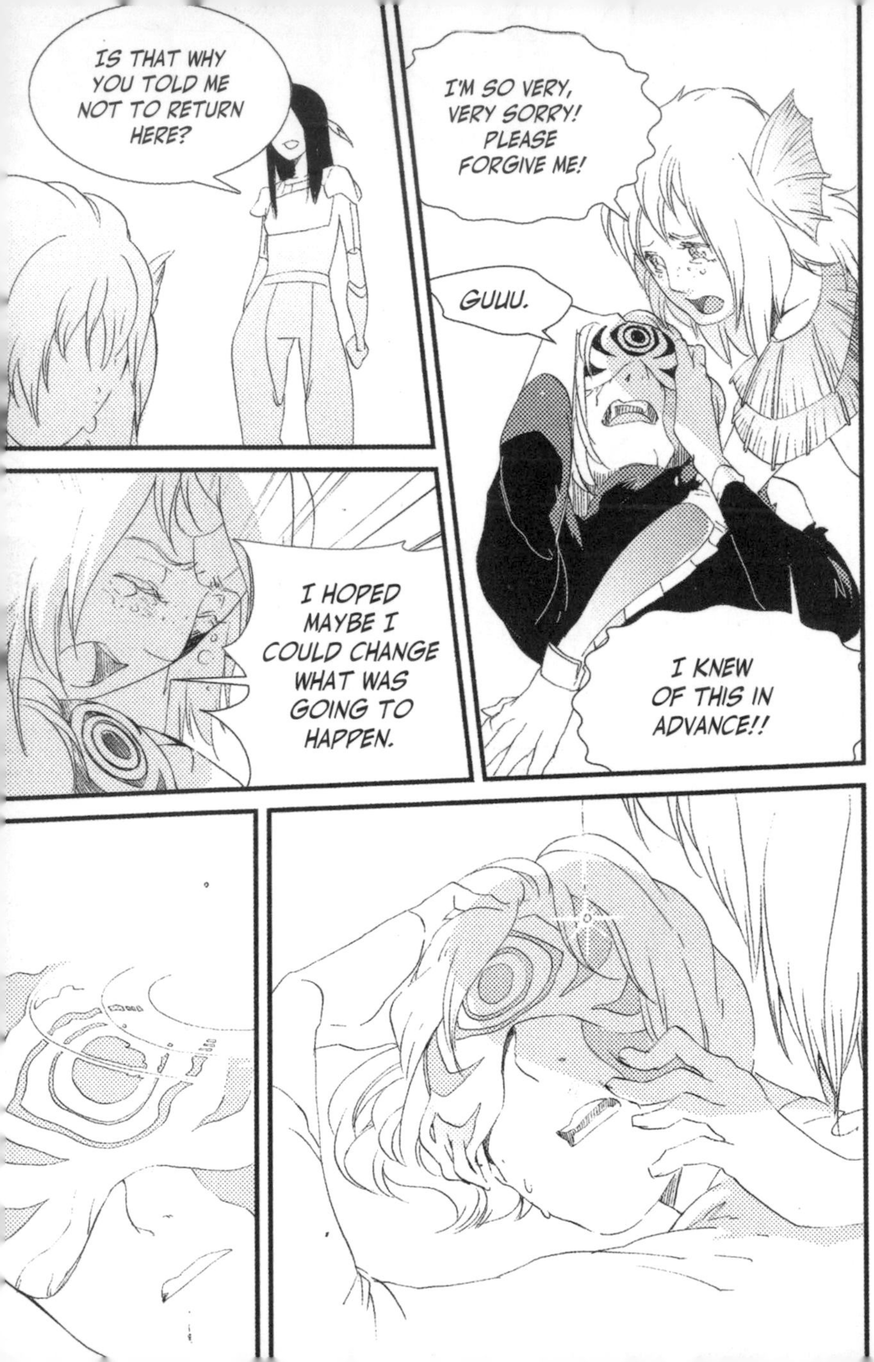
IS THAT WHY YOU TOLD ME NOT TO RETURN HERE?
I'M SO VERY, VERY SORRY! PLEASE FORGIVE ME!
GUUU.
I KNEW OF THIS IN ADVANCE!!
I HOPED MAYBE I COULD CHANGE WHAT WAS GOING TO HAPPEN.

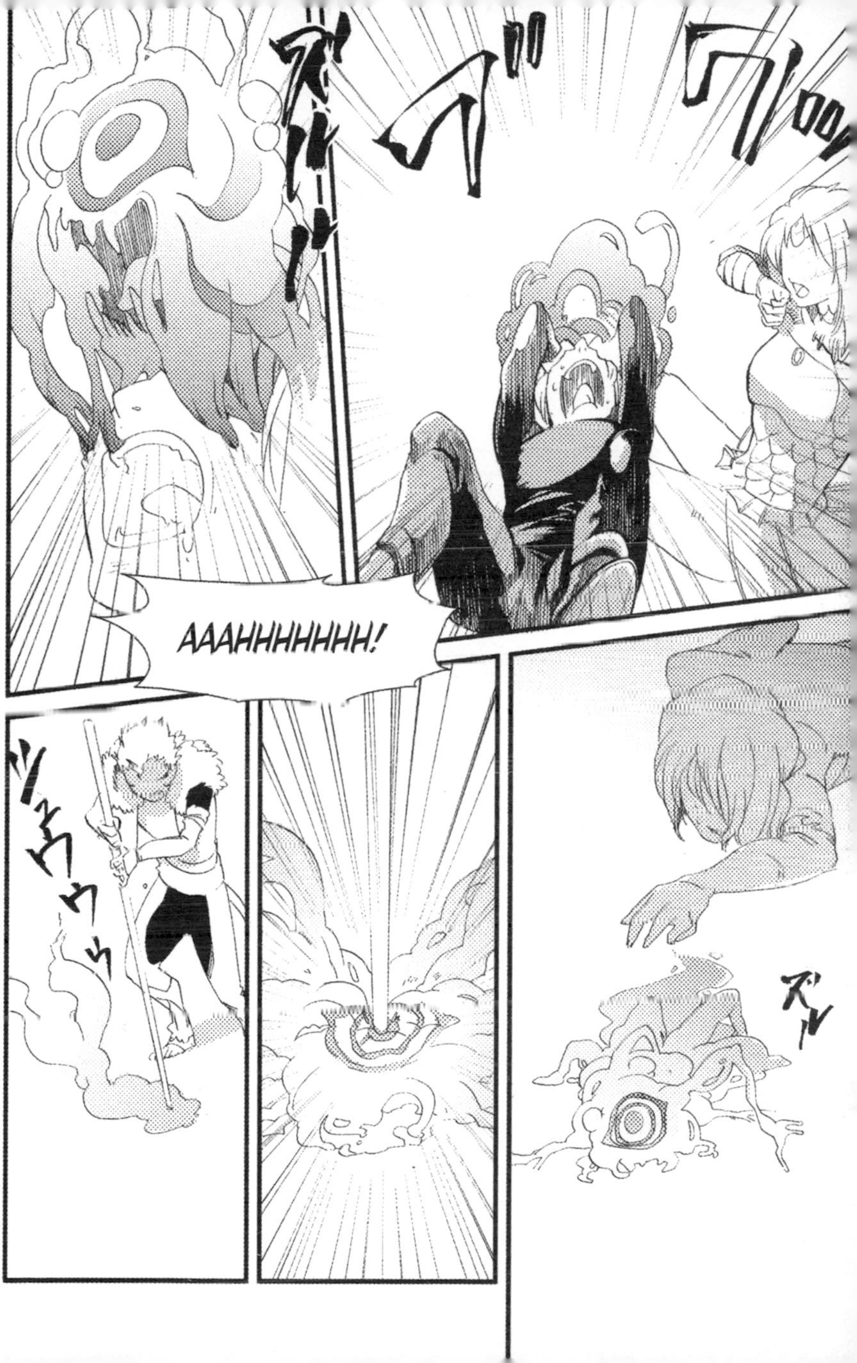
AAAHHHHHHH!

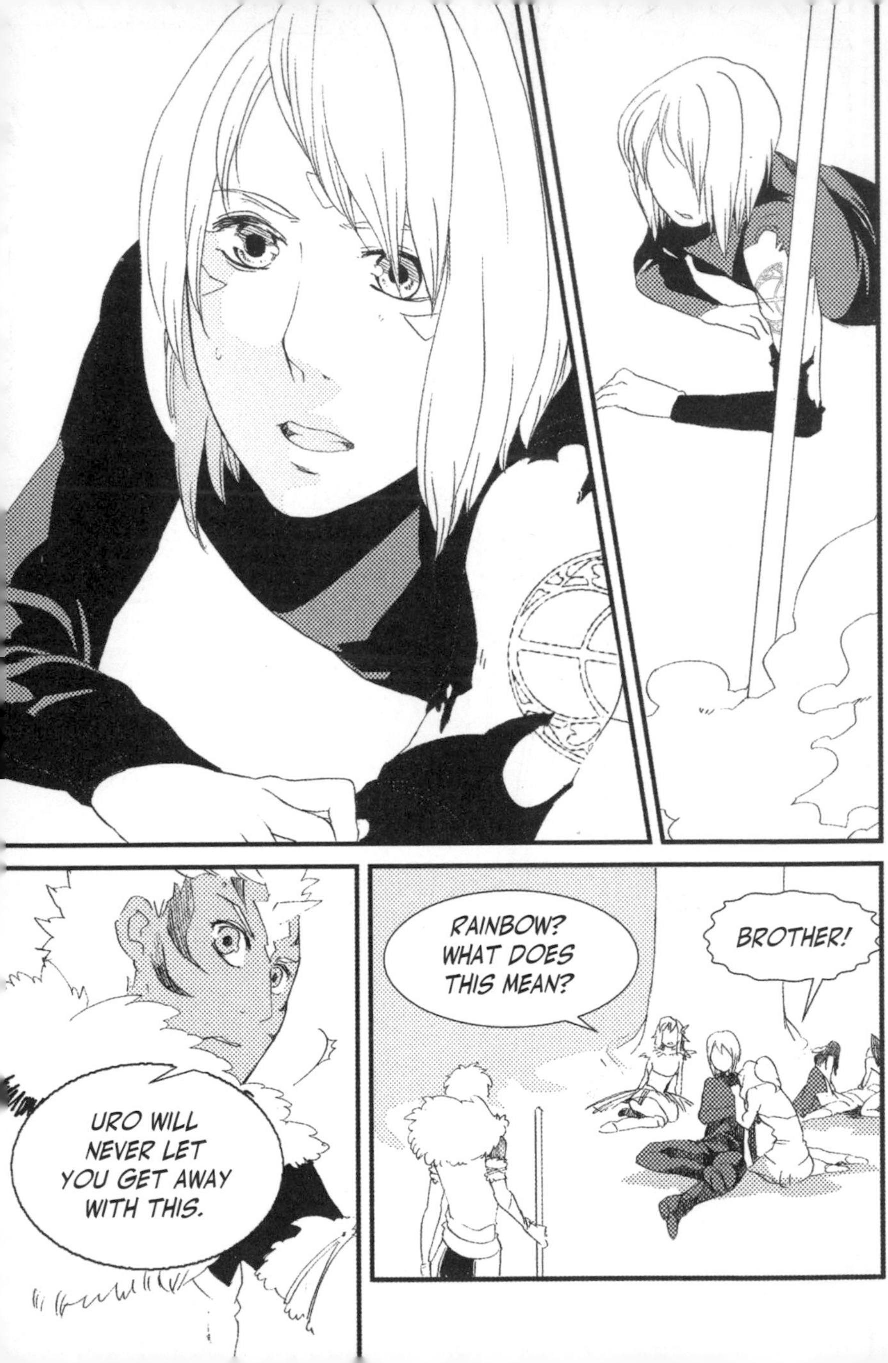
BROTHER!
RAINBOW? WHAT DOES THIS MEAN?
URO WILL NEVER LET YOU GET AWAY WITH THIS.

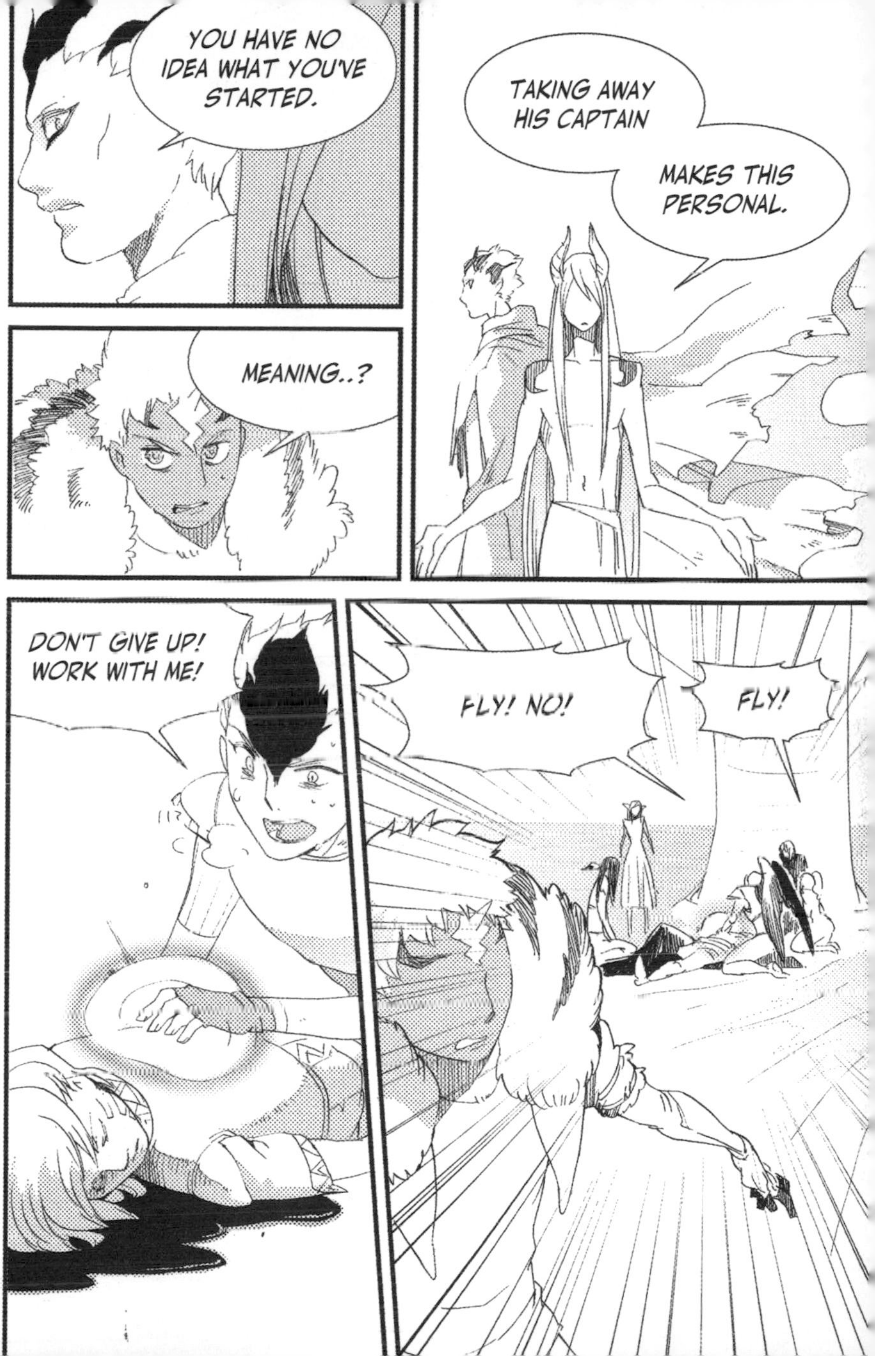
YOU HAVE NO IDEA WHAT YOU'VE STARTED.
MEANING..?
TAKING AWAY HIS CAPTAIN
MAKES THIS PERSONAL.
DON'T GIVE UP! WORK WITH ME!
FLY! NO!
FLY!

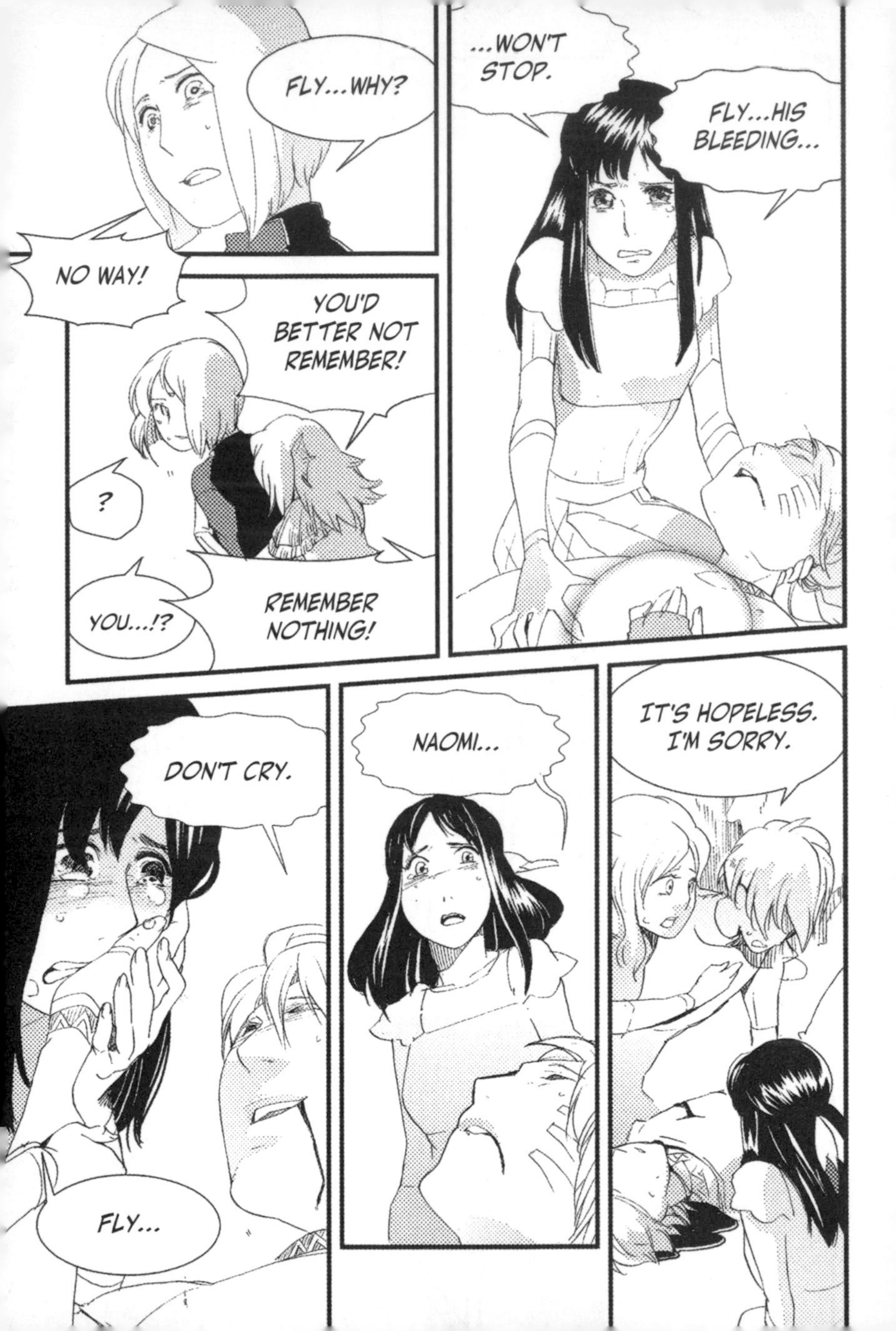
FLY...HIS BLEEDING...
...WON'T STOP.
FLY...WHY?
NO WAY!
YOU'D BETTER NOT REMEMBER!
?
REMEMBER NOTHING!
YOU...!?
IT'S HOPELESS. I'M SORRY.
NAOMI...
DON'T CRY.
FLY...

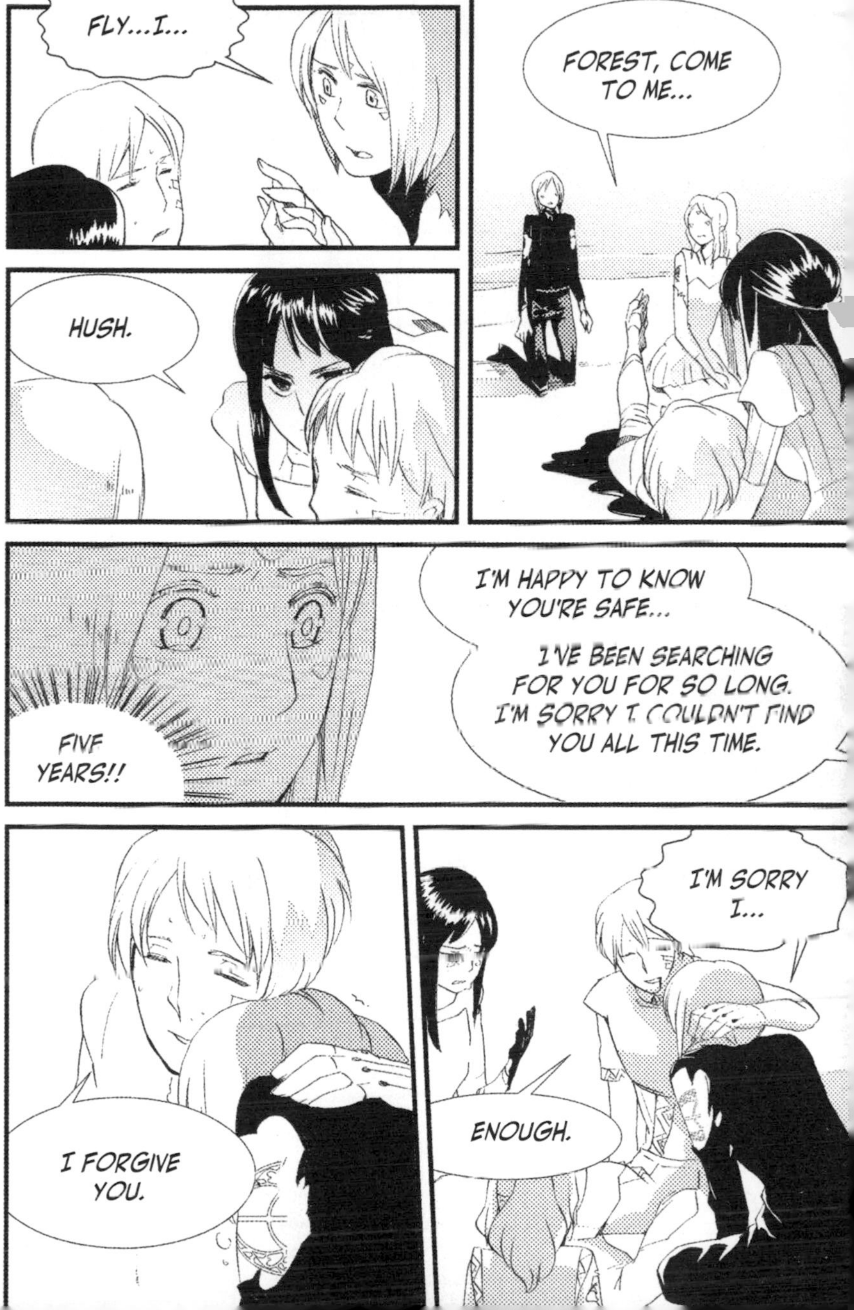
FOREST, COME TO ME...
FLY...I...
HUSH.
I'M HAPPY TO KNOW YOU'RE SAFE...
I'VE BEEN SEARCHING FOR YOU FOR SO LONG. I'M SORRY I COULDN'T FIND YOU ALL THIS TIME.
FIVE YEARS!!
I'M SORRY I...
ENOUGH.
I FORGIVE YOU.

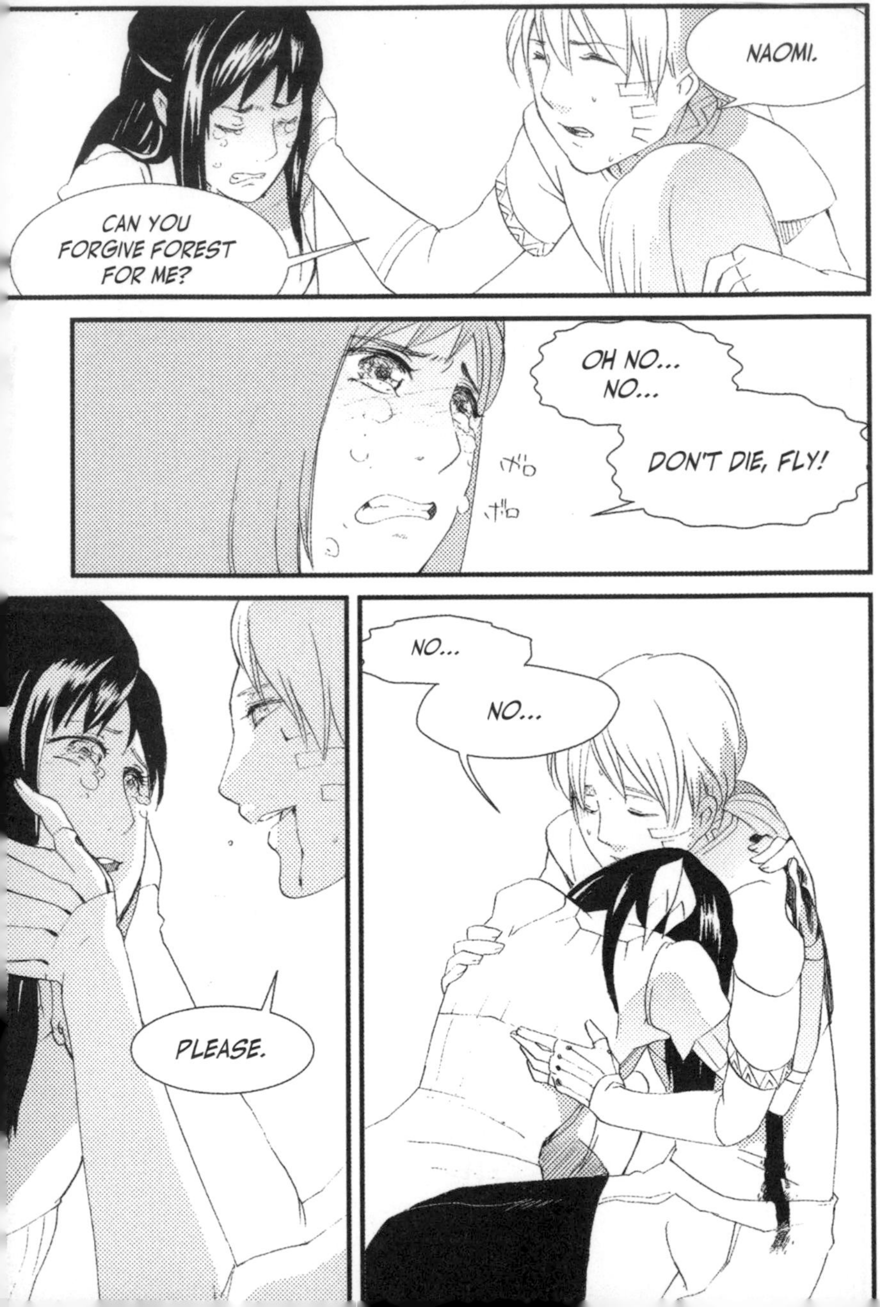
NAOMI.
CAN YOU FORGIVE FOREST FOR ME?
OH NO... NO...
DON'T DIE, FLY!
NO...
NO...
PLEASE.

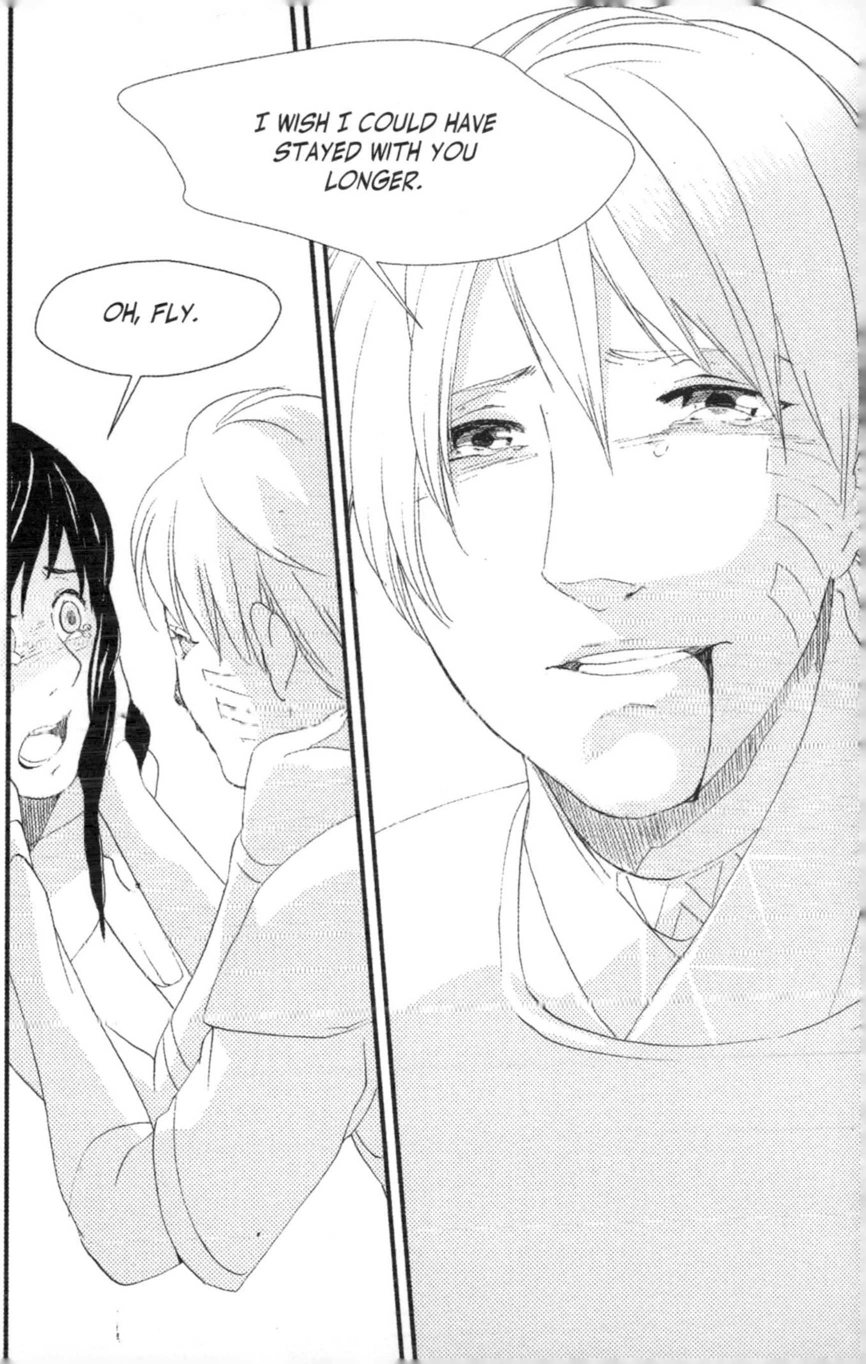
I WISH I COULD HAVE STAYED WITH YOU LONGER.
OH, FLY.

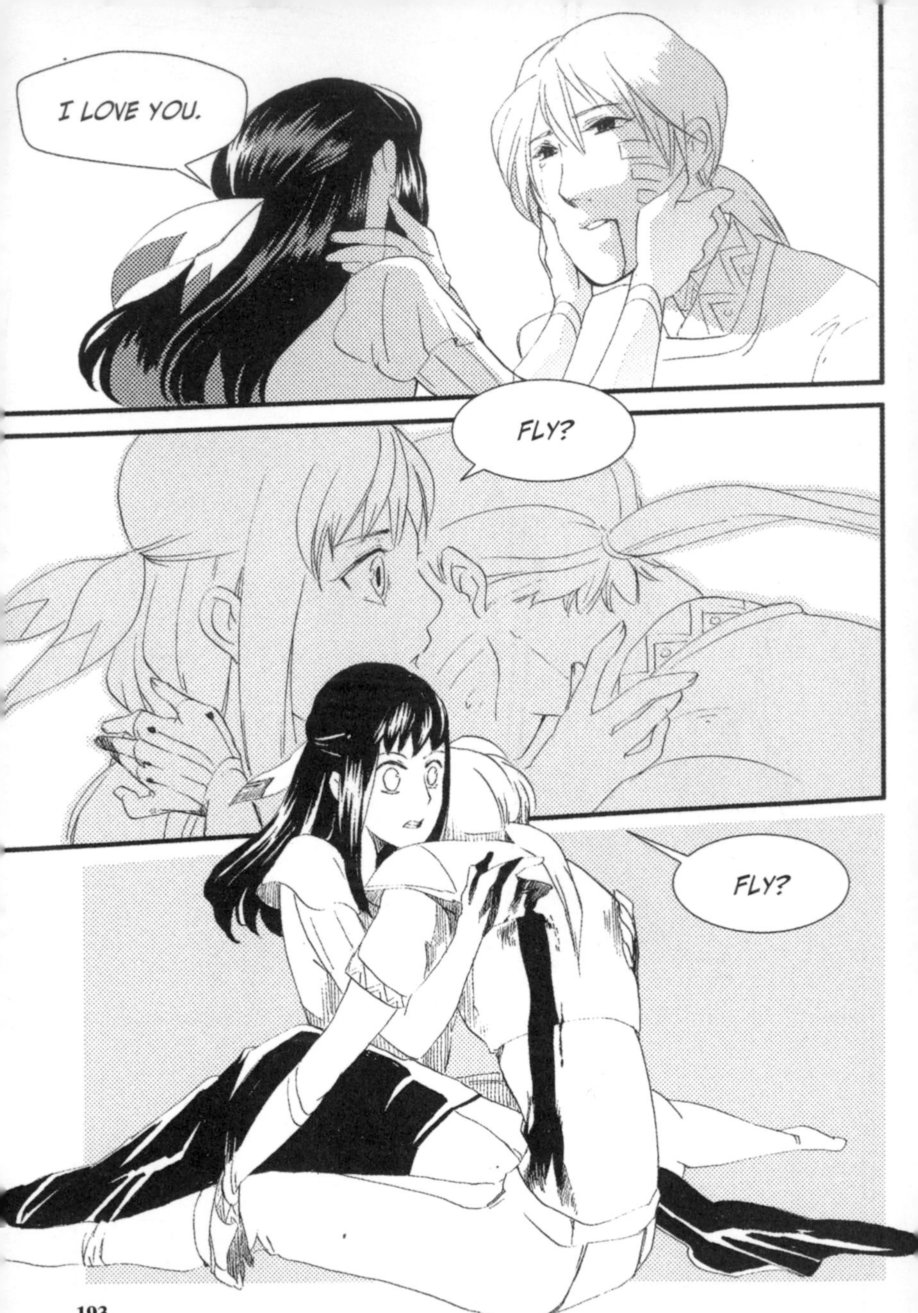
I LOVE YOU.
FLY?
FLY?

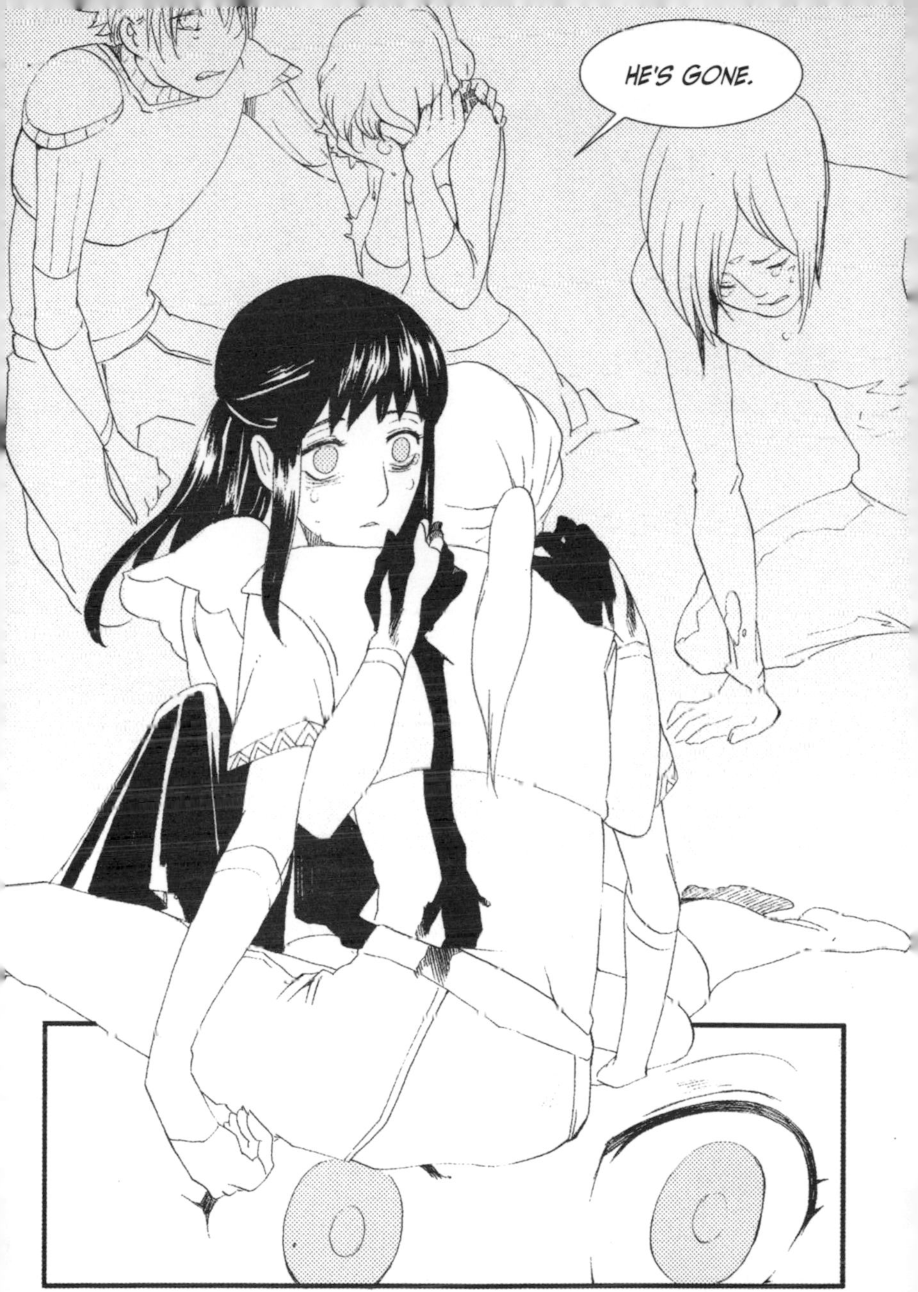
HE'S GONE.

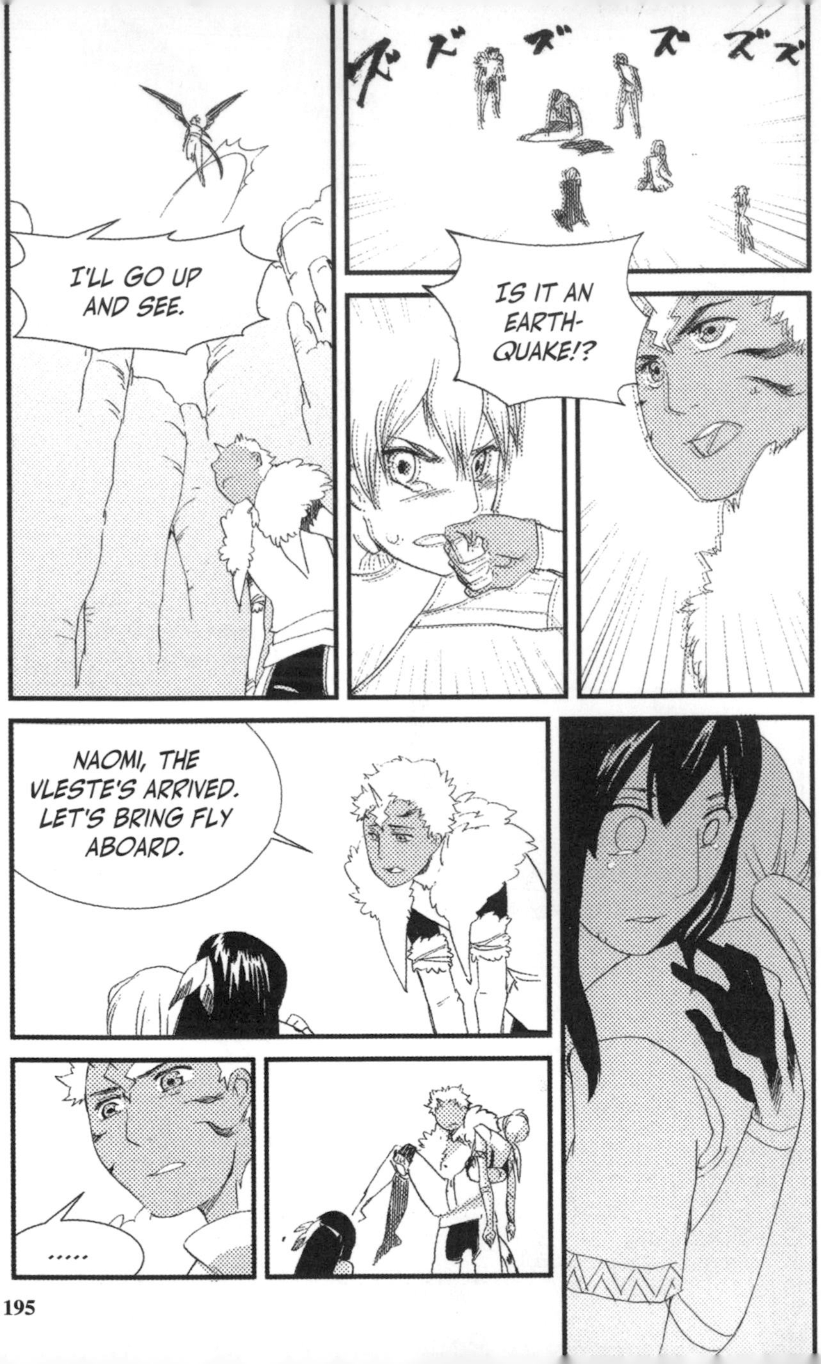
ズズズズズズ
IS IT AN EARTH-QUAKE!?
I'LL GO UP AND SEE.
NAOMI, THE VLESTE'S ARRIVED. LET'S BRING FLY ABOARD.
.....

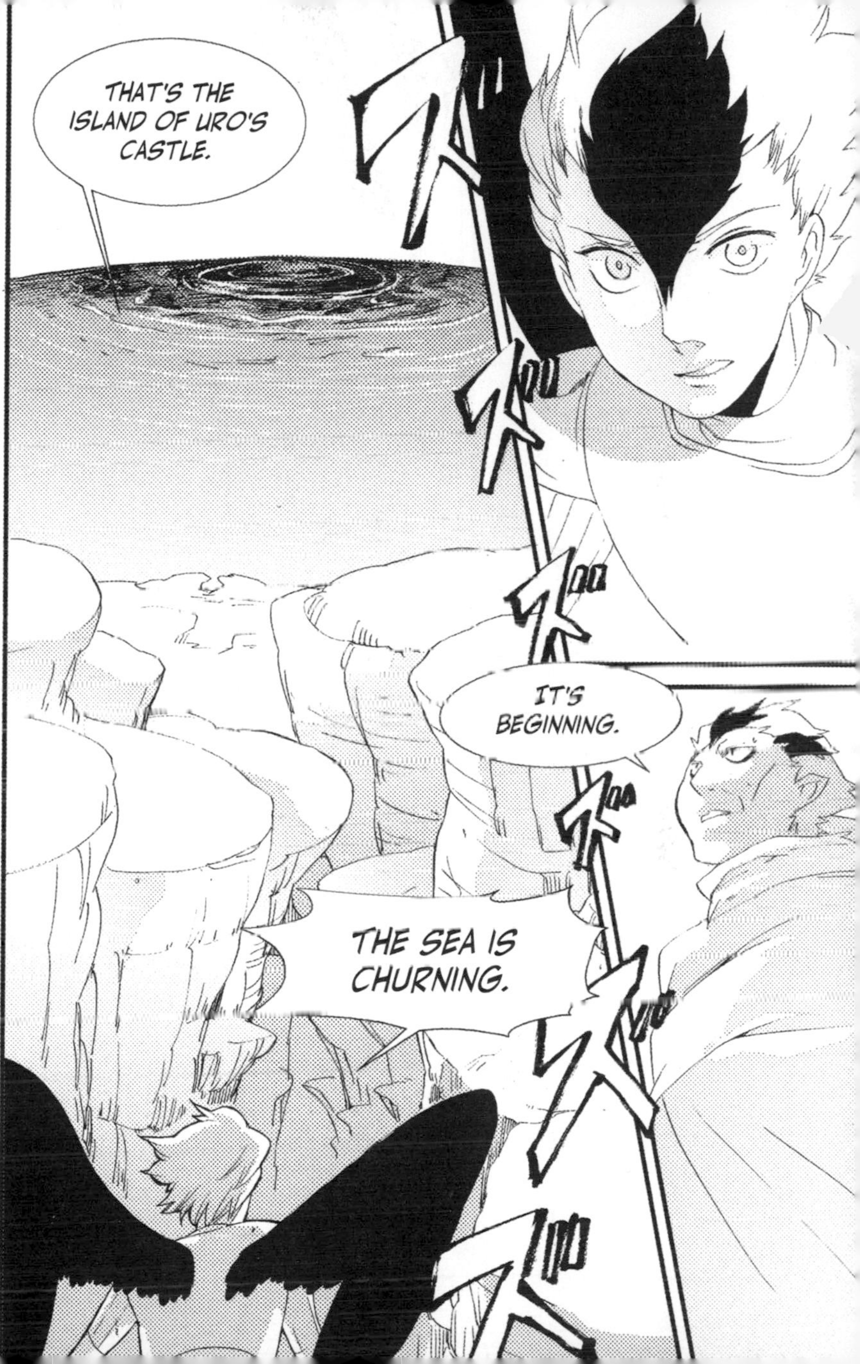
THAT'S THE ISLAND OF URO'S CASTLE.
IT'S BEGINNING.
THE SEA IS CHURNING.

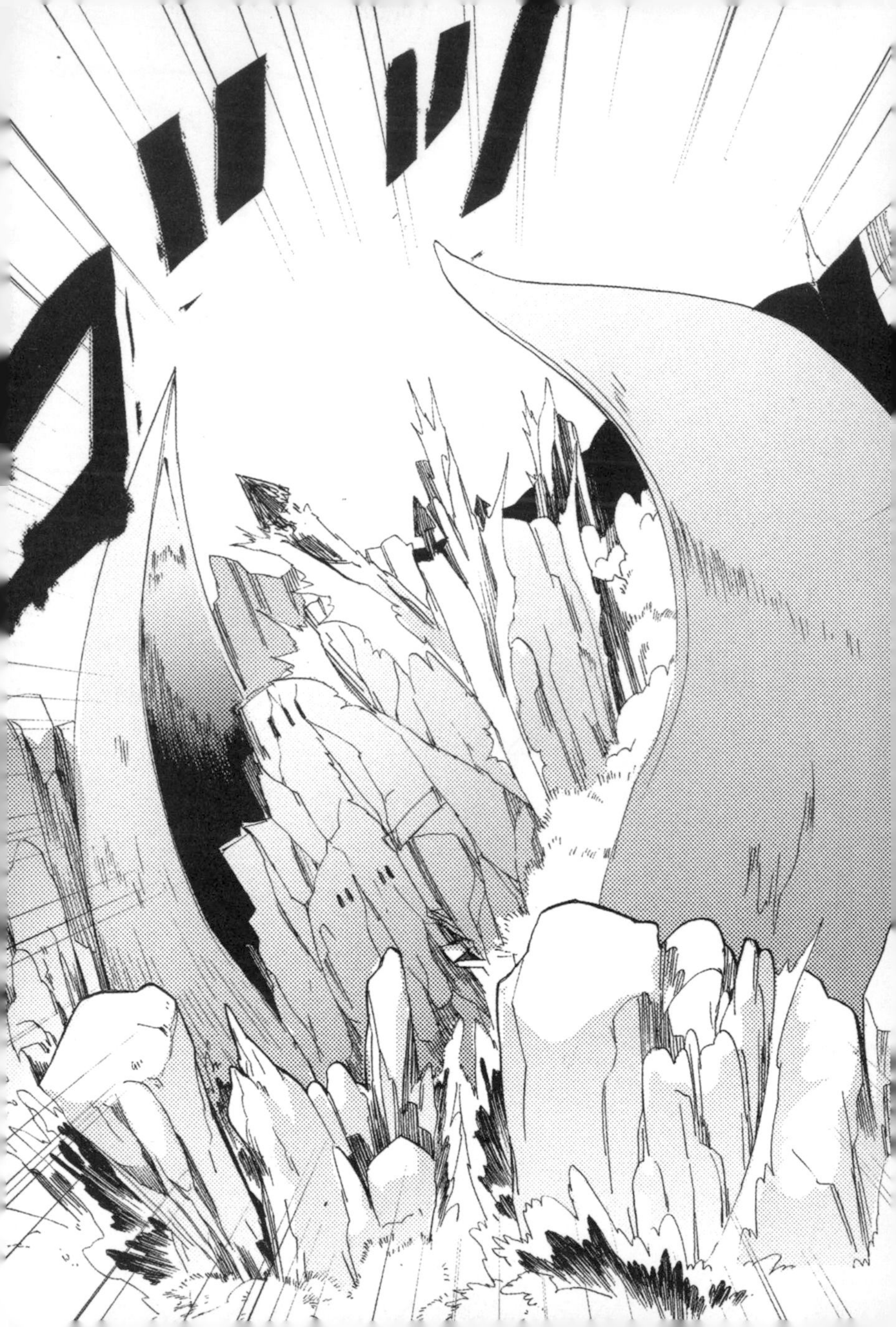

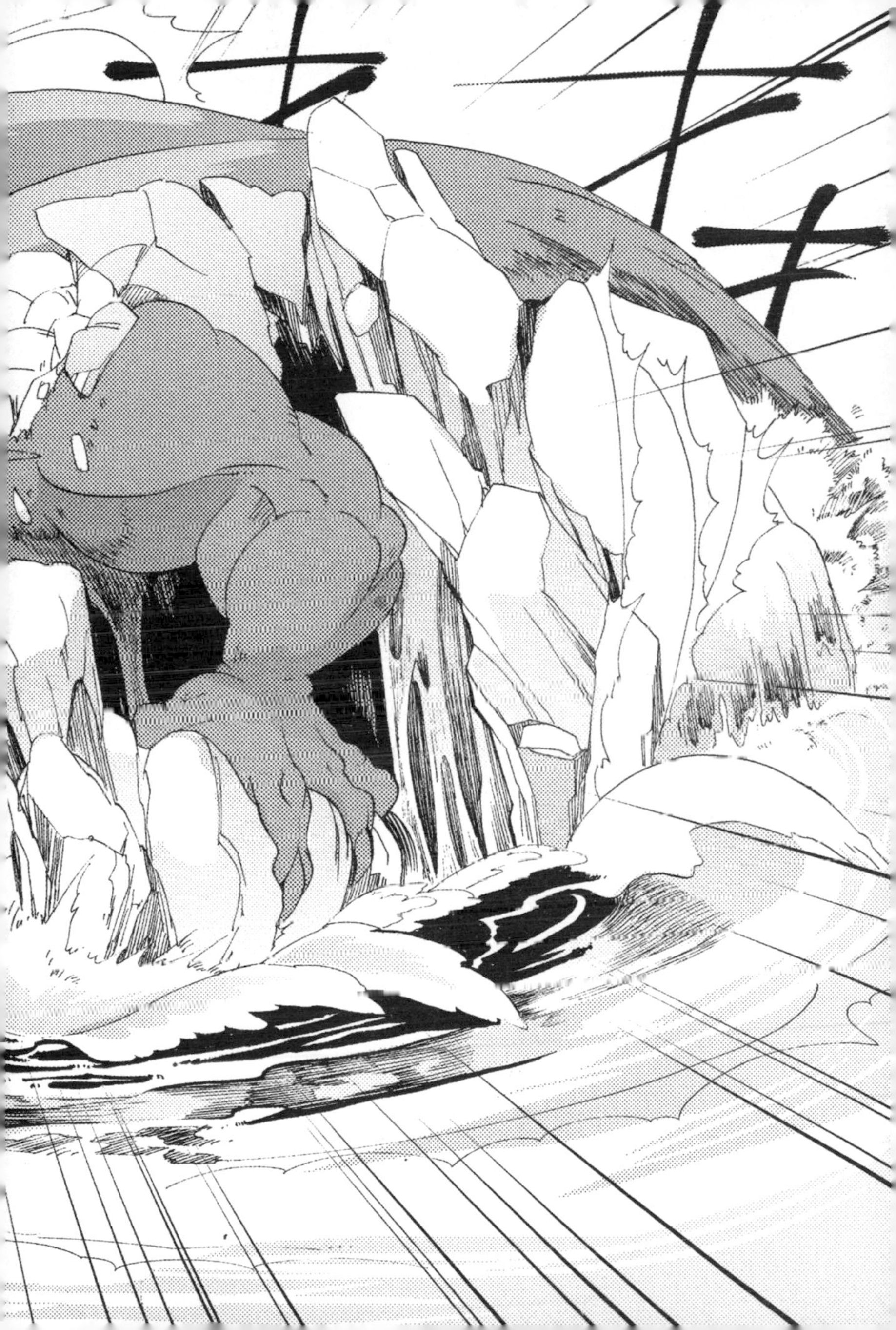

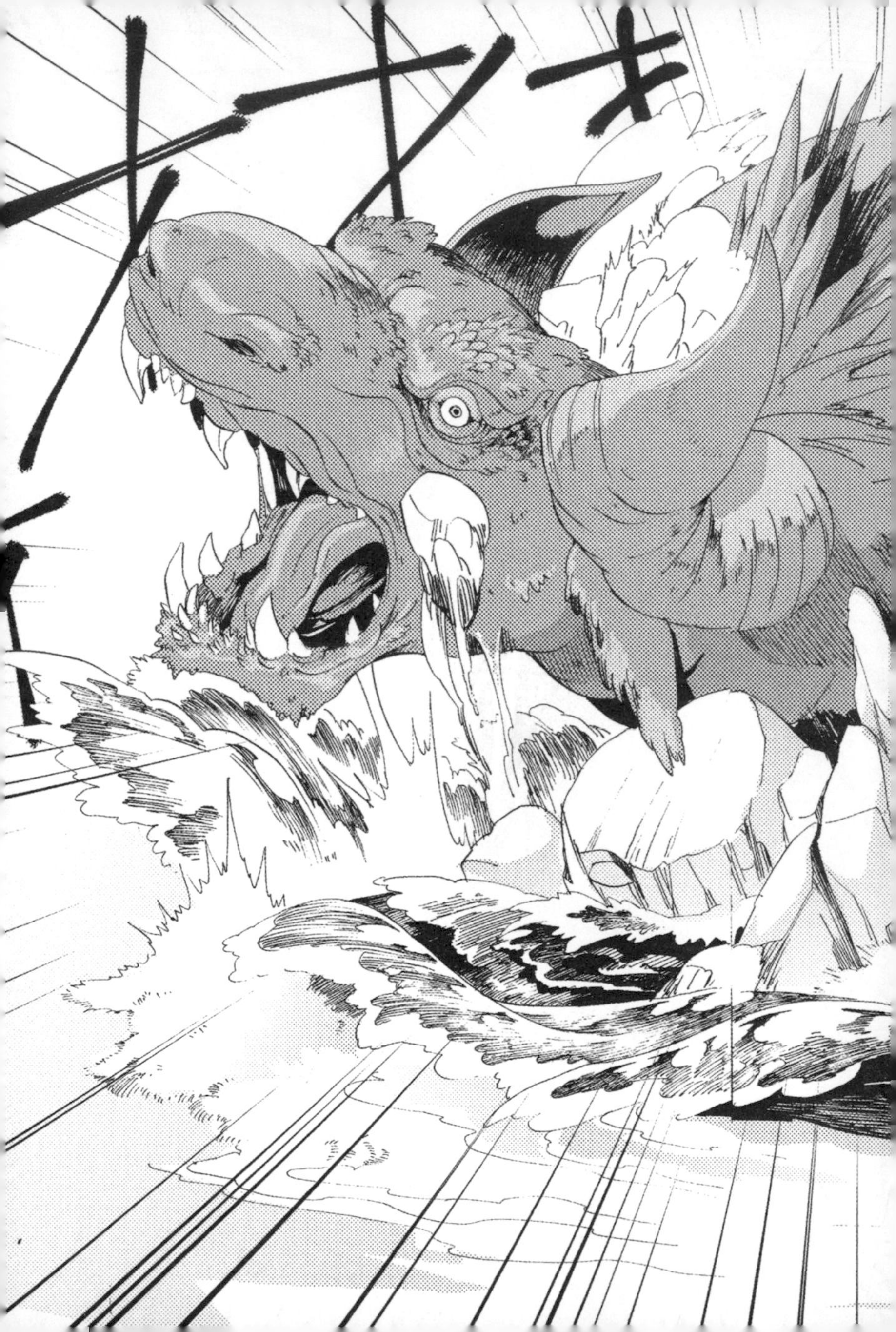

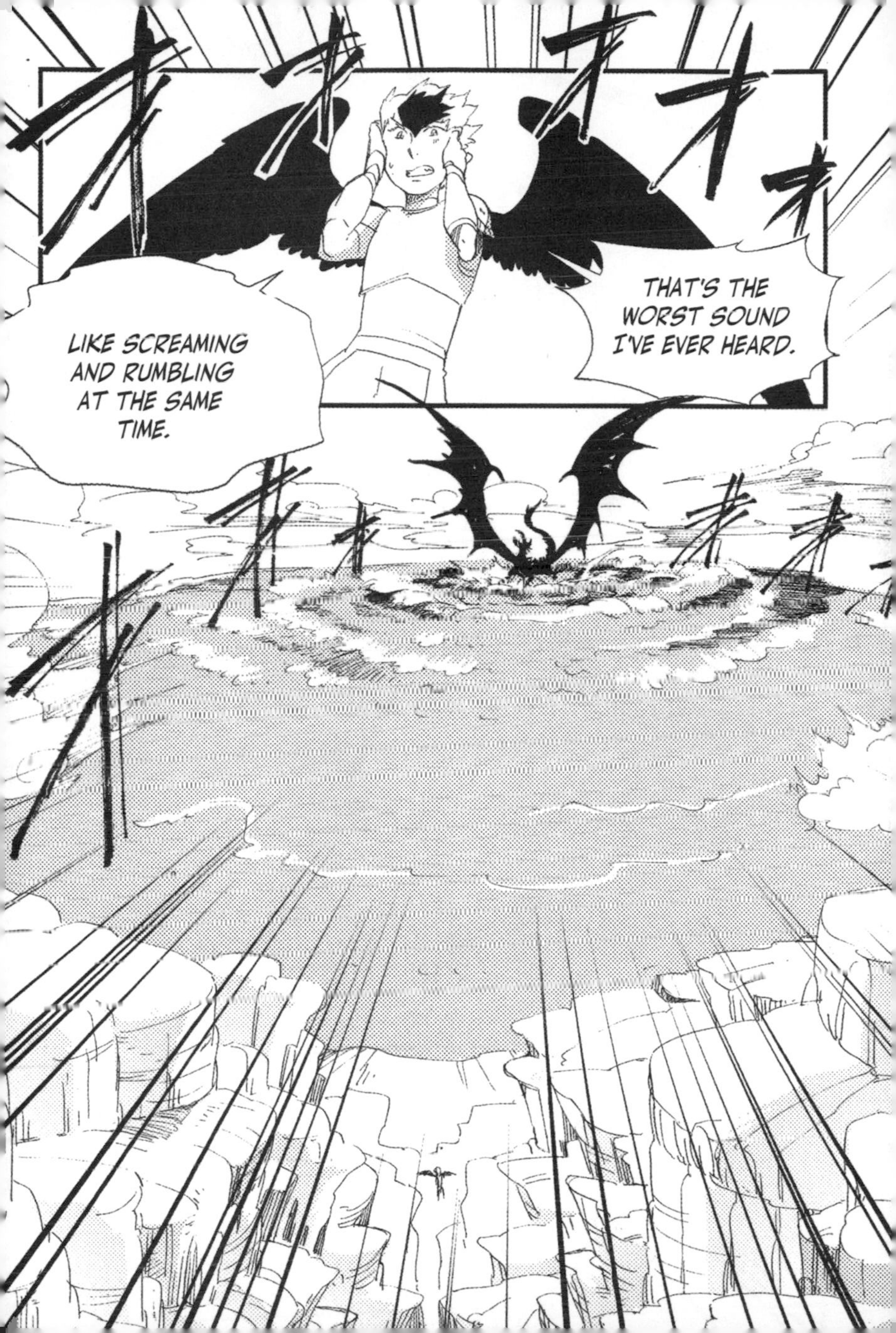
THAT'S THE WORST SOUND I'VE EVER HEARD.
LIKE SCREAMING AND RUMBLING AT THE SAME TIME.

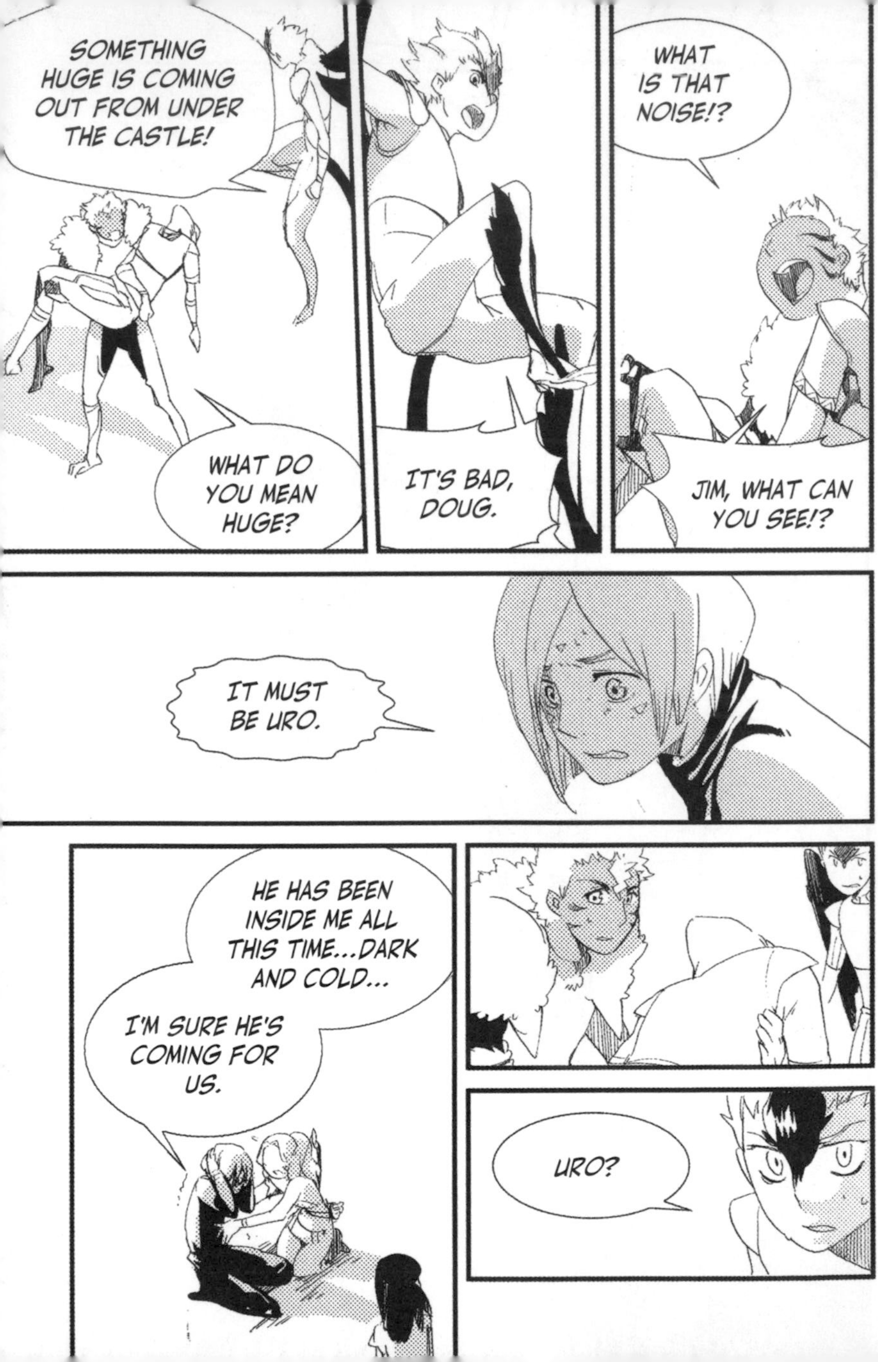
WHAT IS THAT NOISE!?
JIM, WHAT CAN YOU SEE!?
IT'S BAD, DOUG.
SOMETHING HUGE IS COMING OUT FROM UNDER THE CASTLE!
WHAT DO YOU MEAN HUGE?
IT MUST BE URO.
URO?
HE HAS BEEN INSIDE ME ALL THIS TIME...DARK AND COLD...
I'M SURE HE'S COMING FOR US.

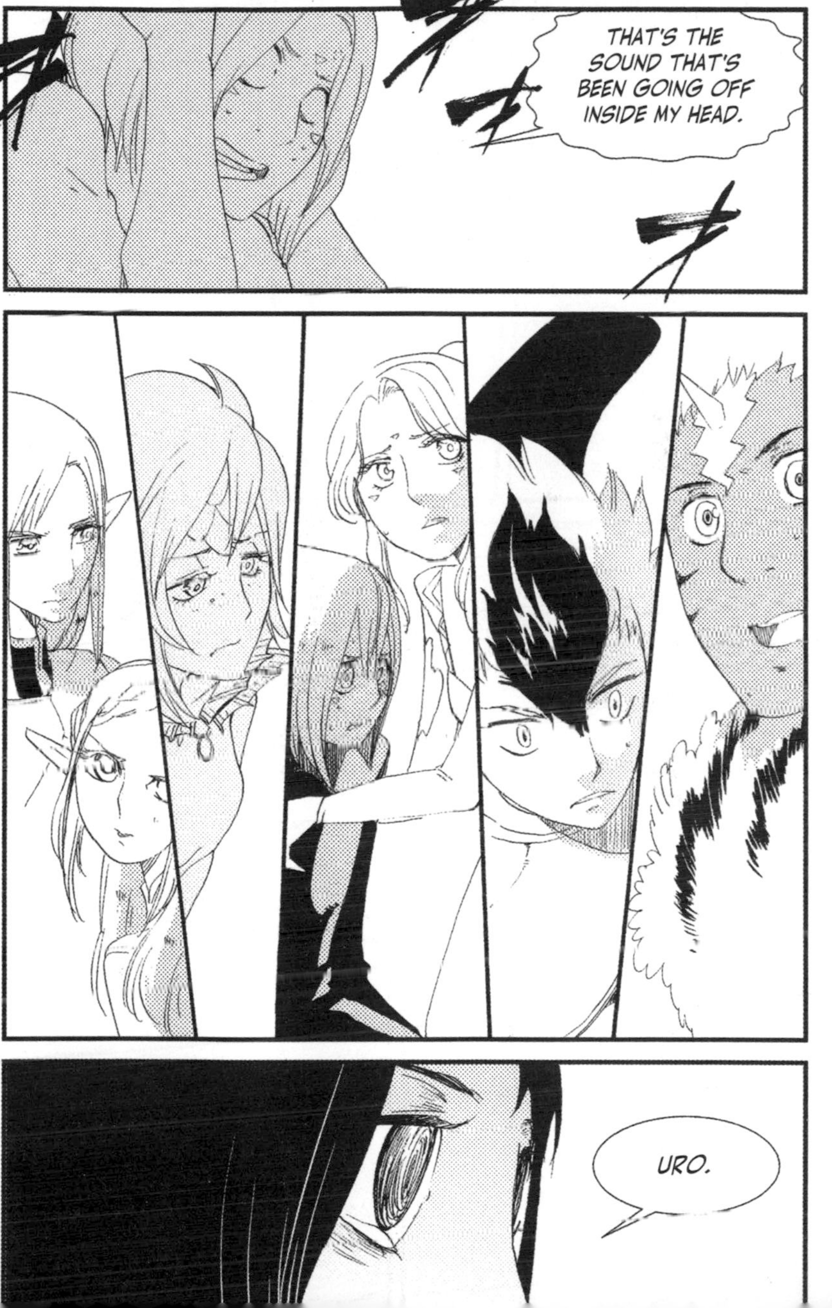
THAT'S THE SOUND THAT'S BEEN GOING OFF INSIDE MY HEAD.
URO.

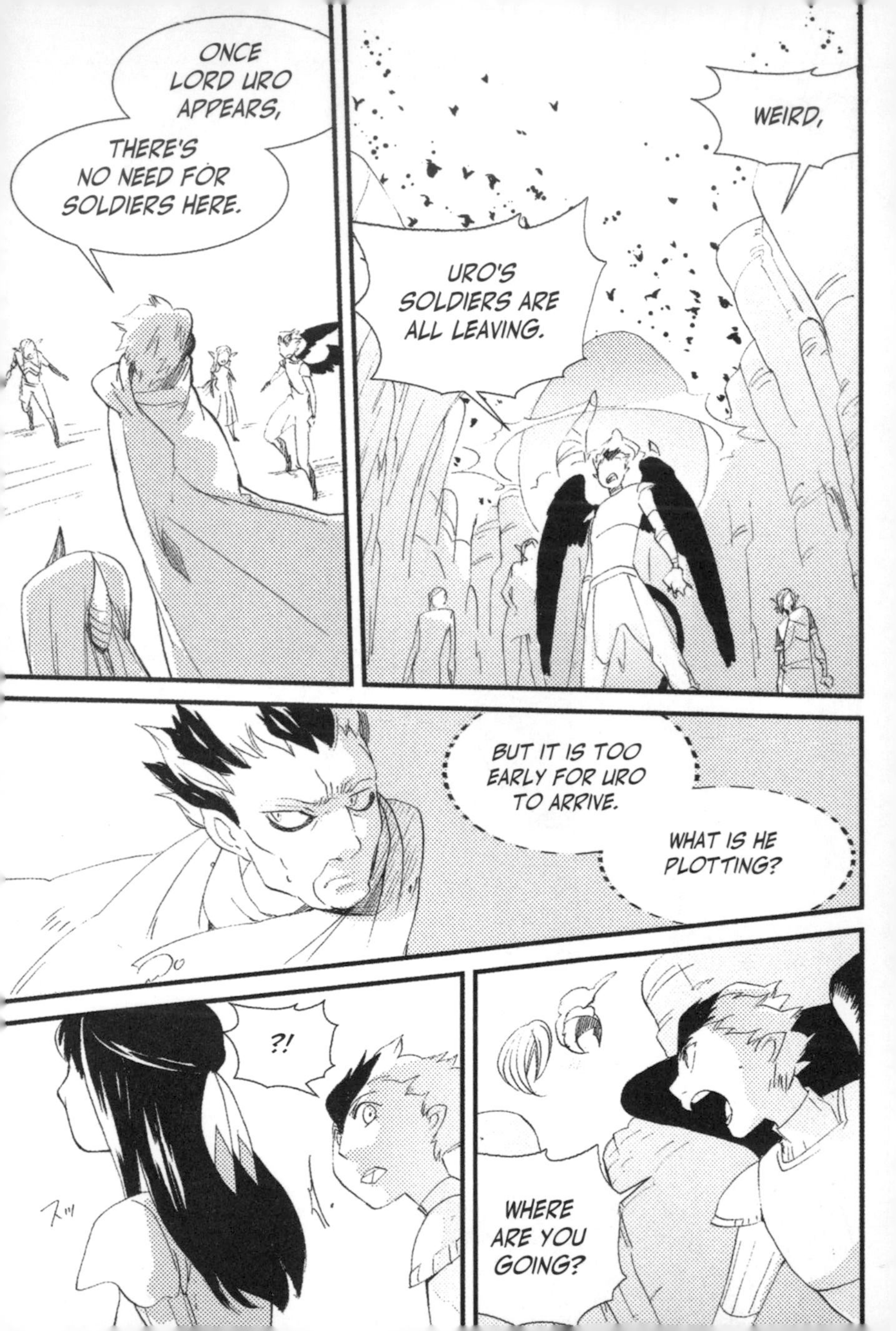
WEIRD,
URO'S SOLDIERS ARE ALL LEAVING.
ONCE LORD URO APPEARS,
THERE'S NO NEED FOR SOLDIERS HERE.
BUT IT IS TOO EARLY FOR URO TO ARRIVE.
WHAT IS HE PLOTTING?
WHERE ARE YOU GOING?
?!

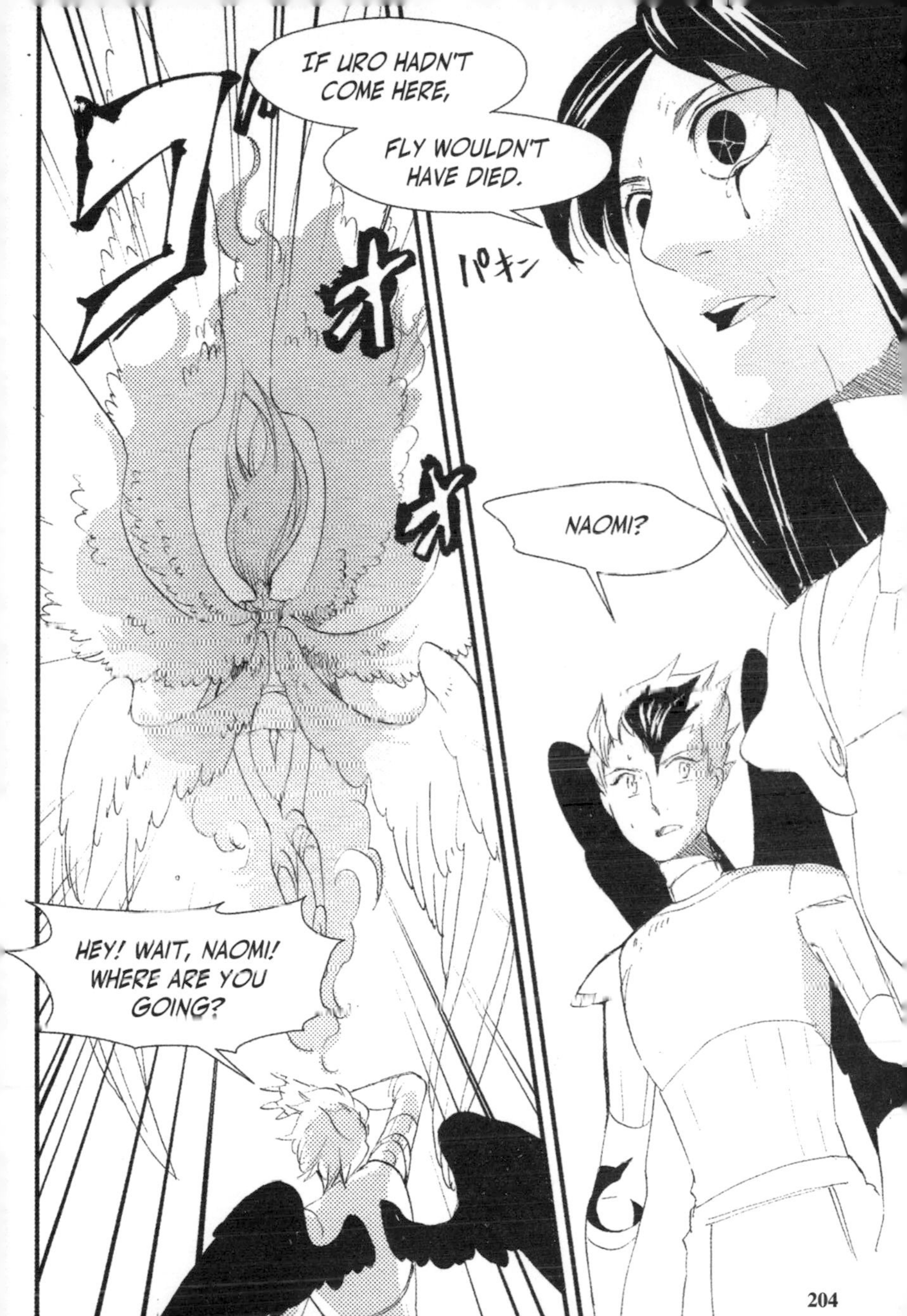
IF URO HADN'T COME HERE,
FLY WOULDN'T HAVE DIED.
パキン
NAOMI?
HEY! WAIT, NAOMI! WHERE ARE YOU GOING?

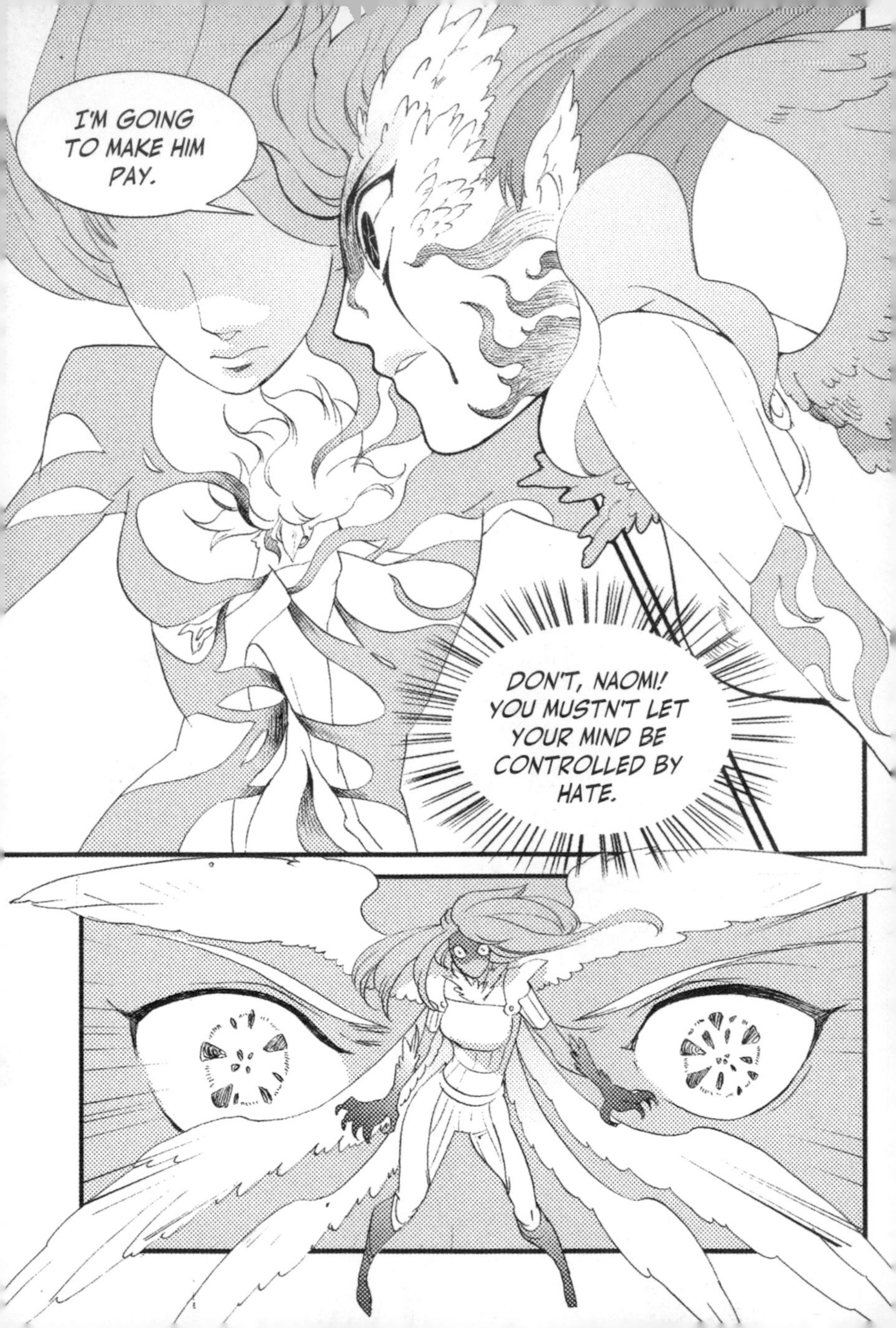
I'M GOING TO MAKE HIM PAY.
DON'T, NAOMI! YOU MUSTN'T LET YOUR MIND BE CONTROLLED BY HATE.

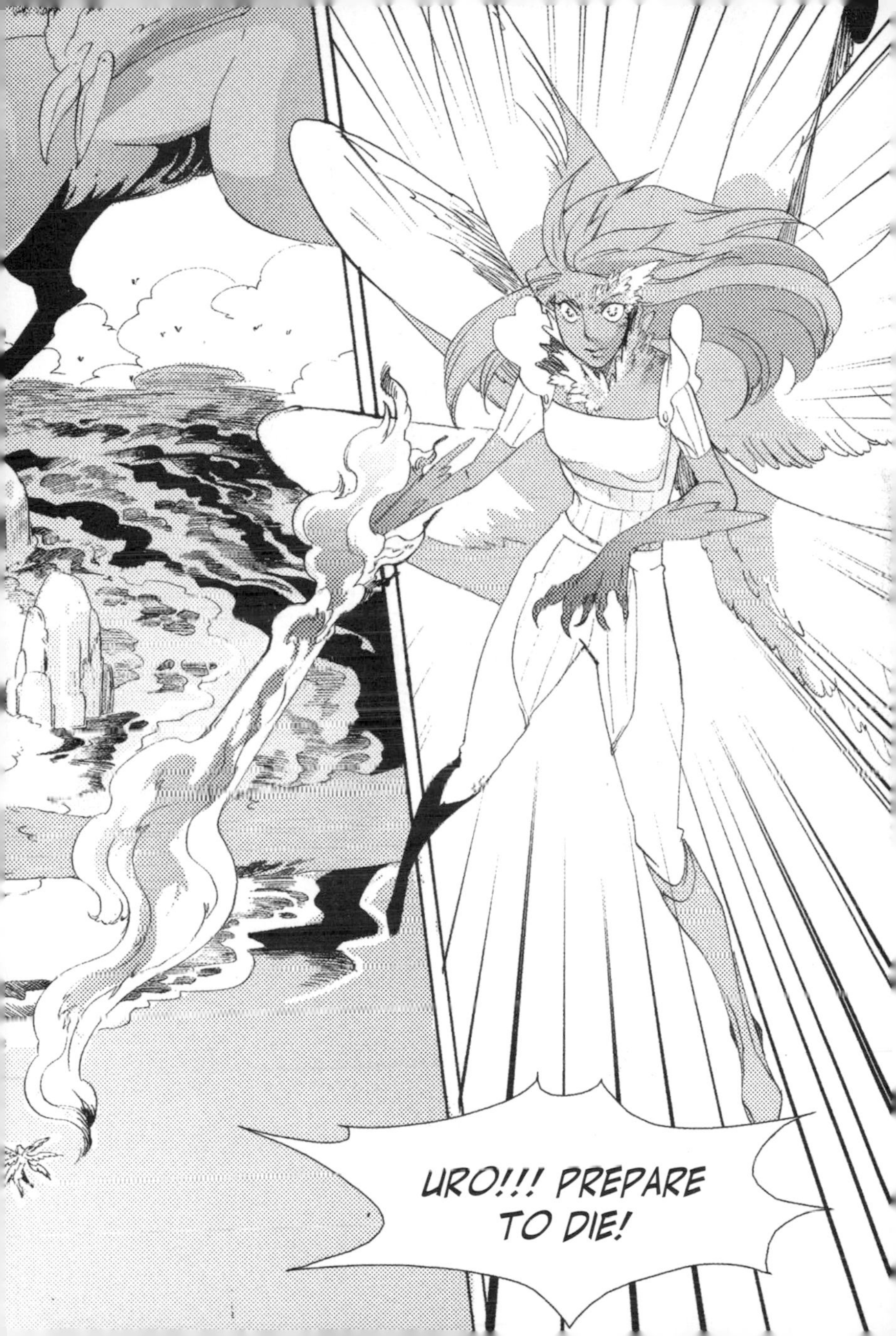
URO!!! PREPARE TO DIE!

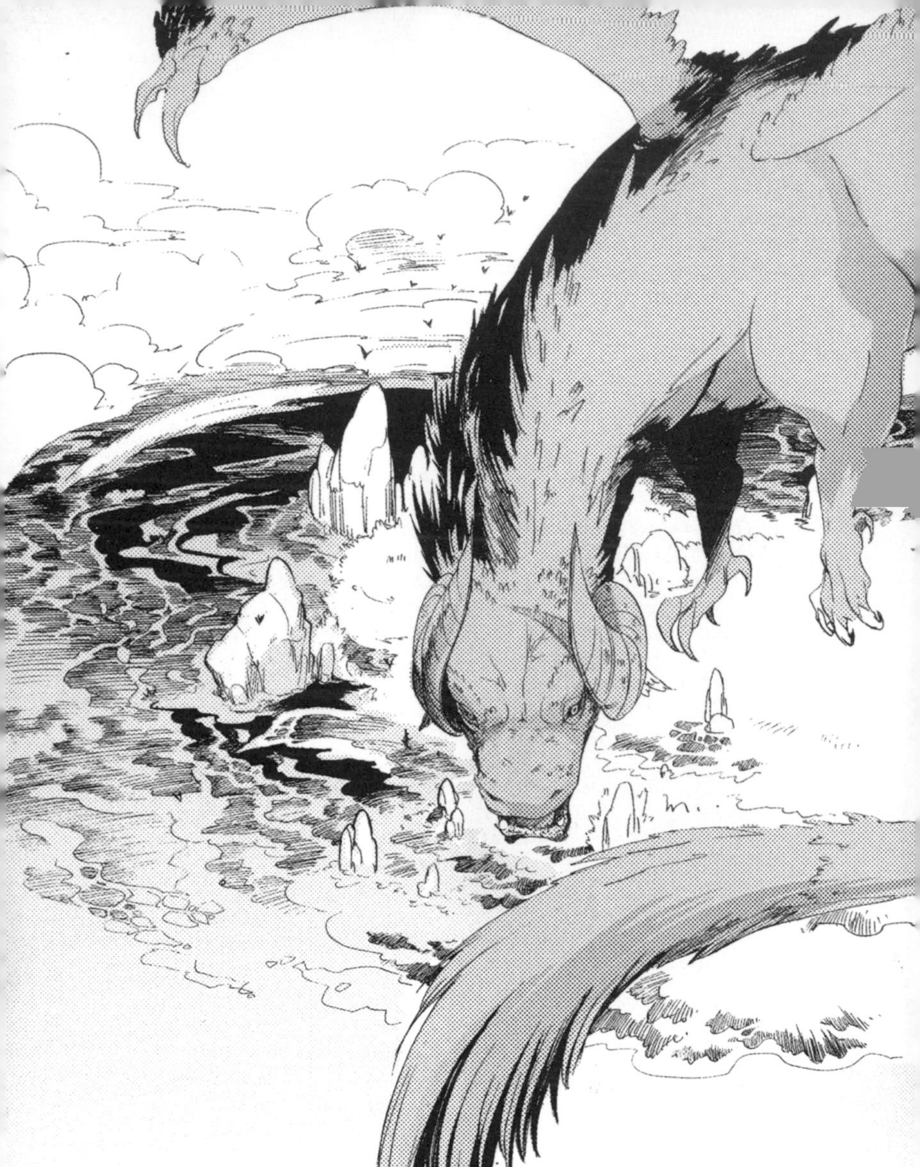

First U.S. edition 2014

Library of Congress Cataloging in Publication Data

Yoyo
Vermonia 7, battle for the Turtle Realm / by YoYo.
p. cm. — (Vermonia)
Summary: Four skater friends fulfill an ancient prophesy as they discover their true warrior spirits in an epic battle to save the planet of Vermonia. The reader is invited to learn more about the characters by playing an online game after finding hidden clues in the illustrations.
ISBN 978-1-6153-3651-7 (pbk.)
1. Prophecies — Comic books, strips, etc. 2. Adventure and adventurers — Comic books, strips, etc. 3. Graphic novels. I. YoYo (Group). II. Title.
PZ7.7 Y69 2014
741.5—dc23

This book was typeset in CCLadronn Italic

Windmill Books, LLC
303 Park Avenue South, Suite # 1280
New York, NY 10010-3657

WWW.VERMONIA.COM

Return of the Queen

Coming soon . . .